Envoy of the Flame

Sylvia Engdahl

* Ad *
Stellae

Eugene, Oregon

Book design and layout by Sylvia Engdahl

Cover art © by 1971yes / Dreamstime.com

ISBN 13: 9798985853223

Contents

As I watch the bright stars shining, I think
    a thought of the clef of the universes
    and of the future.
A vast similitude interlocks all,
All spheres, grown, ungrown, small, large,
    suns, moons, planets
All distances of place however wide,
All distances of time, all inanimate forms,
All souls, all living bodies though they be
    ever so different, or in different worlds,
  . . . . . .
All identities that have existed or may
    exist on this globe, or any globe,
All lives and deaths, all of the past,
    present, future,
This vast similitude spans them, and
    always has spann'd,
And shall forever span them and
    compactly hold and enclose them.
    —Walt Whitman, "On the Beach at Night
    Alone," 1867

However slow the progress of mankind
may be, or however imperceptible the gain
in a single generation, the advancement is
evident enough in the long run.
    —John Locke, 17th century

Preface

The Prologue to this novel was originally published as the story "The Beckoning Trail," co-authored by me and Rick Roberson, in the anthology *Universe Ahead: Stories of the Future* (Atheneum, 1975) and also appears in the expanded ebook edition of *Anywhere, Anywhen: Stories of Tomorrow*. It has had a few very minor wording changes for consistency with the first two books in this trilogy and one name change due to its use elsewhere for an unrelated character.

Those first two books, *Defender of the Flame* and *Herald of the Flame,* need not be read before this one, as it is complete in itself. However, the backstory it contains includes major spoilers for them.

Because this book and the preceding one deal in detail with the Anthropological Service that appears in my "Elana" novels *Enchantress from the Stars* and *The Far Side of Evil*, adults and older teens who have enjoyed those books may be especially interested in them. Please note that unlike the Elana books they are adult novels and contain some material that is unsuitable for middle-school readers.

Is this trilogy set long after or long before the Elana novels? That remains an open question, as it was in *Enchantress from the Stars.* Elana might have lived at the time of our ancestors or our remote descendants; the Service, as I imagine it, is eternal.

It has sometimes been implied by reviewers that the Federation in this trilogy and in my Elana novels was derived from Star Trek. It was not. For the record, I created the Federation, the Anthropological Service, and its strict non-interference policy in a draft of the opening of *Enchantress from the Stars* written in 1957, nearly a decade before Star Trek existed. It is my honest opinion that advanced extraterrestrial civilizations do not contact young species before they are mature enough to be treated as equals, and that this is why we ourselves haven't yet been contacted by any aliens.

Are advanced ETs as much like us as I portray them in my fiction? Of course not. But I feel that showing what people of all worlds have in common is closer to realism than an attempt to imagine differences of which we know nothing. We will learn about the differences soon enough as we explore the universe. What's needed now is awareness that the sapient species that may exist elsewhere are "human" in the most meaningful sense of the word and share the qualities that characterize humanity—including, among others, the capacity for love

.

Sylvia Engdahl, June 2021

Prologue

THE STARSHIP WAS nearing its destination: a solar system far from Earth, much farther than humankind had previously gone. Ardith Moran stood by a viewport looking out into void. There were few stars to be seen while the ship traveled between jump points, as the radiation filters obscured all but the brightest; beyond the port now was mere ... blankness. Nothingness, like the feeling she'd had lately about things that used to excite her. But she was well inured to this. She had been aboard large hyperdrive ships before.

And she'd never intended to board another, exobiologist though she was. Why am I here? Ardith asked herself, turning wearily back to the cramped compartment that served as ship's library. Why did I come when I'd already decided to resign from the Scientific Exploration Corps and take the professorship on LaLande VI? I don't really expect to find anything that will make a difference—do I?

Still, for the first time, after all the empty years of searching, there had been a Message.

Radio astronomers had started listening for interstellar messages centuries ago, in the 1960s. They had believed that sapient races elsewhere in the universe must surely be transmitting, for purposes of their own if not in a deliberate effort to get in touch with other beings like themselves. Many scientists had been convinced that such an effort was inevitable for a civilization advanced enough to be able to afford the power output, and according to statistics, advanced civilizations should far outnumber those at Earth's level or below. There was a real expectation of establishing communication with those civilizations, and of learning from them ways to solve the seemingly-insoluble problems that plagued Earth. Yet failing that, science had reasoned, it should at least be possible to obtain evidence of alien peoples' existence; if any were broadcasting into space, Earth's technology could detect them.

Time had passed. No messages had come, or indeed artificial signals of any sort. And, gradually, optimism had waned; it had begun to seem that the statistics must have lied. It had been said that civilizations didn't survive long enough for there to be much chance of detecting their radio broadcasts, or that they abandoned technology, or that intelligent life of other worlds wasn't in any way human in its psychology. It had for a while been thought that the universe was as hostile to life as early twentieth-century scientists had maintained—that theories suggesting an abundance of life must be flawed. Once interstellar travel began, that proved untrue. The universe was full of life. Ardith herself had studied it in a dozen different solar systems. But nowhere within the areas visited was it as advanced as on Earth. There were primitive forms and in a very few cases, primates; but no sapient ones. No waiting galactic supercivilization. Not even a Stone Age culture. A thorough search of Earth's region of the galaxy would require travel to many thousands of stars, so in the absence of signals, humankind was resigned to being alone.

So we go on, Ardith thought, spreading our colonies from system to uninhabited system, leaving the few with advanced lifeforms for their indigenous species to someday develop. And what good is it? It was exciting, once: it was the Big Dream, the long-awaited destiny, the ultimate challenge. To fly among the stars was humankind's great hope fulfilled. In the beginning I felt all those things— even I, born several hundred years too late. If I'd been born in the Dawn Age of interstellar travel would things have been different? Would I not have outgrown the dream? Would I still see new territory to explore?

She glanced around the compartment at the men and women gathered there, some reading, others talking quietly; and she wondered how many of them shared her depression. Lately it had all seemed very pointless. You lost track of the solar systems after a while. You started questioning whether colonization of another one, or even scientific analysis of another one, could lead anywhere ... though you were not really sure where you wanted it to lead.

I'm old, she realized. I'm not yet thirty, and already I'm old! There had been a time when she wouldn't have considered settling permanently on any planet, not even a newly-opened one like LaLande VI. She would have rejected the offer of the professorship; she would not have begun to suspect that her career, and possibly someday a family, might be all she could expect from life. Once, no opportunity would have outshone her vision of something to be sought beyond the next star. Did it now? Or was it merely that she'd lost the vision?

She'd convinced herself that she didn't care, that it had been a childish dream anyway, as philosophers said humankind's dream of meeting advanced aliens was childish. Then the Message arrived, and it had ruined her hard-won indifference.

There was no mistaking the artificial origin of the Message. The signals received were classic in format, the format predicted by the early radio astronomers: binary impulses that could be decoded to form a diagram. The diagram was of the same kind enthusiasts had always used to illustrate the ease of communicating with an alien intelligence. It contained universal statements of mathematics and physics. It portrayed the solar system of its source. And it showed, as a stick figure, a being definitely humanoid in shape.

The Message was repeated at regular intervals over a period of twelve days. Then it stopped. But no scientist doubted that the content of the recordings had been designed as a greeting. Earth was not alone among reachable technological civilizations after all. Nor was humankind the most advanced species in Earth's part of the universe . . . because the Message had been in transit nearly a thousand years. It had come from a star nearly a thousand light-years away. If its senders had high-power transmitters a thousand years ago, what had they achieved by now?

Or had they survived to achieve anything?

If they had, it was argued—if any civilization that advanced existed so relatively close—Earth should have heard from them long ago. They would have faster-than-light ships, too; they'd have been using them for centuries. Perhaps not enough ships to send everywhere. Yet the Message had not been sent everywhere, either. It had not been broadcast to all of space; it had been beamed directly to Earth. The beam was so narrow that it had not been received in colonized solar systems even as near as Alpha Centauri. That was the most puzzling thing about it.

The odds were incredible that by accident, Earth should have been singled out to receive the Message, a Message sent not only before humankind's initial radio waves could have reached its source, but long before the voyage of Columbus.

Perhaps it was not by accident. Perhaps the senders had faster-than-light travel a thousand years back, and had seen which of the countless solar systems within range were developing civilizations; they might have beamed signals timed to arrive when those civilizations were able to send ships of their own. Maybe they did not plan to pass near Earth again. Earth might not be that important to them. They too might wonder if still another world was worth the trouble, Ardith thought sadly.

She, like the other members of the expedition, had speculated and debated and had finally given up in frustration; though the various theories about the Message were complex, there was a limit to the length of time you could spend going over the same ground. Yet you couldn't concentrate on other work, either. If you had no shipboard duties—and the scientists, unlike the Fleet officers who crewed the ship, had none—then you could only sit and think, or pretend to read, or make small talk . . . and slowly go crazy. We are in limbo, she thought, as the ship is in limbo while outside normal space. This should be the most thrilling trip of our lives, of humankind's history, even—and it isn't! It isn't! It's as if we've lost something. . . .

She sat down, pressing her hands to her forehead, fighting the headache she knew would come. Headaches had been frequent enough these past weeks. At least there were only a few hours left until the final jump. Before long, speculation would have ended; she would know. Know what? Ardith's mind persisted. That they died while our civilization was young, that all that is left are ruins to excavate? Or that they live, so that in them we will see there is nothing new ahead of us?

From the contour chair next to Ardith, Fred Liang smiled at her. He was a young man, perhaps five years younger than herself, but of the astronomers aboard the one she'd found most congenial. Most of the rest were quite sure what they'd find at the destination solar system, at any rate as far as its physical aspects went; their opinions were strong even about the rationale behind the Message. Fred had an open mind.

"Nerves?" he asked, not needing any more words, though it wasn't a thing people commonly spoke of.

Ardith nodded. "I was—wondering why I came."

"We're all afraid, you know."

"You, Fred?" It surprised her; he was too young to be afraid.

"Not of—well, not physically," he explained hastily.

"Of course not." None of them worried about the Others being hostile, or treating them as lab specimens—though it occurred to Ardith suddenly that if you wanted to capture specimens, you sometimes imitated calls that they would heed. Like the mating calls of insects. She laughed; it was a good mask for deeper fears.

But Fred wasn't afraid in the same way she was; he had not yet lost his sense of excitement. Nor did he, like many of Earth's scientists, have mixed feelings about encountering a race that had achieved all they themselves could achieve, long ago in the distant past—a people whose stature might make humankind's own efforts meaningless. "What is it, then, Fred?" Ardith asked, lapsing into soberness.

"I'm afraid I'm not good enough," he confessed. "That I won't meet the—the admission standards, so to say."

"You will if any of us do." She regarded him thoughtfully. "You picture Earth as a—a candidate? I suppose you've been talking to Jacob."

"Yes, but I always did feel we're coming as children, to be taught. Jacob—he doesn't believe that. I don't know what he believes now; our having received the Message runs counter to his theory. And he admits it."

"Which is more than can be said of certain other people! I like him for that." Jacob Stromberg was an anthropologist, and a distinguished one. There had been no question about his qualifications for leading the expedition's contact team. His accepting the post had been odd, however, for throughout his career Jacob had insisted that it was harmful to primitive sapient species to be contacted by more advanced ones. He'd been instrumental in establishing a non-interference policy with regard to any extraterrestrial Stone Age cultures that might be observed by future exploration teams; he had maintained that being of different origin, they needed to evolve at their own speed. And with strict consistency he'd applied the principle both ways: in his view, no superior civilization would contact humankind by interstellar radio or by any other means. Jacob had thought it very natural that centuries of listening had yielded no results, though he favored the early statistics that said such civilizations were prevalent. The Message must have been a blow to him.

"I don't quite see why his theory was affected," Ardith admitted. "I'd think he would merely be afraid that this contact is going to harm us. After all, we don't know the Others were trying to contact worlds less advanced than theirs—not unless we assume they knew of our existence. They could have been searching for superiors, with the idea that if it was harmful their superiors wouldn't answer."

"You can't place the whole burden of the decision on the superior civilization," Fred pointed out. "Because if some worlds do transmit, then space is full of their old messages sent before they knew it was harmful. Nothing can get rid of the old radio trails, traveling on forever at the speed of light; and the farther from the source they are when some world picks them up, the bigger the evolutionary gap between senders and receivers. The damage is already done, Ardith, if contact is bad for us. We've already had contact with them; everybody on Earth knows how far ahead of us they are."

Ardith thought of friends she'd left, friends who were half-hoping that the expedition would bring back answers to culminate their research . . . and half-hoping that it wouldn't. She shivered. "Jacob must be more scared than any of us; he's so sure civilizations can't skip stages."

"He's worried, all right. I've watched his face when he thought no one was looking."

"He wouldn't—that is, there's no chance of his deciding to—"

"Sabotage the mission?" Fred shook his head. "Jacob is too honest. He won't hide truth; he's convinced that humankind can't ever benefit from denying reality. Besides, it wouldn't solve anything for him. What bothers him isn't so much the thought that we might get hurt as that the universe isn't set up with safeguards."

"Good Lord, Fred. Jacob's too bright to suppose that the universe has ever been *safe*."

Fred hesitated. "Of course he is. Like I said, he

knows we could get hurt. We could have blown ourselves up before we outgrew war, too. Or the sun might go nova. But those he considers exceptions—I mean, they don't happen to most sapient species in the normal course of events; they're cases of something going wrong. Whereas if sending interstellar radio greetings is harmful, and it's done before civilizations are mature enough to know better, then sooner or later almost every world would be affected."

"But he could have figured that out before we ever got the Message," protested Ardith.

"He had a safeguard theory, though, one that explained why the danger should be negligible. Till now, the evidence for it has built up year by year; the Message is the first negative sign there's been. It could be a freak, but—"

"But statistically, that's an unscientific assumption," Ardith agreed. "Every step of scientific progress has shown that it's more valid to assume Earth isn't freakish. In fact in the fields where we have data enough, we've found that there are no freaks; there are only patterns."

"Yes. And Jacob thought he saw a pattern, but the Message doesn't fit into it."

"I wonder." All this was so fruitless, Ardith was thinking. These eternal discussions were so tiring, when they couldn't get anywhere—yet you couldn't turn your mind off. "Fred," she asked, "has Jacob ever considered there being a point when contact's good? I mean . . . when there's no other challenge left for a civilization: when we've abolished war and poverty and totalitarianism—all the evils our society's gotten rid of these past centuries—and when establishing colonies is so routine. We weren't given answers to those problems. We found them on our own. And sometimes . . . I wish I'd lived while we were still finding them."

"You're saying contact with other civilizations may come next?"

"Why not? Something has to. Or we'll . . . lose interest. Give up from sheer boredom. I think what scares me most is the idea that the Others may have done that. Seeing they have would be worse than finding them far ahead, whatever Jacob may say."

"I don't think he'd say you're wrong," Fred replied gravely, after a long pause. "I haven't heard him speak of eventual contact; I'm not sure if he believes there's a time for it. Yet he came on this ship, didn't he?"

*

Late in the night, by its Earth-standard clock, the ship emerged from its final jump into normal space and began to decelerate. Ahead was the star Omega, so called by the expedition because it was too dim in Earth's sky to have been formerly known by anything but a catalog number. Ardith did not see it; she was sleeping. But while she slept she began to dream, and the dream was of vast luminous cities and unnamed sensations and other things she could not describe or remember.

She woke in a mood unlike her customary one; for a few seconds she imagined herself back on the first starship she'd traveled in, thinking, There are five glorious new worlds out there, worlds humankind has never set foot on. . . .. But how odd, she reflected, sitting up and reaching for her hairbrush. There hadn't been five worlds in that first new system she had explored; there'd been eight, of which only two weren't gaseous. As for the Omegan system, data in the Message had specified that there were eleven. That could not be verified, though, until the instrument readings were in.

When she went to breakfast she found everyone in a state of stunned dismay. The initial instrument readings showed no planets at all.

To be sure, the ship was still far out; it hadn't been safe to calculate the coordinates too close for such a long series of jumps, and the approach would require several days in normal space. But at this distance planets should be easily detectable. Ardith joined the crowd by the viewport, her heart lifting at the sight of stars spangled against the dark expanse, so welcome after the days of nearly-featureless void. The constellations were unfamiliar here, a thousand light-years from home. Even large planets could not have been identified by the naked eye. Telescopic observation, however, should have found them; the computer should have charted the whole system by this time.

The day passed. Fred Liang and the other astronomers stayed in the observatory; Ardith did not see them. Morale among the rest of the staff was at low ebb. People were too baffled even to discuss the situation. Inexplicably, her own spirits remained high. She could not account for it. Am I thinking that if there are no planets my worst fear can't be realized? she wondered. But then neither can my hope, such hope as it is. The universe will seem emptier than ever! She did not feel empty. She felt more on the verge of discovery than at any time during the journey.

For the others the reverse seemed true. Most of them had anticipated immediate radio contact with the Omegan civilization, yet the ship's signals brought no response. "Perhaps the Omegans no longer use radio," people said, "still they'd listen for a reply to the Message! They'd monitor that frequency and answer us—" What people did not say, at least not aloud, was that the Omegans were evidently gone. Sometime during the thousand-year time lag, either they had been wiped out or they had migrated. What else was there to think?

That night Ardith dreamed again as soon as she fell asleep. It seemed that she was free in space, without gravity, without even a spacesuit to isolate her from the void; but it was not a void. It was filled with light and sound and a nameless presence that she knew not through her senses, but through faculties she'd never before possessed. In the dream this seemed natural. She felt no surprise, nor any trace of fear: she was flooded with joyous anticipation. But what she anticipated she did not yet know.

The impressions of the dream became less vague. Gradually they crystallized, focused, until she was in the midst of spinning globes. They spun in starred blackness, though she herself was enveloped in the warmth of sunlight. How could the solar system have been thought planetless? There were many planets, some circled by moons, and all were of surpassing beauty. But five stood out; they sang to her of things past imagining—it was if her senses were transformed. She heard colors, patterns, indescribable concepts. Space was not silent any longer. . . .

Ardith woke abruptly. For an instant her elation remained; then she was moved to tears of frustration and regret. Why had she been torn back from the place where there'd been something to look forward to?

In the morning, after orbit around Omega was established, she found Fred with Jacob Stromberg, weary-eyed, exhausted from hours of uninterrupted work. "There's no reasonable explanation," he was telling Jacob. "The Omegans might be gone, but their planets couldn't be. Planets can't just disappear."

"Maybe—maybe they blew them up," Ardith ventured, voicing what she knew many people suspected.

"All the planets in their system? And into dust, not mere fragments? There would be evidence! Even if they could do such a thing, there'd still be dust. We're close enough now to detect it. Anyway, that's not the main problem. We'd expect planets here if there had been no Message at all, simply from the characteristics of the sun."

Jacob frowned. "Are you saying astronomical theory isn't consistent with a sun like Omega being planetless?"

"I'm saying we've got to junk all the theory about planetary formation we've got," Fred stated flatly, "theory that's held up in every solar system we have visited. Of course only a small area of the galaxy has been explored—but the same physical laws apply everywhere."

"Yes, but ... well, I'm no astronomer. Still, rejecting a fundamental theory sounds a bit drastic."

Shrugging, Fred countered, "What do you do in anthropology when the theories don't fit the data?"

"We may not have all the data here," Jacob declared.

"The instruments have been checked and rechecked and cross-checked about fifty times."

"I can guess what you're thinking," Ardith said to Jacob, feeling a strange, cold thrill. "The Others—the Omegans—could be influencing the readings."

"Influencing our instruments?" demanded Fred. "That's impossible. The readings for everything else are okay. What we've learned about this sun itself matches data from Earth's telescopes. We use the same equipment for different purposes, you see—"

"Fred," argued Jacob, "I don't say the instruments themselves could be affected; you know more about that than I. But we all know basic scientific method. You tell us the theories about presence of planets apply to every known solar system but this. There's just one other way in which this system differs: it was the source of the Message. It was once, at least, the home of a technological civilization. What are the odds against the only two variables being unrelated?"

"You have a point," Fred admitted. "We'd be fools to write it off as random chance. No gambler would take such odds, that's for sure."

"Which means the Omegans either did something with their planets and moved on, or . . . they're hiding from us. They have a way to shield their worlds from detection."

"Why all their worlds?" Ardith asked. "Why not just the five inhabited ones, so astronomical theory wouldn't seem invalid?"

"That wouldn't work; we could tell from the orbits of the others—" Fred broke off. They stared at each other. She had said five. . . .

"I don't know why that slipped out," she murmured, embarrassed out of all proportion to the incident. "I had some silly dream last night; there were planets in it." Which was natural enough, when that was what she and everybody else had been concentrating on. Why should it impress Fred and Jacob, as it obviously did; why weren't they laughing it off?

His frown deepening, Jacob said slowly, "That they're shielding is most probable. I—I had hoped it would not be so."

"But it supports your own theory!" exclaimed

Fred, surprised. "If your ideas about the harm in contact are right, the Omegans *would* shield. They'd have learned by now that they shouldn't have sent the Message."

"No. You don't understand. If messages are sent that should not be received, the safeguard theory is wholly demolished. We must either concede that or say Earth is a freak case, and the odds that it is are even longer than those we were just discussing." Jacob smiled ruefully. "People thought it strange that I favored this expedition. Some feared I came to ensure its failure. But the truth is that I still trusted in universal safeguards, factors in the design of the universe that keep most worlds from coming to harm. And as for Earth being an exception . . . well, I bet on the alternative with the best odds."

"There's another alternative," said Ardith. "Contact may be harmless to us now." Somehow she felt surer of this than when she had mentioned it before the past nights' dreams.

"I know," agreed Jacob, in a tone that told her he had known and hoped for a very long time. "But if that were so, why would they shield their worlds?"

She could think of no cheerful reply. Finally she said, "Isn't the fact that they can shield at least an indication of safeguards, as you call them?"

"Ardith, think," put in Fred. "We crossed a thousand light-years! Suppose they discovered the shielding process only within the last century or so— it must be very advanced; our science can't conceive of any way such a thing could be done. What about all the worlds at closer range? Besides, knowing that a race so far ahead of ours exists may in itself be damaging to us."

"I've never heard this safeguard theory," she admitted. "I don't know what it involves."

"That's not an official name, of course," Jacob explained. "And it's not actually a theory; it's a mere hypothesis—an educated guess—though the fact Earth listened so long before receiving signals does provide some evidence. Essentially, it's an assumption that interstellar radio greetings are never transmitted in the normal course of a civilization's development: transmission's just too expensive before a species is far enough along to realize that less advanced worlds' evolution can be upset by contact. In other words, everybody listens and nobody sends. After all, Earth never transmitted more than a few primitive experimental messages; a project like that couldn't have gotten funded unless we'd received a message prior to the invention of faster-than-light travel."

"If the transmission of greetings was normal we'd have picked up broadcast signals years ago, according to statistical probability," Fred added. "Broadcasting a general beacon is much easier than beaming to countless specific solar systems; if a civilization was trying to find what others exist, that would be the natural way of going about it. To be sure, beaming takes a lot less power. But if the destination's so far off that one beam can reach many stars, you can't hope for replies."

"Then the fact that the Message was beamed to Earth selectively—"

"Might be encouraging." Jacob nodded. "I let myself be encouraged, again because the odds of that happening by chance were so incredible. But there is always the possibility that the Omegans discovered Earth at a time when the question of whether contacting younger species does harm was controversial among them, as it still is in our own civilization. We have faster-than-light travel, and my ideas aren't supported by all my colleagues. What, for instance, if we were to find a developing civilization near here, a thousand light-years from home—isn't it conceivable that someone on Earth might beam a greeting to it, in case we don't come back in a thousand years? To send a few beams is cheap; it might well be tried."

"Or," Ardith reflected, "there's the possibility that some worlds may pick up signals not meant for them."

"The chances of that are small enough to fall in the 'freak' class," Fred told her. "Early radio astronomers once supposed they might eavesdrop on signals not intended as greetings at all, but we've never received any, and there were a lot of advances that they didn't allow for. They figured high-level civilizations would form associations by radio instead of developing faster-than-light travel; and they even assumed a long period of local signal leakage. From Jacob's standpoint, things look safer than they used to."

Ardith watched Jacob's face, feeling confused and uncomfortable. "I am not sure," she said, "that we should want to be so safe. Do you really believe it is wrong for us to seek knowledge of higher civilizations?"

"No!" he replied intensely. "That's a misinterpretation of everything I've ever stood for, Ardith. It's never wrong for us to seek knowledge! It wasn't wrong for radio astronomers to listen, and our mission here is vital to humankind. If what I believe about safety factors in the universe is true, we won't find things beyond our ability to cope with—but we must keep on searching for whatever we *can* find. How else will we advance? It's wrong only to force knowledge on those unready to seek it for themselves."

"If there should be a way to—to penetrate the Omegans' shields, then you wouldn't oppose it?"

"I'd be the last person on this ship to do that," Jacob assured her. "Wait and see: if there is any chance of penetrating, I'll fight for it . . . and the rest of the staff will vote me down."

*

Again, both that night and the next, Ardith dreamed so vividly that she was reluctant to come back to consciousness. But in the daytime she was not sure what she had dreamed.

Music . . . like the "music of the spheres" the ancients had written about, she thought, trying to sort out the traces accessible to her. No, not music . . . not even sound, perhaps, but something for which no words existed. We think in words, she realized, and that limits us. We think in terms of what we already know. There's something here we've never met before. . . .

She was torn in two. The dreams elated her; waking brought back all the anguish of losing purpose in life. Maybe there were not really five inhabited worlds in the Omegan system, she told herself; maybe she merely wished there were. Yet half the time she did not wish it; she was afraid . . . afraid that the real worlds would not be like the ones of which she dreamt.

Almost everyone aboard seemed to have recovered from the initial disappointment of finding no planets; though Jacob and Fred presented the shield theory in a staff meeting, it was dismissed as fanciful by a large majority. Maybe the others have the same fear I do, Ardith found herself thinking as she talked this over with Fred. Maybe they're afraid the Omegans have nothing worth shielding, nothing far enough from our level to be a challenge . ... maybe they'd rather leave without knowing. Perhaps, if contact is harmful despite our having solved Earth's problems, that is why. The Omegans may want to spare us the final disillusionment.

"But that's inconsistent!" she burst out aloud.

At Fred's puzzled look, she explained, "I was wondering what the Omegans need to conceal. According to what Jacob believes, mature civilizations don't reveal themselves to immature ones because if they tried to spare them trouble it wouldn't really help. If you help a butterfly out of its cocoon its wings won't get strong, and it will die. By that reasoning, it's understandable why they never gave us answers. But now, if the worst thing we face is finding nothing left to look for, they wouldn't try to spare us that knowledge; it would be the next problem in sequence for us to solve."

He appraised her, startled. "Ardith, do you honestly think there's nothing left to look for?"

Equally startled, Ardith whispered, "No. No—not anymore." The fear drained out of her, and her heart began to race with excitement she had not felt for years. She *knew*. The dreams weren't mere symbols of her own suppressed longings. They were—contact. In sleep she had already begun to penetrate the shield.

When she next slept, she lay in darkness that melted into the light of strange new perceptions. She was in space no longer. She stepped into regions belonging to the planets themselves; yet she did not walk there, or fly through their skies—she was simply aware of them, without apparent bodily contact. There was no coherence to it; she was shifted from one scene to another in the way of dreams, and always there was the singing that was not singing. She heard no melody, no words, but only voices glimmering through mist like colored flashes seen from the depths of a luminous pool. She clung to sleep, struggling to rise to the surface of the water. . . .

And awakened in bitter disappointment.

Being now beyond all embarrassment, Ardith sought out Jacob Stromberg. "Yes," he told her, "I've dreamed, too, and so have others—more than will ever admit it. We can't force the issue. There must be no open discussion until each person who's receptive is independently sure."

"It's a crucial phenomenon, though! It may even signify—"

Jacob sighed. "Talk to Meiko Yamanashi; you'll see what I mean."

Ardith found Meiko, a young chemist whom she didn't know well, alone in her quarters. The girl was evidently quite upset; at the mention of dreams she wavered between defensiveness and an irrepressible eagerness to speak of them. "Look," she said to Ardith, "I don't claim there's anything supernatural about it—"

"No one's saying you do," Ardith assured her, though she saw from Meiko's face that some people were indeed saying that.

Meiko was convinced that five planets in the Omegan system were heavily populated. "I know they're here— the Others," she insisted, twisting her fingers nervously. "Dr. Gordon says it's wish-fulfillment—"

"Gordon? I thought he was trained in parapsychology."

"Sure he is. He calls it telepathic contagion; he treats me as if I were a carrier or something. He wants to put me under sedation at night, but I've refused. They are *good* dreams."

"Can you remember many details about them?" Ardith asked, hoping desperately that Meiko could draw back the curtain that descended whenever she herself tried to recapture specific images.

"Not many," Meiko confessed. "I just—well, I find knowledge in my mind. I have a rough idea of the planets' distances from Omega, for instance, as if someone had told me."

"You mean the Omegans talk to you?"

"No. It's not like that. It's more like clairvoyance; I believe I'm sensing things by myself."

"Can you do it while you're awake?" Ardith persisted.

"A little, now. I know what's real and what was an ordinary dream." She added, "I never had ESP talent before. That's what's so strange about it; if it were in my history, I suppose Gordon would accept it."

Ardith pondered this. "I wouldn't bank on that," she said, reflecting that a parapsychologist who'd joined the expedition with the idea the Others might be telepathic ought to be fascinated by Meiko's testimony. Also, the senior astronomers ought to have figured out the possibility of deliberately shielded planets long before Fred and Jacob had.

"Meiko," she continued, "why did you join the Exploration Corps?" She was groping toward something she couldn't yet define. "An exobiologist like me has to go to different worlds, but there are plenty of opportunities for chemists on Earth. Was it too crowded there, or what?"

"I didn't grow up on Earth; I'm from the colony on Ceti IX. It wasn't crowded and there was plenty of interesting work, but it didn't seem enough, somehow. I thought the Corps would be different."

"And it wasn't."

"You feel that too—as if there has to be more, somewhere? More even than meeting other species with high civilizations?"

"Yes. But most of the people aboard this ship don't. Maybe they did when they were kids, but now—well, they shut it out, the way they do these dreams. They might as well be in research labs on Earth; they'd function just the same there, if not better."

"They—oh, I don't know how to express it—but it's as if they can't bear the longing."

"You express it perfectly," said Ardith. "What they can't bear, they won't acknowledge even to themselves. If Omega had been what they were picturing, a system of worlds that could be analyzed by the old rules, it would have been okay. But without the framework of those rules their lives will fall apart . . . and there *is* something more here."

"Something besides just seeing these five worlds and their culture," Meiko declared positively.

"The dreams won't show it clearly, though. We won't know what it is if we leave without finding the worlds."

"The Omegans can't hide them from us, Ardith. From the machines, yes, but not from us. We are—sensitive. There are millions of other sensitive minds out there, and subconsciously we feel their presence. I think ESP must be more highly developed among the Omegans than in our species so far; that's why sensing them takes less talent than sensing other minds on Earth."

Ardith laughed. "It's easy to say, but the majority will not believe it; they'll trust the instruments more than they trust themselves."

"I know," admitted Meiko. "We'll be torn away, a thousand light-years back, and for the rest of our lives, jumping from solar system to solar system—colony to colony—we'll know that we're not getting anywhere. That we failed to follow the only forward trail."

We can't let it happen! Ardith thought fiercely. Yet we can't prevent it. We're ahead of our time, we few who believe in our own dreams.

*

She went to bed early that evening, hoping to dream more; but sleep would not come. Her mind would not rest; over and over it explored all the frustrating channels. This was how evolution worked, she told herself. She was a biologist; she'd studied evolution; she could apply the principles beyond the realm of biology. Always, steps forward were taken by the few, not the majority. In the fullness of time humankind might be ready for Omega. For the present, the dreams of the few would remain unfulfilled. The forward few always suffered; the first creature to crawl out of Earth's primeval sea had no doubt found it painful to breathe air. Yet preferable to returning to the sea. . . .

Ardith sat up in her dark cubicle, pulse pounding. What was happening to the expedition was *not* how evolution worked! Had that struggling creature been forced back to water when it was ready for air?

The majority of the public had not been ready for the moon in the 1960s, yet the few who cared had managed to get men there. The majority had not been ready for the stars when the dissatisfied few had begun to colonize other solar systems. As Jacob would say, the universe had built-in safeguards. The way forward always existed. Those who chose it might suffer or fail, but they *could* choose it; they were not condemned to waste their lives feeling they'd been born centuries too late—or too early. No species could evolve if the way were barred to the pioneers.

She wanted to cry out silently, Oh, help me, help

me, whoever you are here—you Others on the bright invisible worlds that orbit this sun! Show me the way and I'll come! I won't be like the rest; I won't turn my back on what the Message trail's led us to find . . . but no. That was almost a prayer, and they were not gods. They couldn't help. They wouldn't even if they could; they were wiser now than when they had sent the Message.

Or were they?

With shaking hands she reached for her clothes, slipping into them hurriedly. Fred might still be up. She could not wait till morning to ask the question that suddenly occurred to her.

She barged into the observatory center, heedless of the two other astronomers who were sitting with Fred at a computer console. "Maybe this is stupid," she began without preamble, "but how do we know the Message came from Omega's solar system?"

Fred looked up, startled. "Why, because it came from precisely this direction—telescopes picked it up only when accurately focused on this star."

"But have we any proof that it traveled a thousand years?"

"The speed of light and radio waves through space is a constant; you know that. We know we came about a thousand light-years to get here, and that's simply another way of saying radiation from here takes that long to reach Earth."

"Suppose something else generated the radiation, something directly in line—"

"If there were a closer solar system in direct line, we'd never have seen Omega from Earth. And if there were a farther one, Omega would have interfered with the signal waves."

"Yes—yes, of course. But a ship, for instance. If a ship relatively near our system had been precisely in line with Omega, and had sent the Message, there'd be no way of telling the difference, would there? We couldn't tell that the signals hadn't actually come so far."

"Since we can't verify the original frequency, no," Fred agreed. "Not unless the source was close enough to show parallax, which means very close because the beam wasn't received outside our solar system."

"Only a few light-years," put in one of the men with quick interest. "We didn't receive for long enough to detect parallax on Earth, and Mars was on our side of the sun; the distance between planets wasn't great enough for much parallax measurement."

"But it's fantastic, Ardith," Fred objected. "The odds on a ship being in exactly the right position—"

"I realize it couldn't happen by chance."

The older man's face lit up. "A hoax," he said. "It accounts for the selectivity of the destination, the tightness of the beam, everything! I wouldn't have thought anyone in Fleet could astrogate that well, let alone an outlaw crew; still it's the only sensible explanation."

"That wasn't what I was suggesting!" exclaimed Ardith. But in the relieved expressions of Fred's colleagues she could see that it was too late to amend her words. Unwittingly, she'd provided the safe, logical way out they'd been hunting for.

"Let's see who we can round up," said one of them. "I want a staff meeting the first thing tomorrow morning—there's no point wasting any more time in orbit." They left hurriedly, ignoring Fred as well as Ardith.

Fred looked troubled. "I'm sorry you said that in front of Ivanson," he told her. "The hoax idea will be the clincher—not that it will alter what he was trying to do anyway. In orthodox scientific terms we've collected all the data we can here. Ivanson's been pushing for a jump to the nearest similar star hoping it has no planets either; he's rewriting planetary theory and as chief astronomer aboard, I think he's got his eye on the Galaxy Prize. The chiefs of the biology and geology departments will support him; their people are going batty without planets to study, and they want to get moving."

"I suppose that's the official explanation for the dreams," observed Ardith bitterly.

"What else?" He met her eyes. "Ardith—what were you getting at, if not a hoax?"

"I—I guess I was backing up Jacob's safeguard idea."

"That we're unlikely to have gotten a message we shouldn't have? But we did receive one—" Fred paused thoughtfully. "Oh, you mean that if we can't prove the senders are a thousand years ahead, no damage has been done. Maybe not; still it doesn't save Jacob's theory. It doesn't provide for the case of worlds receiving signals before the senders have learned to shield their own planets from detection."

"There may not be any such cases," declared Ardith. "Don't you see, I'm saying he could have been right in the beginning about no harmful signals ever being transmitted! An Omegan ship could have sent the Message—recently—to bring us here."

"Because we're ready for contact with them? Then why shield their worlds from us?"

"Not necessarily from us; perhaps from other passersby. But also perhaps from those of us who aren't really ready."

"Like Ivanson."

"And like our blind parapsychologist Gordon. Fred, suppose Jacob is right all the way. Suppose he's even right about there being a huge hidden supercivilization, the kind imagined by twentieth-century radio astronomers—"

"In that case," interrupted Fred, frowning, "we should have found suns like this before without visible planets. They'd be shielding many."

"Maybe they deliberately avoided colonizing systems near Earth, at least those of stars we'd be likely to visit. There are thousands of solar systems a supercivilization could choose from; and besides, some of its member species may have environmental requirements different from ours. We've known all along there must be other civilizations in the galaxy, that our not finding them was a matter of the odds against stumbling on them—and the same goes for shielded systems."

"True. A federation of species could manipulate the odds. What's more, if a people did come across a shielded system prematurely, that wouldn't do any harm."

"Only for us it's not premature," Ardith went on, her exhilaration growing. "If there's a supercivilization, and we've reached the point in our evolution when we're to be admitted, how would contact be made? Surely the Others wouldn't land UFOs on Earth as if they were creatures out of an old-time space opera."

"No," Fred agreed slowly. "The old assumptions were all wrong. They'll never come to us; we had to come to them—in more ways than one." Watching him, Ardith knew that he too had dreamed, and that his longing to respond to the dreams equaled her own. He cursed softly. "We came, yet we're going to blow it."

"Are we? I think if they'd expected everybody to react the same way, we'd have met the welcoming committee by now. Why not land their ship on Earth, if not to give us personal choice?"

"Ardith, you know what will happen if we present these theories in a staff meeting. Jacob will back us, and Meiko Yamanashi, and perhaps a few others. We won't sway the majority. The ship won't wait to investigate."

"We don't need the majority, or the starship either. Just one lifeboat. You've done some piloting, haven't you?"

"Orbit to ground, yes. But I can't astrogate without—"

"Without knowing where the planets are. Fred, if I'm right, Meiko can . . . locate them. Can you establish an orbit once you're close to a planet?"

He drew breath. "Yes. I'd like to try. It's insane not to try when we've come a thousand light-years! But a lifeboat can't gather any more data than this ship's instruments; I doubt if the Captain will authorize it."

Ardith laughed, feeling buoyant and reckless and young again. "Who said anything about consulting the Captain?"

*

From the lifeboat, three days later, the four of them stared at the blazing stars—groupings they now knew well—and tried not to reckon the minutes that were passing. So little time left, Ardith thought, and if we fail we'll have no second chance. . . .

Getting away unnoticed had been no problem. This being a scientific expedition staffed by known researchers, Fleet had no need to limit access to the ship's facilities, as would be done on an ordinary charter trip, and the idea that someone might want to make an unauthorized excursion in a lifeboat had never occurred to the Captain. The small-craft bay had been deserted, as it always was while the starship was in deep space. There was no reason for anybody to go near it when no planets were thought to be close. Fred had been able to program the lifeboat's astrogation computer without fear of detection during the time it had taken the others to assemble the few things that could be taken aboard.

But a second chance was out of the question. If they docked to restore their dwindling life support, they would not be permitted to separate again. That had been only too obvious from what had been said over the radio they'd finally turned off.

And over half the time for which their life support was adequate had now passed.

"I don't understand," Meiko said wretchedly. "I know there's a world nearby. We're in the right area! We've been approaching! And still no sign—"

"We could see it with our eyes by now despite whatever keeps the instruments from picking it up," someone protested. They had come far from the starship in the sixty hours since they'd left it; the lifeboat was fast enough to circle Omega. They had not needed to circle, however. Meiko's sensing ability had led them closer to the sun, but no great distance in the new orbit, before they'd all begun to know they were in range. Asleep, dreaming, they had known positively.

"We can't guess how the shielding works," Fred pointed out. "It's possible that a world might be hidden from our eyes as well as from instruments."

So much was hidden. The lifeboat's radio could not be tuned to the frequency on which the starship was signaling to the Omegans, which was of course an astronomical one, the one on which the Message had been received corrected for the presumed thousand light-years of travel to Earth; neither the starship's call nor any possible reply to it could be detected. What else is there in the universe, still invisible, that we've never even imagined? wondered Ardith. Have we ever really searched? Do we know how to search? Or were we too busy founding colonies to care?

"The colonies were necessary," Jacob said. Ardith wasn't surprised that he'd answered unspoken thought; it had happened frequently, among all of them, these past few days.

"Necessary," Jacob continued, "but not the real purpose of travel between the stars. They were only a beginning, a jumping-off place. The real purpose of interstellar exploration is finding evidence for ideas— ideas that we've called pure philosophy, or maybe even religion. If there is a supercivilization, that is the sort of exploring it does."

"We shouldn't have named this sun Omega," said Ardith in a low voice. "We were naive."

"Very naive. Even those of us who, three days ago, were so proud of being more perceptive than our shipmates."

"And now we're paying for our pride," added Fred.

"No!" Ardith insisted. "This isn't Omega, yet all the same we had to come here. We got the Message; we simply haven't discovered how to answer it."

"We expected it to be easy," said Meiko. "Just the way astronomers on Earth once thought all they'd have to do would be to decode binary data sent by superior civilizations and get solutions to Earth's problems. And the way our own expedition set out thinking the Others would hand us the key to the city, so to speak—or start to negotiate for setting up diplomatic relations."

"Humankind's vision of the stars was childish after all," Fred muttered.

"We are not children now," declared Jacob. "Either we follow through, or we betray what we are and what we may yet become."

Ardith said slowly, "You've known from the start that it wouldn't be as anyone thought. You knew most of the staff wouldn't want to follow through, wouldn't dare face anything too far from what was expected. Do you know what more is demanded of us?"

"No," Jacob admitted. "Only that we can't give up yet, and that nobody will show us the way forward."

"And there is a way." The way forward always exists, she reminded herself. That's the only reason any species evolves.

"Logically, it's impossible that we're all deluded. One or two cases of strange dreams might be mental imbalance. Four of us, separately convinced—" All of them looked at each other. There was no use in talking about it any longer, and in fact they had never talked much about the dreams; what happened in the dreams was too hard to express. Nevertheless their knowledge of it was shared.

By unspoken agreement they lay down once more to seek sleep. The small ship, for the time being unpowered, sped in its orbit around the alien sun, carrying them toward unknown regions. Ardith closed her eyes and felt herself falling, though she was well accustomed to zero gravity. She was dizzy, perhaps from hunger; they were stretching their rations as far as possible, and fasting, they knew, might intensify their dreams. It was a risk: on Earth, the dreams of fasting seers had not always been as valid as they seemed. Yet now only desperate measures were left. . . .

She fell into black space. The worlds were tiny and very distant. For the first time her dream verged on nightmare. Somewhere a long way back were Earth and LaLande VI and all the other safe, familiar planets where humankind belonged, where the pattern of things was lucid; but she was cut off from them. She was cut off from everything. She could not find her way to the worlds of the Others. They were there and they were beautiful, but it was an alien, terrible beauty, past all comprehension. And there were perils there, also. She was not equipped to cope with such perils; she wanted only to withdraw . . . even to withdraw into nothingness. Though it was fearful, she feared the bright worlds more; and of her longing and her fear, she was not sure which was worst. . . .

Ardith came to herself, cold and trembling. While the dream stayed clear in her mind, she recalled snatches of past ones, too: both the wonders and the terrors. There had been terrors; why had she not recalled them consciously? Why had she sought a universe where human works were the games of children; where human symbols were abandoned toys, cherished for past value, but no longer of real use? Once you entered such a universe, you could never go back.

And they would have to go back—soon, if they failed, if their life support ran out before they found the way through the Others' shield; but anyway, eventually. Wouldn't they?

No, Ardith saw suddenly, not if what they were seeking was a real step in evolution. Evolution didn't work like that.

With rising fear, she began to perceive the way forward.

*

"It's the only answer," she told the others, now all awake, clustered around her in the dimly-lit compartment. "We're not committed. We are still thinking of going back."

There was silence. Finally Jacob said, "I believe

you're right. We can't have it both ways. Oh, we may return to Earth someday—we, or others like us—once we've found what it lies within us to be. We are still members of our own human race; they are not gods, and they won't do anything to change us. We're pioneers, not deserters; we'll play some role in changes already happening to humankind. We'll become emissaries, perhaps. But we must not count on going back in any manner we can foresee."

"Because they won't accept us on those terms?" asked Fred.

"It's not a matter of their accepting us. They've issued an invitation to our world; it's up to us to accept *them*."

"To trust them," Ardith said. "Or at least to trust our own dreams."

No words were required for the rest of the answer. They all saw it: for their trust, for their commitment, there must be proof. There must be proof in their own minds, whether or not any outside agency demanded it. They would not penetrate the shield while they held any tie to Earth's starship in reserve.

The time was not ripe for full-scale contact between cultures; that must come gradually. And the safeguards did exist. Earth would not find what it was not quite ready to find. So the starship could not return and arouse a controversy, as would surely happen if some were aboard to report a discovery not yet truly sought by the majority. It could return only to report the majority's view that the Omegan system was planetless and the Message a fake; that there was no known superior civilization; that the people who insisted on following dream trails had been lost in a small craft with less than three days' life support remaining. . . .

The time would never be ripe for contact if no one took the first step.

"There's an old legend," murmured Ardith, "about burning one's own ships—"

"Very ancient," said Jacob. "A sixteenth-century explorer named Cortez set fire to his fleet so that his expedition couldn't turn back from the New World. It wasn't the first such incident. It won't be the last; the principle is valid."

"And how would we . . . manage it here?"

"If I clear the memory of the astrogation computer," Fred answered, "we can't find the starship again. If I rip out certain tracking circuits and then alter our course, it can't find us. The Captain will try until time runs out for our life support; after that, his natural assumption will be that we no longer exist."

We're crazy, Ardith thought, to stake our lives on what's really only a guess . . . on what, underneath, we fear as much as we long for! Yet evolution always does require that a being adapt or die. . . .

"How much of our time—"

"To do it? A couple of minutes. Close your eyes and it's finished, if that's what we all want."

One by one, they nodded.

For an instant Ardith's mind was brushed by terror; then joy spread through her, crowding out the fear. She saw the stars as if for the first time, the long-ago time that had seemed past recapturing: the time when they'd been symbols of glories to reach for. How many had worlds shielded from the uncommitted? To how many suns, how many galaxies, would humankind someday be led by her refusal to deny the Message? Along how many beckoning, radiant trails?

She shut her eyes; the ship rotated and through the viewport, the light of the star once called Omega shone warm on her face. Almost at once she saw images from the dreams, though she remained conscious. Soon she would be more fully aware of the universe ahead.

Part One: Ydoril

~ 1 ~

The alien ship loomed out of nowhere, as if it had been waiting for them—which it probably had been, Ardith realized. If the Others were telepathic they would have known when the commitment was made.

It was a large ship and the entire lifeboat was drawn into it under some sort of automatic control that Fred made no attempt to counter. Their fate was out of their hands now. What was to come, would come; if any choice was available to them, they would be told. But she sensed that their arrival was viewed with gladness—greater gladness, in fact, than the circumstances seemed to warrant. It was as if they were not merely welcome, but needed.

The hatch opened and a tall figure wearing a coverall and face mask beckoned them through. A breathing mask inside the ship, when they themselves had been given none? Briefly puzzled, she turned to Fred. "The air's apparently been adjusted for us," he said in a low voice. "It's not their air, but they know what we require."

And indeed, though there was an airlock on the inner wall of the shuttle bay they were not taken through it. Instead, to Ardith's amazement, they were escorted through an adjacent hatch into a comfortably-furnished compartment that looked more like a living room than a section of a ship. Weak from stress and lack of food, she sank into one of the chairs, which although large and shapeless immediately conformed to her body. What sort of bodies had it been designed for? she wondered. There was nothing in the place to suggest anything alien.

A roboserver appeared, offering her a steaming mug of some sort of soup, which she drank gratefully, finding that it tasted good and quickly revived her. Looking around, she saw that the others were also reviving. A tall arch stood open to another compartment, inviting entry, and since their needs were evidently being met, she realized that it must lead to a bathroom. By unspoken agreement she, as the oldest female among them, rose to use it first. But once inside she saw that there were privacy booths and called to the others to follow.

In the center of the bathroom was an actual bath, a wide, deep pool containing far more water than any of Earth's ships could have devoted to that purpose. From a rack near it hung bright-colored robes of varying lengths. Emerging from her booth, where she had left her clothes in a bin apparently meant for them, she descended into the pool and let it absorb the remainder of her weariness.

"If I weren't so eager to know more about our hosts I'd be enjoying this," said Meiko. "But I guess we should get ready . . . for whatever's coming." They climbed out, finding that a blast of warm air near the robe rack eliminated the need for towels. Ardith chose appropriately-sized sandals and a silky blue robe that came just below her knees. A few, she saw, would have been long enough to trip on and then some; more than one race of beings must use this ship—which, though no sleeping area was visible, had obviously been designed to accommodate passengers unlike its crew.

The robes were self-fastening and apparently intended to replace other clothes for the time being; she wasn't sure if she would ever see her own again, and she really didn't care. Styles worn by the aliens were undoubtedly quite different. She was starting afresh here, and felt no eagerness for reminders of the old life that had been so frustrating.

When they returned to the main room, someone awaited them there, a figure clad, surprisingly, in an ordinary pullover shirt and trousers. As he turned, Ardith gasped in astonishment. He was not alien, but a vigorous white-haired old man she might have met anywhere on Earth.

With a warm smile he said in Anglo, "Welcome to the Federation of Allied Worlds. I'm Radnor of Maclairn, and I'll be your mentor here."

"But—but you're *human*," Ardith burst out.

"We're all human in the most meaningful sense of the word. But if you mean I'm a member of the species native to Earth, yes, I am. You're not the first of us to meet others."

"How can that be?" Jacob protested. "For years I've been in touch with everyone who has any interest in searching for extraterrestrial civilizations. Surely such a secret couldn't have been kept—"

"It was essential that it be kept. You of all people, Jacob Stromberg, must know what the reaction on Earth would have been if such meetings had been made public."

"You recognize me?"

"Of course—I've viewed recordings of your speeches and read everything you've ever written, starting long before there had been any contact with extraterrestrials. And it will save a lot of explanation if I simply tell you that your theory is 100% correct. The Elders—species that evolved long ago on different mother worlds—do not reveal their existence to young species not mature enough to join the Federation as equals. It would preclude their evolution to that level, and the loss would be not only theirs but everyone's, since each 'human' species has a unique contribution to make as a result of its independent development."

"Are you saying we're mature enough now?" Ardith asked skeptically. Surely the scientists aboard the starship hadn't been.

"Not all of us. But as a planetary civilization we meet the minimum criteria." Motioning them to sit, Radnor went on, "Of course all the member species are at different levels of maturity, since they have existed for different lengths of time. We are the youngest admitted so far, and we have a lot more growing up to do. But we have passed the three essential milestones: we've built interstellar ships and colonized planets of many stars; we no longer make distinctions between people based on physical differences; and a sufficient percentage of us have enough telepathic ability to communicate with the Elders and thus hold our own in a telepathic culture."

"I'm not so sure about that last," Meiko declared. "There's still a lot of prejudice, not against individuals with ESP like during the Ku Klux Klan era a century ago, but against the mere idea of psi faculties. And it's growing. Once, many people believed in the mind powers promised by the Captain of *Estel*, that we'll someday be able to cure sickness and pain by our minds alone, as well as end misunderstanding by communicating without speech. Now, in most places such ideas are simply laughed at. Parapsychologists are interested only in lab experiments. They don't care about the real world."

"There was a backlash," Radnor agreed. "When it began to dawn on scientists who'd put their faith in materialism that the Captain of *Estel* knew what he was talking about, they got scared and intensified efforts to squelch the Estelan movement by making fun of it. The majority of psi advocates went underground."

"Was the Captain of *Estel* a real person?" asked Ardith, surprised. "I've always thought he was a folk hero, that his role in bringing down the Klan was mere legend."

"He was very real," said Radnor. "He is, in fact, my father, though I didn't know that until I was already an old man. And he is still alive."

"Oh, my God. Was he in contact with aliens all along?"

"He was the first, not counting those who met Federation agents unknowingly. That's a long story. For now there are more immediate things you need to know."

"Yes," declared Fred. "Like why we were brought here as we were if other civilizations are already in contact with Earth."

"Not with Earth, just with people whose ancestors were Earthborn. There is a colony named Maclairn, secret from all but a few other humans, where psi powers are highly developed—it is my native world. Fifteen Earth-years ago my father went there as ambassador of the Elders, who do not show themselves until invited. He convinced its leaders to accept extraterrestrials into our midst. But no one on Earth except Maclairnans has yet been told." He paused and then continued intensely, "That, if you are willing, is to be your role, and it's not an easy one. We had to find telepathically-sensitive volunteers with the courage to take it on."

"You mean you contacted us by telepathy intentionally?" Ardith was surprised; she'd assumed they had simply sensed the presence of the wondrous alien worlds.

"We did," Radnor replied. "A few very advanced telepaths have the ability to reach receptive minds distant in space."

"Why haven't you—your colony's people——told anyone about the Elders?" Meiko asked, puzzled.

"We will, in due course. But we can't do it alone because we would not be believed. Fringe cults have been claiming to be in contact with extraterrestrials since the twentieth century, and as the League government is already suspicious of our reliance on psi powers, we'd be viewed as merely another one."

"It has to come from reputable scientists, then," Jacob agreed. "Is that why the Elders sent a message aimed specifically toward astronomers?"

"It was the best way to learn which of the researchers interested in contact were sincere enough to risk their lives for it. We'd have gladly accepted the whole staff of the expedition and the Fleet crew as well, if they had pursued the investigation. But I don't have to tell you that we didn't expect them to. You four alone proved qualified."

Ardith frowned. "I don't think we'll be believed either, if we go back to Earth and say we've met aliens."

"Sure we will," said Fred. "They'll have to believe us because officially we're now dead. We were lost in a small lifeboat a thousand light-years beyond where any other starship has gone. Our life support has run out. If we turn up alive, they'll know we had help."

"Yes," Radnor agreed. "That was why we induced your starship to come so far."

The claim would be unassailable, Ardith realized.

By law only the Earth League government's paramilitary force, known simply as Fleet, could own large starships. It used them to police space as well as for passenger or freight transport, and sometimes chartered them to organizations such as the Scientific Exploration Corps. Small ships, useful only to courier services, free traders, and pirates, could not carry enough fuel for the jumps such a long distance would require. There could have been no rescue by humans.

"There have been many alleged contacts with aliens," Radnor continued, "but never any proof, and a legitimate claim would be dismissed for that reason if no proof could be offered. Your DNA and implanted IDs will provide it. But it's not that simple."

"They won't *want* to believe," Meiko said sadly. "They'll pretend the proof doesn't exist."

"Unfortunately, that's true," Radnor agreed. "The authorities will not welcome the proof and they'll try to suppress it. You'll have a hard time getting it seen by those ready to know we're not alone in the universe."

Through her growing telepathic sensitivity, Ardith grasped more than Radnor had said aloud. The majority of people on Earth did not want to face the fact that they weren't safely isolated from the universe. They perceived the vast region beyond the colonized worlds as threatening, full of unknowns, if not hostile forces then at least ideas that might shake their deepest beliefs. They'd do just about anything to avoid having to confront such ideas. . . .

My God, she thought, he's saying that if we do turn up alive, we may not stay alive! The easiest way for opponents to suppress the evidence would be to eliminate us.

~ 2 ~

"I don't understand," Fred protested. "Some species in the Federation must be physically different from us. If they went to Earth there'd be no doubt that they were alien."

"Think, Fred," said Jacob. "This is the same situation that has been discussed by speculators for hundreds of years. For aliens to suddenly appear on Earth would produce shock. Some people would assume they were hostile, others would expect them to be godlike beings able to put an end to all its problems. And still others would be literally xenophobic—while there's no racism left in regard to our own species, they'd be repelled at the sight of nonhuman bodies, and some might turn violent. In any case, there'd be cultural upheaval and the Federation's long avoidance of disclosure would prove futile. So the knowledge of its existence must be absorbed gradually."

"But if the Captain of *Estel* is still alive," Meiko said, "surely he could prepare people, just as he inspired them to want new capabilities."

"He's no longer physically strong enough to travel, let alone speak to crowds," Radnor explained. "He is very old now and the end of his life is approaching."

"And so we are expected to take on the job?

"That's right," Radnor agreed. "It will be a long, slow process that began when Federation agents were first secretly based on Earth. They have never shown themselves in UFOs, by the way. They are sworn to die rather than reveal their alien origin. But they've encouraged the belief in the possible existence of extraterrestrials that's already well established in the population's collective unconscious. Now, more specific preparation is needed. It has started with the integration in the secret colony Maclairn. The next step, a perilous step, is liaison with the League government that represents Earth and its recognized colonies. There must be joint planning for the eventual public revelation."

"Through us, the four of us? I don't think I'm ready for that responsibility," Jacob said slowly.

"Not yet. You have much to learn and many challenges to meet before having to make that decision. You're not obligated to accept the mission. The Elders never force anyone into an unwanted role; if you go, it will be as genuine volunteers."

Why would we want to volunteer? Ardith asked inwardly. Haven't we just seen that most people, even scientists who joined the expedition, don't really want to meet aliens? I never liked Earth, was never content in any of its colonies. What makes him think I'll choose to return there as an envoy the authorities may try to get rid of?

"I don't really see why it's important to tell everyone," she confessed. "They might be happier not knowing."

"Is Earth a happy place now?" Jacob asked.

"Well, no. Most people are bored and depressed. But knowing there are aliens won't make them any happier."

"The Captain of *Estel* thought it would," Meiko recalled. "In one of his famous speeches he said that finding other worlds, worlds full of exciting new sights and ideas, would be our best hope for a brighter future."

"He still believes that," Radnor declared. "Like the Elders, he's sure that contact with those worlds is the way—the only way—to keep Earth's civilization from sliding further downhill. It saddens him to know that he probably won't live to see it."

"And it can't happen until most of Earth's people accept aliens as our equals," Jacob said. "So if we can help bring that about, I'm willing to try."

While they ate a light meal brought by the roboserver, Radnor explained that the ship wasn't taking them to one of the five planets they had perceived from space. "It's too soon," he said. "They are populated mainly by the oldest species in the Federation, the one with the strongest psi powers. Only skilled seers of that species are capable of reaching distant untrained minds through dreams, and you would be overwhelmed if you tried to communicate with them now, while awake. You wouldn't be able to grasp the concepts and images that fill their thoughts."

Ardith looked away, stricken by disappointment. She had anticipated seeing the place the dreams had shown her, mysterious, incomprehensible, but inspiring. . . .

"We'll jump to a solar system with a planet whose inhabitants are used to dealing with new-comers," Radnor continued. Ydoril, he said, was an artificially-constructed world designed to meet the needs of diverse biologies. It was the headquarters of the Federation's Anthropological Service, an organization responsible for observing peoples not yet mature enough for Federation membership and establishing contact with those that had reached the threshold.

"There is no native population," Radnor told them, "except children of the few Service agents who choose to raise families. The long-term residents, apart from administrators and data analysts, are all either in training or retired. But many others come for breaks between assignments, or to bring guests from recently-admitted worlds."

"How much red tape will there be to get Earth admitted?" Fred asked.

"As far as the Federation is concerned, it has already been admitted. But for a world's species to attain full membership two things have to happen. First, it must be judged to be sufficiently mature; that judgment has been made. And second, a significant number of its people must seek contact—the Elders don't go where they're not invited."

"How did they go about judging us?" Ardith inquired.

"The Service has evaluated Earth over a period of millennia, and since the twentieth century its agents have lived incognito there, sometimes undergoing modification of their bodies in order to pass among us. When the time was ripe, *Estel*'s copilot Liam revealed himself as an Elder and took my father to Ydoril, then eventually to another world to be mind-probed by the man we call Eldest who is the closest thing the Federation has to a leader. His power is purely ceremonial, but some sort of ceremony is needed on such occasions; my father told me later that it was deeply moving. Through him, as a representative of our species, Earth was declared a Federation world."

"But what if the League government won't sign the treaty?" Fred asked.

"It's not a matter of treaty. The Federation has no central government—its worlds are independent, and most have outgrown the wish to be governed even internally. Representatives of the members meet to discuss issues of common concern, but apart from the ban on contact with immature races and some restrictions on relations with new members, there are no overall laws. Earth will be prevented from harming other planets or their citizens, by force if necessary; but otherwise it will remain autonomous."

Jacob frowned. "Radnor," he said, "I've had a long career and studied countless cultures, past and present. I have enough knowledge of human nature to make me a realist. And what you are describing sounds too much like utopia to be credible. There have been many attempts to do without government, and they have all ended in disaster, with the worst people preying on the best. Sooner or later the same must happen with worlds."

"That's what I thought, too, before I studied Federation history," Radnor said. "What's hard to grasp at first is that you and I have seen human nature only from the perspective of our own point in our species' evolution. We underestimate progress because we have forgotten what life was like in earlier eras and have had no way to see what it will be like for our descendants."

"True, but biologically, our nature is a constant."

"The behavior of sapient species isn't determined by biology. Think of all the barbarisms abolished in the past—mass slaughter of enemies; war viewed as glorious, with rape and pillage as its accepted aftermath; slavery; the subjugation of women; the poor even in peacetime allowed to starve—and then say humans don't gradually become wiser and more humane."

"The Federation can't have abandoned violence completely," Fred declared, "if it's prepared to prevent Earth from harming other peoples by force."

"Well, that depends on what's meant by force," Ardith pointed out. "The Federation worlds are shielded, presumably from harm as well as from sight. No doubt they can shield younger species' planets too, if they choose."

"They can and do, to prevent their discovery," Radnor agreed. "But as far as mass violence is concerned, that wouldn't be necessary. It's inconceivable that a starfaring species would seek to colonize an inhabited planet, for instance. We wouldn't have considered it even as far back as the twenty-first century, if interstellar travel had been possible then."

That was true, Ardith thought. Stories about war with aliens had always been analogies based on Earth's past rather than a reflection of current views.

"The more likely scenario is harm to Federation visitors on Earth," Radnor continued, "or vice versa, through unintentional interference—and for that reason there's an unbreakable policy that prevents anyone not officially authorized by the Service from setting foot on young worlds. Earth won't be cleared for tourists for a good many years to come."

"Surely there will always be disputes between Federation worlds," Jacob argued, "even if they're settled by negotiation."

"Disputes over what? If you think they have cause to fight, you've been reading too much old-time science fiction. Earth's colonies don't fight each other, after all. Conflict between inhabitants of a single planet involves either land or resources, and there's no lack of either, once a species can travel between stars. The universe is full of resources, not to mention uninhabited planets. It costs less to develop unused ones than it would to seize those already claimed."

"But you've implied that all civilizations evolve in much the same way," Meiko protested, "and aren't humans naturally aggressive?"

"No. Humans and other sapient species have a natural drive to meet challenge—to overcome obstacles, such as a lack of resources they want or a fear of losing those they have. There is nothing inherently aggressive about this drive; it leads to aggression only while a species is confined to a single planet with resources that are finite."

"I guess that's why interstellar colonization is one of the requirements for admission to the Federation," Meiko reflected.

"It's true that our colonies don't come into conflict with each other," Jacob said. "Yet there's plenty of aggression on Earth itself caused by gangs and terrorists."

"Yes, because no constructive challenge is open to them. Earth hasn't enough resources to go around; it's overpopulated and most people aren't free to move to the colonies. So conditions are bad there, not just the violence but the inertia born of frustration that affects almost everyone. It's a temporary stage that will last until new challenges are taken up—unless the situation there deteriorates further, which it may if contact with the Elder worlds can't be established soon enough."

Jacob frowned. "If it can't be, they'd intervene?"

"Only in an emergency, and then only if a large enough segment of the population asks for help. Normally it's not a matter of intervention. People on Earth will be invigorated by knowledge gained from other civilizations, now that they're ready for it, and it will inspire them to deal with the problems by themselves."

Ardith looked down at her plate, feeling little interest in food that was all too similar to that served on the starship she had left. She wasn't sure what she had expected from her first hour in an extraterrestrial civilization, but certainly not this—not a philosophic discussion that might just as well be taking place at the university on LaLande VI where she'd been due to teach.

She liked Radnor; he reminded her of the grandfather she had adored as a child. But she wasn't a child now, and she had anticipated meeting extraterrestrials. What had happened to the feelings that had aroused such joy in her, such conviction that alien contact was the key to a more fulfilling life?

"When my father spoke out as the Captain of *Estel*," Radnor went on, "it was to give people hope for a new kind of challenge, one that doesn't depend on Earth's society but only on powers of their minds. Hope—that's what the word 'Estel' means, why he chose it for his ship."

"He faced down the Klan," Meiko said, "and rescued a lot of refugees before that. So he was well aware of the violence. Did he really believe no one's violent by nature?"

"Of course not," Radnor said. "There will always be individual evildoers—but they become more aberrant as time passes. Local police can deal with them; when conditions on Earth improve they won't be able to attract followers, as they do when people are frustrated. The history of the Federation worlds proves this, but those worlds are centuries, in some cases millennia, ahead of ours. You'll study their history while you're here."

No wonder the Elders didn't make young worlds prematurely aware of them, Ardith realized. It would be tantalizing, just as she herself had been tantalized by a taste of a something still far beyond her understanding. Would she ever be shown the essence of it? Abruptly it occurred to her that being in the vanguard of evolution might be more difficult than she'd expected.

~ 3 ~

Radnor stood up and pressed a switch that illuminated one entire wall of the compartment, which proved to be a huge holoscreen. "We've dropped into normal space near Ydoril's star," he said. "The shield will be lowered in a couple of minutes, and you'll be able to see where we're going."

As they watched, Ydoril loomed suddenly into view, close, nearly filling the screen. Blue-green and sparkling—sparkling in a way Ardith had not seen on any other world—it pierced her low mood with its beauty. The initial disappointment of first contact faded, and with a surge of excitement, she felt young again.

"What makes the planet sparkle?" Meiko asked. "I don't see any water."

"There are domes, large transparent ones, among the trees," Radnor explained. "Not all the residents need the same atmosphere. We're among those who can't breathe outdoors without masks."

Quickly, he told them what to expect on landing. "It's evening by our dome's time," he said, "and there'll be an informal gathering in what we call the Sky Room. You'll be welcomed there by a variety of people. Most of them, even those of different species, speak Anglo; they have worked as observers on Earth or in Earth orbit, or have visited my home world Maclairn. A few do not, but you'll be able to pick up the gist of their words telepathically."

Dismayed, Ardith protested, "I'm not telepathic except in dreams."

"Unconsciously, you are. Your ability to grasp thought consciously will grow through contact with stronger telepaths."

Their clothes, Radnor told them, had by now been

measured by a robovalet and new ones were ready in the booths where they had left them. These proved to be loose optionally-belted tunics, again in bright colors, and mid-calf grey pants that seemed sturdy although soft against her skin. Recyclable underwear was also provided, along with lightweight bags in which to carry their robes and other belongings.

Dressed, they watched in fascination as they drew closer to the planet's surface. In less than an hour they reentered the shuttle bay to board a round pilotless craft, which Radnor said would take them directly into the dome where they were to live. "We'll talk again later tonight," he said. "I'm not going down yet, but the shuttle will be met when it lands."

The descent was so smooth that with her eyes closed Ardith wouldn't have known the ship was moving, and in fact it was not even equipped with seatbelts; the Elders evidently had a way to control gravity. The bright landscape below shrank as they moved toward the night side of the planet until, by the time they were close to the ground, the land below was dark—except for the domes, which shone from light within. Awed, she began to grasp their immensity—taller at the center than any skyscraper, each one must accommodate thousands, and their outer shells appeared to be composed entirely of windows. No wonder they sparkled with reflected sunlight when seen from orbit.

The ship was taken in near the bottom of a dome through a port that dilated as they approached and sealed itself behind them. After a brief wait for the air pressure to equalize, the hatch slid open and the four humans rose to be greeted by two extraterrestrials.

Two *people*. She must think of them all as people, Ardith realized, for there was no other term for sapient beings. They were human in shape and dressed as she was, but there were obvious differences. One of them had yellow skin—a clear light yellow with no trace of brown—a flat nose, and sparse fuzzy white hair. She wondered, suddenly, whether this was a man or a woman. The familiar clues being absent, there was really no way to tell.

I'm female, the person told her silently, having grasped the question telepathically. And then, aloud in a voice that was obviously synthesized, she said slowly, "Welcome to Ydoril. We are very happy that you have come."

The other alien was taller and of a different species, with facial features unlike those of his/her companion and purple-tinged skin. "My name is Coris," this person said, "and as Coordinator of contact with Earth I wished to greet you immediately. Korela, who is a student at the Academy here, will show you to your sleeping quarters and then take you to the Sky Room, where many others are gathered to welcome you."

Though their words were formal, no doubt because Anglo was not their native language, the two did not seem cold—they radiated warmth and friendliness. Neither of them offered a hand to shake, and perhaps hand-shaking was a purely human custom; after all, the hands of various species must be shaped differently. Abruptly it dawned on Ardith that it was unnecessary to touch physically when so much could be conveyed by the wordless touching of minds.

Meiko, Fred and Jacob were silent, and she found that with them, too, there was no need for words. The experience was shared fully enough without them, and it was so overwhelming that comment would have been superfluous.

The corridor through which they were taken was wide, bright, and spotlessly clean, as could be expected on a world with AI technology far surpassing that of Earth; but there was nothing sterile about it. Planters containing greenery and flowers, brilliantly-colored flowers, lined its walls, and she could see that they weren't artificial. During the day light must pour through the now-opaque outer surface, and water must be piped in.

Following their guide, they stepped into an alcove on the inner wall and were amazed to see that it had no ceiling—through a shaft far, far, above them they could see the star-studded night sky. Only when its semitransparent walls slid gradually downward, revealing an opening to another corridor, did Ardith become aware that it was an elevator. Like the lander, it was powered by some effect of gravity that eliminated any sense of motion. Several floors were passed before it came to a stop and they were led into a narrower passageway off which many doors opened. A green light above one of them marked it as their destination.

The room they entered was quite small and contained facing sofas made of the same body-conforming material as the starship's chairs. The outer wall, like that of the main corridor, was featureless, apparently to permit full daytime transparency. Openings on each of the two side walls led to a narrow space beside two huge beds, one above the other—not like bunks but separated by a floor halfway between the main floor and the high ceiling. This arrangement, Ardith realized, gave all the beds access to the window wall without consuming extra space. Bath/dressing rooms, one on each side to be shared by its occupants, were across from them.

They left their bags in the dressing rooms and sat in the main room of the suite while Korela gave them tablets and explained their use. Translation was automatic, she said; the AI to which they were linked had been programmed for Anglo after agents brought written materials from Earth. There were maps of various sections of the dome on which their location was tracked so they could easily reach their room, or any other chosen destination, from wherever they happened to be. With these in hand they followed her back to the elevator, which took them rapidly to the top of its translucent shaft.

Here, at the crest of the vast dome, the whole ceiling was crystalline. The stars shone through with startling brilliance, almost as bright as if seen from space—Ydoril's atmosphere was evidently thinner than Earth's. The room appropriately called the Sky Room occupied an immense rotunda, surrounded by a tall circular half-wall behind which, Korela said, were the conference and dining rooms used for important meetings. Their air could be adjusted through the use of force fields to meet the needs of different species, as could that of the center room, now arranged as a lounge with a large round buffet table and informal groupings of chairs. Sometimes, she told them, it was converted to an assembly hall for formal ceremonies.

The room was crowded with extraterrestrials of many species. Their heights, skin and hair coloring, and facial shapes differed widely, and a few had body hair or fur. But no details of bodily form could be seen under the brilliant loosely-fitting tunics they all wore—a symbol of unity, Ardith decided, since surely fashions must vary on their birth worlds. Again, she wondered how strangers could determine gender, and then it occurred to her that it might not matter. This mixed culture might make no distinction between men and women; it would have significance only for members of species sexually attracted to each other, who could presumably recognize potential partners.

Everyone was very friendly, yet for all its conviviality the gathering seemed too quiet. At first puzzled, Ardith suddenly realized that this was to be expected among telepaths—people who could communicate with one another silently had no need to fill a room with noise. She found that it indeed made little difference whether they greeted her in Anglo or merely telepathically since the feeling behind their words was unmistakable.

That wouldn't come across to a denier of psi power. The Federation's requirement that young species must develop telepathic capability before admission was wise, she reflected. Sight alone might well lead to the misinterpretation of a strangely-shaped face as hostile.

She wondered how she herself appeared to them. Shoulder-length brown hair, grey-blue eyes, white skin—she saw no one with skin as pale as hers although since they lived in a dome with an unbreathable atmosphere outside, their darker or brighter-colored skins couldn't be due to tanning. Many were superficially no more different from her than Meiko, who had short jet-black hair, or Fred, whose skin was a light chocolate brown. Yet differences in shape, often subtle differences, marked them as separate species, so that to them the Earthborn must look strange.

"They don't seem curious about us," she said to Korela during a lull when no one approached her. "Is it because they've met people from Maclairn?"

"They treat you just as they would any other newcomer," Korela replied. "It's discourteous to take note of someone's race; Service ID records don't even include that information, except in medical files. You are Federation citizens or you wouldn't be here. What you look like in comparison to others is of no concern."

Tired from the long day since waking on the lifeboat and somewhat shaky from excitement, Ardith sat down next to Meiko as people crowded around to greet them. She had lost track of Jacob and Fred. Someone brought her small, sweet cakes from the buffet and a cool drink, which she sipped gratefully without attempting to guess what was in it. Closing her eyes for a moment, she glimpsed a mélange of the alien faces she had seen, almost as if in a disturbing dream—not a nightmare, for she knew they were kindly faces, but . . . *unnatural*. What would it be like to live among them? How could they ever be welcome on Earth?

She was startled back to full awareness by Coris, who appeared beside someone unlike anybody she'd met previously. "This is Varel, who'll be your instructor in Federation history," he said.

At first sight Ardith thought Varel was of Earthborn descent, a Maclairnan like Radnor although younger and completely bald, but she quickly became aware of differences—larger eyes, a narrower face, a skin tone halfway between yellow and deep gold. They were not, however, differences that left her in doubt about this being a man. He smiled at her and in a surprisingly deep voice said, "I'm glad you're here—I've long been especially interested in your world. I'm looking forward to working with you."

"So am I," Ardith said, feeling relief at the thought of being taught by someone so much like a human being. Perhaps she would get used to interacting with extraterrestrials, but it was going to take time.

~ *4* ~

Meiko joined the conversation, and Jacob and Fred, soon appeared. Varel sat down across from them. He was a member of the Service, he told them, but not one who visited young worlds. His specialty was the study of their history and how it compared to the histories of countless older worlds in the Federation. He was familiar with Earth not only from this study, but because he had spent some time visiting Maclairn, and he spoke Anglo as fluently as someone born there.

"We were really surprised when we were met by a fellow-human," Ardith said. "He seemed to hold some sort of official position here—does he too belong to the Service?"

"No, Radnor is a special case," Varel said. "Just what did he tell you about himself?"

"That he's the son of the man known on Earth as the Captain of *Estel*, who we'd always assumed was no more than a legend."

"Did he also tell you that he's the son of Kathryn Bramfield, the Earthborn attorney who negotiated the agreement between Maclairn and the League, whose grandfather was one of the wealthiest men in North America? Or that he's heir to what was left of that fortune after she donated most of her inheritance to the Maclairn Foundation, which runs the mind-training program on Earth, and that he was in charge of that program for more than half a century?"

"What mind-training program?" Meiko asked.

"The one run by the Maclairnans. You're familiar with what the Captain of *Estel* stood for, what led to formation of the Estelan Party—the belief that someday humans will have full conscious control over their bodies and will be virtually free of sickness and pain as well as of dependency and control in a political sense—"

"I can't get used to knowing that he really exists," Meiko said. "My family were Estelans, but we took it for granted that he was just the apocryphal author of the writings attributed to him. He wasn't the actual founder of the party, surely. It began on a colony world named Ciencia where its leaders were political activists."

"He was imprisoned on Ciencia for having led a conspiracy there," Varel said, "but the party wasn't formed until later. It was inspired by what he said at his trial and by the memories of people whose pain he'd healed."

"Is *that* true, too? That he was a healer?"

"He isn't a skilled one like some Maclairnans I know, but it's true that he can relieve pain through telepathy."

"Seriously?" Jacob said slowly, "As an anthropologist, I'm aware that individuals in some cultures have possessed what our own would label supernatural powers. Yogis and shamans have done some amazing things. But the Captain of *Estel* didn't come from such a culture. He's said to have been an experienced jump pilot and a talented hacker who managed get his ideas into a wide variety of supposedly-secure   ."

"Yes, that's true. He started out as a Fleet officer, an explorer pilot."

"Has Radnor actually seen him relieve someone's pain through mind alone?" Fred asked.

"Perhaps not, but he has often done it himself, and has taught many others to relieve their own pain. Anyone willing to be trained can learn that."

Speechless, they stared at Varel. "The aim of Maclairn is to spread these skills, along with

telepathic ability, to all humankind," he said. "We—
the Federation—have long been aware of this, and we
waited until the project was well along before
accepting you. But the existence of Maclairn has been
kept secret from all but a few people on Earth."

"I can see why," Ardith said. "During the Klan era
a colony with that aim would have been in danger."

"As much from corrupt League officials as from
the Klan, and in fact there was collusion between
them. In any case, Maclairn is protected from
discovery by a Fleet cruiser under an arrangement
known only to the League government and the crew
involved. Radnor's father Terry went there as a young
officer and soon married Kathryn Bramfield. But
before their son was born, through a tragic error on
the part of our agents he learned about the Elders.
Reluctantly, they sent him into exile on Ciencia to
make sure he would never again have contact with
gifted telepaths, or with his wife, who would have
absorbed that knowledge from his mind."

"That was cruel!" Meiko exclaimed.

"Sometimes cruelty is unavoidable, when there's a
lot at stake—in this case, the independent evolution of
Earth's culture. It wasn't ready for contact then, well
over a century ago."

"Wait a minute," Fred burst out. "If it was that
far back, and he didn't see his wife again—"

"Radnor is older than you'd think," Varel agreed.
"Long life is one result of using the mind powers."

Over a hundred years old, when he'd looked no
more than seventy? It was incredible, Ardith thought,
yet there was no reason to doubt Varel's account. As a
professional historian he surely wasn't confused about
dates, and in any case she could sense that be
believed what he was telling them.

"His father's presence on Ciencia had far-reaching

effects that couldn't have been foreseen," Varel went on, "synchronicities too significant to be mere chance, including not only the Estelan overthrow of tyranny there, but the saving of Maclairn from a terrorist attack. The biggest mystery of life, which even the oldest race of Elders cannot solve, is how such things come about."

"Coincidence is strange," Jacob agreed. "But are there really grounds for thinking they're more than that?"

"Statistical analysis, for one," Varel replied. "If we rely on statistics in scientific experiments, which we do, we can't turn around and call them irrelevant to other events. And synchronistic events occur on all worlds—as a historian, I can't ignore them."

"It's true that a young Fleet officer wouldn't have become the influential figure he did without being exiled," Jacob admitted. "That alone makes the error that caused it a deviation from normality."

"Yes," Varel agreed. "He eventually escaped from Ciencia, and soon after, during another brief contact with the Elders, he was given the ship *Estel* with the understanding that he would stay away from worlds where there were trained telepaths."

"I suppose that's why he never went to Earth except the once, to confront the Klan," Meiko reflected. "I've often wondered whether he could have made a difference—inspired hope, as he did in the colonies."

"Earth was already past the stage of becoming hopeful," Jacob said ruefully.

"It was," Varel said, "though the situation there wasn't yet as bad as it is now. And the mystery surrounding *Estel* was part of what made the colonies take notice. Even the Maclairnans weren't aware until his return that the famous captain of that ship was the man they'd known as Terry Radnor."

"Why does Radnor use just the surname?" Fred inquired.

"It's the only name he has. Mclairnans use single names, as we do in the Service, so Terry dropped his surname and gave it to his son."

"Where is he now?" Ardith inquired.

"On Maclairn, where Radnor's lifemate is caring for him. *Estel* still exists, by the way, and is used for transport between here and Maclairn. Terry is too near death to make the trip now, but it's flown by his long-term Elder copilot Liam, who's only a few years older than Radnor and is of a species with a slightly longer lifespan."

How old was Varel? Ardith wondered. He appeared to be in his early thirties, but his lifespan, too, might be so different as to make age in Earth-years meaningless. To her surprise she found that they connected telepathically, somehow, beneath his spoken words; she sensed that the details of Earth's past meant more to him than a record of historical fact. His emotions were engaged in a way she couldn't decipher.

"So Radnor went to Earth and taught mind skills there?" Jacob asked.

"Yes, he succeeded his predecessors as director of the program, which has existed since before his birth. Now that he and his lifemate Clarys have retired to Maclairn, he's considered the foremost mentor there and is slated to take over as head of the colony's government when the current one dies. You four are the most important people on Ydoril right now; the Service wouldn't have called on him for anything less."

Stunned, Ardith said, "We didn't know any of that. He said something about being our mentor and I assumed that was just a word for teacher."

"Mentors are much more than teachers. They're the highest rank on Maclairn and they serve as doctors, psychotherapists, and even something like priests, though not of a formal religion. They have many years of education—the equivalent of a medical degree—and serve a long apprenticeship before being appointed."

"And they run the government, too?"

"Not entirely, but only mentors are eligible for the top positions. Maclairn was founded for the purpose of developing mind powers, so everything centers on that."

Jacob said, "I think we all want to know more about these mind powers. Just what do they consist of besides telepathy?"

"Remote viewing—clairvoyance—for one thing. And learning to control the inner processes of our bodies. Some people also have talent for psychokinesis, the moving of objects by mind alone, but it's not common among species as young as yours and can't be taught to individuals who lack aptitude. You won't see it on Ydoril because Service agents are forbidden to use it here; if we got in the habit it would be too easy to forget and use it on young worlds where we have to conceal what we are."

"If I've followed what you've been saying, the Captain of *Estel* had mind powers at the time he was on Ciencia," said Fred. "Did he get them from the Elders he met or come by them naturally? Or were they already common on Maclairn when he first went there?"

"He was initially taught by a Maclairnan mentor as a condition of being assigned to the Fleet crew deployed to protect the colony. They are universal skills available to all sufficiently-evolved species— someday I'll tell you how Maclairn became the first human society to make wide use of them. Its long-term plan is to introduce them gradually throughout Earth and the colonies."

"Do you mean there'll eventually be an effort to give them to the general public?" Meiko asked.

"They're given to selected members of the public now. Centers have been established where mentors live and work under assumed identities, choosing and training people with the most aptitude who can be counted on to keep quiet about it. If any of you had been known to the recruiters you would have been offered the training then, since your latent psi talent would have been detected."

Ardith drew breath. "Is there a chance we could get this training now?"

"Yes, of course. That's what Radnor's here for—it's best for you to get it from a member of your own species, and he's an exceptionally skilled instructor. But it won't be easy. The first stage is extremely painful, more so for adults than for kids."

"Painful? I thought the idea was to eliminate pain," Meiko said, puzzled.

"That's true—once you've learned a new way of dealing with it you'll be immune to physical suffering for the rest of your life, as well as having some more spectacular skills. But the only way to learn is through experience."

It was a sobering thought, but Ardith was too absorbed in all the other things they'd been learning to be dismayed by it. Gradually the crowd in the Sky Room thinned and Varel said good night, leaving them to find their way back to their bedroom suite with the aid of the illuminated route shown on their tablets. Right now she felt more than ready to get into one of those large inviting beds.

~ 5 ~

When they reached their room they found that Radnor, now dressed in a teal-blue tunic styled like their own, was waiting for them. "I know you're all tired," he said. "But there's something you need to know before you sleep."

Ardith watched him, wondering how she could ever have thought him ordinary-looking. It wasn't just his being a centenarian that now impressed her. Despite the white hair and the evident aging of his face he was strong, vital, with eyes that revealed not only wisdom but a kind of confidence in himself that made her feel safe in his presence. There was no doubt about his worthiness for the status he had evidently earned.

She noticed that he wore a small copper-colored pin in the shape of a flame, which had also been on the lapel of the shirt in which they'd first seen him. Curious as to what it signified, she was surprised when he responded to her silent question just as the aliens had. "It symbolizes the evolving power of the human mind," he said. "Not just in Earthborn humans but in sapient beings of all species. On Maclairn it signifies a formal commitment to the extension of that power, but when we met the Elders we found that a flame has similar meaning to many of them. The concept, though not this particular insignia, became a bond."

"Because they all have psi capability?"

"Yes, but much more—volition and even spiritual qualities. The things that make us human."

She had more questions, but sensed that now was not the time for them. Radnor's attention was focused on something else.

"You've been experiencing some very powerful

dreams," he said to them, "dreams inspired by uplifting thoughts intentionally sent to you. But it's not going to be like that tonight. Here, you will dream in the normal way without any purposeful input. And it may not be entirely pleasant." He looked at Jacob. "Are you familiar with the concept of the collective unconscious?"

Jacob nodded and Meiko said, "I am, too, a little. Estelan literature mentions it."

"The term has been used in different ways at different times on Earth. But our modern concept, as understood on Maclairn, is that the collective unconscious of a world consists of all the many attitudes and impressions of its people transmitted by unconscious telepathy to a deep well from which everyone draws. Everything anyone thinks or feels about a subject gets into that well, often in metaphorical form, and your own thoughts and feelings are influenced by it. Consciously, you're not aware that this is happening, though you sometimes receive inspiration from what seems to be an unknown source. But in dreams, ideas and images come through. The extent to which they're random is unknown—no doubt a lot of them are, yet at times they may depend on what troubles you or what you're searching for."

"You mean if you're trying to solve a problem, the answer may come to you in a dream?"

"Sometimes. But more commonly what you pick up will be meaningless to you, which is why you have weird experiences in dreams. You may absorb the fear other people have felt about a thing and find yourself fearing it later, while awake, without knowing why— that's often the origin of phobias. Or you may come to believe strongly in something without any apparent reason. But usually there's no logical connection between dream images and anything in your real life;

they simply express feelings, and the feelings of others."

"All kinds of feelings? Do you mean that all the evil and hatred in the world gets into this well, as you call it, and affects everybody's unconscious mind?" Ardith protested.

"Well, that's indeed how it spreads among those who are susceptible, and why those who aren't sometimes have nightmares unrelated to their own lives. But most people aren't swayed by evil—in the collective unconscious good predominates, as it does in most aspects of life. Evil influences aren't the main issue."

"Then I don't see what you're warning us about. We've been dreaming all our lives."

"Yes, but only on worlds you are used to. The collective unconscious does not extend from world to world. If it did we would all be bombarded by impressions from minds on billions of worlds throughout the universe—we would go insane with a mere fraction of that input. So our minds evolved to filter out what comes from distant ones. In Earth's colonies the difference isn't a problem because the inhabitants, or their ancestors, came from Earth; their cultures are similar and much of the content is therefore the same. You're familiar with it; you've been in contact with it since babyhood.

"But here, the collective unconscious is entirely different. It comes from the minds of people of different species who grew up on worlds unknown to you. So you will be exposed to a barrage of ideas and images unlike what you've encountered in the past— not unpleasant in themselves, but foreign. There will be symbols whose significance you can't grasp, or worse, mean the opposite of what they would on Earth. And so your dreams are likely to be disturbing for awhile. While awake, you won't recall them, just as you never recall most dreams; so you may feel disturbed without knowing why."

Jacob said slowly, "There's more to it than our dreams. If this material is absorbed into our unconscious minds it will affect us all the time, not just in sleep."

"Yes, until you get used to it and learn something about the worlds where it arose. Service personnel are trained to control unconscious telepathy while awake so they won't contaminate the collective unconscious of young worlds they visit; that's one reason we have brought you to Ydoril first, rather than to a world with a typical population. Being here will minimize the discordant input you receive. Nevertheless, it will take awhile to adjust. The thing to remember is not to worry if you don't feel as good as you've expected to during your first days here. That's normal, and it will pass."

Dismayed, Ardith went quietly to her bed, scarcely noticing the marvel of the automated bathroom fixtures or the small round platform that lifted her magically to the top bed of the stacked pair. She had counted on experiencing the kind of dreams she'd had in space, the ones that had impelled her to bet her life on a chance to experience the reality behind them.

Yet she shouldn't have, she thought ruefully. She had been told earlier that those dreams had been telepathically transmitted from worlds far from Ydoril. Her future here would not be dreamlike. It might even be more frustrating than the life from which she'd escaped.

She slept restlessly, haunted by the strange images and sensations Radnor had predicted, and on first waking she felt nameless dread. But it dissipated as she came fully awake and pressed the button Korela had said would let in daylight. To her surprise the whole outer sidewall of the bed cleared and she looked out on a bright sunlit landscape, a green meadow bordered by trees that partially obscured the sparkle of another dome.

The bed was nearly twice a long as needed for her height, evidently to accommodate different species. Like the chairs, it conformed to her body and felt soft without sagging. She had slept in her silky robe under a light coverlet, having been told that a fresh one would be provided in the morning. Now she lay back, reluctant to move, and let Meiko use the bathroom first. When she got there she found that it had cleaned itself and that new clothes were waiting for her. After a hot shower she put them on, feeling reenergized.

Korela appeared and took them to breakfast in a cafeteria several floors above the bedroom suite. It was long and narrow so that all the tables were by the window wall, with an automated buffet opposite. The food was delicious, though mostly unidentifiable— sweet rolls, a cheese-like substance, and a lightly grilled red fruit resembling tomatoes.

"There are eateries on every floor," Korela told them. "The map in your tablets will show you where they are, and you can eat in any of those with air breathable for you, though the most popular ones are sometimes crowded."

Didn't anyone have to pay for food? Ardith wondered. As usual, Korela picked up the unspoken question. "Apart from guests, everyone on Ydoril is a member of the Service," she said. "That's a lifetime commitment, and the compensation includes all living expenses, even after retirement. No one here is paid— students do all the jobs in the domes that aren't done by AI. It's not like an ordinary Federation world."

"I'm not really clear about how the Service is set

up," Jacob said. "It must be tremendously expensive to send starships to developing young worlds and keep agents on some, in addition to maintaining this whole planet and all its residents. If the Federation has no central government with the authority to tax, how is it funded?"

"The individual worlds do tax their citizens, and they all contribute. It's viewed as a basic responsibility, because without the Service, some races of sapient beings would come to harm—or might pose a threat to others. And we might never be able to integrate newly mature ones into our alliance."

"But then if Earth is now a member of the Federation it will be expected to contribute, too," Fred said. "That's not going to go over well."

It certainly wasn't, Ardith thought. It would be hard enough to get aliens accepted on Earth without trying to get the League government to pay them.

Korela smiled. "You need to start thinking in terms of longer time frames," she said. "No one expects a young civilization to recognize its responsibility to the rest of the universe as soon as it's contacted—a lot of people don't even recognize their responsibility to their own planet. That's an awareness that has to grow gradually, as they begin to accept the fact that no world exists in isolation from the cosmos as a whole. In the beginning citizens who understand what's at stake will be exceptions."

Troubled, Ardith said, "The League isn't likely to put the right sort of exceptions into power."

"Probably not," Korela agreed. "The Earth League has a very immature form of government—it claims far too much power over individuals. The question isn't whether the right sort of people hold that power but whether it should exist at all."

"You're not suggesting that we should revolt!" Meiko was horrified.

"Not violently. But once the majority of the people develop mind powers, they won't tolerate being told what to think or how to live their lives. Federation history tells us that interplanetary governments eventually become less intrusive and more oriented toward voluntary acceptance of responsibilities." She hesitated, then sadly continued, "I've been told in my history class, though, that under the present conditions on Earth, things are likely to get worse before they get better. It's ripe for takeover by tyrants."

"Earth abolished totalitarianism long ago," Jacob pointed out.

"Yes, but if the current government is uncaring and corrupt, evildoers could get into power," Korela replied. "And most people on Earth are too apathetic to do anything about it. At least that's what Varel says."

Varel, Ardith recalled, had told them he was an instructor at the Service Academy as well as a historian and data analyst. Ydoril was the home of the Academy, although that was an organizational entity rather than a physical one. Young men and women admitted to the Service were classed as students for several years before taking the oath of commitment,

A special history seminar had been scheduled for the prospective envoys. She found that she was eager to get started—perhaps that would take her mind off the nagging disorientation engendered by her dreams.

~ 6 ~

Since all bedrooms and eateries seemed to be next

to windows on the surface of the dome, Ardith
wondered at first what the vast interior was used for
apart from kitchens and utility areas. A study of the
map in her tablet soon revealed gyms, swimming
pools, sanctuaries for meditation, and lounges of
various sizes where people with similar backgrounds
tended to congregate. Much of it, however, was filled
with conference rooms and study facilities, duplicated
so that the air of separate rooms could be adjusted for
different species.

In the center of the dome was a larger computer
complex than Ardith had ever imagined. Containing
data from thousands of Federation worlds plus all the
Service had collected about young ones, it dwarfed
any such installation on Earth, despite the fact that
its technology was more advanced and data storage
occupied less space. They would have full access to the
Federation data, Varel told them, but not the data
about immature worlds, which was restricted to
Service personnel.

The conference room to which he took them was
equipped with a giant holoscreen, on which he began
showing them scenes from some of the worlds that
had established the Federation thousands of years
before the appearance of humanoids on Earth. It was
overwhelming at first, but Ardith soon found that she
absorbed more than the pictures, more than the
narration—she could sense Varel's interpretations of
the scenes and perceived that he was projecting them
telepathically. She *knew* what those worlds were like,
insofar as she could comprehend them. Not facts
about them, but simply feelings about how they
differed from Earth and from each other, and how
they had changed over time.

It would take years to grasp it all. This was just a
brief and superficial introduction to a very few of the

countless planets that now comprised the Allied Worlds. What they were being shown merely increased the longing she had always felt to see something more than colonies that were all alike. But it made her aware that in time that longing could be satisfied.

During the break for lunch in the dining room to which Varel took them, she watched him with an increasing awareness of how very human he was. She had already lost sight of the physical differences, and despite his baldness he struck her as handsome. She wondered whether he had a family. Radnor had said that few Service members chose to have families; why, when they seemed enough like Earthborn people to want homes and children?

By now she was used to having her silent questions answered, so it didn't surprise her when Varel said, "Most members are field agents; they go where they are sent and couldn't take kids to young worlds in any case. Occasionally they have children who are reared by retired great-grandparents, but it's not common."

"They must have grown up in families on the planets they came from. Don't they miss having that kind of home life?"

"Well, joining the Service is a choice, after all, a binding one made in youth with full knowledge of the pros and cons. Besides, with such a variety of species living on Ydoril, the chances of falling in love with a member of one's own aren't large. Relationships are more apt to form between members of similar species who find each other attractive—and of course no offspring can come of such unions, however much they might be wanted."

Ardith nodded. As an exobiologist she shouldn't have needed to be told that; for partners whose ancestors had evolved on separate planets to have children would be genetically impossible. This also explained why the Federation worlds remained so completely independent. Intermarriage, if it occurred, could not result in blending of their populations, only of their cultures.

She and Varel, seated side by side, went on talking while the others across the table were absorbed in Jacob's comments about one of the worlds they'd been shown. He himself lived full time on Ydoril, Varel told her. As an analyst rather than a field agent, he didn't visit young worlds. But he liked the planet where he'd been born and still owned a house there for use during his vacations. He was due for one, but had cancelled it when assigned to be their history instructor.

"You gave up your vacation just to teach us?" she asked in surprise. It was becoming more and more evident that they were being prepared for a task their hosts considered highly important—why, when it surely would be many years before more than a few of Earth's citizens were ready for interaction with the Elders?

"I like teaching," Varel replied, "and I'm deeply concerned about current conditions on Earth, which are going to get worse until its people make contact with the Federation." Smiling, he added, "It's turned out to be a good thing that I did stay—I'll enjoy getting to know you better, Ardith."

To her surprise she sensed something behind the words that she could never have anticipated. If such a comment had been made by a new acquaintance on Earth, it wouldn't have been hard to interpret, and the telepathic undertone of it made clear that its meaning here was the same.

That night she dreamed again, and the dreams

were troubled by random mixtures of images from the worlds she had seen on the screen, accompanied by feelings that were not her own. Once she woke, shaking, aware that she'd been on the verge of reaching for something she longed to possess yet was terrified to touch. She fell back into sleep, fearful of what might await her; but in the morning the sun was bright and she told herself the fear was foolish.

The days passed, full of excitement about all she was learning. In addition to the seminars with Varel that familiarized the four of them with cultures of various Federation planets, Ardith began to consult the database about their biology, which was, after all, her own field of study. It seemed almost futile, as knowledge of exobiology on Earth and its colonies was so hopelessly behind what was known here, and for the first time she fully understood why premature contact with an extraterrestrial civilization would have been a setback for human science. Nevertheless she was fascinated by it and didn't feel it was a waste of her time. Unlikely though it was that she would choose to return to Earth—a prospect that now struck her as unthinkable—if she ever did go she would have much to teach her former colleagues.

She was impatient to actually see ET lifeforms beyond the flowers grown in the dome, which flourished in an atmosphere like Earth's, so one afternoon Varel took her outside. Once she'd learned to deal with the unfamiliar breathing mask they headed for a patch of yellow ground cover she'd seen from her window. Crossing the meadow she felt buoyant, light on her feet, although the gravity was no less than she'd been used to on some colony worlds. It was almost as if she were floating. She reveled in the sun and the deep blue sky, and tried not to remember that she would not be a guest of the Service forever and the aliens she met elsewhere night not be such good company.

In the evenings they went to the Sky Room, which except for invitational events was open only to guests and faculty members, as it wasn't large enough for more than a fraction of the dome's residents. Its spectacular view of the stars made it preferable to the less crowded lounges available. Meiko, Fred and Jacob soon made new friends, but Ardith generally found herself with Varel—if she didn't see him when she entered the room, before long he appeared at her side.

There were endless things to discuss or simply absorb, wordlessly sharing each other's impressions of Earth's culture and of the worlds shown in holos. She had never been interested in history until she viewed it through his eyes, seeing how it progressed from era to era in similar ways on many planets, dark times alternating with bright ones successively over the centuries. "From what I read of Earth's literature," Varel said, "people don't grasp that. They see evil in their own era and forget that former eras were worse. They think they're the first generation to believe disaster is coming, not realizing that many former ones felt the same way. Of course disasters do occur. Occasionally worlds are destroyed. But these are exceptions. On the whole, the more worlds I study the firmer grounds I have for hope."

"But isn't Earth in worse shape than the others?" Ardith asked, thinking of the deteriorating cities and bleak landscape of the home world she remembered.

"Currently, yes. It's facing real danger," he admitted. "But it doesn't have to be like that forever."

She sensed that he was troubled but not hopeless. Inexplicably, her mind and Varel's meshed in a way she had not experienced with anyone before. It wasn't just that he was telepathic—she didn't interact with other telepaths that way. Perhaps it was because of the background music, a strange but stimulating tonality that entranced her. Her whole past life was a distant memory compared to this place where she at last felt that she belonged.

They often lingered in the room after most others had left. Ardith told herself she did so because she dreaded the night's dreams, and in fact she did dread them, though for the most part they were less foreign than at the beginning. Radnor, whom she saw often, said this was nothing to worry about. Knowing him to be telepathic she was embarrassed to discuss them with him—he was after all a psychotherapist, among other things. But if he sensed any personal details, he passed no comment. He simply reassured her that in time she would no longer be troubled by the strangeness of them.

Then one night she dreamed she was back aboard the lifeboat, but it was taking her away from the bright worlds of the aliens, not toward them. Not back to Earth, just into a terrifying whirlpool of empty space. And she felt an unbearable sense of loss, as if she were being torn from all that she needed to remain human. Looking down at her body she saw that it was not human, nor was it like those of any extraterrestrials she had met—it was misshapen, a mass of flesh that wavered between human and alien form. . . .

This was not like dying. It was nothing as natural as dying. She knew she would be forever trapped in emptiness with nothing to hold onto, not even her identity as a sapient being. In terror she cried out, *Help me! Please help me, Varel, I'm falling apart—*

Ardith? Ardith, where are you? I was asleep— It was Varel's voice, and Varel's hand reached out to her, and she had a hand of her own again to grasp it. . . .

And she woke up, shaken, at first paralyzed by dismay at what had just happened. It had been a nightmare, not real, yet Varel had come to her. She had called out to him and he had heard; she was absolutely sure that his presence hadn't been part of the dream. Telepathically, he had sensed her call and responded.

Oh, God. What had possessed her? In her terror she had called out to Varel—not to Radnor, the fellow-human psychotherapist to whom she might reasonably have appealed, but to a man not even one of her own kind with whom she had nothing in common beyond enjoyment of conversation.

The next day passed in a haze of confusion. During the seminar she could not meet his eyes, but she was aware that he knew. He himself had not been dreaming; he'd been awakened by her call and had come to her consciously. She knew too little of telepathy to judge whether that was merely the customary response to a person with bad dreams, but she suspected that it was not. If telepaths normally sensed and contacted anybody having a nightmare, they would get no sleep. It was more likely that they shut out random input from everyone but their closest friends and loved ones.

Should she thank him, or would that embarrass him? Perhaps it would be better to let him think she believed it had all been a dream. Carefully she avoided him that afternoon and had dinner with Meiko. But she couldn't stay away from the Sky Room—that would look as if she were angry.

"I—I don't know what to say," she admitted when they met in their usual seating area near the far wall of the dome.

"Don't say anything," Varel replied. "Just know that I'll always be there if you need me, Ardith, at least while we're on the same planet."

~ 7 ~

A few days later Radnor introduced the subject of the mind training. He called the four of them together and said, "Varel has told you a little about what it entails. Adolescents on Federation worlds all receive such training, but for Earthborn adults it's more difficult. It's up to you, individually, to decide whether you want me to give it to you."

"Of course we want you to," Ardith declared with elation, thinking that of all humans she had known, this man seemed most trustworthy. "Why would we want anyone else?"

"The question isn't whether you want me as your instructor, but whether you choose to have the training at all. It will be helpful to you on Earth—you'll be protected against most sickness, and your telepathic sensitivity will be enhanced. And you'll gain confidence for dealing with challenges. But the first few sessions are an extremely painful ordeal. On Maclairn kids go through it at the age of thirteen; it's the rite by which they attain adulthood, so of course they want it. And it's easier for them because they don't have past fear of pain to overcome—they are used to having their parents telepathically relieve any pain they've had and they know what it feels like to enter a state that prevents suffering. An adult from a culture like Earth's doesn't have that advantage."

Jacob frowned. "You intentionally inflict pain on people?"

"How else could they learn to end it? Deep aversion to pain is genetically hard-wired in all organisms as a protection against injury. It's an alarm that an animal, small child, or semi-conscious person can't turn off. But the alarm is in the brain, not the body. Once you have gained voluntary control of neurological functions that affect your state of consciousness, you can turn it off by yourself."

"You mean like turning a switch in your brain?" Obviously, Fred was skeptical.

"That's right. You will feel the physical sensation of pain, but you won't mind it—assuming that you use the skills you've acquired, you will never again experience what we think of as physical suffering."

"Well, if everybody on Maclairn and the Federation worlds has gotten through," Fred declared, "I guess l can steel myself to being trained."

"That's just what you can't do, Fred," said Radnor. "Willpower won't work, because the type of volition needed to control unconscious responses is the exact opposite. Unfortunately nobody believes this until shown the hard way, so I won't try to explain it now. Briefly, what's needed is willingness to stick it out. You have to be truly willing, not just trying to look brave—I can tell the difference, and if deep down you aren't, then I won't proceed, not only for ethical reasons but because the training methods wouldn't work on an unwilling person."

"I think I'm willing," Meiko said. "I pretty well have to be if I want to live up to Estelan ideals. But I don't quite understand why teaching everybody in the universe to turn off pain is worth their going through this. Painful situations aren't very common in the real world nowadays."

"It's not about pain," Radnor said. "I talk about that first to get the bad news out of the way and because immunity to physical suffering is easier to understand than the main goal. But what we're aiming for is something far more important, the acquisition of full voluntary control over our minds and bodies. That is literally a step forward in evolution, one our species is just beginning to take."

"I'm not sure what you mean," said Ardith. "We can already control our bodies, can't we?"

"Only to a limited degree. Evolutionary progress can be measured by how much volition an organism has. Most forms of life have none—they act by instinct alone. Fish don't consciously decide to swallow little fish, and birds on Earth don't intentionally migrate thousands of miles when the seasons change. The amount of volition involved in mammals' action is controversial, but it's safe to say that a mouse doesn't deliberately choose to run from a cat, and anybody who has owned a cat knows that while chasing mice may be instinctive, cats do make deliberate choices about their interactions with people."

"I never thought of it that way," Jacob said. "Primitive humans made an increasing number of choices at successive stages of culture. The use of language involves far more volition than simply building shelters—it's not just that it requires greater intelligence, but that we *choose* our words."

"Yet some theorists claim that even modern humans have no volition," Ardith said. "They say free will is an illusion."

"The Elders know better," Radnor said. "That theory was discarded when their science began to investigate the so-called 'paranormal' powers of the mind."

"But you've said telepathy is usually unconscious. So how does that relate to volition?"

"Volition is what it takes to use it consciously, once a person knows how. In a telepathic society children pick up that skill naturally, just as they do language. But our species is just beginning to develop the degree of volition required and so with adults, training is needed to make use of it. You will become far more telepathic, and gain other psi skills, after you have had this training."

Fred said, "There are biological limits on what we can do through volition. For example we can control our breathing but not our heart rate. Are you saying you'll teach us a way of surpassing those limits?"

"Control of heart rate and bleeding, are among the simplest things gained from mind training," Radnor told them. "Through more complex skills you can control the neurological processes that determine sickness or health. Mind, not biology, sets the limits, assuming an organism has a sufficiently complex brain."

"You mentioned states of consciousness," Jacob said, "Of course we know that some individuals can voluntarily enter altered states—among mystics it is common. Is that what you mean?"

"It's part of it. There are other natural states, such as the one in which there's no physical suffering and the one in which psi powers can be intentionally employed. The big difference is that in the past individuals learned to control consciousness only after long practice, and often only at the cost of being detached from everyday life. With Maclairn's methods you can get a good start in a few days without losing your ability to think and act normally."

"Just what are those methods?" Fred asked. "Apart from the infliction of pain, I mean, which I don't really see the need for."

"We have to use pain in the initial sessions since it's the safest means of producing the extreme stress needed for a breakthrough in mind control and it can be stopped instantly when need for it is past. As to the other training methods, neurofeedback is one of them. And telepathy, of course—such training couldn't exist without telepathic instructors. Because you four have some past experience with telepathy you will learn much faster than people in whom that faculty is merely latent."

"What good does extreme stress do?" Fred persisted.

"It alters what an organism is capable of. For example, there are many known cases of people not suffering from pain under extreme stress, such as soldiers in battle and athletes while performing extraordinary feats—spontaneous analgesia is the technical name for it. But such a state is brief and can't normally be entered by choice. We teach you to do that, but you must experience it under stress to begin with to learn how it feels. Once you know, and can switch into it, you can switch into other supernormal states as well."

It began to make sense. "There's a step in the training that's secret because its effectiveness depends on surprise," Radnor continued. "For this reason, you will be separated until you have all been through the initial training so that unconscious telepathy between you won't give it away."

During the next few days he interviewed them in private one by one to make sure they really wanted to go through the ordeal and were psychologically fit to benefit from it. Then Korela helped them move temporarily into single rooms on separate floors. "The other people here have known the secret all along," Ardith protested. "If we might pick it up telepathically, why haven't we already done so?"

"Service people are taught to shield their minds against unintentional leakage," Radnor said, "and in any case their mind training was long ago, so there's been no reason for the details to rise to the surface."

But for Varel there was a reason, she thought. He knew she was about to undergo an ordeal, and he would worry about it; he had promised he would always be there for her. If she was frightened and in pain, she might cry out to him again. . . .

"You might," he agreed when they said their temporary goodbye, "and I'm not sure I'm strong enough to resist contact with you, now that it's happened once. So while you're in isolation I'm going away in a friend's ship. If I were here on Ydoril I would share your suffering whether or not you called to me, and I don't think I could bear that."

"Is it really so bad, then?" Radnor had warned her, but she'd assumed he was testing her motivation.

"Yes. But what you'll gain is worth it. No one I know has ever been sorry afterward."

Ardith clung to that thought the next afternoon when Radnor took her to a small windowless room somewhere in the heart of the dome, strapped her into one of the reclining chairs there, and fitted an ominous-looking helmet over her head. "There are two kinds of fear," he said. "There's rational fear that you will be harmed, which you don't need to be concerned about—you know I will not harm you. It will feel as if you're being injured, but that's an illusion. Your body won't be damaged in any way. Okay?"

At the moment she was not okay, but she felt too weak to say so. She was shaky and glad she'd been forbidden to eat breakfast or lunch.

"The other kind of fear, emotional fear, can't be reasoned away," Radnor said. "You feel it when confronting something unknown, even when you're aware that you're not in danger. And we don't want to lessen this. The more terrified you are, the better, because strong emotion increases telepathic sensitivity, and much of the instruction I give you will be telepathic. It involves concepts that can't be expressed in words."

"So you scare me on purpose?" She could see why; it was terror that had enabled her to reach Varel while dreaming.

"Yes, because we can induce fear when we can't, or wouldn't, induce equally effective emotions such as love or hate, both of which have strong influence on the telepathic spread of attitudes in society. It's not groundless fear, though. The fear of losing control of yourself is real."

Ardith's skin felt clammy with cold sweat. Control . . . volition . . . it all fit together somehow, but she was in no condition to figure it out. In a low voice she asked, "What happens if I crack up?"

"I'll have data input from your brain and I won't let you come to harm. Of course you'll be free to quit—this training is entirely voluntary, and if you ask me to stop, the pain will end instantly. But it's a final choice, Ardith. If you quit, you won't get another chance."

"Not ever?" she whispered. In the future she might not feel so sick. . . .

"If there were no lasting consequences for quitting nobody would ever get through it."

Oh, my God, Ardith thought. Helplessly she watched as Radnor opened her damp tunic and attached a heart monitor, knowing that despite her misgivings she had no choice but to consent.

~ 8 ~

She wasn't sure, later, just what had happened. All she could remember was pain more overwhelming than anything she had ever imagined, tearing into her until she was couldn't tell where in her body it came from—agony so fierce that everything she'd thought she cared about fell away. There was no knowing how long it had lasted. She had fought to endure it, had resolved never to ask that it stop . . . and then without conscious choice she had been screaming, and it *had* stopped, and the next few minutes were blank.

She found herself still in the chair, fully reclined, but the straps and the helmet were gone. Radnor was not in the room. There was no pain anywhere in her body now, which seemed odd because she clearly recalled that her arm had been burning. There should be blisters if not charred flesh, but it looked and felt perfectly normal.

She had failed. But did that matter, when the new worlds that had held so much promise were inhabited by beings who could do such things to people routinely, who had no regard for mercy, no compunction about inflicting intolerable suffering in the name of education? It was inhuman. . . .

Of course it was inhuman. They were aliens. Their culture was alien; why had she thought it could ever be compatible with Earth's?

But Radnor wasn't an alien. The Maclairnans had been doing this to people on Earth since long before they ever encountered the Elders. Varel had told her so, and she could not doubt Varel's word.

He had also told her no one he knew who'd taken the training had ever regretted it.

Hers was a real failure, then, and it did matter. She didn't see how she could face him. What was wrong with her? Why couldn't she bear what countless other people seemed to have borne, when in the past she had never considered herself a coward?

Ardith lay back, wanting to sleep, wanting to shut out the memory not of the pain itself, but of her weakness. She wondered whether she could ever sleep peacefully again. The dreams would be worse now, and if she dreamed of Varel. . . . Oh, God—would he know? Would they tell him when he returned to Ydoril? Of course, because she was not fit to be trained for an envoy's role now, not fit to represent the Federation on Earth even if she volunteered. She would be treated kindly, but as a child; it had been said that the training was the rite by which Elders and Maclairnans became adults. . . .

Eventually she did sleep, fitfully, and when she came fully awake Radnor was at her side. He didn't say anything, but of course he was telepathic; he knew what she was feeling. His own mind was closed to sensing. She wondered how he felt about having misjudged her.

"What are you going to do now?" he asked.

"Do I have a choice?"

"Certainly. Life goes on. You can continue with the history seminar—"

'Oh, no." She couldn't work with Varel again.

"Or you can study exobiology on your own. Eventually, you can go back to Earth if you wish. Your presence there would still prove you've met aliens."

Ardith was silent. Radnor went on, "The training was voluntary, after all. You can do whatever you would have done if you hadn't chosen it, go wherever you want to be."

"I can't be happy anywhere now, Radnor."

"No. You can't," he agreed. "Do you know why?"

"Because I failed, of course."

"Really? Or is it because you think you'd fail again if you ever faced another challenge?"

Stunned, she realized that he was right. No one but her friends here would ever know about her failure. Others would view her as dependable, perhaps even respect her for her knowledge of alien biology. On Earth or in a colony she might be offered another professorship. But *she* would know, and she would never again have confidence in her ability to deal with a crisis.

"I promised I wouldn't let you come to harm," Radnor said, "and psychological damage is as much harm as a physical injury would be. So I can't just drop this. We have to find a way through it."

"Psychotherapy, then." She had been told that he was well qualified.

"Yes, perhaps for a long time. But there's a quicker and surer way."

"How can there be? We can't undo what happened and it's impossible to wipe it out of my memory." Struck by a new thought, she added, "Or is it? Do the Elders have technology that can do that?"

"They do, but you would end up insane. It's used only as a last resort for people who are already mentally ill."

"Then I don't see—"

"What you need is to be sure you wouldn't back away from a challenge, isn't it?"

"Yes. Maybe I'll never be in another bad situation, but I'll always wonder—even wonder about dealing with things I used to take in stride."

"Then face a bad one now, and stop wondering."

"Nothing would be bad enough to work, short of turning back the clock."

"That's what we ought to do, Ardith. Repeat the training session."

Horrified, she burst out, "I couldn't! I couldn't go through that again, and anyway, I'd just fail. Besides, you said I wouldn't get another chance."

"The point isn't whether you can get through it without cracking up—it's already been proven that you can't. The point is whether you still have the ability to consent. Whether you're helpless if confronted with challenge, or have enough volition to choose—because that's what it was all about in the first place. Not endurance or lack of it, but volition."

"Oh, God. You're saying that all I have to do is go through the same thing again, and I'll be cured?"

"You're not sick, so 'cured' isn't the right word. But you'll get your confidence back if you're willing to face failure."

She'd be crazy to go along with this, Ardith thought. But what had she to lose? It wouldn't harm her body, and it couldn't make her more unhappy than she already was, whereas to refuse would only add to her shame.

Without consciously deciding, she let Radnor strap her in again and attach the helmet. When she tried to speak her mouth was so dry she was capable only of saying yes or no, and when he asked her, she said yes.

"Don't fight to control yourself," he said. "Just relax. Let yourself scream if you feel like screaming. It won't matter since you can't hold out indefinitely anyway."

The assault on her senses came directly to her brain through the helmet, she perceived as the burning spread through her. It had never involved her flesh. Was knowing this the reason she didn't feel like screaming yet?

"I have something to show you," Radnor said. Suddenly the whole wall of the room opposite the chairs became a holoscreen filled with a jagged graph-like figure, violet on the left and progressing in rainbow order to deep yellow on the right. "It represents data from your brain," he told her, "but it's symbolic, not raw output. The rainbow colors represent intensity of the stimulus. This is a recording from your first session. See anything strange about it?"

"It—it isn't complete. It should be red on the righthand side."

Radnor didn't reply. Instead he turned off the image and replaced it with one in black and white. "Here's today's recording, in real time," he said. "What color do you think it has reached right now?"

"Green," she said without hesitation. "Go ahead and turn it up—this isn't going to work if you make it easier." The pain was not yet nearly as bad as it had been before, and all she wanted was to get it over with.

"I'm not making it easier, Ardith. You are. You're relaxing instead of fighting. See what a difference that makes." The image burst into color and to her astonishment, the rightmost side of it was bright orange.

"Oh, my God," she gasped. "That's not possible."

"Yes, it is. Relaxing is the first step toward learning to do away with pain entirely."

"*Now* you tell me, when it's too late for me to learn?"

"It is not too late. You didn't fail the first time— you never consciously quit. Neurologically, you were past the stage of having a choice; I had to take it to that point because your choice—your volition—was the only thing that mattered."

He pressed a button on his remote and the pain stopped abruptly. She stared at him, not understanding. "You knew I'd crack up, and let it happen?"

"That's the secret step in the training, Ardith. It is not possible to overcome pain while fighting it, but instinctively everybody tries. If I simply told them not to try, they'd try anyway, or else they'd quit before making enough effort and would assume that trying harder would work. It won't. But the only way to convince people of that is through demonstration."

"You could have explained this without leaving me alone for hours thinking I'd failed," she protested indignantly.

"No. You had to feel low enough to see that trying was futile before you could give up and relax. That had to be kept secret because if you'd known you hadn't failed, you'd have harbored a suspicion that it might be possible to hold out by willpower."

It was true that she couldn't have relaxed if she hadn't been hopeless, Ardith realized. Slowly absorbing the implications, she persisted, "You do it to everybody? But then what about those who won't consent to a second session?"

"That would be disastrous for them, but it never happens. I take care not to select anyone to whom it might."

"You *knew* I'd consent?"

"Absolutely. Telepathically, I have more access to your subconscious mind than you do."

"And the others? Jacob and Fred and Meiko?" It was hard to imagine Jacob giving way to despair.

"They'll be fine. Fred cursed me, but underneath he knows it was necessary."

Varel too had known, Ardith reflected, and he had managed not to reveal what she was in for. No wonder he had gone away. It was not the few minutes of her intense pain he couldn't bear, but her hours of believing she was a failure.

There'd be more pain to come, of course. She might have to consent many times. But now she had confidence, both in herself and in Radnor's methods. If everyone on Earth were given training, then someday no one there would suffer from pain, any more than the Elders or the Maclairnans did. And in how many other ways might they be able to go beyond instinct?

"A lot more," Radnor said. "The key is being able to control how your brain operates, first by choosing to relax and then by voluntarily entering a specific state of consciousness. Tomorrow you'll start learning how to do that."

Her eyes fell on the flame pin he wore, which he'd said symbolized the evolving power of the human mind. The power of increased volition, according to his later remarks about evolution. The training, too, was symbolic, however great its practical benefits turned out to be—it was demonstrating that there were no built-in limits, that as humans evolved their power to choose would keep on growing. It occurred to her that there might be more than one reason for it to be given to prospective envoys.

~ 9 ~

`Ardith went to her room totally exhausted, scarcely able to eat the food brought to her. But she slept soundly and did not dream. Not until the next day did she fully grasp the significance of Radnor's words.

What she was being taught would be heresy to scientists on Earth, she knew. As a biologist she had taken it for granted that living organisms did not control their brains; their brains controlled them. What was a mind, if not a brain? According to orthodox science they were one and the same, and if she said otherwise she would be considered superstitious. Yet she had seen concrete evidence that what she felt depended more on her state of mind than on the input her brain received—and during the past weeks she'd gotten endless information via telepathy that hadn't been available to her from any other source. She wondered how many other tenets of Earth's science were antiquated in comparison to that of the Elders.

Her session with Radnor wasn't scheduled until late afternoon, as he was dividing his time among the four of them. When she got to the training room, guided by her tablet's map, she felt nervous but not seriously afraid. She sat quietly while Radnor placed her helmet on her head, and then, to her amazement, sat down in the adjacent chair and put on an identical helmet of his own.

"This is a form of neurofeedback," he said. "The dual patterns on the screen will represent states of consciousness, and the aim is for you to match yours to mine."

They were different from yesterday's images, not graphs but three-dimensional patterns without a time axis. "Again, they're symbolic, generated by computer analysis of neurological data, rather than pictures of your physical brain," he told her. "The colors are simply part of their complexity without specific meaning—what's significant is the pattern as a whole, the gestalt. They will shift as the activity of our brains shifts. Once you memorize a pattern and are aware of the state of thought that produced it, you will be able to enter that state whenever you choose."

"And there's one that means not suffering from pain?"

"That's right. But it's only an example. We use such patterns for a great deal more. Controlling pain is one of the easiest to learn because you won't have trouble focusing on it—when in pain your mind won't wander."

That was reasonable, Ardith realized. The need for the training to involve pain became clearer. "We'll start with ordinary everyday consciousness," Radnor said. "Watch, and notice how similar our two images are, and how they change when the pain begins. Then mine will change again and yours may become more like it. That's what we want, but you can't force it. Just relax and let it happen."

She fixed her eyes on the two patterns, which were nearly identical. After a while the pain started. Don't panic, she told herself. Just watch. Both images had abruptly changed form, but then Radnor's began to shift, the colors blending in new ways. Hers wasn't altered, it just shimmered.

"Imagine your own pattern shifting," Radnor advised. "Don't try to make that happen, just imagine that it already has." She stared at it, losing awareness of everything but the pain and the screen. Slowly, it became a little more like Radnor's, and as it did so the pain lessened.

Over and over they repeated the process, until her image shifted almost as fast as his did. "Why can't I just match with a recorded image?" Ardith asked, "Then you wouldn't have to keep generating one that looks like a state of suffering."

"Recorded images don't work; it has to be live, and real. There's telepathy involved, you see."

"Oh. But if I'm learning through telepathy, what do I need the image for?"

"So you will remember it and associate a state of consciousness with the pattern. Then when you visualize the pattern you can enter that state without the telepathy."

"I don't see how you keep generating the image that goes with suffering, so that you can shift out of it," she admitted, puzzled. "Just by associating it with a memory?"

"To produce that image, the pain has to be real. It's possible for the brain to generate real pain by association—in fact that's often the cause of illness. However, to do it off and on, quickly, it's much easier for an instructor to use the helmet."

"You mean you're getting the same I am?" She was appalled; he had been sitting here all day doing this with one person after another.

"The worst thing about suffering is the sense of helplessness, and I am not helpless," Radnor said. "I can turn it off mentally whenever I choose. So I don't really mind *not* turning it off when it's useful, just as athletes tolerate pain when it's necessary for improving their performance."

Somehow this made the whole process easier to understand. There was nothing supernatural about it—you could choose whether to turn off suffering, just as you could choose whether to move an arm or a leg. In either case the brain produced the body's response, but *you* told the brain what to do. The only difference lay in how much it would do by instinct in the absence of a conscious decision. How could science ever have gotten so confused about this? How could she have gone along with the notion that humans didn't control their own brains?

They went on matching patterns until Ardith could shift easily as long as nothing distracted her. There was no way to describe how she did it; the sensation was quite unlike anything she had experienced in the past. It was like adjusting a holo that was out of phase—the image on the holoscreen didn't look right, so you kept correcting, and then abruptly it was sharp.

"Can you initiate the switch without matching?" Radnor asked her after many repetitions.

Ardith pictured the pattern in her mind. "I think so," she said, as the now-familiar shifting began. Suddenly the holoscreen went blank and, startled, she let the mental picture fade. New pain swept through her and she almost cried out; it was more intense than it had been just seconds ago. . . .

"Picture the pattern," Radnor said sharply. She managed to get it back, as clear in her mind as it had been on the screen. And the pain faded again. It was still there, but she scarcely felt it.

"You're a fast learner," said Radnor, turning off the stimulus. "Very few people can do that on the first try. Do you understand what you did?"

"It—it wasn't just that I saw the image in my mind. It was remembering what it was *like* to see the image."

"That's right. Now, with practice, you can reduce any pain you feel by entering that state of consciousness. So tomorrow we will try turning off suffering entirely. The first time you do that is called breakthrough, and it can be achieved only under great stress. But once you've experienced it you'll be able to repeat it, and to learn other patterns for control over other bodily processes."

When they sat down in the chairs the next afternoon and Radnor informed her that he would be using a more intense stimulus than he had previously, Ardith almost forgot to relax. He reached over and gently took her hand. "Fear is your friend," he said. "Remember, it increases telepathic sensitivity. I'll help you more than I've been doing so far. Your brain will resist your control, but if you link to my mind you'll know how to override it."

Pain engulfed her and as it mounted she probed desperately for the link, finding him there and steady, although his image on the screen showed that he too was in a state of suffering. *Watch the patterns!* he commanded. *Follow me! Match mine!*

His voice in her mind was clearer and more

powerful than ever before, compelling her to concentrate on the screen. The images blurred as his pattern shifted; her eyes weren't working, or perhaps her brain was too fully occupied with the pain to accept input from them. Vaguely, she realized that it was seizing her attention in an attempt to prevent her from ignoring physical injury. Neurologically, there was no difference between stimulation from the helmet and the effect of a mortal wound.

She was in no shape to reason this out; the knowledge came from Radnor's mind to hers. But she understood, and it enabled her to ignore the insistent prodding of her brain and turn to matching the screen images. Gradually, he shifted into the state represented by the pattern she remembered. Her own screen image was shifting, too. . . .

The pattern in her mind came suddenly into focus. She felt calm, free of her brain's outraged protest; Radnor must have turned off the stimulus. . . . No, it was still there, a strong sensation, but it didn't bother her. It was just the activation of a nerve. She couldn't imagine why she had ever suffered from such a feeling.

And then she felt an overwhelming surge of elation. Oh, my God, she thought—I must be getting high. She had never taken drugs that made her high; she knew that what they forced on a mind was artificial, a perversion of feelings that if roused naturally would be good. But this was the real thing. It *was* good, it was like being transformed. . . .

Still linked with Radnor, she was aware that he too felt it. And for a moment, dismayed, she feared that he had given it to her, that it wasn't her own feeling at all. Quickly he reassured her, *I'm not projecting, only sharing what's in your mind.*

Why do I feel like this, instead of just relief?

It's a natural high. It comes from taking control of your brain through volition.

Because of having been in pain? That didn't seem right; it would mean pain should be welcomed.

It has nothing to do with pain—you'll get it in other situations, too. From surpassing the programming built into your brain. Functioning by choice instead of by instinct. Becoming fully human.

Always?

"Not after you're used to it," Radnor said aloud. "Only at first, or after a new breakthrough. There's a physical component, the release of hormones, but it's your mind that triggers that."

"Is it the same as the high people say comes from altered states of consciousness?"

"Yes, if they enter such states naturally without drugs, but of course they're influenced by the effects of the state itself. Mystics, for example, experience something else. And athletes who perform record-breaking feats feel still another way. Anyone who achieves something requiring sudden, extraordinary effort can get it in one form or another."

Evolution, Ardith thought. There's joy in going beyond instinct; if there weren't, we'd never make the effort to progress.

She felt energized, about to float from the chair, and could not bear to sit there any longer. Radnor rose and unfastened her straps. "This will wear off after a few hours," he said, "and it's customary to take advantage of those hours. I think Jacob will still be in a mood to celebrate, too, so let's look for him in the Sky Room."

~ *10* ~

Breakthrough was considered an occasion for festivity, Ardith discovered. In the Sky Room people of all species crowded around her, congratulating her warmly, as they did Jacob, whose breakthrough had occurred earlier that afternoon. Their own breakthroughs had been many years ago, in early adolescence, but they remembered, and she knew from the telepathic ambience that this had been a major highlight of their lives.

Fred and Meiko were not present, and she realized that it was not yet their time to celebrate. There would be a party for them on another night; the enthusiasm of the crowd suggested that a second one would be welcome. Since the room would accommodate relatively few of the dome's occupants, she wondered how Coris had decided whom to invite.

They're the ones who have studied Earth or have visited Maclairn, Radnor told her silently. His `telepathic voice was stronger in her mind than in the past, and she realized that this was a permanent effect of the extreme experience they had shared. Once exposed to that level of communication while under stress, the mind remained sensitive to it—this, he'd said, was why the training increased psi capability as well as other forms of volitional control.

Gradually, she became aware that she was picking up more from other people, too—not just those who spoke Anglo but the ones she hadn't been able to communicate with before. They had always been friendly, but now their greetings to her took the form of silent words. It was as if mere background noise had turned to music.

Flowers decked the buffet table and there were tiered trays of delicious food, some of it new to her despite her weeks of living on Ydoril. But no intoxicating beverages, although wine had often been served on previous nights. It came to Ardith that this was an acknowledgment of the heightened state she was in. She did not need wine; any enhancement of her mood would have been an anticlimax.

Before long the seating was pushed back against the wall and musicians appeared. She stared at them, fascinated by the instruments that produced sounds she had previously heard only in recorded form. The blend of them excited her; it made her feel as if she were being lifted above the confines of her body. Was it merely because she was high, or would the augmentation of her senses persist?

Soon people began dancing, an informal line dance facing the musicians with a row added whenever the parallel one got too long for the space. Since with most species she couldn't distinguish male from female she couldn't tell whether the arrangement involved partners. In any case they did not touch, which considering the variation in species' forms, was the most practical way of preserving equality. Only minds touched in the dance.

More dancers were joining the line closest to her, and before she knew it Ardith found herself pulled in, not by anyone's hand but by the drawing power of many minds and the hypnotic beat of the music. She didn't know the steps, but it didn't seem to matter; she could stay with the beat by simply treading to it. She lost track of time. She was too high to feel tired, too transported beyond her normal state to notice when a line formed behind her. And then, impelled by an inner voice speaking her name, she turned—and came face to face with Varel.

She hadn't looked for him here; she'd believed he was still away from Ydoril. Breathless from the exertion of the dance, she didn't attempt to speak. She was scarcely aware that her heart was racing rather than slowing down. He led her out of the dance line and as he took her arm she shivered, though the touch of his alien flesh was anything but chilling. It felt warm. steadying . . .

"I thought you were on a ship somewhere," she said, keeping her voice even.

"Did you think I'd miss your breakthrough party?" He let go of her arm, and to her surprise she wished he hadn't.

"How did you know it would be tonight?"

"I called Radnor. I had to be sure you were okay."

They sat down on a vacant bench and he brought her a cold drink from the buffet. "Are you happy that you came here?" he asked. "Is it worth the risk you took to make contact?"

"Of course. I wouldn't want to be on Earth. I never did, really. I always knew there had to be some place I'd fit better."

Varel frowned briefly, and didn't reply. Before she could wonder why, he reached for her hand and squeezed it. "I'm happy that you came, too," he said. "You deserve a taste of what's ahead for your world, brief as it has to be."

Later, in her room after the party was over, Ardith recalled that remark, thinking she should have set him straight. Earth wasn't her world anymore. She could never go back, even to one of the colonies; she wasn't the same person as she had been before her breakthrough. There was so much more to learn, so many more worlds she had yet to see. Besides. . . .

Slowly, it came to her that her liking for Varel was based on more than just friendship. It had never occurred to her that such a thing might happen. She was twenty-nine and had had more than one past relationship, but never anything that stirred her as being with Varel did. What they felt for each other wasn't mere physical attraction—she was astonished to find that such attraction could even exist.

Interspecies unions were common; she had known that since the day he'd told her that they didn't produce children. She hadn't given any thought to their other aspects. What would sex be like with an alien? Would there be—differences? Surely not, when what she could see of his body was so human. The attraction itself proved that it would be natural and good.

During the next few weeks the bond between them strengthened. When at the breakthrough party for Fred and Meiko they danced side by side, Ardith found herself wishing it were an Earth-type dance where they would touch.

She saw him every morning in the history seminar, of course. He was now presenting worlds only a century or two ahead of Earth—worlds that had once been in bad shape, yet had become more like the older ones after joining the Federation. It wasn't clear to her what brought that about. The Elders hadn't done anything specific for newly-admitted civilizations. They had left each to develop on its own, just as they had before contact. Those worlds had remained independent. Yet their major problems had been overcome. Was this just a matter of time? Perhaps she'd been right in the first place in her perception of evolution as involving only the people ready for it—what good would it do to force knowledge of the aliens' existence on Earth's population?

In the afternoons they often went outdoors again, sometimes accompanied by one or more of her fellow envoy candidates. They visited other domes and twice Varel took them in an aircar to see regions of Ydoril where Service students were taught to cope with environments simulating those they would encounter in the field. But Ardith found it hard to keep her mind on exobiology during those trips.

She was fully focused on learning only during her daily turn in the neurofeedback room. She no longer needed to practice pain control; now Radnor was teaching her more complex skills like the control of her temperature, heartbeat, and even of bleeding. There were different visual patterns to learn for different types of skill, and she became adept at match-ing, and later recalling, whatever image he presented on the dual screen. Having once grasped the connection between a visualized pattern and a state of consciousness, she could do it with many; he told her that eventually she would be able to prevent illness and even cure minor ills in her own body. And in fact, the headaches she used to have were already gone, though perhaps that was only because she was happier than she'd been in the past.

She and the others had moved back to their original suite as soon as they all had achieved breakthrough. But they weren't as close as before, as they'd each made different friends with whom they shared meals and recreation. If they noticed that she spent all her free time with Varel, they didn't comment on it. Radnor did, however. "You're setting yourself up for sorrow, Ardith," he warned.

"No, I'm not. He's not the kind of person who'd lead me on."

"Varel would never intentionally hurt you. But the circumstances are as they are."

"Yes. We can't change the way we feel about each other."

Radnor sighed. "I suppose not. These things happen faster between telepaths than among those without inner knowledge of each other, and unlike physical sensations they can't be controlled by volition. Telepathic affinity, even when unconscious, is too powerful to deny. Well, I wish you the joy of it while it can last."

Why wouldn't it last? Ardith thought. And then it struck her: Radnor assumed she would go back to Earth. She hadn't told him that she didn't plan to, that she'd never choose a pointless and perhaps futile mission over happiness on Federation worlds.

Not many days later she and Varel found themselves in the Sky Room after everyone else had gone. As usual they had lingered, talking or simply sharing thoughts, not consciously hoping to be alone together but reluctant to part. It wasn't until Varel's arm tightened around her that Ardith realized that no one else was in the room. And then, when she didn't resist, he pulled her close to him; and in the next moment his skin was warm against hers and she raised her face to his kiss, knowing that all her life she had waited for this and it was better than she had ever guessed.

Time stopped. She didn't try to look ahead—there was no place they could go for full privacy. For the time being she was content to remain as she was, unconcerned about the future, her mind merged with his. . . .

But not quite merged. He pulled back tele-pathically before drawing away physically, and the shock of it was even worse than the shock of what he said.

"We mustn't start this," he declared painfully. "It would be wrong."

"Wrong? Surely not," Ardith stiffened, totally bewildered. There were no sexual taboos based on species. Nor were there any formalities attached to relationships; on Federation worlds consensual sex was unrestricted and partners might or might not choose to be considered married.

"Wrong because I'm sworn to the Service," Varel told her. "I'm allowed intimacy only with fellow-members."

"But *why*? Is there some sort of prejudice—"

"Because I can't make other commitments. I could be sent to a young world where only Service agents are permitted to go, and my oath would require me to leave you. In any case, you'll be going back to Earth, and for us to be together here would make that harder for us both. I love you, Ardith, and now I know that once we started, we couldn't bear to be anything less than lifemates."

"I'm not going back to Earth," Ardith confessed. "I don't want to, and Radnor said we would go only as genuine volunteers."

Varel stared at her. "You don't *want* to?"

"Why would I? I was never happy there or in its colonies, and I might be locked up or killed to prevent me from presenting evidence that extraterrestrials exist."

"But there are only four of you to provide the evidence, and you may not all succeed. Isn't it your responsibility to try?"

"Responsibility? Most of Earth's citizens don't want to know that there are aliens, and those who do will eventually find out one way or another. I don't see why the Elders set up such a complicated scheme to create proof—there's no rush to tell people something they're not ready to hear."

Stunned, Varel was silent for a moment. Then he said, "Ardith, I thought—I assumed—that you understood. Earth's civilization is on the verge of collapse, and only contact with the Federation can save it."

~ 11 ~

"I don't understand at all," Ardith protested. "I thought the Federation kept its existence secret so as not to harm young worlds. How can you turn around and say that at some point only contact can save them?"

"It sounds like a paradox," Varel agreed, "and it's complicated. I can't explain here, tonight." He was too torn emotionally to explain, she realized. He was full of remorse about having led her to think there could be a long-term relationship between them.

"I thought we both knew what we were getting into," he told her. "I thought we could enjoy the time we had. It didn't occur to me that you weren't planning to leave—or that I'd come to love you too much to face losing you if we went too far."

To her dismay, his mind was now telepathically closed to her. She wondered if they could ever share thoughts again, or whether she could comprehend his if they did. How could the theoretical fate of a world not his own seem more important to him than love?

She couldn't believe that it was her responsibility to save Earth's civilization. The idea was ridiculous. No individual could make a big difference to the mess it was in. If the Federation wouldn't take action— which the history lessons had made clear that it would not—then simply convincing people that it existed wasn't going to help matters. As a professional historian Varel surely knew that, and he must also know that if on the unlikely chance that he was sent away despite not being classed as a field agent, it would be no worse than never having been happy. He evidently had some other reason for avoiding intimacy with her, and failed to see that it would be less painful for them both if he were honest about it.

Rather stiffly they said goodnight, and Ardith went to her suite. She wanted only to crawl into bed, but Meiko, Fred and Jacob were in the central room having a late snack; she couldn't just ignore them.

Nor could she hide her inner turmoil. Meiko, the most telepathic of the three, picked it up immediately. "What happened, Ardith?" she asked with sympathy.

"Varel says we have to go back to Earth," Ardith replied.

"Well, of course we do. We were told that in the beginning."

"Were we? Radnor said only if we volunteered."

"That was a formality," said Jacob. "They won't force us, but they've accessed our minds telepathically so they know they won't have to."

"If they accessed *my* mind, they know I never wanted to, and that I haven't been planning to do it." It was odd that Varel hadn't known, she thought. They had been so close telepathically. . . .

"They know more than you do about what's important to you subconsciously," Jacob replied, "just as Radnor knew we'd consent to a second session of mind training. It's not like reading conscious thoughts—those are private unless intentionally shared."

"Ardith, think about it," Fred said. "Look at all the trouble and expense they went to, setting this up. A powerful telepath sending us dreams night after night, maybe having to be drugged to reach so far. A luxury-class starship waiting for us in orbit light-years from here. All our needs met since we arrived: accommodations, clothes and gourmet meals, and every one of the residents going out of their way to be friendly—not to mention the mind training, or the fact that Radnor, who's a top official on his home world, has devoted his full time to us for many weeks. Did you think they were doing all this without expecting us to take on the job they recruited us for?"

She *had* thought so. She had assumed it was a matter of hospitality to guests, or perhaps just of wanting to observe inhabitants of a newly-admitted world. "But why is making themselves known on Earth so important to the Elders?" she protested. "Why is it more important to Varel than his own feelings?"

"He's Service," Meiko said, "and to Service people their personal feelings don't matter compared to the fate of worlds. They swear an oath to put the best interests of young worlds ahead of all other considerations, and they mean that literally—Korela told me that they'll die rather than break the oath, and some of them have."

Was that why he took the possibility of her being killed so lightly? She and Varel had never communicated much about the Service, Ardith reflected. It was true he had mentioned an oath, but she had assumed it was a formality like the oaths of office-holders. As a data analyst rather than a field agent, was he bound by the same strict interpretation of it? Apparently so. Apparently, if he thought Earth's future was at stake, he could not in good conscience do anything that might prevent her from fulfilling what he believed to be her destiny.

That was easier to accept than the idea he'd had second thoughts about his feelings toward her. But how could he possibly believe that simply knowing about the Federation would save Earth?

"I never stopped to think that the rest of you might not see why our mission matters," Jacob said. "I've believed so long that Earth needs contact that when they confirmed it I felt only relief. It was why I originally became an expert on the search for extraterrestrials, you see—"

"But you believed we wouldn't find them! That they'd hide from us, as we now know they did."

"I believed they'd hide *if we weren't ready,* and that their failure to appear meant we weren't. That was why I was so happy when we got the Message, why I went on the expedition to its source—why I was willing to risk my life clinging to the hope that they did send it. It wasn't just that I wanted to meet aliens personally and learn from them. I wanted to bring word of them to Earth before it's too late."

Ardith frowned. "What good will it do? Radnor told us conditions on Earth aren't going to improve for a long time."

"But there will be challenge, Ardith. At least on the part of a minority, there'll be the knowledge that there's somewhere to go from where we are."

"Right now there's no hope," Meiko said sadly. "Everybody on Earth is so depressed by the futility of making effort that they don't try to achieve anything new. Mile after mile of run-down buildings, full of people who don't care about getting off the couch as long as the robocart delivers food and beer—"

"They're afraid to go out because of the gangs that control the streets," Ardith pointed out.

"And if they wanted to work there'd be nothing much to do," Meiko added. "They couldn't get materials for building and there's no vacant land left. There's no way to produce food or clothes outside the robo-factories. Only artists and athletes have any real goal."

"We were lucky; we all had science to occupy us," Fred said slowly. "Yet we weren't learning much of anything new from science, were we? I know I wasn't accomplishing a lot by cataloging more and more stars."

"Nothing really new has been achieved for a long time, not since automation eliminated poverty," Ardith reflected. "If it hadn't been for the colonies—"

"If it hadn't been for the colonies the human race would be extinct by now," Jacob said. "Even with materials from the moon and asteroids Earth couldn't have supported a growing population, and confinement to a single planet would have resulted in war. We were able to end war only because of the outlet, and the challenge, that exploration and colonization provided. But now that challenge is wearing thin. It's been done so often it's not really challenging anymore."

"Just settling more planets the same way seems pointless when there's room for more people in existing ones," Ardith agreed. "That's why I wanted to see new worlds."

"Developing psi powers offers challenge," Meiko said. "The Captain of *Estel* said so—and for the four of us it has certainly been true."

"Yes, and Radnor told me that's Maclairn's aim, why they set up the mind-training program on Earth," said Jacob. "But it won't be challenging indefinitely. There's only one lasting challenge, one never-ending hope—the absorption of new ideas from alien civilizations."

"Ydoril's culture isn't that different from ours," said Ardith. "I admire it, but it could get boring, I think."

"Ydoril is not a complete, naturally-evolved culture; it was created purposely by the Service as a base for its agents. Think of all the past cultures that developed on Earth, and how they blended—it's the blending that produces new ideas—and then picture thousands of cultures on different worlds."

"That's why the Federation doesn't interfere with young ones," Fred reasoned. "The separate planetary cultures have to develop, not just for their own sake but because the Elders need the variety. You knew that all along, Jacob? That was the basis of your theory?"

"Yes. Every time in Earth's history that there has been major exploration leading to discovery of new lands and different cultures, there has been a renaissance—excitement, new ideas, not merely borrowings but creativity. That's a well-known fact, and there's been worry because it can no longer happen."

"But if we make contact with extraterrestrials it *can* happen," Fred continued, "and it will go on forever because the Federation keeps finding new worlds—countless worlds in this galaxy alone, and someday it may reach others—"

"And it's time for it because there's no cultural diversity on Earth anymore," Meiko said. "The blending has all been done. That's how they know we're ready, not just because we passed the milestones."

"Yes," said Jacob, "and it's why Earth's civilization is doomed if we don't make contact. Our very survival is endangered because in the long run a sapient species without a thriving civilization will die out. So I'll do my best to prevent that, and if I'm killed for it, so be it."

Ardith's heart sank. Oh, God, she thought—it was becoming obvious that she should go back to Earth with the others, not because she was convinced by Jacob's argument, which seemed rather speculative, but because Varel wouldn't respect her if she refused. But she couldn't make herself believe she would achieve anything by it.

"Contact with alien cultures isn't going to get rid of the gangs and the terrorists who have nothing constructive to do and channel all their energy into destroying things," she declared. "And it's not going to provide occupation for the people who are idle. They can't even get passage to the colonies, let alone alien planets. So it's not likely that we can save civilization, whether our story is believed or not. How can action by a few individuals be expected to save it?"

"Every step forward ever taken began with a few individuals who weren't sure where it would lead," Jacob said. "That's how evolution happens."

Evolution? Once she herself had said things like that. When she'd boarded the lifeboat she had believed it was her destiny to be one of the few. She hadn't balked at risk then. She had looked forward eagerly to the challenge. What had happened to her?

With chagrin, she realized what had happened, and it wasn't just her failed relationship with Varel. In the lifeboat, she had been headed toward bright, beckoning worlds where she expected to see wonders. Now she would be going back to the dreary world she had left. She was not even sure it was worth saving.

While talking she'd felt a headache coming on after all, as they had so often during her old life and now probably would again. Resigning herself, she lay in bed for nearly an hour before she remembered that with her mind training she could turn off the pain.

~ 12 ~

During their last days on Ydoril before touring other worlds, Varel showed them holos of planets that were comparable, he said, to what Earth would someday become—or at least should become, if all went well. Jacob was right, he told them. Challenge and variety were among the key factors. They went over the whole argument again in the history seminar, and Ardith had to admit that the evidence he presented was strong. But she still had doubts about their ability to have an impact.

"The thing to remember," Varel said, "is what Earth will be like if it cannot be saved. You may think conditions can't get any worse short of a devastating war, but they can."

He turned on the holoscreen. "I'll skip the pictures of nuclear disaster," he said, "because Earth's film industry has produced countless simulated ones and you don't need to see the real ones in our files. We have come upon other dead worlds, and archeology has told us what happened. In the most tragic cases, the people had never crossed space—but though colonization is essential to long-term survival, that alone is not enough to keep the mother world's civilization alive."

A sick feeling came over Ardith and she sensed that she was still closely enough attuned to Varel to have picked it up from his mind. "The species that evolved on the world I'm going to show you," he said, "is not extinct because it did have colonies. But its home world has been abandoned; it is no longer habitable by more than a tiny fraction of its peak population, and the colonies aren't strong enough to restore it."

The scenes that appeared on the screen were appalling. The land surface of the planet was a virtual desert punctuated by vast areas of boxlike structures that apparently had once been living quarters. There was little sign of vegetation. "Those who died, died slowly," Varel said, "because people hadn't the skill or the gumption to maintain the level of technology on which their civilization was dependent. They just let things go."

Puzzled, Fred asked, "What do you mean, let

things go? You mean they ran out of resources?"

"No, in the past their ancestors had adapted to dwindling resources as they had to climate change, just as all species either adapt to changing conditions or die. The ability to do this through technology is what makes humans a more successful species than others that evolved on Earth. But nostalgia for ancient times led people to forget that; some blamed technology for their problems, while the majority were merely apathetic. Few bothered to become engineers or technicians—robodevices provided everything they needed, and they didn't stop to wonder what kept such devices going."

"But what killed them?"

"Well, the freshwater supply had long been inadequate, so when the aging desalination plants failed, millions died of thirst. Millions more starved because crops couldn't be irrigated. The power satellites went offline due to lack of maintenance. Transportation came to a halt, leaving people to die in their homes or in the streets. We think some resorted to cannibalism."

"Couldn't you have intervened?" Jacob asked.

"We didn't find this planet until it was in the state you now see. But even if we had, direct intervention on a world not in contact with us is permitted only in the very rare case where nothing else can prevent extinction of a whole species. These people had thriving colonies, so it wasn't a question of extinction. We would have attempted to initiate contact, however—they had passed the three essential milestones."

"Including widespread telepathy?" Meiko asked. "Why didn't that make them aware of what was happening before it was too late?"

"Their excessive focus on telepathy and other mind powers was part of the problem," Varel said.

"People devoted themselves to attaining new states of consciousness and ignored the demands of physical existence. A civilization needs both inner powers and technology. They have to stay in balance if it is to survive."

Ardith frowned. "Is there a real chance that Earth could go the same way as this world if it has no contact with the Elders?"

"What do you think, Ardith?" Varel asked pointedly. "You don't like Earth the way it is now, after all."

She flushed, feeling suddenly chagrined by her own insensitivity. He had told her Earth's civilization was on the verge of collapse, and she had not asked him why. She had assumed that his obvious emotional pain was due entirely to the state of their personal relationship.

"It's a real danger for the long term," Varel went on. "However, it's not our chief concern for the immediate future. You may have wondered why we in the Service, and the Maclairnans, are giving your mission such high priority. It may seem that there's no hurry about revealing our existence to Earth when we know that a large share of the population isn't ready to accept us. And we haven't explained why there is, because there'd have been no point in your worrying before learning enough about the Elder worlds to feel hopeful about the future and to offer that hope to others. Now, though, it's time for you to face the facts about what you may be up against."

Startled, the four of them stared at Varel in bewilderment. What, short of the devastation he'd shown them, could be worse than the dismal conditions on Earth with which they were all too familiar?

"When people are as stressed and apathetic as they are on Earth," he continued, "they are ripe for rule by tyrants. We have seen this over and over again in the histories of hundreds of worlds; you have seen it yourselves in Earth's history if you've studied it even superficially. All it takes is for a strong, evil-minded person, one who is unconsciously telepathic enough to gain a following despite lack of any real leadership qualities, to declare himself the boss and back up his supremacy with force. For example, look at the twentieth-century dictators Adolph Hitler and Joseph Stalin.

"For the most part, past dictatorships have not been worldwide, and they haven't been in possession of technology as sophisticated as Earth's now is. On the few planets where they were, civilization was set back for at least a century because all the enterprising people, the ones who would normally overthrow such a regime, had gone to the colonies. They won their own freedom but were too busy surviving to care what happened to the mother world."

"My God. You think such a thing could happen to Earth?" Fred burst out.

"Unfortunately, we know it could. The signs are all there. Oppressive though the League government now is, that's nothing to what it has the potential to become. In the past its leaders have been corrupt or ineffectual, not seekers of extensive personal power. There's one on the rise now, however, that we've been keeping a close eye on. We can only hope that there'll be enough time for you to have an impact before he decides to take over. I don't think I need to spell out how much more difficult your task will be if it runs out."

"Can a takeover be averted if we succeed?" asked Jacob, looking more troubled than Ardith had ever seen him.

"We hope so. It depends, of course, on whether enough people are inspired to wake up and think about the future."

"But if it's not, are we going to be living under such a government for the rest of our lives?" Meiko asked in dismay. It had always been understood that they could not return to the Elder worlds, but they'd thought it would be no worse than what they'd been used to.

"You're free to decline the mission," Varel said. "It's up to you to decide whether the chance of saving Earth's civilization is worth sacrifice."

Ardith thought about it throughout the day, and lying awake in the huge bed she kept thinking. At dawn she cleared the opaque window beside it and looked out at the green meadow where she and Varel had walked together; and she resigned herself to giving up the worlds she'd dreamed of, and even to the new and frightening idea of someday having to live under a truly tyrannical government. It wasn't just that he wouldn't respect her if she failed to accept the responsibility. In her heart, she knew that she wouldn't respect herself.

Yet she still didn't see how it was going to work.

The others didn't either. "I'm not sure just what we're supposed to do," Fred complained. "Who do we tell, and how is the word going to spread?"

After lunch Radnor met with them in their suite to explain more. The goal, he said, was to get as many people as possible aware of the Federation—and willing to confront the vast, mysterious universe beyond Earth's colonies—before the government heard about it. "The officials in charge will resist the knowledge, and as you've been warned they'll try to suppress it," he said. "Sooner or later they will find out—and in fact they *must* find out if contact is to occur. But we need to have a large enough segment of the public on board when that happens to demand that it be brought into the open. That doesn't mean a majority—there's not going to be a vote on whether to establish an official relationship. There just have to be enough people to insist that the rest of the population is informed."

"How can four of us possibly contact that many people when we have to keep it secret from the media?" Ardith protested.

"We'll go into the details of the strategy later," Radnor promised. "Above all, it will depend on your ability to provide proof. For centuries people have claimed to be in contact with aliens and many have had followers, but however strongly they believed it was true, they had no proof of it. You four, and only you, can present objective evidence."

"I suppose we'll be suspected of being like those early believers," Meiko said.

"Yes, you will. That's why it's important to speak only to people who have the means to check your identity. If word were to get around that you were spreading wild speculation, nobody would listen."

"What if someone suspects that our IDs are fake?" Fred asked. "ID forging is pretty common, after all."

"Yes, so you can't depend on your implanted ID—the only really reliable evidence is your DNA profile, which is stored in a database that's virtually impossible to hack. You'll have to let the person you need to convince see you collect the saliva sample and submit it directly for robotic analysis, so that no chain-of-custody question can arise."

"Won't medical analysis be too slow?" Meiko protested.

"The public DNA-search machines are very fast," Ardith informed her. "They can't detect genetic disease, but people use for them for ancestry and paternity tests."

"Eventually, you'll have to get the government involved," Radnor went on, "and since I worked on Earth for many years I have some idea of who would be receptive. Unfortunately the best prospects are not in power at present—there was a League election, and the side most likely to support us didn't win."

"Is it a political issue?" Ardith asked in surprise. "Apart from the general political situation that may lead to dictatorship, I mean."

"Oh, yes. It always has been, ever since the League government learned about Maclairn. That's the main reason why Maclairn is protected by a cruiser, and why it has been touch and go to keep the cruiser deployed for well over a century."

Puzzled, she protested, "But until recently the Maclairnans didn't know about the Federation."

"We knew the potential of psi powers, though," Radnor replied, "and had the specific aim of expanding their use on Earth. We taught people to take full control of their own minds. And if there's anything an authoritarian government fears, it's the prospect of people gaining that ability. It makes them resistant to control by its leaders. That's one of the main reasons why we think that our mind-training program combined with alien contact may enable Earth to stave off the imposition of tyranny."

"You once said there was collusion between the League government and the Ku Klux Klan." Fred recalled. "The Klan was persecuting people with psi powers, wasn't it?"

"Absolutely, and if the Captain of *Estel* hadn't exposed those responsible, it would have attacked Maclairn in force. Conspirators within the government encouraged it—we believe they even funded it. Though the new administration promised freedom of mind, under a more repressive one that promise wouldn't be kept."

"So then especially because the Elders have advanced psi abilities—"

"For the public to find out that psi capability is an evolutionary advance is the last thing Earth's government wants. Just knowing that, without any actual contact with the Federation, would undercut its power."

"This puts a different face on it," Jacob said. "For years I've been focusing on the probable public reaction to contact with aliens, but it didn't occur to me that the government might have reason to oppose it beyond the cultural disruption it's bound to cause."

"Well, it makes sense," Ardith said. "Is this part of the reason you need us to make the revelation instead of the Maclairnans?"

"Yes," Radnor agreed. "For Maclairn to do it would alert them immediately to the fact that there's a connection with psi. We're hoping that because you're not known to be psi-gifted it will take them a little while to reach that conclusion."

~ *13* ~

They were scheduled to leave soon on a short tour of typical Federation worlds. Radnor was going with them as their guide to unfamiliar cultures and customs. Varel would also go along to interpret the historical significance of the places they went. Ardith wasn't sure whether this was part of the original plan or whether he had talked the Service into it before they split up. Now it was bound to be awkward.

On their last evening before departure there was a formal farewell ceremony in the Sky Room. Ardith wasn't looking forward to it; she hadn't been in that room since breaking up with Varel and she was afraid it would bring back too many memories. But when she got there she found that it had been transformed. The seating had been pushed back and a dais placed in the center of the room, surrounded by a low bank of white flowers. And in wall brackets around the circular perimeter of the room were blazing torches.

The people, more people than she had seen gathered at one time, stood in concentric circles around the dais. To her surprise, they were all dressed in white, a color she'd never seen worn on Ydoril. *Those are Service uniforms*, Radnor told her, *which they reserve for ceremonial occasions*. He too was wearing white, which he said was also the ceremonial color on Maclairn. She and her companions had been given green tunics, more tailored than the ones they usually wore, to symbolize Earth. He led them to places on the dais itself, facing Coris and an older reddish-skinned person she did not know.

Looking outward around the circle she saw that Varel was in the front row. Her heart quickened in spite of her resolve to treat him casually. There was nothing casual in his bearing; the uniform made him look like a prince in a fantasy holo. Was that what it had been all along, a fantasy of a universe that had never been meant to be real for her? In only a little while, after a few more glimpses of that universe, she would be plunged all the way back into reality. Would the memory then hurt no more than recollection of a dream?

A sparkle on Varel's chest caught her eye, and looking closer she saw that he wore a pendant made of some brilliant metallic substance with innumerable facets that reflected light. Having once spotted it, she noticed that many others also wore them. *It's the Emblem of the Service,* Radnor explained. *Members wear them always, under their tunics when not formally dressed. The students don't have them since they have not yet taken the Oath.*

The Oath. It set members apart, then, not just as a rule to follow but as a daily reminder of what they placed above all else. If she and Varel had ever reached the point of taking his shirt off she'd have known they could go no further, she thought ruefully, for she'd have asked him what it meant—and *he* would have known what he'd tried, for a while, to forget. For the first time she grasped what his conflicted feelings must have cost him. She longed to reach into his mind and forgive him, but that would only make their separation worse.

The music that filled the room faded and Coris began to speak. "We are gathered tonight to celebrate a new relationship with the planet Earth, a world that all of us here in this room, in one way or another, have studied," he said, "and to consecrate those who will first reveal to its inhabitants that they are part of a larger universe. This celebration is different from our usual practice in that those we entrust with the task are not members of the Service, but citizens of the new member world itself.

"They have been judged worthy of the role. They will be supported by our agents on Earth and by others of their own kind from its colony world Maclairn, with whom we long ago established friendship. But these four people alone will bear the responsibility for paving the way toward open contact with their mother world. It is a difficult task and perhaps a dangerous one. We fear that trouble on Earth will soon increase and they may be caught in the middle of it. Though they cannot wear the Service

Emblem, it is fitting that they receive some token as a symbol of their commitment and of our trust in them."

Ardith drew breath, wondering what was coming. She didn't feel consecrated and was not sure she should pretend to. "Throughout the many worlds of the Federation, as well on Earth," Coris continued, "fire is a symbol of the human spirit—of wisdom, of transformation, of the link between the spiritual and the mundane. The discovery of fire marked the first step in the evolution of human culture as we know it, and it is essential to all civilizations that have arisen since. It can also be seen as a symbol of fellowship: humans on all planets have sat together around campfires to share light and warmth not available to them alone, as we the Federation join our worlds to share the light of our knowledge.

"The rituals of most cultures have involved sacred fires, candles, or torches. Both in our own Service ceremonies and on Maclairn, the torch symbolizes the continuing evolution of the human mind and the effort to extend new powers to all with whom we are in contact. It is a bond between the Elder peoples and the Earthborn."

Turning to the four envoys he said, "Therefore a flame, much like the insignia of Maclairn's Stewards of the Flame but worn as a pendant like our symbol of light from countless worlds, will be your token of our confidence in you and our blessing on your mission. Receive it now from Larendus, Director of the Anthropological Service."

The older man moved toward Jacob, and instantly Ardith knew him for a more powerful telepath than Radnor, far wiser and stronger than anyone she had met. From Coris he took a pendant she could not clearly see. "Jacob Stromberg, will you accept this token and the responsibility it represents?" he asked.

Jacob stood proudly before him. "I will," he said in a firm voice, bowing his head for the chain to be slipped over it, and she was sure that he said it joyfully. This was the fulfillment of his lifelong quest.

She knew she would be next. All at once, as she stepped forward, she became aware that the Director had probed her mind more deeply than she herself could probe it; the question would be superfluous. "Ardith Moran, will you accept this token and the responsibility it represents?"

Trembling, she bowed her head and whispered, "I will." And suddenly she knew what he had known before he asked. Whether this knowledge came from the Director, from Radnor, or from somewhere deep within, she became aware that she had never really doubted her willingness to play a part in saving Earth. She had told herself it was foolish, that no good could come of it, but underneath she hadn't believed that. She hadn't even wanted to believe it. She had merely been afraid—not of the dangers involved, but of finding herself unequal to such a mission. And Varel had known this. That was why he'd assumed she understood that their relationship would be temporary.

She blinked away tears as she looked down at the necklace. Flame-shaped but larger and brighter than Radnor's copper pin, the translucent orange-red pendant was unset, yet somehow bonded to its delicate chain so that it appeared to float unsupported. She was irresistibly drawn to gaze into it, and didn't even hear the question put to Fred and Meiko.

Then all around her the assembled people began to sing, a melody unique in the range of timbres produced by voices of different species. *The Service anthem,* Radnor informed her, *which closes all their ceremonies.* She could not understand the words, but no knowledge of the language was needed to sense their meaning.

In the silence that followed the Director said to them, "It has been our honor to have you here on Ydoril. Go now with our blessing to see many worlds, until you come to the one where the Eldest will give you his own blessing in the name of the Federation."

After the breakup of the assembly the four were offered refreshments, as always, along with the congratulations and farewells of all their friends. She accepted them in a daze, elated but at the same time bewildered. Radnor approached her and she asked silently, *What came over me tonight? I didn't understand why people felt so strongly about what we're doing—and then in the next minute I* knew.

That's what ritual does, he told her. Aloud he said, "You perceived the idea telepathically from more than a hundred people who believed it and were simultaneously focused on it. That's what rituals are for, not only in all religions but in ceremonial observances of other kinds—even in spectator sports—on all worlds. The fact that in some cultures it's not recognized as telepathy doesn't matter; even when unconscious, that's what goes on. But because you are now consciously telepathic you feel the effect more strongly than would someone who isn't."

Varel must have felt it too, many times, she realized. That was why the Service had very nearly the same status in his eyes as a religion. She understood now, but it was not until he appeared at her side, almost a stranger in the formal white uniform, did it occur to her that something had to be said.

They would be living with the others aboard a small starship for weeks to come. They could hardly go on avoiding each other, afraid of intensifying the hurt. He believed what had happened was his fault, when in fact it had been hers—if she'd known herself as well as he had known her, they wouldn't have gotten so deeply involved. Now she didn't know how to get back to being just friends.

Ardith, you don't need to speak, Varel told her, smiling. *Don't you realize that telepathy makes it unnecessary to spell things out? All you have to do is form the intention to share your thoughts.*

At long last, comprehension came to her. She and Varel had exchanged many thoughts about Federation worlds but few about their own lives. Coming from different backgrounds, different species, they had not learned to share the essential things. Thoughts were private unless intentionally shared, but you *could* share them. You didn't have to put them into words in order to prevent misunderstanding. Wasn't that the whole idea of how psi powers could create harmony among worlds?

I will always care for you, Ardith, he told her, *even though we can't be lovers. Since friendship is all we can have, let's make the most of it.*

Deeply moved, Ardith turned her eyes to the clear vault overhead and the stars above it. The beauty of them would stay with her always. No matter how dreary or perilous her life on Earth proved to be, she would have this place to remember. There would be more wonders to recall, but nothing could surpass what she'd felt here, however long she might live.

Part Two: The Elder Worlds

The next morning they left Ydoril, accompanied by Radnor and Varel. The small AI- piloted starship they traveled in was fast; unlike Earth's ships, which spent days in normal space when nearing or leaving a star, it needed only a few hours and thus could visit a different one every day or two. Being designed for the use of Service agents on the job, it provided fewer amenities than they'd become accustomed to. However, the beds were long and wide to meet the needs of different species, and they would sleep aboard even while orbiting destination planets, Radnor said. Its lander needed no special port facilities.

"Visiting Federation worlds will be challenging enough without your having to sleep there and be exposed to disturbing dreams," he told them. "The planets will be larger than Ydoril and populated almost entirely by the species native to them, who have never known any culture but their own. The collective unconscious of each world, built up over centuries, will be different from all others. You'll find that confusing and somewhat upsetting at first."

On Ydoril they had encountered only trained Service members who went out of their way to make them feel comfortable. On other worlds they would be among people who had had little if any contact with strangers. Despite the pictures she had been shown Ardith had always thought of "Federation planets" in a generic way as similar, but of course they weren't—they were independent and no more alike than they were like Earth. Their citizens didn't often travel from one to another, which was, of course, expensive. That was one reason young people joined the Service, she had been told. It gave them a unique opportunity to see diverse worlds.

She and the others had been given different clothes, closer-fitting and of more subdued colors than the brilliant tunics worn on Ydoril. "You can't avoid standing out in a crowd, though," Radnor said, "because few people on these worlds will have seen anyone of our species before. Maclairnans have kept a low profile."

Climate, he explained, would not be an issue. The weather in populated areas of the Elders' planets was never extreme since it was controlled by their advanced technology—hardly surprising, Ardith thought, considering their engineers' ability to shield whole planets from sight. Species did, however, have varying preferences about temperature, so use of the body-temperature control they'd learned in mind training would be essential.

On some planets they would need breathing masks. They were somewhat used to them since they'd been outside the dome on Ydoril several times, and compared to similar devices on Earth's colony worlds they were not bulky. Still, they were uncomfortable and she hoped it wouldn't be necessary to wear them often.

As they orbited their first destination, Ardith felt a thrill of excitement. This was what she had longed for. This was the reason she had wanted to meet aliens. A new world, unlike any she had ever seen. . . .

It was a world very much like Earth—Earth as it had been in the twentieth century, long before the envoys, or even the founders of Maclairn, were born. She recognized it as similar to the still-famous photograph taken when her forebears first crossed space. Looking out at the blue globe patched with brown, green and white, Ardith suddenly grasped why there was still an instinctive love for Earth, based on memories handed down from generation to generation and absorbed into the collective unconscious. The surge of awareness startled her.. Earth looked mostly grey now due to its befouled atmosphere, and she didn't look forward to seeing it again. But now she knew that for the sake of its ancestral glory it was worth preserving.

"Is this a younger world?" Meiko asked."No," Radnor replied. "It is older, much older."

"How did they manage not to spoil it?" inquired Fred.

"It wasn't always like this," Varel said. "It went through a normal phase of industrial development. But they were wise enough to move heavy industry into orbit before it was too late, and after their colonies were well established the home world was restored."

"That's why we chose it to show you," Radnor said, "so you could see that there's hope for Earth worth the hardships you'll face."

It would make no difference to the survival of species if its home world was devastated and abandoned, Varel told them later. Its colonies could make contact with the Federation. But unless at least one colony was large enough to serve as a focal point, there could be no true blending of ideas. The unique civilization built through millennia would be absorbed and lost.

They landed on the Earthlike world and, in the days that followed, on many others. The most impressive thing about the Federation planets was that neither their atmospheres nor their landscapes were polluted. Despite their reliance on high technology, there appeared to be no industrial facilities. She soon learned that this was because all such facilities were in orbit—planets were restricted to residential use, civic centers, and parks. Earth's failure to be further along in the process of moving heavy industry offworld was one of the main reasons for its decline, Varel told them.

Most civilizations had also built living quarters in space, with homes and gardens on the inside surface of enormous orbital cylinders. This, Radnor said, was proposed on Earth as far back as the 1970s, when it was thought they might be used to house space workers, but it turned out that nearly all space labor was performed by AI. And even after colonization of Mars, which had priority, people had been too short-sighted to see the need for orbital habitats near home.

"I guess that accounts for the endless acres of cramped, run-down housing most people have to put up with," Jacob said ruefully. "Living in orbit would be more comfortable, besides allowing Earth to become more park-like."

In some ways being with Varel all the time wasn't as difficult as Ardith had feared it would be. They were always in the company of others, and they refrained from private telepathic communication. It was just as well that they hadn't been in the habit of it.

On the other hand, she couldn't keep her longing for closeness with him out of her mind. They visited a wide variety of planets and cultures, large and small, ancient and relatively recent on the evolutionary time scale. At last her desire to see something different was being satisfied. But everywhere they went, the invisible curtain between them was a barrier not only to communication, but to her enjoyment of the sight.

How could his presence have so much power over her? she wondered. She was twenty-nine years old, far past the stage of girlish infatuations. And though the physical attraction she felt was strong, that was not what made her crave contact. It was the touch of his mind, the sharing of his inner self, that was missing. Having once experienced that, she could not feel whole without it. Seeing wonders with her eyes, she reached for the view through his eyes, and came up against a wall. It took awhile for her to grasp what tremendous effort on his part was required to raise that wall and keep it standing.

Was it always like this between telepaths? Radnor had said it was. He had said love develops faster between telepaths and that telepathic affinity, even when unconscious, was too powerful to deny. Would it last for the rest of their lives, unfulfilled, tingeing everything they saw or felt with a sense of something missing?

She tried to ignore this feeling and focus on the varied worlds she had wanted so much to see. She had not guessed how different from each other technological civilizations would be, despite their commonalities. Most striking was their architecture. Buildings were strangely shaped, yet all seemed to fit appropriately into their settings, whether they were of natural materials, steel, or synthetics more advanced than anything known on Earth. Some societies stuck to neutral-toned buildings, while others favored brightly-colored ones. On low-gravity planets people tended to live in tall, airy structures clustered in dense cities or sometimes, scattered in forests blending with the trees; whereas in high gravity they spread out more, with all living space close to the ground.

The predominant colors of the vegetation varied widely, too, depending on the climate and the characteristics of the sun—or suns, as on some planets more than one was visible. This was also true of Earth's colonies, of course; but there, people copied what they were used to, terraforming as much as possible and building according to conventional plans. The group didn't visit enough of the Elders' colonies to know if they attempted to copy their mother worlds; perhaps they did. After all, many were established prior to their species' admission to the Federation. But they were unlike anything she had ever seen.

There was another major difference from the worlds of the Earth League. Mind training, she found, covered far more on Elder worlds than what Radnor had taught her. The most prevalent form of psi apart from telepathy was remote viewing, which he said anyone with telepathic ability could learn easily since the two were related. He and Varel used it routinely to find their way in strange cities and even to determine which were likely to have favorable weather on the other side of whatever planet they were visiting. It could be used to see farther in case of pressing need, but not, he said, over interstellar distances.

Many people on the older worlds were adept in psychokinesis, the manipulation of material objects with their minds. Even on Maclairn children born with the ability used it in games and a few gifted individuals developed more advanced skills, but as a species evolved it was increasingly put to practical use. In addition to simply lifting objects to avoid getting up to reach them—which had been banned on Ydoril lest agents get in the habit but which Varel now demonstrated to the group's amazement—PK was used for artistic and industrial purposes. Metal could be melted and shaped without heat, for instance. The exceptionally psi-gifted could even move stone. Ardith was awed by the beauty of some of the psi-built sculptures they saw.

The worlds they visited were all, of course, far in advance of Earth. Earth's civilization had just barely reached the level of maturity required for Federation membership and planets ready for admission were not found often. Furthermore, they were not open to tourists until much later, when safety of visitors could be assured. There was, after all, still violence on Earth, not just on the part of individual criminals but among organized gangs. And according to what Korela had said, the Earth League's current government wouldn't be considered mature even if it could be prevented from turning into a dictatorship.

"Do all mature worlds have the same kind of government, then?" Jacob asked, clearly troubled by the thought. It seemed arbitrary.

"Not at all," Varel answered. "As you know, each world, with its colonies, runs its own affairs. Most have some form of democracy, though it's organized differently from place to place; but there are a few that have constitutional monarchies, technocracies, or even theocracies. And in some very advanced civilizations all citizens are well enough informed, and concerned enough about the public good, to control the government directly by vote without the intermediate step of representation."

"The one thing that's not acceptable," Radnor declared, "is any type of totalitarianism. It doesn't matter what it's called; if a government gives its people no voice in its actions and uses force to control anyone other than criminals, it's given provisional status in the Federation. That's the only situation in which the Service is permitted to intervene in internal affairs, and then only if the world's people ask it to come."

"But a government has to use force against groups that threaten others, even if they haven't yet committed crimes," Fred argued.

"It can defend its people against those who take up arms," said Radnor. "If someone threatens violence, that person is no longer entitled to freedom, while those who are nonviolent must be free to do whatever they want. But virtually all young worlds' governments claim the right to tell peaceful citizens what they can and can't do, which in addition to being morally wrong, is asking for trouble."

"Don't you have laws saying what people can and can't do on Maclairn?" Meiko inquired.

"No. We have no laws other than a general one prohibiting violent harm to others, or the threat of it. There's no need to ban theft or fraud because the telepathic awareness of their peers prevents kids from becoming dishonest."

"You have to remember, though, that Maclairn is a small society founded by a selected group of people," Varel said. "You couldn't suddenly switch to such a system on a whole planet—evolution can't be hurried. So the transition has to occur gradually."

"Telepathy, conscious and unconscious, plays a big part in that," Radnor added. "In a society where everyone is telepathic, people know how others feel and don't get angry enough to fight over misunderstandings. And on the other hand, if someone is harboring an intent to become violent, they know it and can stop it before it happens. More than that, as an increasing majority begins to find violence objectionable, the collective unconscious of the world discourages it."

No wonder the Maclairnans were offering mind training, Ardith thought. Earth still had a long way to go. But she knew that. She knew that she and the others would be in danger of becoming victims of violence as soon as they got there, no matter what state its government was in. She had better make the most of this interlude among Elders, suppressing as best she could the thought of the final parting with Varel.

~ 15 ~

As they visited more worlds, walking through the awesome cities of the Elders, Ardith began to feel on edge. Their encounters with people they met troubled her. She was too used to Ydoril now to be impressed by the fact that they didn't look like Earthborn humans. They seemed happy and prosperous, and though they weren't especially friendly, she assumed that was merely because they weren't used to seeing visitors unlike themselves. Certainly they, like all Elders, were telepathic. Nevertheless she couldn't connect with them; it was as if they were figures in a holo rather than live and real.

"It's because you're not even a guest here, just an observer," Radnor told her, "and because the collective unconscious of these worlds is too unfamiliar for you to draw on,"

Varel also seemed troubled, not by anything on the planets where they landed but by some inner source of worry that he did not want her to be aware of. She wondered whether he knew more about

Earth's peril than he had told them; whenever she thought about going there he stiffened and she realized that he was still attuned to her mind although unwilling to share what was in his own.

"What will you say about your impression of extraterrestrials when you describe them on Earth?" he asked her once. "Besides explaining that they're people rather than mere creatures, I mean."

She hadn't given much thought t0 that. That they were friendly and had brought them home, of course, but her own impression? That except for those who'd hosted her, she couldn't connect with them? She certainly wouldn't say that; she could hardly explain about the collective unconscious. She would talk about their superior knowledge, their peaceful society, their amazing technologies—but none of that would convey the essential thing, that they were *human*. People would be shocked if they knew she'd have welcomed sex with one. Coloring, she hoped Varel hadn't picked that up.

Increasingly, she worried about her coming mission. Earth was in such a mess that she found it hard to believe that mere contact with the Federation could save it, let alone that she herself could help in any important way. "Are we really sure our species can someday become like these advanced ones?" she asked Radnor one evening after they returned to the starship. "We haven't ever behaved very well— everybody has known that for centuries. Maybe we're just defective."

"There are no defective species," Radnor said. "There's nothing inherently wrong with us, we're only immature."

"And so world problems aren't cause for guilt on the part of people who didn't personally cause them," Varel added. "The collective guilt humans on Earth feel is part of what brings on the depression that's creating worse problems."

"Yet you say our civilization is about to collapse. What has gone wrong?"

"Nothing. It's a natural stage, like everything else that seems to be a failing.'

"But some civilizations do fail, she protested. "Surely you don't think that what happened to the world you showed us was a natural stage—"

"It was," Varel said, "but it went on too long. Here's how the process works: a civilization gains the ability to colonize space, and unless something does go wrong, it throws all its energy into the effort. That's good, because if it doesn't, the species won't survive after the resources of its home world give out. But eventually almost all the enterprising people go to the colonies. Those left on the home world are either apathetic or frustrated and they stop making any effort toward progress. And so the mother world is degraded, as you saw in the holo, if its people aren't revitalized by contact with other civilizations. Its own civilization then dies out because the colonies are busy surviving and while small, they lack the means to do much else."

"Then are all advanced civilizations automatically doomed if they don't join the Federation? That doesn't make sense. What would happen if there weren't any other civilizations? If we were alone in the universe like everyone on Earth now thinks, or if the only other sapient species were still in the Stone Age?"

"That's like asking what would happen if there weren't any other suns. The universe is as it is, and we can't get anywhere wondering what it would be like if it were different."

"But somebody had to be first," Meiko argued. "If mother worlds are doomed without contact, how did the Federation get started?"

Varel frowned. "There were two at about the same level, and one found the other by chance. It's true that it might never have happened."

"I'm not so sure it was by chance," Jacob said.

"Are you implying something like God?" Ardith asked, surprised. Jacob had never appeared to be religious.

"Not a conscious, personal God," he replied. "That's a metaphor. But the patterns we see in the universe seem to favor the continuous evolution of life and civilizations, and for contact to be statistically unlikely wouldn't fit those patterns."

"Like your safeguard theory, Jacob," said Fred. "You couldn't believe the universe was set up to put most worlds in contact prematurely, and you were right. Are you now saying it's set up to provide for eventual contact?"

"I guess I am. There have to be enough of them to ensure that at least two will find each other and then combine to find others."

"But what if a few don't get found?" Ardith asked.

"What if a few receive radio messages too early? As I said before, it would be an aberration. Reality doesn't function like clockwork. The patterns are a matter of probabilities, just as they are in physics."

"There are no guarantees," said Radnor. "If there were, there'd be no room for free will."

"You mean I wouldn't really have a choice about undertaking this mission. You're making it sound as if we—the four of us—will determine the fate of our whole species, and if we fail it will be an aberration with respect to the way the universe works. It can't be like that! Nobody has that much power. Nobody who's not insane would want it."

"Every one of us has it whether we want it or not, Ardith," said Varel. "What if I hadn't told you what's at stake? Would you have agreed to go back to Earth?"

"Maybe, because I cared what you thought of me."

"So either way, *I* had the power."

He could have made love to me, asked me to stay, and I'd have done it, Ardith thought. He must have felt it was his responsibility to save Earth as well as mine. . .

"And what if we hadn't come on the expedition," Jacob added, "or if there had been no expedition to investigate the Message? Or if the message hadn't been sent? Every person has power to affect the fate of worlds, but nobody has it independently. We can't trace events back to any particular decision on anyone's part. There are too many variables involved."

"Far too many, even in principle," Varel agreed. "The patterns aren't planned, they just come into being—and yet they aren't random. We can predict on the basis of what we've seen in the past, just as in science there are 'laws' that permit predictions, even mathematical predictions, to be made."

"One case isn't enough to base a prediction on," Ardith protested.

"Of course not. Did you think the case I showed you was the only one? The Federation has existed for thousands of years. All of what we know about the extinction of species and the fall of civilizations is based on observation of many, including more than a few that didn't make it."

"It must not be much fun to be a historian," Meiko remarked.

"Not all the time. But if there's one thing I've learned as a historian, it's that there is always hope. Yes, there are some tragic cases, but they are aberrations. For the vast majority of worlds, the dark times always pass and the future gets progressively brighter. People can't perceive that when it's dark and they tend to think it will grow even darker, but looking back they can see if they choose to look. And I can see, because I can look back through time at countless worlds and the overall trends are invariably hopeful."

My God, Ardith thought. She had always pictured him as a teacher, explaining histories of the Federation planets to young students as he had to the four of them in the seminars. Yet his main job was as a data analyst, specializing, he'd said, in comparing histories of young worlds. She hadn't realized what that job entailed. It was hardly surprising that he felt so strongly about the potential decline of Earth. How could she have been so insensitive?

Interested as she was in seeing diverse cultures, it was tiring to deal with a different telepathic ambience every day; even at night aboard the ship, alien images followed Ardith into her dreams. So she was glad of the breaks from contact with people when they visited wildlife preserves. On nearly every planet there were areas where the unique animals that had evolved there ran free to be observed from border stations or from the silent, low-flying lander. As an exobiologist she found them fascinating and craved a closer look; but the tour was nearly over and time was running out.

The last world they visited before Federation headquarters was Everne, Varel's home world. It was a slightly smaller planet than Earth and colder, as it was farther from its sun; and though not a water world, it had an unusually large proportion of water to land. Several of the largest cities rose out of the sea, warmed, Varel said, by underwater springs. Seen from a distance, they looked like floating bubbles with shining towers thrusting through their tops.

There was a spectacular view of them from the porch of Varel's house, which was in a hillside village on the edge of a blue-green forest. It was a historic brown brick structure that had long ago been converted from a library that had held physical books. Inside, it was modernized with all the electronic equipment needed for remote access to Ydoril's database, but it still had the feel of a cozy retreat.

He loved the house. "I was born in it," he told her. "Giving it up for most of the year was the hardest part of joining the Service. I have vacations, of course, and I come back every chance I get. I suppose I should have sold it when my parents died, but I don't need money in the Service and I like just knowing it's here."

How would it feel to live in a place like this? Ardith wondered. She herself had been raised in one of Earth's depressed areas and had never had opportunity to visit one of its few remaining rural areas, much less a large individually-built home. On Earth such luxuries were only for the wealthy. If only she could have stayed on this planet, come here with him. . . .

For the first time during the trip they didn't sleep on the ship—Varel's house had room for all of them. While the others settled to relax in the living room, she and Varel went for a walk outdoors. If she hadn't learned to adjust her temperature via mind-training she would have been cold; there were patches of snow on the hillside behind the house. On the other hand, she didn't think she could ever be cold, holding his hand.

They looked up at the stars, the constellations unfamiliar to her but well-known to him, and thought of the different ones visible from the Sky Room on Ydoril. It was their first time alone together since their parting there, and it would be their last. Tomorrow they would go to Federation headquarters on Andoval, from which she would go on to Maclairn with Radnor and thence to Earth.

When they returned to the porch they lingered for long moments there, not wanting to go inside. He gripped her hand tighter and with a burst of joy she sensed that the wall between their minds had fallen. She turned her face to him and whispered, "Just once . . . for us to remember . . . would it do any harm?"

No spoken words were needed, for she sensed that he had resolved a conflict that had torn him for weeks. *I don't care if it does or not, if you don't,* he responded, and took her into his arms. His kiss was warm and comforting; they both knew that they must not let it become passionate when it was an ending rather than a beginning.

~ 16 ~

Early the next morning they went back to the ship, and after an immediate jump, emerged near the small yellow star they had called Omega—the star to which the Message had brought them many weeks ago, where their lifeboat had been picked up. It seemed as if a lifetime had passed since then. Certainly Ardith felt she had been reborn, short though her new life might well be.

Tentatively, she reached out to Varel's mind, only to find that the wall was back in place. She hadn't had much hope that it wouldn't be; after their kiss he would be more reluctant than ever to give his feelings full rein. Yet what could it matter when it was their last day?

"Are there really five inhabited worlds here, like in the dreams?" Meiko asked.

"Yes," Radnor replied. "Eleven planets in the system, but some are outside the habitable zone. We'll survey the four colonized ones from orbit, then land on the mother world, from which the dreams were sent."

Ardith's heart leaped, and she found that she was shaky. It was frightening to think that she might be disappointed.

They all shared that feeling. This was the reason they had cut their ties with Earth, the cause of their firm resolve to meet the Elders—it would be the culmination of all that had happened to them on Federation worlds. And it would be their last contact with them. After this they would be back among their own kind forever.

"The people on the worlds of this star are the most highly evolved we know of," Varel said, "the very first to contact another civilization and thus establish the Federation. They are the eldest of the Elders."

Soon after emergence they found themselves already within visual distance of its outermost planet—or rather, moon, since it orbited a gas giant. It had been settled only a few centuries ago. Warmed by its inner ocean. the habitable area lay beneath an icy surface and its buildings were not visible from orbit. The technology that supported sapient life in such as environment was, according to Varel, among the most advanced to be found in the Federation.

The next two planets, more conventional colonies, were ancient and as fully populated as many mother worlds. To see them better than from orbit Varel suggested using the lander, on autopilot, to fly over portions of the surface.

By this time Ardith was used to the fact that not all pleasant worlds had green space—Maclairn itself did not, Radnor had told them. These planets had wild mountainous areas and a desert ecology, although parkland with imported vegetation had been created. Buildings covered vast areas but unlike the run-down ones on Earth, they were beautifully designed, clean and new-looking due to the synthetic materials of which they were constructed.

"There's no real need to see them from the ground," Varel said, "as they are very similar to colony worlds you've already visited. They are quite crowded and people live close together, but they have used the best of the technologies developed here and elsewhere to keep their surroundings attractive. And of course their industrial facilities are in high orbit, so there's no pollution."

There was nothing about them that suggested the magical aura of the worlds they'd seen in the dreams. "I *saw* them," Meiko said. "Five of them! Where are they?"

"We couldn't have seen five together," Fred pointed out. "Orbits are too far apart to see more planets than one as anything but stars."

"Of course, but the telepath who sent images to us must have gotten them from somewhere, even though they were combined. It wasn't like an animated holo— I sensed that they were *real*."

The fourth world they orbited was closer to the sun than the mother world but nearer to the starship's present position. They took a look at it, again from the lander, before proceeding. It was tropical, but the growth of vegetation had been controlled to make room for a limited number of settlements. "It's mainly a wildlife preserve," Varel said, "and there are more kinds of animals here than in the others we visited, plus various species of large birds with brilliant plumage. They blend in because of the many-colored foliage. I wish we could see it up close, but a permit to land here takes years to obtain."

Much as she would have enjoyed landing, Ardith was rather glad. She was impatient to reach Andoval, the world from which the dream telepathy had come.

The first thing that struck her as they approached it was that unlike so many other mother worlds they'd seen, it had no orbital habitats, or even much orbiting industry. Yet it was green, almost entirely green with few oceans.

"How can it look so unspoiled when it has been inhabited so long?" Fred asked.

"It wasn't always like this," Varel said. "It never had orbital settlements since there were planets suitable for large-scale colonization nearby in its own solar system. Nearly everyone eventually went there, even the people who in the case of most species would have stayed behind and let their world decline. But of course it did have polluting industry that needed to be cleaned up. In time, the colonies became rich enough to spearhead that, and by then, these people's psi powers had advanced to the point where they no longer needed local industrial facilities. What's not imported they create by psychokinesis."

"Everything in their world?" Ardith asked in amazement.

"Well, it's a specialized world. Most members of their species live in the colonies. Andoval is home only to the psi-gifted, the aged, and those who come for interworld conferences or spiritual exploration."

She looked out at the shining green globe, puzzled and a little let down. It wasn't at all like the dreams. It was just an ordinary planet—a beautiful one, but in no way ethereal or mysterious. She had not expected to hear inner music, but she had thought it would in some way arouse the feelings that the dream worlds had, satisfy the yearning that had entranced her in the beginning.

Flying low over the planet in the lander, they saw homes of many styles nestled among the trees. It was largely a wooded world; in its early days the forests had been cut down, as was usual when planets became crowded, but they had long ago been replanted. It was hard to realize that since the Federation had existed for millennia, this, the site of its birth, had been inhabited even longer. There were no ruins. The sites of ancient cities had been restored to their former glory. "The people here honor their history," Varel said, "as representative of the history of all sapient peoples. But in the modern cities they honor progress toward the future."

He had shown them holos of this world's cities, of course; they'd been among the first they had seen in the history seminar on Ydoril. But nothing could equal the awe they felt on arrival in its capital. Most of the tall buildings appeared to be made of greenish glass, not translucent like the domes on Ydoril, but clear. There were hundreds of them, spaced in clusters surrounded by plantings, reflecting the sunlight so that from above the effect was dazzling. Everything was as clean as if newly washed, which Varel said was due to technology that repelled dust and rain.

It was all so perfect that something about it nagged at Ardith, some disturbing factor that she couldn't define. She sensed that the others felt it, too. Fred finally put it into words. "Varel," he said, "we're all agreed that challenge is needed to keep civilization alive. But these people seem to have met all the challenges. There's nothing in their world that needs improvement. So what challenges *them*?"

"That's a good question," Jacob agreed. "You've said that once contact with the Federation is made there will be new challenges forever because we'll never run out of new worlds to see. Yet the ancient race of this world has been finding new ones and blending elements of their cultures for millennia. I'd think there'd be a limit past which there was no further they could go."

"They could go to other galaxies," Meiko suggested.

"Yes, and their scientists are preparing for that, but other galaxies are too far away for exchange of information,' Fred pointed out. "So it doesn't answer the fundamental question. Where do the oldest species in the Federation go when there are no problems left to solve?"

"They go deeper into their minds, explore phases of reality you and I would find incomprehensible," Varel said. "The material universe is not the only aspect of existence—anyone concerned with spirituality, or even with psi, knows that. But our knowledge of any other is very limited. Even the eldest Elders have much to learn."

"Is this what you meant when you said some of the people on Andoval have come for spiritual exploration?" Meiko asked.

"That's right. It's not necessarily connected to any religion, though religious metaphors are often helpful; but it does involve ideas traditionally considered mystical. Having solved all the problems of physical survival that's the only area left for sapient beings to explore."

"In other words, a new step in evolution," Radnor reflected. "It can't just stop here."

No, Ardith thought, it can't. To stop moving ahead would be the same as death, a death with no form of existence afterward. And if evolution wasn't ongoing, why were they giving up everything to stop the decline of Earth?

By now it was evening by their clock and by that of the capital city, so they delayed landing until morning and returned to the starship. Ardith was eager to get to bed. *Will we dream as we did in the lifeboat?* she asked Radnor.

Possibly, though not as vividly since now no one's purposely aiming to reach you. The collective unconscious is more pervasive here than on other worlds, and contains more inspiring concepts. You have been sensitized to dream input and may receive concepts in that way,

It was evidently the only way she could hope to see what she'd been searching for, Ardith admitted, since none of the worlds they'd seen had been like those in the space dreams. She couldn't help being disappointed about that. They had been told that the dreams had been sent to them. Where had the sender found the content? Was the Service hiding worlds, shielding them as the Federation shielded planets from discovery? That must be the explanation, but it was odd that Radnor hadn't said so.

She lay in bed, at first too excited to sleep. When she finally drifted off she saw no wondrous worlds and heard no inexplicable music. Instead, she found herself enveloped in light and warmth and a feeling of absolute safety, of certainty that all was well. And in the next moment, Varel was there beside her. *We will never be apart,* he said. *Because the worlds intersect, you see, and this place where we are now exists in all of them.* He took her hand and they stood in the light of many suns, orange and blue and yellow, more than they had seen in the sky at once on any planet they had visited. She saw them not with her eyes but with some faculty that revealed more than eyes, and she knew that even when it was dark she would be with him in sunlight. . . .

Shaken, she sat up feeling not quite sure how much was real. Had Varel really shared that dream? He had not come to her consciously, as in the nightmare long ago. She was sure that he had vowed not to, and she didn't doubt that he would keep that vow. But unconsciously, if he too had been dreaming. . . . Reaching for her clothes, Ardith found to her surprise that yesterday's soft grey tunic had been replaced by a white one. How very strange—white was the Service's ceremonial color and she had not thought it was ever worn on other occasions. Mystified she dressed and headed to the ship's lounge for breakfast.

~ 17 ~

The others too were wearing white, and Varel had put on his Service uniform. "Today you will receive the blessing of the Eldest," Radnor announced, "as the Director told you on Ydoril that you would."

In dismay Meiko asked, "Why has he noticed us, let alone chosen to bless us? We're important only to Earth."

"Well, there's something I need to explain," said Radnor. "I didn't tell you sooner because I thought anticipation of meeting him might make you nervous. You see, it was the Eldest who sent you the dreams across space."

Stunned, Ardith managed to say, "How did he even know about us then?"

"He believes in the importance of saving Earth— of saving every world of which the Elders know. He admitted Earth to the Federation ceremonially through my father Terry Radnor, who was also taken to meet him. So when later told of its peril he helped formulate the plan."

She turned to Varel. "My God, Varel, you have always known this! Why did you let me think it was just a Service scheme?"

"Because your choice had to be your own. Knowing that the sender of the dreams planned the mission might have influenced you."

Yes, it might have, Ardith realized. The memory of the dreams had made her want to stay; she'd felt that going back would be a denial of them, even though she'd known the Service had somehow arranged them. Underneath she had resented its desire to send her away. Yet Varel, knowing this, had not used the one argument that might have prevented her anger at him.

"Will it be a formal ceremony?" Jacob asked.

"Yes, but a private one, with no spectators."

"He doesn't have underlings or a palace guard or something?" Fred put in.

"He's not like that. Not royalty or even a political figure, and certainly not a religious one like the Pope or the Dalai Lama on Earth. He's just a very wise old man whom everyone respects, and who is therefore viewed as a symbol of Federation unity. He was chosen, among other reasons, because he is the strongest and most skilled telepath now alive."

They boarded the lander, which set down in a park-like area near the city center and a moving walkway took them to the largest building of all, which appeared to be made of many-faceted crystal. It dazzled so that eyeshades were needed in addition to the breathing masks; Varel explained that the eyes of the native species were adapted to a wider range of light than those of Earthborn people.

"This is the headquarters of the Federation," Radnor said. "There aren't as many offices as you might expect, since there's no central government and what there is lacks the trappings of bureaucracy. Mostly the building is used for conferences between delegates from different worlds."

"Have you come here before?" Jacob asked.

"No, but as you know, my father did, and he's told me what to expect. Each conference room is separated by invisible force fields into areas with different atmospheres so that people of different species can meet without masks. We will take ours off before we meet the Eldest."

They entered the building directly into a rotunda, shaped like the Sky Room but much larger and illuminated by a shaft of light that descended past many floors from a skylight in the roof. It was dominated by a wide moving staircase on which all six of them were able to ascend abreast. On the level to which it took them they were met by a young person with short yellow hair who led them to an ordinary controlled-gravity elevator, and from there to a room on the top floor. Varel, after conversing with their guide in a language the rest of them didn't know, said it was now okay to remove their masks.

They were early for their appointment. Though the chairs in which they sat to wait were comfortable, Ardith couldn't relax. She kept clenching and unclenching her fingers, afraid that she might not know how to respond to a man viewed as the wisest of all the billions who inhabited the many worlds of the Federation.

What would he be like, this man who had sent her dreams? How could any single being convey such awesome feelings to multiple people, powerful telepath though he was known to be? While only she and her companions had picked up enough of them to be swayed, they had potentially been received by the whole starship crew! To communicate them, he must have the wonder of them deep in his mind—they couldn't have been based on mere imagination. Was he an explorer of the mystical, as Varel had implied?

She didn't know much about mysticism, but what she'd heard didn't fit her experience. On Earth, she'd been told, mystics entered a state in which they felt as if all minds were one. Yet in the dreams she hadn't felt one with the whole universe or lost her sense of self. That wasn't consistent with what Radnor had taught them about volition. Evolution of the mind progressed through increased capability for volition—that was how they'd gained mind powers—and volition was a wholly individual faculty.

According to Radnor it was a matter of opinion as to whether mystical "enlightenment" of the sort that denied individuality was to be desired, let alone viewed as the evolutionary advance some claimed it was. Clearly he felt that it was not.

"We are not 'all one mind,'" he'd declared. "Our minds are all *connected*, which is something quite different. It's like Net connections—any computer can communicate with any other, but they are still separate computers that can function independently. And the sapient beings of a world, much less of all the worlds in the universe, are not inseparable either. We are linked through unconscious telepathy."

That had to be true, Ardith thought. At the moment of their kiss she and Varel had shared each other's minds, feeling no barrier between them; but that didn't mean they *were* one. To say they were would leave no room for loving each other.

Nor did it allow for the Eldest, or any person, being wiser than others. So maybe the beliefs of Earth's mystics were wrong. Maybe they were just misinterpretations of the connection between people on the part of those who didn't understand that most telepathy is unconscious or recognize that a lot of it comes from a planet's collective unconscious.

Whether or not he had some special source of wisdom, the Eldest must be aware of all worldly things, too; mere telepathy could give him that. Suddenly she wondered, will he know? Will he know how much I want Varel, want him as more than a friend? There was no reason to be ashamed of it. She wasn't ashamed, just embarrassed at the thought of someone knowing anything so private. Radnor wasn't aware that they had kissed, might not realize how deep her feelings still were.

Fred sensed her discomfort, though not its cause. "We're all nervous," he said. "I think I'm back to wondering whether I'm worthy."

"Of course you are," Jacob said. "We were declared worthy in the ceremony on Ydoril. But I confess to wondering whether he can make me feel more capable of living up to that than I do right now."10

"Me too," Meiko admitted. Ardith was silent. The time for wondering was past. Their choice had been made, and whatever was going to happen, here or on Earth, was beyond their ability to foresee. Oh God, she thought, let it not be for nothing! Let him give us some sign that it's worth the cost!

The inner door to the room opened and their guide beckoned, speaking in the language only Varel understood. "Since there are so many of us we'll be in a conference room rather than the Eldest's office," Varel said, relaying what he had been told. "We'll be behind a force field, as he breathes the atmosphere of this planet—it's invisible so we won't be aware of the barrier unless someone touches it. All communication with the Eldest will be telepathic, and since that's instantaneous the interview will be brief. But we can speak aloud for the benefit of each other."

Resolutely they rose and followed the guide. The room to which they were taken was softly lit, although no lighting fixtures were visible. It was furnished with a row of comfortable chairs positioned on one side of a long table, but not drawn up to it; a line down its center marked the location of the force field. The wall behind them was decorated with holos showing landscapes of different worlds.

The holo on the opposite side of the table was huge, giving them the feeling that they were actually in a green forest with sunlight streaming down between the trees. In front of it, in a large low-backed chair, sat the Eldest.

Welcome, he said to them silently. *I know that your custom is to extend a hand in greeting, and I'm sorry that the force field prevents me from doing that.*

He was a small man with blue-black skin and golden eyes that seemed too large for his face, eyes that revealed deep wisdom and compassion. Ardith knew instantly that there was no need to be shy with him and that he was to be trusted above anyone she had ever met. She knew, too, that if this man thought her presence on Earth was necessary, it *was*. The last of her doubts melted before the power of his gaze.

It was obvious that the others were similarly affected. "Venerable Eldest, we are honored by your invitation to us," Radnor declared. No one else said anything aloud, but they were drawn into rapport with each other as well as with the Eldest, and they recalled the dreams as if they were happening here, at this moment, instead of weeks ago in space.

Once again Ardith was aware of myriad worlds, countless and yet not separate, as if transported beyond her body; and they were embedded in music without words that she could feel rather than hear. She was transfixed by their beauty, and by the marvels sapient beings had created, generation upon generation, building civilizations that blended into an ever-changing whole. It was *real*, no longer a dream but tangible, the place she had always longed to be. . . . It was clear now, too, that these worlds were not for her. They had beckoned and she had glimpsed them, but it was not her destiny to stay. She had been born a century too early—or had she? Perhaps only someone who'd had an early glimpse could fill the role she'd been assigned.

As the room came back into focus she became aware that the Eldest had been communicating with all of them simultaneously, and after that, privately with Jacob. But now he addressed her alone. *Have I your consent to probe your mind?*

Wordlessly she assented, not knowing just what he meant but willing to submit herself to whatever this man wanted to do. Then for a while—perhaps a moment, perhaps longer—she had no thoughts or even feelings, and it wasn't until her mind was clear again that she realized he now knew everything she had ever felt in the past. While telepathically joined they had merged, unconsciously on her part, yet she didn't feel violated or even judged. The blessing he gave her was superfluous—he *knew* her, and that alone was enough to give her confidence in her fitness to become an envoy.

She sat quietly while the Eldest probed Fred, Meiko, and Radnor, one by one, and blessed them. Then, to her surprise, she saw Varel lean forward and knew that he too was being probed, which they had not expected. And when in his face she saw apprehension followed by unexpected joy, she knew what the probe had revealed.

Varel rose from his chair and came to her. She too stood, and when he reached for her hand she gave it to him gladly, while in their joined minds they heard the Eldest say, *Love is not wrong. Love can never be wrong as long as no one is hurt who has not consented.*

Whether the others heard this, she did not know, nor did she care. Nothing mattered except that their love was so real, so right despite all that stood between them, that the Eldest himself believed it should not be denied. Her heart swelled as he himself stood and continued, *Will you, Varel and Ardith, be faithful to each other while united and will you abide the grief of your parting?*

There was no need for them to answer; the Eldest had known before he asked. Nevertheless they both nodded in assent. He smiled and went on, *Then love each other for as long as you have together. Go, now, with my blessing on your union.*

Wordlessly they turned, hand in hand, and left the room with the others following. Any farewell would have been an anticlimax. Not until they had descended all the way to the ground floor did anyone speak.

"What was that, at the end?" Fred asked. As the least telepathic among them, he hadn't picked it up.

"I—I think it was a wedding," Ardith said, still dazed with shock at the marvel of it, the unforeseen bliss.

"So it was," said Radnor, "and my doubts about the wisdom of it are overridden. Tonight you will sleep in the room where I was born, for from the Eldest I received word that my father is dying, and we must go to Maclairn at once."

Part Three: Maclairn

~ 18 ~

To get to Maclairn, it was necessary to rendezvous with a larger Service starship that was patrolling near its star and transfer, after a short wait, to the historic ship *Estel*, which came to dock with it. Only *Estel* could approach the planet because of the Fleet cruiser that was stationed there. Fleet didn't know about the Elders and could not be allowed to find out; if its officers knew, they would be obliged to report it to the League government, and that would be as disruptive to Earth's civilization as the sudden appearance of aliens.

For fifteen years, since the return of Terry to Maclairn, *Estel* had been a direct link between the colony and the Federation. It had taken Maclairnan mentors to Ydoril and Service members to Maclairn, its secrecy maintained by its status as a privately-owned ship under the control of Maclairn's council. Fleet respected the wishes of the Council in all things, so it obeyed the decree that *Estel* must never be challenged or boarded.

All the same, Elders who looked significantly different from Earthborn humans were not brought in; there was too much risk of their being seen by Fleet officers who came to the planet's surface.

Some Elders, such as *Estel*'s pilot Liam, were indistinguishable from humans—to work as agents on Earth, they had been surgically altered in youth. Varel, who had come once before, was a borderline case. With a long-sleeved hooded jacket provided by the Service starship to cover his skin color and baldness and distract attention from his face, he could get by as long as he stayed away from places where officers might see him at close range.

He hadn't expected to come this time; the need to instruct the envoys was past and to Ardith's sorrow he'd been scheduled to go back to Ydoril. But under the assumption that the Eldest's blessing took precedence over standing orders, he had joined them without obtaining permission from the Service. There really hadn't been time to ask for it, since they'd returned to the ship within an hour after leaving the Eldest.

It was just getting dark when *Estel's* four-place lander set down for the second time at Maclairn's small shuttleport, on the rim of a canyon half-filled by a narrow lake. Varel, who'd been in the second group, pulled the hood of his jacket around his face as they disembarked and Liam secured the lander. They had to walk down a succession of terraces to the water's edge. The night air was cold by the time they got there; Ardith shivered before remembering to raise her body temperature. She'd been told that Maclairnans were dependent on that ability, since in the daytime the planet was scorchingly hot.

They were to be transported to the city by boat as far as the dam at the lake's end, and then by rail. It was a large boat; as it came in Ardith saw that its deck was crowded with people, obviously in a holiday mood despite the relative silence among telepaths to which she was now accustomed. To her amazement, when it reached the dock they began to sing. She couldn't make out the words, but the intent she sensed was unmistakable—it was a welcome, a joyous one, as if the travelers were celebrities.

"Why are they so glad to see us?" Meiko asked. "Is our mission to Earth important to the Maclairnans?"

"Not just the mission," Liam said. A quiet, self-reliant man whose white hair belied the impression he gave of youthful vigor, he informed them, "It's a traditional festival song. We're on our way to the wedding feast."

"Feast?" Ardith questioned. "Who told these people about what the Eldest said? Varel and I don't want any fuss made about it, we just want to be alone together."

"I'm afraid you can't avoid a celebration," Radnor replied. "You can slip away before it's over, but you'll have to accept a lot of congratulations first."

"I don't understand—" she protested. But she was escorted into the boat before she could get an answer, separated from Radnor and even Varel by the crowd.

As she stood at the rail, bewildered, Liam came up to her, accompanied by a tall silver-haired man he introduced as Gabriel, the head of the on-site Service team for contact with Earth. Radnor had said that Liam had been his father's close friend for over a hundred years, since long before revealing his alien origin—though it would have been hard to hide since he now had the vigor and unlined face of a man who hadn't even been born a hundred years ago. Hoping he had some authority here, she said in desperation, "Please, can't you get me and Varel away to someplace private? We're not really married, you know—we have only a little time left to be with each other."

"By Maclairn's custom you're paired even though not lifemates," Liam said. "I don't think you realize how important an occasion this is."

"Important to people besides me and Varel? Why?"

"Because it is the first union between a member of your species and an Elder," he replied. "It marks recognition of your tie with us, your membership in the Federation."

"More than that," Gabriel added, "It's an acknowledgement of your species' equality. Did you think your feelings alone were considered? The Eldest is wise as well as compassionate."

At Ardith's baffled look, Liam said, "She needs an explanation, Gabe. She can't be expected to know anything about Federation politics."

Turning to her, Liam went on, "Ardith, the most fundamental rule the Service has, second only to the ban on revealing our existence to immature species, is that we are forbidden to have intimate relations with them. Partly this is so that the native of the young world won't suffer grief when the agent leaves without explanation, but it's also because a line has to be drawn. Individually all humans are equals, but as species some are mature and others are not, and we often deal with primitive ones whose members are physically attractive. It's like the age of consent law concerning sex between teenagers—an older boy can't have sex with a girl of twelve even if she happens to be mature for her age."

"But if there's a line, didn't we cross it when Earth was accepted into the Federation?"

"There are some people on the Elder worlds, and even some in the Service, who believe Earth isn't quite mature enough to be brought in," Gabriel explained. "There has been controversy about it, and those of us who believe Earth is ready have won, but others are unhappy. The Eldest has always favored admitting Earth, but he can't say so because his role is ceremonial and he's not allowed to take sides on political issues. Ceremonially, once the Service's decision had been made, he admitted Earth through Terry Radnor, and again through the four of you; but that isn't enough to satisfy the opponents. So what could he do to make his position plain? He gave his blessing to a sexual union between you and Varel, an act that would be shocking if your species were not on Federation level."

Ardith didn't know quite what to say. Was she merely a pawn in a political fight? Was Varel? "Does Varel know this?" she asked.

"Yes, of course. In his position as a data analyst he could hardly be unaware of it. But he didn't know what the Eldest was going to do. I doubt if the Eldest himself knew until he probed Varel's mind and sensed his love for you."

"You don't think he was just—matchmaking, instead of judging our feelings?"

"Oh, no, Ardith," Liam assured her. "If he approves of your relationship, it's because he became aware of those feelings' strength. He has deep understanding of human emotions."

That was true, Ardith realized. She had been sure after his probe that he knew her, and that he was absolutely trustworthy in all respects. There could be no doubt that he'd known Varel also.

"If the Service directorate thought Varel knew beforehand what would happen, he'd be in a good deal more trouble than he is already," Gabriel added.

"Trouble? What trouble?" Ardith asked in dismay. But just then Varel reached her side, and she got no answer.

As the boat proceeded down the lake they stood arm in arm by the deck railing, pressed close together against the night chill. People crowded around, and they did their best to accept the attention graciously, then and later aboard the railcar. When they reached Petersville, Maclairn's main city, Radnor and Liam went to his house to be with his dying father. The others walked some distance farther along a broad stone-paved path to the house of the Council head, which served as the headquarters of the colony.

It was a huge house built largely of stone, which like most of the older homes on Maclairn had once housed several generations. Now its many bedrooms were used as guest rooms, most recently for visiting Elders. Ardith and Varel were shown to a large one on the top floor. "This is the room where Radnor's parents started their life together, and where he was born after his father went away," said their hostess. "He asked that you be given it."

They changed clothes—not back to their formal ones since Radnor had said white wasn't worn for weddings on Maclairn—and after a longing look at the wide, low bed, they went down to join the party.

The great room of the house was dominated by a huge circular stone fireplace with a hammered-copper hood, which Varel said had historical significance dating back to before Maclairn's founding. It was surrounded not by chairs but by many large floor cushions on which people were sprawled; in this colony, he told her, all seating and even dining facilities were customarily placed at floor level. Food and ale were plentiful and everyone, including Jacob, Fred and Meiko, seemed to be having a good time.

After a greeting from Kenard, the aged head of the Council, they found an unoccupied cushion near the fire and sat down, immediately becoming a focal point for people who approached them to offer good wishes, telepathically if not aloud. It was more like a gathering on Ydoril than on Earth, Ardith thought. She might never again have such an experience; she should savor it. All the same, she was impatient for the evening to end.

At last, when people started leaving, they felt justified in going upstairs. It had been a long day—— she now realized it was late morning again by the clock on Andoval, where they'd awakened—and what they needed most was probably sleep. But it would be some time yet before they did any sleeping.

Varel, she asked silently, *Gabriel said something about you being in trouble. What sort of trouble?*

It's nothing, just a technicality, he replied. She could tell from the undertone of his thought that it was not nothing, but now wasn't the time to worry about it.

The bed, like the other furniture, was set on the floor, but its mattress was thick enough to raise it to sitting level. They settled on it, facing, and slowly undressed each other, discovering the formerly-unseen differences between their bodies. She had not expected the variations in his skin, a darker shade of gold in some places than on his face and hands, nor had she known that he was not only bald but totally hairless. He was surprised that her body wasn't, and by the upward curve of her breasts.

She could feel the telepathic current between them stronger than ever before. *Has Radnor told you what will happen in our minds?* he asked. *How when joined, we will feel each other's sensations as well as share thoughts?*

She lay back on the bed, welcoming him. Radnor had mentioned that sex enhances telepathy, but she'd had no idea of what that meant. At first, fondling each other, she knew what Varel was feeling, but then in the fullness of their union she *felt* it; she could not tell which sensations came from her body and which from his. And their thoughts merged so there were no secrets between them; all the experiences of their past lives were as clear to both as if in memory, except for details intentionally kept private.

Afterward, nestled in his arms, she could not look back or ahead. This moment alone was real and important, and she shut out all thought of what was to come.

~ *19* ~

The next day, shortly after the noon meal, Radnor came to take them to see his father. Meiko was ecstatic and the others, too, were thrilled; it seemed incredible that they were about to meet the fabled Captain of *Estel* after a lifetime of assuming that if he'd been a real person he must have died long ago. He was, Radnor said, a hundred and forty-one years old.

"How is that possible?" Fred asked. "As far as I know, medical science on Earth hasn't made much progress in extending life since the average lifespan reached a hundred. It has all the experts puzzled."

"Medical science starts from the wrong premises," Radnor replied. "Except in the case of accidents and infection by virulent microorganisms, poor health is caused by accumulated stress, and people who've had mind training are able to manage the effects of stress so that it doesn't damage their bodies. On Maclairn we generally live into our hundred twenties, a little longer in exceptional cases."

It took a minute or two for this to sink in. Then Meiko said, "Are you saying that we ourselves will live to be a hundred and twenty because we've had mind training?"

"Probably not quite that long, since you didn't have it until you were past adolescence. But you should reach an age well over a hundred."

"Your father didn't have the training until his twenties," Ardith pointed out.

"Well, in his case the Elders modified his body somewhat at the time they gave him *Estel*, because they wanted to make sure he'd live long enough to become the first contactee."

"I'd have thought they'd have learned to make people immortal," said Fred. "Futurists have been anticipating that for centuries, yet no one on Ydoril ever mentioned it. Haven't they made any progress?"

"Surely you don't believe that old notion, Fred!" exclaimed Jacob. "After the mind training we've had, how can you not see the fallacy in it?"

"What fallacy?"

"That life depends only on physical factors—in other words, that the mind and the brain are the same thing. Scientists used to think they were; some on Earth still do. And so they thought they could keep minds in enhanced bodies going like machines, or even transfer their minds into computers. But the Elders must know better. If it were true we couldn't control our brains' actions with volition the way we do, or use any kind of psi."

"But why can't our minds keep the brain from dying, then?" Meiko asked.

"Because that's just how the universe works," Radnor said. "We don't know why death is inevitable any more than we know why we're alive in the first place. We know only that the maximum length of life doesn't exceed about one hundred fifty Earth-years for any sapient species, no matter how much tinkering with the body is done. The lifespans of the Elder species are all surprisingly similar. People not killed prematurely die when they are subconsciously ready to die, as my father is doing now."

"And medical technology can't keep him alive?"

"Keeping bodies alive indefinitely was tried, disastrously, on the colony planet our ancestors escaped from," Radnor said. "Their horror of the stasis vaults was what led them to leave and found Maclairn. Now on Maclairn, as on the Elder worlds, medical technology is used only for mechanical treatment such as limb replacement and for control of virulent disease. Other health problems that can't be eliminated with self-healing are treated by psi-gifted healers."

"Have the healers tried to cure your father?" Fred asked.

"Yes, several including my lifemate have examined him, and they say his body is simply shutting down. That's what always happens when old people die here."

"Can't they stop it?" Meiko protested.

"No, and he doesn't want them to—neither we nor the Elders view death in old age as an evil. He knows it's time for him to go. He hasn't been sick or disabled in any way, as the elderly on Earth are when medical science tries to prolong the natural process. He was still flying *Estel* until shortly before you arrived. Since then he's been getting more and more tired, and soon he'll simply not wake up from sleep."

"Very old people often do feel it's time to go," Jacob said, "and I've always thought it was tragic when they were subjected to medical intervention they hadn't asked for. Or when they accepted treatment merely because it was considered the customary thing to do."

"Different societies have had different conceptions of death," Radnor agreed, "and on Earth, in the dominant culture at least, it has been viewed as the worst possible outcome of any situation, something to be fought—which is ridiculous considering that everybody is destined to lose the fight. All sorts of military terminology has been used in connection with fatal disease—fight, enemy, attack, assault, struggle, battle, and even war—which has come down from a time when few people lived into old age. The Elders have outgrown that attitude. They don't know any more than we do about death or what, if anything, comes after it; but they have recognized the fact that it's an aspect of life's underlying nature."

"If death is determined by the subconscious mind, is illness?" Ardith asked, "And if so, does the collective unconscious influence it?"

"Absolutely," Radnor said. "That's why people in a society that doesn't rely on technological medicine are generally healthier than those who live where it's considered appropriate for routine use. The Elders give very little thought to their health, since on their worlds most disease too invasive to be prevented either by skills learned through mind training has been wiped out."

"Haven't they progressed in enhancing their bodies by now, though?" Fred asked. "It has been claimed for centuries that we'll eventually become cyborgs and it's strange that we haven't gotten as far toward that as people expected."

"Would you *want* to be a cyborg, Fred?" Meiko asked in dismay. "Would it help you do anything you really care about doing? And are you sure it wouldn't spoil your relationships with your loved ones?"

"I guess not," Fred admitted. "I wouldn't want my kids to be part machine, if I had kids."

"Well, that's why the Elders haven't pursued the possibility," Varel said. "In theory it sounds like an advance, but there's no market for it. History is full of ideas that were dropped for lack of demand."

"The human body has evolved as it has for a reason," Radnor added. "There are tradeoffs—for example, increasing input to the brain, which was once advocated, would decrease a person's ability to process it effectively. The sheer amount of it would be overwhelming."

"It's hard to keep track of all we know now," Jacob pointed out. "Just think of what it would be like to have direct access to the entire contents of the Net. It would be distracting, to say the least."

"Our bodies don't need improvement," Radnor declared. "We have external technology to do everything an enhanced body could do; which is the way the evolution of sapient species has progressed since the very beginning."

They walked the short distance to Radnor's house; Maclairn had no local vehicles other than robocarts, since the elderly were not disabled and there were few if any younger people with disabilities. Like Kenard's, it was a large, old house built of wood and stone. His mother had purchased it during his infancy when she inherited her grandfather's fortune, and had lived in it until her death at age one hundred thirty-three, a few years after Terry's return.

While Radnor was on Ydoril his lifemate Clarys had stayed on Maclairn to care for Terry, assisted by their children and grandchildren who visited frequently. She was both a healer and a mentor, and had worked with him on Earth giving mind training until they retired. "I'm happy to meet you at last," she told them. "And congratulations, Ardith and Varel, on your pairing."

She led the way into Terry's room. He was sitting up in bed, a slender old man with sparse white hair and a face that looked far younger than his age. "Here are the Federation's envoys to Earth, Captain," she said.

"I've waited for this day," said Terry. "Come closer, and let me see you." The four moved closer to the bed, Varel remaining in the shadows.. "It's a been a hundred and fifteen years since I first met the Elders," he said, "and ever since, I've looked forward to the time when Earth would be transformed by contact with them. I was among those who took the first step, the transport of Maclairnan mentors to Earth. Later, I spent many years persuading people in its colonies to want mind powers. I had the honor of being the first Earthborn person to visit Ydoril, and I convinced Maclairn to accept the Elders. I thought then that the mission fate gave me was finished. But lately I've become aware that knowledge of their existence must be spread sooner than I once believed, and have felt helpless because I can't take the next step."

"You already achieved more than anyone could have foreseen," Meiko declared. "If not for you there'd be no next step to take!"

"Yet I saw no way it could be managed, and I fear the time for Earth is running short. So when Radnor told me about the plan my joy was greater than you can imagine. Now, meeting with you, I know my work will be completed. I'm thankful beyond measure that you've come."

"It's an honor to be here, Captain," said Jacob, and the others echoed it. Meiko, visibly shaken, gazed at him in awe, her eyes bright with tears.

Ardith was tongue-tied. He was expecting too much of her. Didn't he know how bad things were on Earth, and how doubtful it was that they could make a difference? How unlikely that they could even survive the attempt, let alone persuade anyone there to accept aliens?

He was telepathic, of course; she soon realized that he did know. *It was the same for me,* he told her silently. *I didn't know what I was going to say to people before I said it, the wording of it was a surprise to me. Yet it swayed them. Enough of them became Estelans to tip the balance.*

She was shaken, overwhelmed, by the touch of his mind. No one, saving only the Eldest, had ever made her feel this way: as if she were somehow empowered to become more than the ordinary person she knew herself to be. It was because *he* had become more, she realized—though he'd started out as a mere space pilot, unaware of any ability to change the world, he had brought about its potential transformation. Could that happen to her? Could she really make a difference on Earth?

"I've learned a lot since I first went to Ydoril," he said aloud. "I've been back many times, and visited many Federation worlds. And I know that we are part of a larger pattern, a pattern even the Eldest cannot fully understand. But he knows much that the rest of us don't know. I'm told that he has blessed you, and blessed the pairing between one of you and an Elder. Which of you was that?"

"It was me, Captain," said Ardith, and Varel came forward to stand by her side.

"I get glimpses of the future more and more as I grow older," Terry said, "and they have shown me that this union will bring you greater joy and greater pain than you foresee. A mysterious destiny was predicted for me in my youth, and that proved to be a true seeing. So I dare to predict that on you rests the future of our birthworld."

Nonplussed, Ardith dropped her eyes to the flame

pendant she always wore, drawing it from under her tunic to gaze at it. "What is that?" Terry asked, noticing,

"It is a token of our consecration by the Service," she replied, leaning over so that he could see. "All four of us have them."

"A flame—like my pin," he said, and she saw that on his nightshirt he wore a pin like Radnor's, as had most of the Maclairnans she had met.

"It is fitting," he continued. "Years ago on Ydoril I was taken to see my first friend among the Elders, who had chosen me long before to become the first contactee. She was dying. And she said to me, 'Though I will not be here to see the culmination of our mission, I have been given the privilege of seeing you pick up the torch.' I now say the same to you four, who will carry it after I'm gone. There will be torches at my funeral, as there were at hers, and they will symbolize not my passing but the light of the mind powers all humans share."

Turning to Radnor, he went on, "Let them light candles from the Ritual torch, and do not blindfold them. They have as much right as any of you to affirm their commitment."

~ 20 ~

"What did he mean?" Ardith asked, after they left the room. "Why would you blindfold us?"

"He was referring to the ritual we will hold at the end of the funeral," `Clarys explained. "The Ritual is our most sacred ceremony on Maclairn, which is held on various occasions by the Stewards of the Flame— those of us who are voluntarily committed to advancing our use of mind powers and spreading them to all humankind. Membership is what the flame pin signifies."

"The rite involves a dramatic form of psi that we don't let children—or anyone else who hasn't been initiated—observe, because to see it would interfere with their own initiation later on," Radnor said. "Ordinarily only Stewards are allowed to attend. At the rare times when guests are present they are blindfolded, but we have made an exception for Liam and a few other Elders, and my father has now asked that the same exception be made for you. As there's no chance that you will become Maclairnans in the future, I'm sure Kenard will agree, especially since you've had enough mind training to grasp telepathically what you'll need to do."

"It's a sign of Terry's high regard for you," Clarys added, "because the Ritual meant a lot to him. He was initiated the night before he left Maclairn, and during his exile he was influenced by it in what he said as Captain of *Estel*. He cherished his flame pin above all else."

That night Terry died in his sleep. Despite the short time they'd been with him they grieved, and Meiko, who had idolized the Captain of *Estel* since childhood, was in tears.

Traditionally, funerals for mentors and other prominent Maclairnans were held on the beach at the Old Settlement adjacent to the shuttleport, reachable only by boat. The bodies were then submerged in the lake, a form of burial once universal on Maclairn but now, with the increased population, reserved for a few. There wasn't room on the beach, or even on the narrow terraces above it, for all who wished to honor Terry. So attendance, too, was limited; separate memorial services would be held later in many localities.

There were several large boats and a number of small ones, but even so it was necessary to make many trips up the lake. The guests were taken last, since Varel couldn't mingle with other attendees; who included Fleet officers who had known and respected Terry; again he covered his bald head and face with the hood of his jacket. By the time they got there the steep terraces rising above the beach were crowded with people. Rows of blazing torches lined them, an array of flame like the torchlit circle in the Sky Room but far more spectacular. Awed by its beauty, Ardith recalled what they'd been told about the symbolism of flame being a bond between Maclairn and the Elders.

The telepathic ambiance of the crowd was overpowering—all four of them, and Varel too, were caught up in it. They were seated near the lake shore among the members of Radnor's extended family, who were solemn but not sorrowful. Because Terry's was not a premature death they would mourn not for him but simply because they missed him. The funeral was a celebration of his long and momentous life.

"There's a stone monument at the end of the beach where lists of names of the dead are engraved," Clarys told them. "Terry's name was added prematurely more than a century ago, when he was lost in space and Maclairn believed he had died there. He'd had a premonition long before at the sight of that monument, sensing that this was where he'd eventually come to rest."

A small platform had been built at the water's edge, and next to it the boat bearing Terry's wrapped body was anchored. That boat was illuminated by clusters of tall, fat candles affixed to blocks of wood. More of them bordered the platform on which Kenard, Radnor, and Liam stood. As the music that had been playing stilled, one by one those who had known Terry best came forward and paid tribute to him, recounting episodes from his life. Others spoke of his historic achievement as the Captain of *Estel*, which had been anonymous at the time it was occurring and a surprise to Maclairn when revealed upon his return after a century-long exile.

Finally, Liam told of his long friendship with Terry as his copilot, omitting mention of the Elders because Fleet officers were present. Watching him, Ardith sensed the depth of his feeling and became aware that he was much more than a pilot and Terry's first guide to Ydoril. She knew that he had been born on an Elder world and had come to Earth straight from the Service Academy over hundred years ago, having been chosen for the team that would initiate contact and surgically modified to pass as Earth-born. He had been assigned to secretly guard Terry long before becoming known to him, and later, when flying with him, he'd kept to himself, never allowing his inner strength to show lest he influence him prematurely. Far from his family and heritage, he'd had no life of his own and was seemingly a mere sidekick, but underneath he'd possessed deep knowledge of Earth's affairs and the ability to deal with whatever crisis might arise. Now she realized that once Liam's grief for Terry lessened he would become a counselor to the Service and Maclairn alike.

When the music began again, the candles from the platform were added to those already on the boat, which then pushed off, heading toward the center of the narrow lake. When it was halfway to the opposite shore they were put overboard to float on their buoyant bases, drifting away as the body was dropped over the side. At that moment the recorded music hushed and the people began to sing, their voices echoing across the water from the cliffs on the other side. Though she could not make out the words, she picked up the gist of them telepathically.

May the radiance of candles we light now
amidst our tears
Fuel the rising flame within us to be passed
on through the years.

"That song has been sung at every funeral since the death of our founder Ian Maclairn, over three hundred years ago," said Clarys when it ended. As she spoke the dock light flashed three times, a signal for the children in the crowd, the Fleet officers who had come down the terraces from the spaceport, and a few other adults without flame pins to go. Radnor left the platform briefly and came over to the group of guests.

"It goes without saying that what you will see tonight is absolutely secret," he cautioned, "because if it were known, future initiates' success in the psi that's involved would be at risk—it has to come as a surprise to them. So I must ask you to pledge never to reveal it to anyone, anywhere."

Individually, they assented. Then Radnor said, "Reach out telepathically and you will know what to do. I won't be able to communicate with you personally because my role in the Ritual will require my full attention, but this is a large enough crowd to convey the essence of it. Don't be frightened by what happens at the end. It works like the breakthrough in your mind training—the full participants, and some of the onlookers, will get a tremendous lift from it, a natural high."

Unlighted candles were now being passed to the assembled people; Ardith took the one she was offered. Radnor returned to the platform to stand in a semicircle along with Kenard, his lifemate, and

Clarys. Between them and the platform's edge stood Liam with a tall torch, also unlighted, which he held upright.

The crowd hushed, and Kenard began, "As we hold the Ritual tonight in honor of Terry, we recall that the most significant thing he did for Maclairn was his introduction of the Elders, which has transformed our view of Earth's place in the universe. Yet when he first told us of them, we doubted him—I myself, to my everlasting regret, believed him to be insane. Tonight there are four among us who will soon make this same revelation to some of the people on Earth. It is fitting that they, and we ourselves, should hear in Terry's voice what he said during the Ritual on the night be convinced us."

The recording was as clear as if Terry himself were alive on the platform and speaking directly to them. He said, "The Flame we touch, the Flame we all wear, is a symbol of our commitment to the use of mind powers, but in a larger sense it symbolizes the ongoing evolution of humankind. That is what we mean when we say it will illuminate future generations. That's what it has always meant, what it meant to Ian Maclairn when he chose those words.

"Whether you judge my own experience true or illusory, keep in mind that worlds and peoples different from those we know *must* exist, for if they don't, there is nowhere to go from here—no hope to inspire future generations. Someday if not now, humankind must encounter a new universe to explore, or civilization can only slide further downhill. Don't let doubt about one man's sanity rob you of that hope."

Ardith let out a long breath. If even the people of Maclairn had resisted the thought of there being aliens, those on Earth surely would. How could she or any of the others hope to make them believe? Yet Terry had faced the same doubt and had succeeded. In asking that they attend the Ritual he must have meant them to feel inspired.

There was a brief pause before Kenard pronounced the customary invocation: "In silence, let us commend ourselves to whatever Power we hold highest, each of us in our own way."

Then suddenly, after a few minutes of quiet, the torch held by Liam burst into flame. Ardith gasped. No one had come near it and there was nothing to light it from; it blazed up all by itself.

No, not by itself. Telepathically, she absorbed the knowledge that this was done by psi. She had never heard that such a power existed, but it must be common because some people's candles were now also burning. Other people went to the torches nearest them to light theirs. Liam extended his toward the onlookers, holding it horizontally so that it was within reach, and she went forward to light her own from it. Varel, at her side, told her, *I think I could have done it with psi if I'd had warning. And I can sense that something harder is coming, so try to be prepared.*

When all the candles were alight Kenard began to speak again. The words were formal and obviously traditional; she understood them without the need for telepathy.

"Unfaced fear is the destroyer. We will acknowledge fear and accept it, we will go past it and live free.

"We will trust the power of the mind over all restrictions, whether imposed from within or by the world outside.

"We will act always through volition, allowing neither internal nor external pressures to enslave us.

"We will support one another unfailingly in fulfilling this pledge.

"We believe that we are stewards of a flame that will illuminate future generations.

"And we now seal our commitment with the symbol of the mind's power, which is fire."

Liam turned the torch toward the platform, again holding it out horizontally. Then, incredibly, Kenard and the other three on the platform plunged their left hands directly into the flame.

Ardith did not have time to be astonished. It was as if time had stopped, and the voices of all the people spoke to her at once; but the strongest was Kenard's, and she knew he was channeling the power of their assembled minds into a force that could protect even the weakest of them from harm. Unhesitatingly she did what the others were doing, and passed the fingers of her own left hand through the flame of her candle.

It did not hurt, of course, for unconsciously she shifted into the state of not suffering in which she had been trained. But more than that, it did not burn her skin. When her fingers were withdrawn she could see that there was no mark on them.

Everything blurred after that. She was high, as she had been after her breakthrough, and not really aware of what was going on around her, except that people were embracing each other and she herself was in Varel's arms. In this moment, if not forever, all doubt about her ability to meet challenge was gone.

~ *21* ~

Going home on the boat, Ardith was still scarcely able to believe what she had seen. It was one thing to touch flame and be unharmed, but a whole hand. . . .

"How did any of you dare to try it in the first place?" she asked Radnor. "How could you know you were psi-gifted enough not to be burned?"

"Actually it doesn't take a special gift," he said, "Anybody who's had a successful breakthrough in mind training can do it. All four of you could, and if you were Maclairnans you probably would, because it is the only way to get a flame pin. But it's true that if you'd seen it, you wouldn't have the nerve to try. That's why we don't let potential candidates see it."

"You mean you just tell them to put their hand in the fire, and they agree without even seeing that others aren't harmed?"

"They aren't told beforehand—like the secret step in mind training, it depends on surprise. When the time comes they do it instantly without thinking, as you did with the candle. Of course it requires a great deal of telepathic backing—nobody, not even a mentor, can do it alone. For an initiation we try to have as many strong telepaths as possible present, and no one else. We wouldn't have let you watch an initiation because any hesitation at all among the onlookers could affect the focus of the novice."

"The power comes from everyone, then?" Jacob asked. "It wouldn't work without the candles?"

"That's right," Clarys answered. "The focused state of consciousness has to be simultaneous, and just watching wouldn't produce that. The presiding mentor has to channel it and at the same time probe the novice to verify readiness. The backup mentors are there for support in case something goes wrong. It very rarely does, and it's not a disaster if it happens because we can heal burns very rapidly, but it makes it virtually impossible for that person to try again."

"Does Kenard always preside?" She was thinking that she'd sensed some special power in him that explained his being Maclairn's leader—and Radnor was scheduled to become leader after him.

"With initiations he normally does. Any mentor can preside when all the full participants are experienced. We use the Ritual to focus psi power for many purposes, for example, bringing rain. The lake would dry up and then flood if we had no control over it."

"There are rare cases on Earth where something similar is done with fire," Jacob said. "Anthropologists reported it as far back as the twentieth century. And other spectacular forms of psi have been used by many groups throughout our history. Some secret societies were mere social organizations, but not all of them."

"If such things are possible, they must be done on the Elder worlds," Meiko said, puzzled. "Yet we never heard of anything like it on any of them."

"Well, for one thing, it's secret on all worlds for the same reasons it is here—where there's a larger population than Maclairn's, it's kept from everyone but those directly involved. There are people on Andoval who know what's done with advanced psi elsewhere, but it's not publicized. The mentors here know what the human mind is capable of, but not the ways of triggering power that have built up in the collective unconscious of any planet but our own."

"I'm beginning to think there's a lot on the Elder Worlds that we weren't shown," Ardith said.

"There is," Radnor agreed, "and I haven't gone deeply into it myself. Terry went a little further after his return; he visited Andoval, but tactfully avoided telling me things I wasn't ready to understand. By the time he died he knew more than he'd known as Captain of *Estel*. But he, like the rest of us, was *homo sapiens*, and some of the Elder species are much,

much older and further evolved. We can't begin to comprehend what goes on in their minds."

She turned to Varel. "You must have been aware of this from studying history. Yet you never mentioned it."

"I guessed a little of it. But my species isn't among the oldest, Ardith, and those the Service mainly draws from aren't, either. We have to focus on practical issues to do our job."

The Eldest was the oldest member of the oldest species, Ardith recalled. He must deal with concepts and capabilities far beyond the understanding of most Federation peoples. It wasn't surprising that she couldn't grasp all that lay behind the feelings he had given her.

And then she was struck by another thought. Of course she had not seen any worlds like those she'd been shown in the dreams! They existed only in the mind of the Eldest. They were simply symbols of what he'd wanted her to know—that there was good in the universe, and in the Elder worlds, that was worth seeking, worth risking her life to pursue. That the only answer to the depression she'd felt was to move ahead to a place beyond her imagination.

And that was true of Earth, too. That was why only contact with the universe beyond what was known could save it.

"We understand very little about the depth of the mind," Clarys said. "We're learning here on Maclairn, but we have a long way to go before we're at the level of the Elders."

"The Ritual is our attempt to acknowledge that humans are more than material bodies, that our minds have power that overrides physical laws," Radnor said. "That's why Terry wanted you to see it. When you go to Earth you may need mind power beyond what you consciously understand, if only to inspire others to believe in a brighter future."

When they got back to the city Varel went off somewhere with Liam, who though retired was still a member of the Service, while the others returned to Kenard's house. They sat for awhile by the fireplace in the great room, still too awed to feel like talking much. Ardith had put off thinking about the coming mission during their tour of Elder worlds, but now she couldn't avoid it. She had no idea how they would go about doing what they were being asked to do; Radnor had said they would have a meeting tomorrow to discuss the practical details. But however they proceeded she didn't see how they could make listeners understand that aliens were not weird beings but simply people to be met as friends.

And she didn't see how she could endure separation from Varel. When just this one evening seemed empty without him, how could she get through a lifetime?

Of course it wouldn't be total separation, forever. Though it had been understood from the beginning that she could never return to the Elder worlds, Radnor had said they could meet on Maclairn. A Maclairnan ship, *Promise,* went regularly to and from Earth under cover of secrecy. If she survived, it would be possible to make a brief trips even if her responsibility to the mission meant living on Earth permanently. Varel had come to Maclairn twice and he could come again, on vacation if not assigned here; they could meet for a little while, at least. Why hadn't he ever said so?

It was late when he got back to the house. She had waited in the great room, watching the door and getting more and more agitated as time passed. Finally he appeared and took her in his arms, but he seemed to be in a surprisingly low mood considering the lift they'd gotten from the Ritual. Though his mind was closed to her, she could sense it even without telepathy.

In their room they undressed quietly. Hoping to cheer him she ventured, "Have you any idea how soon we'll be able to come back Maclairn?"

Varel's reaction wasn't what she'd expected. "I'm afraid that's unlikely to happen, Ardith," he said painfully.

"Why? If the mission's succeeding there should be no harm in my taking a short break. Radnor and Clarys say we'll be welcome."

"Well, I told you in the beginning that I'm forbidden to have committed relationships with anyone but fellow Service members."

"But everyone was so pleased by ours, saying it's a symbol of Earth's acceptance into the Federation."

"The Maclairnans were pleased. Liam and Gabriel were, too, along with the majority of the others who've heard of Earth. But not everyone. And in any case, the main objection isn't to your being from Earth, it's that you're not a member of the Service."

"That didn't bother the Eldest."

"No, and that's part of the problem. The Eldest is not supposed to interfere in politics, any more than the head of a constitutional monarchy is. Some feel that by overriding a firm Service policy he has done just that."

"It wasn't your fault—you didn't expect him to, did you? So how can they blame you?"

"In the first place, they feel I shouldn't have put myself in such a position. I shouldn't have let myself fall in love with you, just as I knew when I tried to break it off. But more than that, Liam told me that some people in the Service are saying I violated the Oath by accepting his blessing."

"You couldn't have stopped his blessing us—it was his own idea."

"Yes, I could. He asked us if we would be faithful to each other while united, and I assented."

"I thought that just meant sexual fidelity."

"It means commitment, putting the person or task to which you give that commitment 'above all other considerations,' as the Oath words it. Why do you think the priests of some religions are not allowed to marry? It would result in divided loyalties. The same is true of the Service, except that it's okay for us to have relationships with other individuals who are also committed to it."

"Maybe after this mission is over I could join the Service."

"Oh, Ardith. You couldn't qualify. You're older than most trainees, and in any case the entrance tests are extremely competitive, physically and psychologically, as well as requiring more education than you could have gotten on Earth. Besides, you'd have to be a student for three years before taking the Oath."

"What happens if someone violates it just temporarily?"

He frowned. "I don't know. Liam and I are going to the starship tomorrow to learn as much as we can about my status—the ship is in communication with Ydoril. But he's not optimistic. It's almost certain that I won't be permitted to visit Maclairn again. I wouldn't have been this time, which is why I didn't ask."

Ardith blinked away tears as, wordlessly, Varel got into bed beside her. The Emblem he wore beneath his clothes gleamed against his naked skin; in more ways than one it lay between them. Not even the enhanced telepathy they experienced during sex would help this time. But there were just a few nights remaining, and so they must make the most of them.

When they'd been blessed, before coming to Maclairn, she hadn't thought they would see each other in the future. Yet now that the hope had been awakened, she couldn't let it go again. It was intolerable to think that they might have to settle for the recorded messages Liam or other agents would undoubtedly agree to carry.

~ 22 ~

In the morning the four envoys met with Radnor, as representative of Maclairn, and Gabriel, as leader of the Service team on Earth, to plan the details of the mission.

The strategy, Radnor told them, would be to speak first to the people who'd had mind training. They would believe in the sincerity of the envoys their mentors vouched for, and they could grasp the information they were offered telepathically as well as from speech.

"We've been giving the training on Earth for well over a hundred years," Radnor told them, "so some of the trainees are no longer living, and others we lost contact with long ago. The mentors at our centers will be able to assemble groups you can meet with and provide leads on more distant people with whom they've been in touch."

"So will the Service agents who've been living on Earth incognito," Gabriel added. "Now that Earth is a member of the Federation they will switch their policy from non-interference to doing everything they can to help spread the word. But they cannot reveal themselves as alien until the government seeks contact."

"Do the mentors know the Elders come to Maclairn?" Jacob asked.

"Yes, they were all informed some time ago. By the way, most of the trainees haven't been told that Maclairn exists; they assume the mentors are League citizens. So you must not mention it to anyone but a mentor unless that person gives you the password, which is 'Stewards of the Flame.'"

"Can we talk to anyone not recommended by a mentor or an agent?" Jacob asked.

"If you know them personally you can. For instance, you and Fred both have university contacts that may be useful."

"I can't contact anyone at my university," Fred declared. "The worst thing that could happen to us would be for Ivanson to hear about it. He was responsible for turning the expedition ship back, which won't look good when it comes out that there really were aliens nearby. And he's staked his reputation on a theory about stars with no planets, which by now he's probably published in the top scientific journals. If anybody wants to see us dead again, it will be him."

Gabriel frowned. "You'll have to steer clear of him, then, which may mean not going to your home city at all. And later on when the word spreads it may be a problem for all of you."

"I'm in touch with scientists all over the world who believe in the search for extraterrestrial civilizations," said Jacob, "and they above all people need to know that contact has been made. But I can travel to only a few of them. Am I allowed to inform them from a distance?"

"Yes, if they know you well enough to trust you

and you can trust their judgment about who to tell. But don't do it over the Net—stick to secure messaging services, phone or fax."

"What do we do if someone we approach just flat-out refuses to believe?" Ardith asked.

"There are two reasons that might happen," Radnor said. "In the first place, a great many people are subconsciously terrified at the thought that Earth isn't safely isolated from the rest of the universe—not as many as there used to be before we had interstellar colonies, but still a lot. For centuries the public knew theoretically how vast the universe is and how many billions of stars there are, but they didn't expect any contact with the strange and mysterious things out there—unknown and perhaps horrifying things. That was a major reason why they were slow to support space travel. Now nearly everyone accepts it, but aliens are another matter. They don't *want* there to be aliens because if there are, a whole new area of mystery opens up, and even if they're not hostile, we might have to change our own way of looking at existence. Even when people aren't consciously aware of this, they're scared underneath."

"Is this why most members of the expedition to investigate the Message turned back?" Ardith asked, suddenly grasping what had underlain their loss of enthusiasm.

"Almost certainly it was. They thought they wanted to discover an extraterrestrial civilization, but when it came right down to it, their subconscious minds balked."

Jacob frowned. "I suppose that could happen with some of my contacts, too."

"It could, so you must sound them out carefully before you offer proof, in case they're predisposed to become antagonists. Opposition from a former supporter of an idea can be much more dangerous than from someone to whom it's new."

"The other problem," Gabriel said, "is that even people with mind training might well doubt your story, because psi over long distance in space or time is unreliable and psi-gifted people have been misled for centuries. Some have actually seen aliens on Earth or on the moon who didn't exist. So if word got around about your claim, the mentors themselves could be discredited. That's why nothing must ever be said about the Elders without proof."

"But we can offer proof to relatively few people," Ardith protested. "Nothing like a sizable segment of the public."

"It will spread both by word of mouth and by telepathy," Radnor said. "Those you contact through the mentors are used to keeping the secret of their mind training, and to judging potential recruits' reliability. The crucial thing is that every chain must start with someone who has seen the proof and been convinced by it."

"And we can use public DNA-search machines?"

"Yes, your expense allowance will cover the fees. As for proving you were on the starship and were lost, people can look it up on the Net with their tablets. Make sure they do it, not just take your word, because if they pass it on they must be able to say they've seen the proof personally."

"Speaking of expense money, who pays for all this?" Fred asked.

"The mentors will provide food and lodging while you're with them, and your IDs will be loaded with enough to buy what you need to elsewhere. The funds come from the Service, which gets local cash by selling platinum as it does for its own agents."

Troubled, Ardith said, "If our IDs and DNA

profiles are checked when we're listed as dead, especially if it's done frequently, won't some kind of alarm be triggered by the surveillance system? It would look like a forger had reused them."

"True, but our agents have the ability to hack the system," Gabriel explained. "We forge IDs for ourselves, and we can prevent the triggering of the alarm for yours, as well as the tracking capability. The hack may be detected eventually; that's one of the ways you may get caught. But it should give you quite a bit of time."

"I'm a little confused about something," Jacob said. "If the Service can hack the system, including creating DNA and biomarker records as you did for Terry when you sent him to Ciencia, why couldn't agents be given ours? Why couldn't they do the job we're supposed to do?"

"For one thing, because their own DNA is alien," Gabriel replied. "Enough changes have been made to their bodies for it to pass a superficial examination, but it can't withstand full analysis."

"Moreover, an agent would have neither credible impressions of the Federation as seen by a newcomer, nor detailed knowledge of your own backgrounds and your experiences on the starship," Radnor said. "He or she might get by with faking at first, but eventually you will be examined by experts, probably under drugs or hypnosis. Your memories will be compared with information from your relatives and childhood friends as well as the other members of the expedition."

Ardith swallowed. She hadn't anticipated undergoing that kind of examination. Would they find out about her love for Varel? It was private and precious; she was appalled by the thought of the intimate details being exposed.

"How much should we tell people about the Elders?" Meiko asked.

"As much as they seem interested in—it will vary, and you'll sense it," Gabriel replied. "The main thing is to make them feel that aliens, as individuals, are neither superior nor inferior to Earthborn humans."

"Remember that there'll be unconscious telepathy going on," said Radnor. "If you contact a significant number of people you will be literally inserting ideas into the collective unconscious of Earth."

"That's an awfully big responsibility," Ardith said, her dismay increasing.

"It is, but all four of you have been evaluated by me, by the Service, and by the Eldest, and you've been judged worthy of it. So don't worry—you'll be okay."

"How long will this go on?" Fred inquired. "Won't there be a time when we want the government to know?"

"Yes, if enough believers have been recruited to influence public opinion at the time of the next League election," said Gabriel. "I will be the judge of that, and if I think we can win I will leak the story to the media. But first I will warn you, and you should then take the initiative in contacting candidates and government insiders. I can give you names of those most likely to be receptive—I'm acquainted with some, and so is Radnor."

"I thought Maclairnans had to hide on Earth," Jacob said. "So how are you acquainted with government people, Radnor?"

"A few high officials do know about Maclairn, and are as eager as we are to keep it secret," he explained. "They provide IDs for the mentors and protect them as much as possible from the bureaucrats. The rest don't know I'm Maclairnan. They know me only as the owner and former director of a chain of health clubs called Bramfield Clubs, which we use as a cover for mind training. Incidentally, the managers of those clubs have all visited Maclairn as observers; the mentors are ostensibly their employees and no one else knows their true identity."

"We'll visit the clubs, then?"

"They will be your contact points for reaching the mentors. You will each be assigned to a different city, and after you've spoken with everyone you can there you'll move on to another. They exist all over the world; we'll start in Anglo-speaking countries but later we will provide translators."

"The biggest problem," said Gabriel, "is getting you onto Earth in the first place."

"Can't you just land us somewhere in one of your ships, like you do your own agents?"

"We could, but that's a little too much like the traditional UFO scenario. You don't want to be associated with that—it would destroy your credibility with the people who matter. And even if we did it secretly, it would eventually come out; there needs to be a record of your arrival."

"But they're going to know aliens transported us somehow," Jacob declared. "The very thing they need to realize is that we couldn't have gotten back to Earth without their help."

"Yes, but to reveal that alien ships are around would be too much of a shock. Better to take it in stages, and come from a colony."

"That's reasonable," Jacob agreed. "They might expect aliens to keep their distance, come to a colony far from the home system."

"Why not Maclairn?" Ardith asked.

"It's too soon to reveal Maclairn's existence to the

public. Besides, when the government finds out they would assume the very connection with psi we need to hide."

"New Tahiti, then. We could be brought in from there on *Promise* without raising any questions." The Maclairn Foundation starship *Promise*, they'd been told, masqueraded as a tourist vessel and made a stop in New Tahiti because it couldn't pass through immigration at Moonbase without proof of its world of origin.

"Our IDs would be checked at Moonbase and we'd be taken into custody right then," Fred pointed out.

"Why?" Meiko protested. "They're legal. We haven't committed any crimes."

"But we'll be listed as dead and would be detained on suspicion of having forged IDs," Jacob said.

"No competent forger would use the identity of people who died so recently," Fred objected. "And in any case he wouldn't leave the status as dead."

"Even so, they wouldn't be likely to just let us pass without some sort of investigation. And since our being thought dead is the point of reappearing, you can't alter that by hacking."

"Entry from New Tahiti is what we've been planning for," Gabriel said. "The hack will prevent the alarm and later tracking. We'll just have to hope that the officer who boards *Promise* doesn't look closely at what comes up—he's not likely to, since he'll be relying on the alarm flashing. And he surely wouldn't suspect more false IDs after finding one, so only one of you will be at risk."

The rest of the day was spent going over more details, including the specific city assignments and how to reach those cities from the spaceport. It was all rather daunting, Ardith thought as they gathered in Kenard's home for dinner. Her head was spinning with the amount of data she would have to memorize during the trip—it wouldn't be safe for them to leave much information on phones or data bracelets, lest they be lost or stolen. The job seemed impossibly hard, and the near-certainty of eventual arrest filled her with dread.

Worse, she still wasn't convinced that success would save Earth. But she had committed herself. From Varel she had learned what commitment meant, and she was resolved to live up to what he expected of her, what the Captain of *Estel* too had expected.

That night she sat alone in Kenard's great room after the others had gone to bed. She knew that Liam had taken Varel to the starship but she had not expected them to return so late. Her hands were cold and every small sound jarred her nerves until at last she heard footsteps in the hall. But to her dismay it was Radnor, not Varel, who appeared.

~ 23 ~

Even without the telepathic leakage of emotion he was trying to hide, Radnor's face told her that something was wrong. "Varel?" Ardith gasped shakily. "He's okay? The ship—"

"He's safe," he assured her. "The shuttle landed a little while ago. Something came up, and he's still with Liam; but he asked me to talk to you before he gets here—he feels it would be too hard on you both if he brought you bad news himself."

She waited, trembling. Painfully, Radnor went on, "Ardith, Varel has been placed on probation. It's expected that on pain of dismissal from the Service he will be forbidden to communicate with you at all, ever again. If they rule that he has broken the Oath, that is what will happen."

Ardith turned white. "Oh, God! They can't prevent it! You and Liam will be going to Ydoril again—you can carry messages even if Gabriel won't, which I think he will, since he approved of our pairing—"

"You don't understand. This will not be made final until Varel has been given a hearing in person, on Ydoril. But if the decision goes against him, neither Liam nor I, and certainly not Gabriel, will help him violate the terms of his probation. You wouldn't want us to, Ardith, because it would mean his sure dismissal from the Service, and that would destroy him."

"Why would it? If it can be so cruel, why would he even want to stay? I'll be surprised if he doesn't resign right now if that's its attitude."

"The Oath is irrevocable; he cannot resign. He is so much in love with you that if it were possible for you to live together he might simply leave, which would be worse than dismissal; but it would go against his conscience and lead to suffering you surely wouldn't wish to inflict on him, in addition to ruining his career. As it is, he won't do it just for the sake of messaging."

She dropped her eyes. "Why would it ruin his career? He could teach at a university somewhere else in the Federation."

"No, he couldn't. Dismissal from the Service would be a disgrace; it is highly regarded everywhere, almost revered. The best he could hope for would be a job as a teacher in the equivalent of high school, and even there he wouldn't be respected."

"I thought the Federation values freedom. What happened to what you said about mature governments not telling people what they can and can't do?"

"That's true, but the Service is not the government. It's an organization that people join voluntarily, giving up some of their freedom to serve its cause and obtain the benefits it offers them."

"Just communicating with me wouldn't interfere with his job," she protested.

"No, since he's not a field agent, it wouldn't, and if it's just a matter of rule-breaking they may allow it. But if they decide the Oath is involved, there must be consequences, because if there were none, other members might not take their sworn word as seriously as they have to. The welfare of the young species the Service contacts depends on strict adherence to the Oath. Field agents are expected to die rather than break it; some have. On primitive worlds some have died under torture when they could have saved themselves by not putting the best interests of the natives ahead of all other considerations. There isn't time to make decisions in such situations, and the Oath, taken once, eliminates the burden of them."

"Well, Varel loving me isn't comparable to situations where people have to die."

"Isn't it? Imagine one where you and Varel were on a young world and he had to choose between possible harm to it and letting you be killed."

"Oh . . . I guess I see," she said slowly. "They don't want to put anyone in that position."

"Exactly. If the partner has also taken the Oath the situation doesn't arise, because the obligation is the same for both. And the principle applies to less drastic conflicts."

"But must the punishment for a minor violation be so heavy?"

"It is not punishment, but an ongoing test of self-discipline, which is a quality anyone in a position to affect the destiny of worlds must have. Once a lack of it has been shown it must be continuously proven."

"Varel must have been aware of this all along," she reflected. "He tried to break up with me and I—I wouldn't let go of hope."

"Don't blame yourself. He knew what he was doing and chose to take the consequences."

"They wouldn't really dismiss him, would they?"

"They could, but Gabriel doesn't expect it; putting him on permanent probation should be enough. In part, it's meant as a rebuke to the Eldest. That's another factor in this case—I'll give him the benefit of doubt and assume that he didn't stop to think that the blame for his action would fall on Varel. He should have, and if it comes as a surprise he'll suffer over it."

"That's horrible, when he meant to make us happy."

"Yes, but his interference with Service politics, subtle though it was, can't be allowed to pass, because a ceremonial leader in his position who intervenes in worldly affairs could become a virtual despot."

"I can't believe we won't find a way around this," Ardith persisted. "How can I leave Varel tomorrow, knowing I'll never hear from him?"

"You made a vow too, Ardith. The Eldest asked if you were willing to bear the grief of being parted, and you assented."

She sighed. "I suppose I did. I wasn't picturing there not even being messages."

"Would you have declined to pledge if you'd known?"

"No, of course not."

"Then don't let this become any harder for Varel than it already is. The ban on communication is effective immediately, to become permanent if that's the final decision. Liam has defied orders by bringing him back here from the Service ship just for tonight. Make it worth the risk they're taking."

When Radnor had gone, Ardith gave way to tears, hoping to get that over with before Varel arrived. It would be their last night. They must not spoil it by bitterness over a decree they could not change.

In bed they clung to each other, not thinking past the moment, by unspoken agreement saying nothing. When their bodies joined and their memories merged telepathically they relived the joy of the past weeks: her breakthrough party, where for the first time he had touched her hand; the Sky Room on Ydoril; the porch of the house on Everne; the beauty of other worlds they had seen together from the starship. They thought of the wedding feast, where everyone had congratulated them on a union that would raise the status of Earth. And finally, they envisioned their meeting with the Eldest and made again, silently, the pledge to be faithful and to abide the grief of their parting.

Later, when sleep wouldn't come, Ardith pondered that. The Eldest had known there would be grief; he must also have known that loving even for a little while would be worth the pain. *Love is never wrong*, he'd told them, *as long as no one is hurt who has not consented.* How could he, a man viewed as the wisest person in the Federation, have been blind to the fact that Varel would be censured?

It wasn't possible. He must have thought that Varel was consenting to the full consequences rather than just to the grief of separation.

The light of dawn was seeping through the window curtains, and she could see that Varel, too, was only pretending to sleep. She had to say something, or he might believe the Eldest had carelessly betrayed him; and there would not be time to talk in the morning.

Pressing closer to him she whispered, "Varel . . . Radnor said the Eldest didn't foresee that you'd get the blame for what he did, and that he should have. But I think maybe he's mistaken. I think the Eldest may have known and not realized how hard they'd be on you."

"Of course he knew," Varel replied. "Besides his being smart enough to figure it out, *I* knew, and he had access to my whole mind."

"You knew the Service would impose a penalty?"

"Either that or dismiss me, yes. They have no choice, Ardith. It would diminish the Oath if people could get away with breaking it."

"Why didn't you tell me that? I wouldn't have let you risk it for my sake."

"It wasn't just for your sake. It was partly for me, because I wanted you more than I wanted to keep my job. And it was partly for the sake of Earth. In a way I honored the Oath better by technically breaking it than I would have by sticking to the rules, because I put the best interests of Earth first."

"Earth? I know they're all saying that our union is a symbol of Earth's people being viewed as the equal of the Elders. But most Elders thought we were ready for Federation membership anyway. Was convincing a few more worth risking your career?"

"There are two ways to look at our union, Ardith——as symbolic of the Earthborn being equals of the Elders, or of aliens being seen as 'human' by the Earthborn."

"My God. That never occurred to me." Not in a positive way, it hadn't. She had thought, somewhat bitterly, of the probable reaction if she said on Earth not only that she had met aliens but that she'd had sex with one. She had shuddered at the headline that might eventually appear in the sensational press, "I Slept with an Alien." It was unthinkable; it would desecrate the most meaningful experience of her life.

Yet it was true that admitting to it would go a long way toward convincing people that extra-terrestrials were the equivalent of humans.

"You're going to have a lot of trouble getting people to accept the idea that the Elders are just people," Varel said. "I've studied history of enough worlds to know that. And in the case of Earth, time is crucial. The more evidence you can present, the better."

Morning came too soon. For weeks she had dreaded her departure from Maclairn; the thought of boarding a ship that left Varel behind was not to be borne. As it turned out, it was the other way around, for Liam had to take him back to the Service starship shortly after dawn. She went with them in the boat that took them up the lake to the shuttleport. And so, on the beach where two nights ago they had shared the elation of the Ritual, the moment arrived for farewell.

"Don't climb the terraces," Varel told her. "It won't help either of us to wait for blastoff. I'd rather remember you here by the lake with sunrise reflected on the water, a picture I can hold in my mind forever."

"Will we be together for a little while longer, telepathically?"

"Only till the shuttle lifts off. Some people can do it from orbit, but you're not experienced enough, and in any case we're not going to stay in orbit; *Estel* will head straight for the starship."

"Will they arrest you?"

"They're not police; they can't confine me physically. On Ydoril I'll simply go to my room and wait to be called."

"Oh, God, Varel. I can't stand to think of you doing that."

"One place is as good as any, if you're not there."

That was true for her too, she realized. It no longer mattered that she would be on Earth, which she hated, instead of the Elder worlds; she could never be happy anywhere now without him.

She struggled to hold back her tears. *We affirmed two things to the Eldest,* he reminded her. *Not just to be faithful, but to endure the grief of our parting. We're still bound by that vow even though we won't have the contact we imagined.*

The Eldest had known what lay ahead, Ardith reflected, and suddenly another memory came to her. The Captain of *Estel* might have known even more. "Varel," she whispered, "was Terry *right*? ,If our love may help to make Earth accept aliens, was it a true premonition when he said that on us rests the future of our birthworld?"

"It's possible," he said. "Premonitions are a common form of psi, but there's no way to know in advance which are true. This one matches what I felt when I chose to break the rules."

From the terrace above, Liam was beckoning. She could not think of any words adequate for what she felt. They embraced, and after a long kiss he broke away. Her last sight of him was as a tiny figure receding up the long series of steps.

But in her mind she heard his voice. *Ardith . . . I will always love you, Ardith. No matter what happens in the future, no matter how much loyalty I give to the Service, you'll come first in my heart.*

I'll try to be worthy of your love, Varel. If I succeed in the mission on Earth, it will be because of you, because of what we've meant to each other. I will love you as long as I live.

For a little while more they shared wordless love, until the moment when his thought cut off abruptly and she knew that the shuttle had lifted.

Part Four: Promise

~ 24 ~

That night aboard *Promise* Ardith dreamed of the Elder worlds, and it was not exhilarating, as it had been in her former dreams, but heartbreaking. She still saw beauty in those worlds but they were receding from her, and from now on that beauty would be beyond reach. When she woke in the dark her face was wet, and she hoped that Meiko, who shared her stateroom, had not heard her crying.

Promise was ostensibly a tourist ship, which was necessary in order to avoid suspicion on arrival at Moonbase. In the past, it had carried three Earthborn guest couples per trip plus a mentor couple on their way to assignment on Earth. Since the arrival of the Elders Maclairn hadn't accepted guests, who after observing its psi-based culture had served as managers of the Bramfield Clubs and recruiters for the mind training program on Earth. So, since tourist ships do not make the long jump from Earth to New Tahiti half empty, additional mentors had been sent on visits to fill the extra staterooms.

On this trip, however, at the last minute it had been decided to send Liam, who had come out of retirement because it was felt that a senior agent with experience on Earth would be needed as a liaison during this critical time. The crew of *Promise* knew him as *Estel*'s pilot and were aware that he had come to Maclairn with Terry, so they assumed he was Earthborn. They would believe the four envoys to be native Maclairnans.

The last morning on Maclairn had been spent packing. Ardith had been given back her own clothes, carefully cleaned and stored during the weeks on Ydoril, plus some Maclairnan garments styled much the same but handsewn—the colony didn't have machine-made clothing since its limited industrial capability was devoted to electronics and life-support essentials. It felt strange now to be wearing anything other than the Elders' soft, indestructible fabric, but the hand-made clothes were beautiful; Maclairnan craftworkers took pride in their work. Ardith was not in the mood to appreciate it.

Her only other possession, other than her original tablet and a new phone compatible with the Net on Earth, was the flame pendant. She had worn it since the day she'd received it, and always would—though it might have to be hidden beneath her shirt on occasions when it could attract comment. As had been intended, it was the equivalent of Varel's Emblem, and if she couldn't have any object he had given her, this at least represented the goal they shared.

All through the leavetaking—the festive farewell meal, the words of encouragement from Kenard and Radnor, the good wishes from friends they'd made at the wedding feast, the final boat trip—she had felt numb. Her sadness at departure from Maclairn itself was overshadowed by her awareness that she was leaving forever the place where she and Varel had made love. Climbing the steps of the terraces that he had climbed hours before, she had struggled to keep back tears.

But now, waking aboard *Promise*, it was time to look ahead. It was going to be difficult to do any planning, since the ship was crewed by three Fleet officers who were present except when in their own staterooms or on the bridge. The crew had a long-standing tie with their passengers in keeping the secret of Maclairn's existence from everyone they met on New Tahiti and at Moonbase; moreover, they'd had mind training and so were to some extent telepathic. It was vital that they not learn that there was another secret, as they would be duty-bound to report it to their superiors, who would inform the government. Thus nothing at all could be said about the mission within their hearing, and that would be hard to arrange.

So Ardith couldn't discuss her next step with anyone, not even Liam, who seemed grim and uncommunicative not only because of his grief at Terry's passing but perhaps because he too was angry about what had happened to Varel. The envoys were no longer being counseled, and Jacob, who had headed the contact team of the scientific expedition, was now their leader. But she missed Radnor, on whom they'd relied ever since their pickup from the lifeboat.

She thought back over her last conversation with him, shortly before leaving Maclairn. All that day she'd sensed that he was troubled, though he'd given no indication as to why. Hoping he wasn't losing confidence in their mission, she had drawn him aside after the meal, saying that she needed to talk privately.

Once they were alone, she had told him, "Varel thinks there will be some who believe I met aliens, yet don't think of them as being on same level as Earthborn humans. No matter what I say, they may picture them as some sort of strange beings we can't have normal interactions with."

"There's that possibility," Radnor admitted. "We've just had to hope there won't be enough with that attitude to make a difference."

"We can try to make sure there aren't. If I reveal that I made love with an alien, they'll know how similar they must be."

"You'd need to be very careful there, Ardith. Reports of alleged sex with aliens have been quite common over the past few centuries. People of both sexes have been convinced they were abducted for reproductive purposes by UFOs—and not necessarily by beings like us. Thousands of women have claimed to have borne hybrid babies. The notion has gotten into the collective unconscious to the extent that intelligent people ignorant of genetics sometimes believe it—not to mention the vast number who believe the human race is the result of interbreeding in ancient times. The last thing you want is to be connected to such ideas."

"That's why I need to offer proof. There was never any proof of those other claims."

"True, but how could you possibly prove it?"

"With alien DNA. I couldn't provide it directly to people I talk to, of course; the result of analysis would have to come from a lab. But later, if the government investigates me, there wouldn't be any question about DNA evidence."

"I'm afraid there would," he said. "If you turn over something of Varel's they'll suspect the DNA traces have been faked."

"Of course. That's not what I mean. I will have his DNA with me, for a little while, anyway."

"How? What could you take, even if there were some way to hide it? And in any case it wouldn't prove that you made love."

"It is in my body, Radnor, already hidden."

"What—" He broke off, understanding her telepathically if not from the words. "My God, Ardith. You couldn't have gotten pregnant with Varel."

"No. But sperm will live for a few days even though fertilization is impossible." As a biologist, she was not shy about such things.

"You can't get an officially-recognized medical exam that soon."

"Yes, I can," she said grimly. "All I have to do is walk into a hospital on New Tahiti and claim that I've been raped. League law says hospitals have to collect forensic evidence even if I don't report it to the police, and they have to store it for months in case I want to do that later."

"Ardith, you're not thinking straight," Radnor said gently. "You're picturing aliens as distant, on the worlds where you knew them. But we are claiming that they dropped you off in New Tahiti instead of returning you to Earth. So if you present the evidence later and there's a record that you reported being raped in New Tahiti, what are the authorities going to think?"

"That I once slept with an alien, of course."

"No. They will assume that it was an alien who raped you."

"Dear God. How could I have been so blind?"

"Because you are suffering from an emotional blow, and you're not in any shape to make decisions right now."

"I—I guess I wanted some tangible evidence, some record to prove that the last few days really happened. I wish I *could* have his child."

"But since you can't, I'm not sure that the mere presentation of an alien's DNA would convince the government that they're people like us."

"That's not the point, Radnor." She hesitated.

"Don't you see, if it's proven that I slept with an alien, it won't matter what the government thinks. It will be clear to anyone who's acquainted with me that I'm not the sort of person who would do that if he weren't the emotional equivalent of a human being, someone on our level for whom we can have human feelings."

"I guess that's true," he said slowly. "When you and Varel paired I was so focused on its showing that we're the equals of the Elders that I never thought about it also working the other way around."

"Varel did. He knew when he accepted the Eldest's blessing, Radnor, and he's sure the Eldest knew too. It's why he blessed our love in spite of foreseeing the consequences."

"They both *knew* there'd be a penalty?"

"Yes."

"I think," Radnor had reflected, "that we've underestimated the Eldest. It seems he's indeed wiser than the rest of us, certainly wiser than the Service on this particular issue. They will never admit it; politics are involved so they can't back down, despite being aware of how much he contributed earlier to setting this scheme in motion. But I'll see to it that everyone I come into contact with knows."

"Varel told me that he honored the Oath more by technically breaking it than he would have by following the rules, because it's in Earth's best interests for us to have made love."

"If he believes that, then he has not broken it even technically—the Oath's meaning has always taken precedence over rules,"

"Then he'll be forgiven?" A surge of hope had risen in her, making her dizzy.

"Unfortunately, no, since to condone it would be an endorsement of the Eldest's blessing. He will have many secret supporters, though, who will admire him for his sacrifice. Don't let it go to waste, Ardith. Put bitterness aside, and prove that what he believes about your union is true."

Now, she couldn't let the idea of getting DNA evidence drop. But how could she pursue it? She could collect the evidence herself, submit it to a public DNA-search machine, but that would achieve nothing; the result would simply be blamed on defective AI or worse, it would trigger an investigation. And in any case it wouldn't prove that the DNA came from inside her body. For that, an officially-recorded medical exam would be necessary.

As she had known to begin with, the only way to get such an exam was at a hospital. She could report symptoms of infectious disease and be tested there, and the result would be placed in her official medical record—but a medical-level metagenomic analysis, unlike a forensic one, would check far more than personal identity. It would attempt to separate the host DNA from the microbiome, and would find complex chromosomes so alien that alarms would be triggered. The hospital, after checking its AI equipment and finding nothing wrong, would surely detain her, not for criminal investigation but for ongoing scientific study. They wouldn't believe she slept with an alien; they would assume she was suffering from some freak disease.

So it was essential that the evidence be from a forensic exam and that it not be released until later, when she'd already convinced a lot of people and wanted the proof seen by the government. How could that be arranged? There was only one way—she would have to find a doctor who would examine her but withhold the resulting analysis under doctor-patient confidentiality law until she authorized its transfer to the authorities. And obviously, the doctor would have to know why this was necessary. Which was impossible, unless. . . .

Her job was to recruit believers. Was there any reason why that couldn't include people on New Tahiti?

There was the very good reason that there were no mentors on New Tahiti and thus no one to vouch for her sanity. Besides which, she wasn't acquainted with any doctors. Yet somehow, she had to make this work. Varel had knowingly incurred censure to make sure that her mission on Earth would succeed, and she couldn't let that go for nothing.

~ 25 ~

It took *Promise* more than two days in normal space to reach New Tahiti after emerging from the jump. During that time they weren't able to discuss the mission; one or two crew members were always present, viewing it as part of their duties to socialize with the passengers, and the walls of the compartments were too thin to permit much conversation in staterooms. The best they could manage was telepathic contact too limited to arouse the curiosity of the crew despite their mind training.

Ardith spent most of her time aboard memorizing information about the cities to which she was assigned and the contacts there she had been given, but in addition she tried to get as much information as she could about New Tahiti. Besides what she found in the ship's knowledgebase, she was able to learn a lot from the crew, who had been stopping over there on every outbound trip. Since there was little else to discuss at meals, it was easy to get them talking about it. The copilot Lt. Galina Lenkov and engineer Lt. Derek Renford, who were married to each other, were enthusiastic—where else in Fleet would they have a chance to spend time at what was generally considered the top resort in the galaxy?

"Of course we don't get a chance to visit the luxury hotels," Lt. Renford pointed out. "The Maclairn Foundation's budget won't stretch to that, so we all sleep aboard the ship. But the beaches are free, and you can find pretty much whatever you want in the way of nightlife."

"Don't ordinary people live there, besides the tourists?" Ardith asked.

"Yes, it's a fairly good-sized colony. But everything's focused on serving the tourist trade, since that's its only source of income. They do all they can to encourage it, which is why they're not particular about where the ships come from or the status of passengers' IDs."

That, of course, was why Maclairn had chosen it as a stopover base. The mentors had officially-forged IDs since they were not League citizens by birth, but they had no travel history, nor was there a record of where guest passengers had stayed between their departure from Earth and their return, any more than there was in the case of the envoys. The less checking done of such details, the better.

What would happen if a passenger got sick? Ardith wondered. The mentors could deal with most illness, but in case something serious required admission to a hospital it would surely access that person's medical record. If the League databank didn't include one, there would be inquiries. The next time she talked to Lt. Lenkov she casually raised the question.

"Provision's been made for that," the young officer said. "We have a doctor lined up who will handle it quietly—she was a guest on Maclairn herself many years ago."

A doctor! Perhaps her scheme wasn't impossible after all. She couldn't ask the crew for contact information, but the mentors aboard, Gerard and Brielle, might know. As it was the sort of question that could be approached by telepathy, she soon found that Brielle had been told by Radnor how to reach the doctor if necessary.

But to explain why it was necessary, Ardith would have to speak to Brielle aloud for more than a minute or two—which meant in her stateroom, so Meiko too would have to know. That night when the captain was on the bridge and the other two crew members had gone to bed, she got them together and quietly spelled out her plan.

"It's risky," she concluded, "but not any more so than what we'll be doing anyway if I have a mentor to introduce me. Will you go with me, Brielle?"

Brielle hesitated. Finally she said, "Yes, I think it will be okay. I have met Dr. Marwen; I was working as a healer when she came to Maclairn over thirty years ago. She has had mind training, of course, as all our guests do."

"Shall we tell the others?" Meiko asked.

"No," said Ardith. "It would be hard to get them alone, and they don't really need to know—though Jacob is leader, we won't need his permission for contacting people once we're on Earth so it shouldn't be necessary here, either."

They landed shortly before noon on the third day. The captain and copilot, after securing the shuttle and arranging to meet them that evening for return to *Promise,* disappeared into the city on business of their own, leaving Lt. Renford on watch aboard the ship. Fred proposed going to the beach, but Ardith and Brielle made the excuse that they wanted to do some shopping first—they'd been told their implanted microchips would cover it, since for tourists not to spend heavily would look unnatural. To their surprise, Liam vetoed both plans.

"We need to talk out of the crew's hearing," he said. "There's a park on the map that looks like a place where we can picnic without being overheard."

Puzzled, they followed Liam to an outdoor market, where they bought food, and then to the park. Settling on the grass, they spread out lunch. It was a clear, hot day; New Tahiti's sun was similar to Earth's but brighter, and the sky was a brilliant blue in contrast to the deep blue-green of the nearby lagoon, Though there were others in the park they weren't close enough to hear what was said, and evidently Liam needed to say something important.

"How much were you told about the political situation on Earth?" he asked Jacob.

"Only that the League is likely to turn into a totalitarian government sooner or later if it doesn't establish contact with the Federation before then, and that the Service is keeping a close eye on a potential dictator."

"Unfortunately it's happening sooner," Liam announced. "A few days ago there was a coup. A small but powerful faction within Fleet took over the government and put a politician named Halorun at its head—the charismatic man we've been watching. He has declared martial law. Several agents were caught up in it and barely managed to get picked up by the Service. Two of them were taken directly to the ship in Maclairn's solar system, and fortunately it was the night Varel and I happened to be there. We waited for them to brief us before taking *Estel* down to warn Kenard and Radnor."

The group stared at him in appalled silence. "We don't see any chance of this blowing over," Liam went on. "Fleet, as you know, has a monopoly on all interstellar shipping except for small craft—this was set up to prevent war between colonies. It has no legal power to act on any planet except in connection with crimes committed in space, or with putting down rebellions against legitimate colonial governments. But legality has little to do with what can be expected now, as it is heavily armed and there is no other armed force in existence except for local police. Though most Fleet officers will oppose Halorun, any who rebel can be easily wiped out by the forces he controls. I don't look forward to breaking the news to the *Promise* crew tonight, but that's what I've got to do."

"Are you saying that Maclairn will be taken over, too?" Gerard asked. "The secret exposed, and our families subject to marital law?"

"Possibly, but that's not the most likely scenario," Liam said grimly. "The government has always feared psi and other mind powers; the existence of Maclairn has been a thorn in its side ever since it was discovered, which is why they agreed to keep it secret. I'm afraid Halorun will decide to eliminate it, which would be easy since the public doesn't know it exists. In his view he already has an armed cruiser on site— he's not aware that the crew of *Shepard* would refuse to carry out such an order. But when they do, he will send other starships."

In shock, everyone turned white. "Dear God, we're defenseless," Brielle said in a low voice.

"No, you're not," Liam assured them. "The Service has kept a ship in Maclairn's solar system for more than two centuries to protect the colony if Fleet failed to do so, as it was known to be essential to your civilization's development of mind powers. We can act without revealing ourselves to Earth—we'll simply shield the planet as we do our own, and when they don't hear anything from it they may assume it has been disposed of. This is already underway as a precaution."

"What's going to happen to the mentors on Earth?" Jacob asked.

"I'm afraid they're in a difficult position. Psi may be made illegal, which will be an even greater threat than its persecution by the Klan was. And by the way, you must not reveal the existence of aliens to anyone without mind training before the government finds out about it, which we hope won't be soon."

"We were supposed to tell more people than that," Ardith protested, "and let them start chains."

"Yes, but that's no longer feasible. The authorities will undoubtedly arrest some telepaths and want to know the names of others. Dictatorships are all the same—when they want information they get it by torture. People with mind training can cope with that; most others can't."

Chilled, Ardith said nothing more. If any vulnerable telepath did find out, at least one envoy would be exposed. She hadn't thought of her training in pain control having much practical value in modern society, apart from minor benefits like being able to stop headaches; it was simply a means to a breakthrough enabling her to learn other skills. And despite her ability not to suffer if she were tortured, pain might not be their only tactic.

"Right now, unless a sufficiently-powerful resistance movement is organized, the Service offers the only hope of staving off long-term tyranny," Liam declared. "Since Earth is now a Federation member we are authorized to intervene. But we can't do it unless its people invite us without any prompting on our part. It would do more harm than good to take away your species' control over its own destiny."

"Which leaves us as envoys with the full responsibility for keeping that hope alive," Jacob said. Ardith and the others did not dare to speak.

"That's true," Liam agreed, "but it's a much harder job than you bargained for when you accepted this mission, and you will be in far greater danger. You have the right to withdraw. That's why Radnor sent me with you on *Promise,* so that you would have a chance to think it over, free of his influence. If you choose to back out, you will be picked up here on New Tahiti and taken back to the Elder worlds. We owe you that much, considering the position in which we unintentionally placed you."

"Are you going back to the Elder worlds?" Jacob asked,

"No. I'm going to Earth on *Promise* with the mentors."

"Then so am I," declared Jacob.

"Me too," said Fred. "I'm sure as hell not going to let a tyrant and his pals scare me off." Silently, Meiko nodded.

Ardith's head swam. Back to the Elder worlds . . . back where she'd always wanted to be and would be safe, where she belonged, where Varel was. . . .

But Varel wouldn't be allowed to see her or even communicate, and he had brought that penalty on himself for the sake of Earth. She recalled how he'd looked when he spoke of Earth's danger, and earlier when he'd insisted that it was her responsibility to return there. Unconsciously she clutched the flame pendant that hung around her neck. There was really nothing to think over. She could not betray Varel's trust in her. No matter how great her peril might be on Earth, she could not turn away.

~ 26 ~

Although no one felt like going to the beach or shopping, much less celebrating at an expensive luau set up for tourists, it was necessary to do these things to maintain the fiction that *Promise* was a tourist ship. This was more important than ever now that closer control over travel would undoubtedly be introduced. The authorities must not be allowed to suspect that its passengers were not what they seemed.

Liam explained that Radnor would tell *Shepard*'s crew about the coup and inform them about the Elders if they chose not to support Fleet's new commanders, which was likely even if no order to attack the colony came. All of them had friends on the surface and a few were married to Maclairnans. They would hardly be willing to impose martial law, and though they would be subject to execution for mutiny if they refused, they would be safe for as long as they remained behind the shield.

Ardith was so shaken that it was hard to remember that now was the time when she'd planned to seek the doctor, but that too was now of greater importance than ever. Public revelation of the Federation might be necessary sooner than had been thought. The ground must be laid for proving that aliens were people Earth-dwellers could view as humans like themselves.

Brielle made the call and set up an appointment for late afternoon. They sat on the famous white sand beach until almost time, and then, with the excuse of buying swim suits, they left the others and went into the city. With only a little difficulty they found their way to Dr. Marwen's office.

In the waiting room, Ardith tried to calm herself. This was the beginning, This explanation was what she would have to give over and over to as many people with mind training as she could find, and later to people without it. If she could not succeed in making the doctor believe, could she ever convince anyone?

Dr. Marwen, a small grey-haired woman with a kindly face, appeared at the door. "I sent the nurse home," she said. "Since the call came from a mentor I knew the problem is confidential. It has been years since I heard from a mentor, though I think of Maclairn often." She smiled at Brielle. "Your face is familiar, but I was there so long ago that I must have met your mother."

"We don't show our age," Brielle said. "I remember you; we met when I was working in a clinic, long before I was chosen to be a mentor. Now I'm on my way to Earth to work in a mind training center." Assuming that the public on New Tahiti hadn't yet heard the news, she didn't elaborate. "But right now, my friend Ardith Moran has a problem with which we feel only you can help."

"It's rare for a healer to be stumped, and I'm afraid I don't have much diagnostic equipment here in the office."

"No diagnosis is required," Brielle said. "I will let Ardith explain, and I ask you to believe what she says, because I personally know it to be true."

Ardith drew breath. She must ease into it and provide proof, even though Brielle had vouched for her. "Have you heard about the expedition to follow up on a message believed to have come from an extraterrestrial civilization?" she asked.

"Yes," Dr. Marwen replied. "I read about it on the Net. It failed, didn't it? And lives were lost."

"Supposedly they were. Several people left the starship in a lifeboat and were never found. I am one of those people, doctor. It's important that you identify me, so would you please look at that article again on your tablet and compare me with my picture?" She provided the Net address of the article, which she had memorized.

Puzzled, the doctor did as she asked. "How strange," she said. "It says the lifeboat ran out of life support a thousand light years from here, yet the woman in the picture is your twin. I don't wonder that you're inquisitive. I suppose this is a case of separation at birth and you want me to trace your genetic heritage, but why the secrecy? You could get ancestry tracing from a public DNA-search machine."

The question of a long-lost twin had never occurred to Ardith, but it was easy to answer. "You can check my ID chip too," she said, "and the fact that my DNA profile matches it—I'm sure you have an AI link to my medical record, and all you need is a cheek swab." The doctor complied, obviously influenced by telepathic insistence from Brielle.

"The woman on the expedition could not have used a false ID," Ardith pointed out, "because all members were required to have government security clearance. That's verifiable. So we are one and the same."

"So it seems. If I didn't know better, I'd say you came back from the dead."

"But I wasn't dead, Dr. Marwen. The extraterrestrials sought by the expedition were there after all—the starship left too soon. All four of us presumed lost were picked up and taken to an alien world."

Her telepathic reinforcement of the truth left no room for doubt. "Dear God," said the doctor. "Evidently they brought you home, but why hasn't this been in the news?"

"What do you think the public reaction would be if it were announced that aliens exist, and have come here, or to Earth?"

"There have been plenty of such announcements in the past and the reaction was that those who claimed such contact were crackpots. If you want to keep it secret that would be the surest way to go about it."

"But we don't want to keep it from everyone, you see. Earth needs contact with the aliens, hope that our civilization will someday become as mature as theirs. We need exchange of ideas, something challenging to keep us from giving up in despair. Here on new Tahiti you may not know——"

"We know. I see it in the eyes of the tourists who come to me with ills caused by the depression even the richest citizens of Earth can't escape. If there really were a more advanced civilization, at least there'd be something to aim for."

"Yes. So we need to spread the knowledge gradually, starting with those like yourself who've had enough mind training to sense that we speak truth. The four of us are committed to the task. But speaking is not quite enough."

"I see that. But how can I help? Oh . . . did the aliens give you some physical sign that needs a doctor's verification?"

"Yes, in a way." Perhaps this would make it easier to broach the subject. "Doctor, what would you expect aliens to be like, if you knew no more about them than I've told you?"

"Friendly. Intelligent, of course. Awe-inspiring, and utterly incomprehensible, even with the aid of telepathy."

"But not loving? Not people like us with whom we could interact as we do with other humans?"

"No, I don't see how they could be that, though I suppose you may have gotten used to them."

"Then would it surprise you to hear that I fell in love with one of them, and that we made love more than once?"

"I wouldn't believe a story like that, and if someone is spreading it, I'll do my best counter it. I can see that you're not the sort of woman who goes in for exotic sexual experiences."

Ardith's eyes filled with tears. Her instinct had been right—people would find it hard to imagine the Elders as comparable to humans. "But it is true," she said, finding her voice. "He's not very different physically, and mentally not at all, except maybe as an individual he's smarter than I am. I will love him for the rest of my life, and I'll never stop grieving because our commitments on separate worlds keep us apart."

The genuineness of her emotion came through telepathically, of course, and the doctor was at a loss for words, In the silence Brielle said, "I have met this man twice—the aliens have been visiting Maclairn for some time. Last week I attended the feast that marked his pairing with Ardith. We celebrated because it was proof that Earth's people are on the same level as the Elder species. Only later did it occur to Ardith that it might be necessary to prove the reverse."

Dr. Marwen said quietly, "I apologize, Ardith. I'm ashamed to find myself guilty of bigotry that we thought Earth had seen the last of long ago. But I'm afraid you're wise in thinking that you shouldn't let the press learn that you encountered aliens."

"Or the government," Ardith said, "because we have reason to believe the government will try to suppress the knowledge, perhaps even to the extent of eliminating those of us whose identity proves it.

That's why I've come to you. Someday we will need to offer evidence to the public that aliens have the same human qualities as we do. So I need DNA proof that I made love with one of them, and I can't get it from a government-run lab."

"If you have his DNA properly preserved I can get it analyzed," the doctor agreed. "I'm willing to do that. But DNA won't prove that you made love."

Ardith flushed. "It will if you record where you got it from," she said. "It was only three nights ago."

"Oh . . . sorry for being dense. You want me to examine you, then?"

"Yes, like a forensic exam. I need you to order the analysis privately. Is it true that doctor-patient confidentiality will prevent you from revealing the result before I ask you to?"

"Yes, of course." Dr. Marwen led her across the hall into a small, very clean examination room with one chair and the typical folding and adjustable exam table.

Ardith cringed. She had thought she would not mind; she'd had similar exams for medical reasons, after all. But now to be touched, even by a doctor, seemed a violation of memories that were private and precious. She closed her eyes and tried not to think about what was happening.

To hear her love for Varel described as an "exotic sexual experience"—and by a physician, not the sensational press—had hurt more than she had ever imagined words could hurt. She had thought those she told would immediately realize that it couldn't be that, and would therefore picture aliens as essentially human. If people who didn't need proof were the only ones to whom it could be shown, then it would be a vicious circle.

She was exhausted from the strain of the day, of

the past seven days, and now there was the prospect of martial law to deal with. Of being arrested, perhaps, and locked up before she could accomplish anything. But there was no use in looking ahead. Wearily, once the exam was over, she and Brielle thanked the doctor and made their way to the tourist district, where they bought their swim suits and went reluctantly back to the beach.

~ 27 ~

When they met at the shuttleport to return to *Promise* for the night, the captain hadn't arrived and the copilot, Lt. Lenkov, was worried. "He's not the kind to be late when on duty," she said. "But I have no way to contact him and since we can't all fit in the shuttle at once anyway, I may as well take half of you up now."

The four envoys went back to the ship, welcoming the chance to talk without being overheard. None of them wanted Liam or the mentors to know how scared they were, or how doubtful they felt about their ability to do what the situation demanded of them.

"We have no choice but to take one step at a time," Fred said. "But I don't like the idea of there being no way to contact each other, or the Service, if the mentors whose names we've been given are arrested."

"We go to the nearest Bramfield Club and give the manager the password," Meiko said.

"That's okay unless they close all the Bramfield Clubs, which they're likely to do if they find out that's where mind training has been going on."

"Besides, the mentors aren't going to know what to do either," Jacob pointed out. "There are hundreds of them throughout the world, and I don't think they'll dare use the Net as they normally do."

"They've got a secure site."

"Supposedly, but they don't reveal anything to do with Maclairn on it, and in any case it won't be secure long once government hackers take over."

"What if they fear Maclairn has been destroyed?" Ardith asked. "If the Service guesses that's what Halorun will do, the mentors may too, and they all have families there, grandkids and great-grandkids."

"Surely the Service will tell Maclairn Foundation headquarters about the shielding," Jacob assured her.

"But the rest won't know unless the mentors there, or Liam—or even one of us—can reach them personally. They'll have no grounds for thinking it's still safe."

"And no reason to believe in a better future," Fred added.

"If only it were possible to bring the Captain of *Estel* back," Meiko said sadly. "He hacked the Net to spread his message and it went viral, and the whole Estelan movement grew out of that."

"But Terry never went to Earth," Fred said, puzzled. "He was barred from it because mentors could have picked up knowledge of the Elders from hi mind. He couldn't have hacked Earth's Net."

"He was in the news the one time he landed there to confront the Klan, and so what he'd posted in the colonies spread when his followers repeated it. People believed him even though a lot of them thought he was a myth, as most do today. If posts about him started appearing again, they'd be noticed."

"He couldn't mention the Elders publicly, so how would that help?" Ardith asked.

"Just by spreading hope. Making people feel

that there's something new coming. What he said on Ciencia to kindle hope started the Estelan revolution."

"The Estelan Party will be the first thing the government shuts down on Earth and in the colonies," said Fred, "considering that it stands for gaining mind powers."

"From what I know about totalitarian takeovers in past cultures, the nonpartisan side of it won't stay shut down," said Jacob. "It's exactly the sort of symbol a resistance movement needs."

"So maybe the Service will start it up again," said Meiko. "It would be easy for them to plant posts on the Net—they have even more hacking capability than Terry did."

"No," Ardith reflected. "It would be *too* easy, and later it would come out that aliens were behind it, which would give the impression that the Service had manipulated us. That's what it has to stay clear of."

"But fostering hope could prevent a lot of suffering if it worked—"

"Ardith is right," Jacob said. "If the Service did everything it could to prevent suffering, no world could determine its own destiny. They'd all end up dependent on the Federation instead of being autonomous, and it would become a de facto ruler."

"I suppose so. It's too bad, though—what Terry did had a big impact on morale."

"I think Terry succeeded as Captain of *Estel* because he was just acting on his own, doing what he believed in," Fred declared. "He didn't have a big organization with committees and policies and all that stuff. He said what he wanted to say, and to hell with what anybody thought who didn't like it."

"On Ciencia he set up an organization with cells," Meiko said.

"Did he? If so I'll bet he ran it, without giving anybody authority to override him. And he was captain of a starship, so he could go where he liked."

"Except that Fleet confiscated it twice. And when he first wrote about *Estel* he didn't have a ship. It was imaginary."

"Really? I didn't know that," said Ardith. The idea itself was a more powerful influence than the ship—somehow that struck her as important. "It's so sad that Terry didn't live a little longer," she went on. "After meeting him, I can't help thinking he would know how to encourage people now."

"When he was dying he spoke about taking the next step," Meiko agreed. "It's as if he knew action would be needed to keep what he started going. Besides what the Stewards of the Flame have been doing, I mean—something equivalent to what he did as the captain of *Estel*."

"He wasn't speaking just in general," Ardith reminded them. "To Varel and me he said 'I dare to predict that on you rests the future of our birthworld,' and when he spoke about picking up a torch he told us we four would carry it after he was gone. And when I told him my flame pendant was a token of consecration to our mission, he said it was fitting."

All three of them stared at her, remembering. After a moment Jacob spoke. "Do you know what you just said, Ardith?"

"Yes, I repeated some of his last words to us—"

"You said it's our responsibility. That the torch has passed to us and he was counting on us carry it. Which means we have to act to counter what Earth's government is doing."

"Oh, my God, Jacob. Are you saying we should take on the whole job of stirring resistance?"

"Not political resistance—we don't have the skills to become freedom fighters. But of shaping public attitudes by posting on the Net as he did, yes. Of offering hope, because the word Estel means hope, and hope is what contact with the Federation is about. After all, the whole point of our mission is to get people ready to welcome such contact, which Terry viewed as the next step in human evolution."

"The Captain of *Estel* has become a mere legend, yet we have spoken with him—we alone on Earth, since he was barred from Earth once he knew about the Elders." Meiko added. "If anyone should carry on where he left off, we should."

Recalling that night, they shared telepathically a sense of where they were headed. They had pledged commitment to their mission not just once but twice—three times counting the blessing by the Eldest—first on Ydoril and again at Terry's funeral with the flame that miraculously had not burned them. . . .

Ardith felt as if she were running down a long passage toward a light she could not see, unable to stop or even to catch her breath. Inexplicably she perceived images from the dreams, then in the next moment realized that this was a memory of what the Eldest had given her, not the blessing on her union with Varel but the one for success in her mission. It had been overshadowed in her mind until now—or were they two parts of a whole?

At that moment the shuttle docked and the others soon burst through the airlock. One look at them was enough to show that there was more trouble.

"Captain Levitt has been detained," Liam stated, "because there's an order in place requiring all Fleet officers to report immediately to their bases—he won't be allowed to fly *Promise*. We assume he has had the good sense not to reveal that his base is on an unknown planet, since only a few at the top level know about the cruiser at Maclairn."

"He won't talk, because he's had mind training," Lt. Lenkov said. "But that means he'll be assumed to be a deserter from somewhere."

Liam was keeping his face impassive, and the envoys, telepathically sensing what they otherwise wouldn't have known, followed suit. Deserters, in a situation like this, would all too probably be shot.

"Why would such an order be given?" Lt. Lenkov asked. "Liam knows, I think, but he wouldn't tell me anything more till we were aboard *Promise*."

"It's complicated, and I need to tell you and your husband together," Liam said. "It will be a shock to you, and we haven't much time because they'll check every ship on this planet before morning."

"How do they think the passengers will get home if the crews all report to base?" Gerard asked.

"I doubt if they care whether passengers are stranded," Liam said, "but they'd probably say the ship owner would find a civilian replacement. Most people wouldn't mind spending extra time at a luxury resort."

Lt. Renford came from the bridge to join his wife, and they sat quietly while Liam brought them up to date. It was indeed a shock, as like others born on Earth who hadn't studied history, they'd had no idea how dictatorships operate.

"We need to take off tonight," Liam told them. "If you want to stay in Fleet you must report to head-quarters as soon as we get to Moonbase; I can provide you with fake IDs showing you're stationed there. But as qualified crew you'll undoubtedly be assigned to ships tasked with subjugating the colonies, and colonists won't be as docile as people on Earth. Fleet officers there will be responsible for a good deal of bloodshed."

Horrified, Lt. Lenkov said, "We won't take part in that."

"You won't be given a choice, and if there's an organized rebellion among officers it will be classed as mutiny, for which Fleet's penalty has long been execution."

The two officers looked at each other despairingly. Liam said, "There's an alternative. You can throw in your lot with Maclairn, as we expect the crew of *Shepard* to do. You'll be charged with desertion if caught, but if you can get back there you'll be safe. You will have to stay indefinitely, but that may be okay with you as I've heard that officers stationed there don't have families with whom being out of contact would be a hardship."

"I'm not so sure Maclairn will be safe if *Shepard*'s crew deserts," said Lt. Renford. "That won't deter us, but you should prepare to be attacked."

"We are prepared, and there will be no fight," Liam stated. "But you need to decide right now so I can forge your IDs one way or the other."

"Who *are* you?" Lt. Lenkov burst out. "The Maclairnans don't have the means to do such things."

"I'm coming to that. But before I can tell you I need you to pledge that your allegiance will be to Maclairn in any conflict with the League."

Unhesitatingly they gave the pledge. Then Liam said, "You're aware that people unknown to you have been traveling to and from Maclairn on the privately-owned ship *Estel*, of which I was copilot when Terry arrived. I am now its pilot, and I'm also a citizen of the world from which its passengers come. Our identity has been kept secret, but that's about to change. I'll let Jacob explain why. . . ."

Ardith listened to Jacob's revelation, hoping to learn more about how it should be approached. As the second shock in a row for the couple, it proved a major one; yet knowing humankind wasn't alone did seem to give them hope. For the first time she felt truly committed to spreading that hope among the people of Earth.

~ *28* ~

Liam had learned that Captain Levitt had already filed a flight plan for *Promise* to depart the next night. So the authorities weren't likely to look for the rest of the crew within the next few hours—fortunately, since he needed to contact the Service ship that had been orbiting New Tahiti in case an emergency arose. After ordering the hacking to provide new IDs for the two lieutenants, who were now abandoning that rank in favor of their first names Derek and Galina, he contacted the captain telepathically and offered what encouragement he could.

Which wasn't much, because when he returned to *Promise* he brought devastating news.

"All of Earth is under a lockdown order," he said. "People must remain in their homes except for essential business, and even for that there's a curfew. Furthermore, all travel is banned. I heard this from the Service; the official notice hasn't come through here yet, so if we take off now we can get away. But we may be stuck at Moonbase, and in any case you can't get to the cities you're scheduled to visit."

"Won't the Service take us?" Meiko asked.

"That wouldn't be a good idea," Liam said. "Later, when the government finds you, there'd be no explanation of how you'd gotten there, which would defeat the purpose of bringing you from New Tahiti in the first place. It would inevitably reveal that alien ships are present on Earth."

"There must be some way we can get there on our own," Fred said.

"Perhaps, later on. The city assignments were more or less arbitrary; all that matters is for you to contact as many people with mind training as you can." Liam paused. "Again, this has become a more difficult task than you signed up for, and it may be a hopeless one. You can go back to Maclairn in *Promise* if you wish."

"I wouldn't want to say it's hopeless yet," Jacob declared. "We've been discussing hope, and we think we may have a way to spread it to more people than we can talk to about the Elders."

"That would be great if you can do it, but how?"

"Revive belief in the Captain of *Estel* On the Net," Ardith said. "His posts once had tremendous impact on people—they encouraged the telepaths who were being persecuted and got others believing in mind powers even if they didn't personally have any training. So the idea that someday we'll meet friendly aliens could be encouraged in the same way."

"How would you get around the fact that the government will try to stamp out anything connected to psi, including *Estel?*"

"Is there any reason we can't say that the Captain of *Estel* himself visited alien worlds? That wouldn't he like saying there are aliens here, yet it's too specific to be dismissed as mere speculation. The kind of people who support government bureaucracy will think the belief that we've contacted aliens is crazy, right? So they'd be happy to have the public believe the two ideas are in the same category."

"But what if it really turns out that way?" Galina protested. "What if people do associate them and reject both?"

"They won't," said Jacob. "Those who have such

powers, or who were inspired by the Captain of *Estel* to want them, aren't going to change their minds. But they might change their view of aliens and start thinking that contact with them would be good thing."

Derek frowned. "The trouble is that in the past a lot of people felt sure alien contact had occurred when it wasn't true, so it's like the boy who cried wolf. People today will be skeptical. Isn't that why you four are here to provide proof?"

"How could people have believed they'd met aliens when they hadn't?" Meiko protested. "Were they insane?"

"No, at least not all of them were," Liam said. "The human brain cannot distinguish between input from the senses and auditory or visual input from the mind. If the mind receives strong psi input, it interprets it according to its experience from the past or draws from the collective unconscious."

"You may actually hear the voice of someone familiar to you who is communicating telepathically," Brielle explained, "and because you're aware that such communication is possible, you don't get confused. But if it's not a familiar voice or image, the input will be interpreted according to expectations. Deeply religious people have literally heard, or seen, saints and angels. In the same way people who believe in aliens have heard their voices as strongly as if the input came through their ears, and have seen beings from UFOs."

"But where did the input actually come from?" Ardith asked.

"Sometimes via unconscious telepathy from others who believed, or a blend of ideas from the collective unconscious. But not all of it can be explained that way. There have been cases where the information was such that no one on Earth could have known it. The details were clearly metaphorical because they didn't match real Federation worlds, yet they involved concepts far beyond Earth's level."

Liam added, "Those cases are a mystery that even the most advanced Elders haven't figured out. Similar cases once occurred on all the Elder worlds, and they're more complicated than ordinary precognition. It has been speculated that like apparent communication with the dead, they involve anomalies in time."

"Time, like ideas from now being sensed in the past? After all, there are real aliens here now," Meiko said. "So the more we get people to believe in them, the more likely their ancestors were to believe when it wasn't real?"

"Well, nobody can claim to understand time paradoxes. But that's a possibility."

Jacob frowned. "Isn't it more likely that the information came from worlds that haven't been discovered yet, perhaps in other galaxies that the Federation hasn't explored? I haven't heard that it has visited any beyond our own."

"That's true," Liam agreed. "We're just beginning to develop technology for reaching other galaxies, and they could be more advanced than ours, which might account for their not having contacted us. That's one reason why we feel that we'll never run out of challenges."

"To get back to the problem at hand," Gerard said, "how do you propose to reach people on the Net? Terry hacked it, but you don't have that capability."

"He started out trying to attract the attention of a society that didn't have the immediate need for hope that exists on Earth, so he had to plant ideas in many places at once," Jacob pointed out. "After it went viral he didn't need to hack; people just repeated it—and they'll repeat ours because they're more desperate than those of his hacking period."

"We can discuss this more once we've jumped out of here," Liam said. "Right now we need to break orbit, or we won't get a chance. Are the four of you sure you want to go to Earth rather than Maclairn?"

"We're still the only people with proof of contact," Jacob said, The others nodded; they were committed regardless of circumstances and they might be able to do some good even if unable to carry out the original mission.

Liam informed the former Fleet officers about the false IDs that the Service had placed in the records their implanted chips would reference, naming Galina as captain of *Promise*, himself as copilot, and Derek as engineer. After they dressed in the civilian clothes he had bought for them, he made a quick shuttle trip to the surface to get rid of their Fleet uniforms. They could only hope that uses of the public recycling machines weren't being recorded.

Would she ever be in another starship? Ardith wondered as *Promise* moved away from the lush green planet below. Or would she be trapped on Earth forever, not even able to visit colony worlds? The idea was appalling. She had longed to get away from Earth even as a little girl, and by majoring in exobiology in college, she'd managed to escape. The colonies had proved less stimulating than she'd expected, but at least they were preferable to the dismal sprawling city on Earth where she'd grown up. She had never intended to look back.

Yet Varel, who had visited countless fascinating worlds, felt Earth was worth the sacrifices made for it.

He really meant for its native human race, she knew; still even though humankind could thrive in the colonies he believed the mother world was important. And he should know, having studied hundreds of them. So she had resigned herself to returning. But it wasn't going to be pleasant, even apart from the current political situation. She dreaded the weeks ahead.

During the two days it took to reach Moonbase after emerging from the jump, they discussed their plans endlessly without reaching any conclusions. No one knew where on Earth they would be stranded if they could get from Moonbase to Earth at all. The best they could do was agree on some Net sites through which they might be able to communicate, based on their past knowledge of Earth's Net. Ardith hadn't been to Earth since she left college, and the two mentors, of course, had never been there at all. The six intended to remain together until they saw the way clear to visit other mentors.

As they established orbit at Moonbase, Ardith began to feel more and more nervous. This was the crucial moment they had worried about ever since learning the details of the mission—the moment when either their IDs would be accepted, or they would be detained for investigation of their recorded status as dead. Would the IDs be checked more carefully than usual now?

"Say what Captain Levitt normally does," Liam instructed, "and don't volunteer any more information than they ask for."

Galina was used to deceiving the controllers, of course, since *Promise* always lied to them about who the passengers were and where they'd been. "Terran Control, this is civilian hyperdrive spacecraft HS *Promise,* inbound from New Tahiti, requesting permission to approach, over."

"*Promise*, state your business and persons on board, over."

"This is Captain Galina Richmond in command,"

said Galina, using the name on her new ID. "I am carrying six returning tourists plus two more crew, all citizens of Earth."

"Have any of these persons landed on any world other than New Tahiti since leaving Earth?"

"Negative," replied Galina calmly.

"Roger, *Promise*. Establish lunar holding orbit at 50 km and prepare for boarding."

Ardith's hands were icy. She tried to keep her face impassive, as the others were doing, when after an unusually long delay two officers in a small shuttle docked and began running their wand over identity chips.

"Our records show that this ship is normally crewed by Fleet," an officer said, after the crew's IDs had been verified without incident. "Where is Captain Levitt?"

"While the ship was on New Tahiti he was ordered to report to his base, as were the other crew members," Galina stated calmly.

"And how do you come to be flying it?"

They had prepared a story, gambling that it wouldn't be checked; it was better to admit to a minor offense than to be caught with forged IDs. "We were on layover there because the free trader we were originally hired for required repairs, and we decided to quit."

The officer frowned. "By a free trader you mean a smuggler. Weren't you aware that you could be arrested for associating with criminals?"

"Yes, sir, so we'd signed on even though we hated what we'd have been doing. We can't be arrested for an offense we never actually committed, can we?" They had no real objection to free trading, considering that Terry had once earned the operating cost of *Estel* by engaging in it; but it was best if Fleet thought they had a strong reason for leaving their previous job.

Sighing, the officer said, "I suppose not—though who knows what policies the new command will impose. But we'll inspect the cargo bay on this ship carefully, so I hope you're telling the truth."

They were carrying no cargo other than the personal belongings in their staterooms, which the officers went through item by item in case the association with smugglers had involved more than a possible flying job. Since this left them little time to look closely at the passengers' IDs, the four envoys were actually safer than they would have been with the normal crew.

Finally, after Galina had affirmed again that *Promise* had not visited any undisclosed planets, its shuttle was given a certified trip transponder and cleared to proceed to the Moonbase orbital station. Whether it would be allowed to proceed to Earth remained in question.

~ *29* ~

The Moonbase orbital station was in chaos, as it was the point of arrival and departure for all ships bound to and from the colonies and all flights had been cancelled. Moreover, Fleet Headquarters was on the Moon and personnel were being called in from outlying bases to enforce the restrictions to which the inhabitants of Earth were now subject. Policing the colonies could wait, apparently, until the home planet was in order.

"At least they'll get rid of the gangs," Meiko said.

"The promise to do that was why many people supported Halorun when he was a mere politician," Fred agreed. "I'll bet they're sorry now."

"Yes—for years they couldn't go outside for fear of the gangs, and now they can't because of the lockdown. Not much was gained, except maybe elimination of the violence."

"Hardly that," Liam said. "He made short work of the gangs; the local police, under Fleet's new command, simply rounded them up and shot them."

"All of them? All the members, without trial?"

"All they could catch. Trials, I'm afraid, are a thing of the past, except where needed for show."

Ardith felt as if she had walked into a nightmare; she had no more idea of what was coming next than she would have if dreaming. The corridors of the orbital station were jammed and the lines at the food stalls were so long that there was little hope of getting anything to eat before having to make a decision about their next move. There weren't accommodations at Moonbase for anywhere near the number of people who were stranded, yet Liam said that to sleep aboard *Promise* would be unwise.

"You might not get back here again," he cautioned, "especially since it would require two shuttle trips each way and you might get separated. In any case I couldn't contact you there, which I'll need to do after I've learned what's going on with the mentors."

She had known that he could not stay with them; Liam, not only their advisor but responsible for liaison between the mentors and the Service agents on Earth, had the whole world to keep watch over. The envoys would have to make their own way. But the reality of that was a good deal worse than they had expected.

"Does Maclairn really need *Promise*, now that it can't make trips to Earth?" Galina asked.

"Probably not; *Estel* can serve its local needs. But we can't spare a Service ship to take you back there."

"Derek and I have been thinking—we can't accomplish anything useful on Maclairn, and we'd hate to run out on the rest of you. But we might be able to get the ship to Earth.

"It's a capital offense for a pilot to make an unauthorized shuttle landing on Earth, Galina. That was true even before the takeover. And you'd need to do it twice." The law was harsh because Earth was too congested and the legal traffic too heavy to permit unexpected ships to approach, as well as because smuggling would otherwise be rampant.

Derek declared, "I think I may be able to modify *Promise*'s trip transponder. That would allow us to reach Earth's orbital station, and if we can talk the controllers there into giving us clearance the actual landings wouldn't be unauthorized."

"We know the Fleet approach codes, which a smuggler wouldn't," Galina added. "After all, we've been there many times before."

"If you did get us there, where would you go afterward?" Jacob asked.

"Well, none of you know where you're going, do you? I guess we can talk to people as easily as those you're trying to recruit can. As I understand it, the only requirements are that they've had mind training and they've seen proof of your identity. We qualify on both counts."

"We won't have any choice about where to go," Jacob said. "If travel is prohibited we'll be given permits good only for reaching our addresses of record. But I guess one city is as good as another to start with."

"My address of record is in the colony on LaLande VI," Ardith said. "Surely they're not going to give us interstellar passage."

"That's a problem," Liam said. "What they'll do is send you to an internment camp along with the homeless. And the rest of you may end up in one if your former housing was given to others after your presumed deaths. If we'd anticipated the lockdown I'd have given you safe addresses as I did for Derek and Galina when I changed their status to civilian."

"Is there still time, Liam?" Jacob asked.

"Yes, if I can contact a Service hacker quickly. The question is what addresses to use. Do any of you have relatives or friends you're sure would take you in?"

"No one who's not connected to my university, and I have to steer clear of that because of Ivanson," Fred said.

"My recorded address is on Ceti XI but I can use my old college dorm address," Meiko said. "They'll find some place with room for me."

Jacob declined to name his friends, saying he didn't want to get them involved in anything that might attract police attention; and Ardith, who had no family, had left Earth so long ago that she knew no one. "The best I can do is give you Bramfield Club addresses," Liam said, "and hope they're still open. We don't keep track of the mentors' home addresses."

Gerard and Brielle, whose forged IDs already listed the address of a Bramfield Club in Oregon, quickly offered to join the mission of the others. So Liam departed to contact the Service through its agent on the moon, while Derek, who had a pilot's license in addition to his engineering credentials, took the shuttle back to *Promise* to work on its transponder. The rest found a place to sit, crowding onto a bench in one of the orbital station's small parks. They decided to take turns standing in line at a snack bar; if they couldn't get some sort of food it was going to be a long, hungry night.

Ardith shut out the noise of the crowded orbital

and tried to think. What good would come of all the weeks spent in preparation if they failed to reach Earth? What would be gained by her separation from Varel, or by the price he'd paid to make aliens seem human? The chance for success in attempting to get landing clearance with an illegally-modified transponder struck her as rather slim. In all probability they would be in prison before morning. She couldn't face that without having made an effort to let the people of Earth know that contact with aliens was something to hope for.

She opened her duffel and retrieved her tablet to start looking at Net sites. Logons from the Moonbase orbital station could be traced through IDs, but she'd been assured that the Service hacks would prevent hers from being tracked. Yes, anything she posted could eventually be associated with her real identity, but at present the government had too much to do checking political sites to bother with those focused on speculative science. She remembered one in particular she'd liked when she was in high school, the one that had inspired her interest in exobiology. Anybody could post comments; the AI filters screened out only spam and porn.

She turned to Meiko, beside her. "Meiko," she said softly, "Do you know what the Captain of *Estel* wrote when he first started, back when his ship was imaginary? Just how did he get people interested?"

"I remember the exact words he posted on Ciencia," Meiko said. "My family had a book of his writings that I read as a child. Let me have that." She took the tablet and in a draft file, wrote:

> There is a ship and its name is *Estel*, which means hope. Its captain came from the stars and his heart is there, but at times his ship

descends to bring the knowledge that's rightfully ours. And someday this knowledge will no longer be hidden.

Ardith studied the words, and after a while she reworded them slightly, then added a paragraph:

There is a ship and its name is *Estel,* which means hope. Its captain came from the stars and his heart was there, but at times his ship descended to bring knowledge of our human heritage. And he promised that someday this knowledge would no longer be hidden.

The Captain of *Estel* revealed only part of his knowledge to the people of his own time, but there is much more to be learned by those of ours. Though its Captain is gone the ship *Estel* still exists, and it carries passengers to and from worlds of which we have known nothing. Such were the beings by whom the Captain was given *Estel,* and the flame of hope they gave him is now ours to hold in our hearts, until the day when we of Earth seek our destiny among them.

"That's beautiful, Ardith!" Meiko said, taking the tablet again. "Look at this, Jacob." It was passed around, and everyone approved, offering a number of suggestions as to where to post it.

"It needs to be posted to as many Net sites as possible, if there's to be any hope of it reaching people," Jacob said, "and yet not Estelan sites, which are political and will be watched."

"Estelans have more sense than to attract attention," Meiko assured him. "We'll shut down our own sites if the government doesn't do it for us. So the question is, where will people like my grandmother, who remember the Captain of *Estel*, be likely to go?"

"Astronomy sites," Fred said. "I've got passwords to some, and since everybody thinks I'm dead, readers will assume my account has been hacked. But a lot will see it before the moderators take it down."

"And religious sites," Galina added. "Because the law requires equality they're used not just by mainline religions but by small offbeat ones, and since freedom of thought is guaranteed, the government can't interfere."

"It can if it wants to," Fred pointed out. "It has already violated most of the Constitution."

"But it won't want to," Jacob said, "because it will assume this is a crackpot idea that may distract people from what's going on here."

"Small offbeat religions include UFO cults," Meiko said, "and we don't want to be associated with that."

"Don't we?" Ardith asked thoughtfully. "We've assumed that we don't, but what harm will it do if some people believe friendly aliens are here in UFOs? After all, they *are* here in ships that are invisible. All the details UFO believers think they know are wrong, yet maybe they should be viewed as metaphorical rather than false. Radnor said such beliefs come from the collective unconscious."

"But some of them think they've had sex with aliens, even hybrid babies," Galina protested.

"Well," said Ardith dryly, "the part about babies isn't true, but there are rational people who wish it could be."

Everyone else stared at her, embarrassed. "Galina," Brielle said, "you and I need to talk later. There are things about the Elders we haven't told you yet."

"No," said Ardith, "not later—now. This is where we test my theory, and if it's wrong I need to know." She turned to Galina. "I'm in love with an alien, and our union was blessed—like a marriage, except for our knowing that we couldn't stay together. Pairings between people of different species are very common among the Elders, but they don't produce offspring because that's genetically impossible. If I could have his baby, I would."

Galina was silent, obviously finding this difficult to absorb. Ardith went on, "On Maclairn, people celebrated our union because they felt it would prove that Earthborn people are the equals of the Elders. But he and I felt it would also prove that the Elders are the equals of humans, because I'm not the kind of person who'd have sex with someone who wasn't. Does that make sense to you? Or am I wrong in thinking I should tell people that I did?"

"No, you're not wrong," Galina said slowly, "I just pictured them—differently, that's all. You see I knew Liam was surgically modified to look like us—"

"Yes, because he must pass inspection. But a lot of the others aren't very different. The ones with major differences simply aren't biologically attracted to each other."

They let the subject drop, but Ardith was shaken. It was going to be more difficult than she'd thought it would be. But for now, the main thing was to get the message onto the Net while they had the chance.

Part Five: Earth

~ 30 ~

Liam saw them only briefly before they left the Moonbase orbital, wishing them a safe journey which they all knew was by no means assured and warning them that he might be unable to contact them again for some time. The Service would keep watch on their flight and let him know when it arrived, but there was nothing he could do if something went wrong. From here on they were on their own.

There wasn't time to tell him about the Net postings.

It took two shuttle trips to get them back to the starship. Exhausted from stress and lack of sleep, they reached it in a daze. Derek went directly to bed, totally depleted by his earlier round trip and the strain of modifying the transponder; but Galina had to keep flying.

"Will our families on Maclairn know whether we make it to Earth or not?" Brielle asked as *Promise* undocked from the orbital station.

"Of course," she assured them. "The Service has rapid interstellar communication capability—they'll keep Maclairn informed."

They would inform Ydoril, too, Ardith thought. Would they tell Varel what was going on? They wouldn't mention her specifically, but as an expert on Earth's history he had the right to keep up-to-date on its political situation. When he heard how bad it was, would he fear she was caught up in it, maybe imprisoned?

With the two pilots alternating they made the thirty-hour trip to Earth's orbital station in agonized suspense, unsure as to whether Derek's tampering with the responder would let them approach. To everyone's relief the Fleet codes he had programmed into it proved adequate. More difficult was the explanation of how a civilian ship happened to be using Fleet codes.

"*Promise* was crewed by Fleet until the officers were ordered to report to headquarters," Galina said calmly to the flight controller. "They didn't bother to change our transponder after we took over."

If questioned, this story would not hold up since the present crew was known to have taken over before leaving New Tahiti, but the harried controllers were dealing with more extra traffic than they could safely handle and did not have time to think about the details. It was unlikely that civilians could have gotten hold of those codes and they recalled that the ship, which they'd seen before, had indeed been crewed by Fleet. Fortunately they didn't recall having seen Galina before, as Captain Levitt had always handled authorization issues.

The check of passenger IDs was perfunctory, as it was assumed that this had been done at the Moonbase orbital, as was the standard procedure. "Why are you bringing returning tourists in at four in the morning Denver time?" a controller asked her.

"Because we found that all the accommodations at Moonbase are full up," she replied, "so we decided to come directly here without bothering to figure when we'd arrive." In reality they had figured very carefully so as to contact the orbital at the busiest time for freighters to be arriving.

It dawned on Ardith that Galina was not merely a good liar, but was reinforcing her claims telepathically, as indeed they all were unconsciously. What seemed like miraculous luck had been more than that from the beginning, as Liam had no doubt anticipated. In any case the shuttle was cleared to land at the Denver spaceport and they were ordered to get *Promise* into a parking orbit fast so that other ships could approach.

Ardith was glad that they were landing at night. It spared her the sight of the miles of deteriorating apartment buildings and tightly-spaced smaller dwellings that housed the residents of greater Denver. Seeing only their lights, a vast glittering panorama, she could imagine the city as beautiful; but she knew it was just like all the rest. Terry had been born here, she recalled; she wondered if his birthplace was still standing. He too had left Earth as soon as he could get away.

As always, two shuttle trips were needed to get the group to the surface. The envoys waited nervously until the second load of passengers was down, dreading the ordeal of inspection at Customs. Having left New Tahiti earlier than planned, they had not acquired the kind of items that tourists normally brought in, and that could look suspicious—not so much in regard to their identity, but again because they might be engaged in smuggling.

"Do we look stupid?" Galina asked the one going through her duffel. "If we were smuggling would we call attention to ourselves by not buying any luxury goods?"

This time, the strategy did not work. One by one they were taken into a holding area and subjected to an invasive body search and an X-ray exam, reducing Meiko almost to tears.

After it was over Ardith, shaken and humiliated, asked the mentors, "Were the examiners latently telepathic? Did they sense that we were lying about something?"

"Perhaps," Brielle said. "But if so, I didn't pick it up."

"It could have been just that the new regime is nervous about people bringing in weapons," said Gerard. "They may think that a laxly-controlled colony like New Tahiti would support resistance fighters—and it could be true."

They lined up for the final ID check that would obtain addresses for their travel permits, hoping that Liam had managed to get forged records in place. There was no way to know, and if asked for their addresses they could not supply even the city; they must rely on the examiners taking them from the screen. But that meant they'd look closely at it! Ardith realized in sudden dismay. They'd counted on their status not being noticed, and during past checks it hadn't been. . . .

Before she had time to worry the examiner was staring at Meiko, who was the last to reach the desk. "What's the meaning of this?" he demanded. "It says here that you're dead."

"Dead?" Meiko echoed in an appropriately puzzled voice. "Well, I'm not, as you can see."

"I see that there's something irregular going on, as I've thought all along. Innocent people don't arrive in the middle of the night without any dutiable baggage, pretending to be tourists—certainly not with forged IDs."

"A forger would hardly leave the status of the old ID he appropriated as 'dead,'" Jacob pointed out.

"Not unless he—or she—was incompetent," the examiner admitted. "But we'll get a DNA check, just in case." He called the medic back to take a sample from Meiko's cheek, and they waited interminable minutes while it was processed by a DNA-search machine.

"Your DNA matches what's on file," the examiner finally admitted. "but the file could have been hacked."

"No forger with the ability to hack DNA profiles could possibly be so stupid as to forget about changing the 'dead' status," Ardith declared. "It's some glitch in the system." Radnor had said hacking of the DNA-profile database was virtually impossible! When the time came to reveal alien contact to the government, would it doubt the match? Could it cross-check using some other form of identification?

That time was not now. No supporters of the Elders had been recruited yet, and if the government wanted to suppress the evidence, it could. What if the examiner decided to look into the anomaly and detained Meiko? If they thought some sort of plot against the dictator was involved they wouldn't hesitate to apply pressure, and her silence alone would reinforce the idea that that an anti-government conspiracy existed. Which meant that all of them were at risk, because their IDs were recorded as having arrived together on *Promise*. Fortunately it didn't occur to the examiner to recheck them here and now.

He printed the travel permits and handed them out——except to Meiko. "The bus for the airport leaves in half an hour," he stated coldly, "and the rest of you are required to be on it. The permits will be accepted as airline tickets because the government now controls the airlines and we want everyone home. You are to proceed directly to your listed address and stay there. If we need you for further investigation you will be contacted. Is that understood?"

Helplessly they nodded, and with a despairing glance at Meiko, proceeded to the bus loading area, shivering in the cold night air. *Don't worry, we'll find some way to contact Liam,* Ardith told her telepathically, sensing that the others were also in rapport with her. But they all knew that reaching the Service might be impossible. They might not even be able to reach any mentors.

I'll be okay, Meiko assured them. *Don't take any chance that might lead them to you. I can tell that this guy thinks I'm in league with an underground—he hopes I am because he'd be rewarded if it were true.*

That explained his refusal to accept logic. Meiko was a more sensitive telepath than any of them except the mentors, and that might work to her advantage. All the same, Ardith was in anguish over having been forced to leave her. Only Jacob's calm, practical words brought her back to their own predicament.

"We can't stay at the addresses on our permits," he pointed out.

"No," Galina agreed. "We will have to stay in the same cities, though, since that's where we'll be transported and travel isn't allowed."

Most of them didn't know which cities those were until they looked. Ardith found that Liam had given her an address in Seattle, a place about which she knew nothing. Presumably it was the address of a Bramfield Club, though of course he hadn't named it.

Her hands were icy and her stomach felt as if she might be sick. Only a few minutes left until they would have to split up. She had been dreading this ever since agreeing to accept the mission, but she'd thought that at least she would be going to a friendly mentor who would help her get oriented and introduce her to people she might convince. Now she would be totally alone and subject to possible arrest, with little hope of finding anyone to whom she dared to speak about the Elders.

They compared the city assignments. "We're going to Portland, Oregon," Brielle said, "as was scheduled all along—we were supposed to work at a new Bramfield Club that's being opened there. There's a chance, a small chance, that we may be able to contact you."

"Contact me? How?" Ardith asked eagerly, "How could you learn my whereabouts when I don't yet know myself?"

"Contact you telepathically. Mentors can communicate consciously over longer distances than people who aren't psi-gifted. We have talked in the past about setting up links to relay information around the world, and now I think the isolated mentors will try. There's no guarantee that it will work, but Portland and Seattle are quite close together and you experienced the dreams telepathically from a distance—that's a hopeful sign."

Ardith's spirits rose. "Could you reach mentors who could contact Meiko?" she asked.

"Probably not. It's a long way from Portland to Denver, with few cities large enough for a Bramfield Club in between."

"We can't be sure she'll be held at Denver," Jacob said. "That's a civilian port, and if they think she's involved in an anti-government plot she'll most likely he taken to the Fleet prison in Earthport."

"With Fleet under the control of the dictator that would be a bad place for her to be," Fred said darkly. "The civilian police are just doing what they're told and they've been rather ineffectual since the last big emigration to the colonies. They're less likely to pursue the investigation."

"We can't afford to have it pursued," declared Jacob. "If they should really verify our identities and believe we met aliens, they would almost certainly dispose of us one way or another."

"Meiko won't tell them anything," Ardith assured him, inwardly horrified at the thought of what might be done to get information from her.

"That's just the problem. If she doesn't, they will assume she has something to hide and won't give up until they find it. Our only protection is for her to *tell* them she met aliens, which they'll dismiss as insanity."

"I'm not sure she'll figure that out," Ardith said in dismay. "I hadn't. I just thought about her being brave enough to resist questioning."

"We've got to let her know," Galina said. But just then the bus came and they had no more opportunity to talk.

~ 31 ~

On the flight from Denver to Seattle Ardith was in turmoil. There was nothing she could do for Meiko; she knew that. She must focus on how she herself was going to survive. And there didn't seem to be much prospect of keeping her freedom. If she couldn't find a place to stay before the curfew she would be sent to an internment camp, where they might or might not arrest her for having a Bramfield Club address.

At the airport she had no choice but to take a bus into the city and a robocab to the address on her travel permit. It was indeed a Bramfield Club and it was closed, not because of its involvement in mind training but because all public facilities were closed due to the lockdown. She was standing in the pouring rain wondering what would become of her when she spotted a small notice taped to the door. Thankfully, it included a phone number.

With shaking hands she pulled out the phone she'd been given on Maclairn and made the call. "I want to speak to the club manager," she said to the woman who answered.

"We're closed, and we don't know when we'll open again. We're not talking to sales reps, as I'm sure you can understand."

"I'm not selling anything. I need to talk to the manager about something personal."

"Well, if you had an appointment for neurofeedback, it's cancelled."

The managers were couples, Ardith recalled; all guests taken to Maclairn were couples. "Either the manager or the assistant will be okay," she said. "Tell them I was asked by a friend to look them up."

"All right, then. What friend shall I say sent you?"

Ardith froze. She could not give the password to a clerk, and even to mention Radnor might be risky; still he'd said his name was known to the public. In desperation she said, "Radnor. They'll know who you mean."

After a long pause a man came on the line. "We haven't heard from Radnor for a long time," he said. "I understood that he was retired. Is he back in this area?"

"No, he's on a colony world, where he lives near a long, narrow lake. He said you would be familiar with the group he works with there, what was its name?"

The man said slowly, "The Stewards of the Flame."

"Thank God!" Ardith burst out. "I've just come

from there, and I need a place to stay. When he sent me to the club he didn't know about the lockdown."

"Take a robocab to the supermarket on 32nd Avenue. I'll meet you by the front door, wearing a yellow shirt."

"My name is Ardith Moran and I'll have a dark blue duffel," she told him.

Apparently shopping for food was allowed, as there were a few people on the street near the store, all carrying shopping bags. When she got there the man in the yellow shirt was waiting for her, and she beckoned him into her robocab rather than let it go. He looked her over, puzzled. "I'm Dirk Werner. You're a Maclairnan? I didn't know they ever came, except for mentors, who are escorted."

"I'm not Maclairnan, but I was there last week. Five of us who were guests came to Earth along with two mentors and two crew members, but we had to split up, and we can't let the authorities find out where we are. It's—rather a long story, and some of it may be hard to believe. You might want the mentors here to join us before I tell it so they can judge me telepathically, unless you've had enough mind training to judge me yourself."

"It's not like Radnor not to tell us you were coming."

"Well, as you know there's no communication from Maclairn except through *Promise*, and the date wasn't set until after its last trip. I wasn't scheduled to come to this particular city, but we found out that the government would require us to go to the addresses of record on our IDs. Since mine is on LaLande VI they'd send me to an internment camp, so a Bramfield Club address had to be forged."

"By the Maclairn Foundation? I'm surprised that they have the means to do that. You really do have a lot to tell us. I think we'd better bring our mentors in now so you won't have to tell it twice."

Fortunately, he and his wife lived in an apartment in the same block as the mentors, which lessened the problem of the lockdown. The mentors, Ron and Emily, were a black couple in their eighties who welcomed her warmly. Ardith drew breath. Here it began. Either she succeeded with these people, or all she'd undergone so far had been futile. *Oh, Varel,* she thought, *I hope I can live up to what you're expecting of me. . . .*

"Has the Maclairn Foundation ever informed you about guests there called the Elders?" she asked the mentors.

Ron and Emily looked at each other, seeming at a loss for words. Finally Ron said, "Yes. Someone from Foundation headquarters came personally to tell us. It's hard to believe, but we can't doubt an official report from Maclairn."

The club managers had not been told; that was her job. She turned to them. "Fifteen years ago, as you may know, Maclairn stopped bringing in guests from Earth. It brings them now from worlds elsewhere in the universe, worlds of species much older than our own. There are many such worlds, united in an alliance called the Federation and kept secret from species too young to be viewed as equals. When our species was judged mature enough, Earth was admitted to the Federation, but this became part of Maclairn's secret because the people on Earth weren't ready to accept alien beings among us. Now, some of them are, and I am one of the people appointed to tell them."

They stared at her, unsure of whether to believe, but the reluctant confirmation from the mentors couldn't be denied. "The revelation must be gradual,"

Ardith went on. "It would cause shock on Earth if it were announced to the public all at once. And so four of us, who are not Maclairnans, were prepared to be envoys. We can provide absolute proof that we have met the Elders and visited alien worlds. But we must do it secretly—more than ever now, because the government will try to suppress the evidence and one of us has been captured."

Dirk nodded. "How can we help?" he asked.

"Hide me—not here, because the government has the club address and this one is associated with it through the phone number. And introduce me to people with mind training I can tell—the goal is to recruit as many believers as possible so that eventually they can prevent the government from concealing it. We thought we could set up meetings. We weren't expecting the lockdown, of course."

"However we hide you, you can be tracked by your ID," said Dirk, frowning.

"No, it's been hacked so that it can't be traced, and the surveillance cameras will ignore me."

"I don't see how the Foundation could afford to hire an ID forger," Dirk said. "Those guys get big money."

"Professional hackers weren't involved. There are representatives of the Elders on Earth. While a species is immature, they can't act, only observe; but once a world has been admitted to the Federation they help people who know about them, and they're experts in hacking the system for their own agents."

"You mean aliens are right here among us?" Emily exclaimed. "Do they look like people, then?"

"They *are* people, just separate species," Ardith said firmly. This was something that had to be established from the beginning. "The agents who visit the surface here have been surgically modified to pass as Earthborn. But they aren't so different to start with as you might think. Various species are of different sizes, with faces shaped a little differently, but otherwise it's largely a matter of color—there are more shades of skin and hair color between species than within any single one, but no more different than black is from white."

They all looked at her, embarrassed. Emily said, "I can't very well fail to think of them as friends, then. It just takes some getting used to."

"What did you mean about one of your group having been captured?" Dirk asked.

Ardith explained how they'd met the Elders, how it had been set up to provide proof that they existed, and how the coup had changed everything. "This is all so much more complicated than I expected," she said. "I'm not a trained undercover operative like in holos, just an ordinary person who wanted to meet aliens."

"I don't think you're at all ordinary," Ron declared.

"For now, you need a meal and some sleep," Emily said. "We've got a spare room, and it's not associated with the club because we don't give it out to anyone but our trainees."

Just before curfew Ardith went home with the mentors, leaving shortly after they did since groups larger than two weren't allowed to be out. Gratefully, she ate the hot food they served to her and headed for the bedroom. The bed was wider than the bunks aboard *Promise,* which had been narrow; the last time she'd slept in a real bed had been in Kenard's house, with Varel. . . .

"Emily," she asked, when her hostess brought in clean sheets, "Have you ever read anything by the Captain of *Estel?*"

"It's odd that you ask," Emily said. "I read

something about him on the Net just last night—it was all over the place, at dozens of sites. I'd heard of him, of course, but I'd thought his following was history. Now people are saying that his ship still exists, and has visited alien worlds. Some say he *was* alien, and that he's alive."

So the message had spread, and had grown in retelling. "He was Earthborn and had lived on Maclairn," she said, "and he was Radnor's father. He went back to Maclairn after you left there—it was he who first told them about the Elders. I met him just before he died."

Emily looked at her in astonishment. "Radnor's father? But Radnor is the son of Terry Radnor, after whom we named the neighboring planet Terry and who was lost in space before I was born."

"Terry wasn't really lost in space, he was exiled by circumstances to a planet where no one knew his true identity, and in time he acquired *Estel*. It's all one idea, you see, the belief in future mind powers—for Maclairn, for the Captain of *Estel*, and for the Elders, it's the same. He wore the flame pin of the Stewards all his life, and the Elders see flame as a symbol, too—they gave me this pendant, and when Terry saw it he said it was fitting." She held it out as she removed her tunic for Emily to see.

Emily looked down at her own pin, fastened to her shirt. "I think we have much in common with these Elders," she said. "And if belief in the Captain of *Estel* can be rekindled, that will go a long way toward making people realize that."

The next day Emily and Ron began contacting their former trainees, using a prearranged code in text messages that signaled a need to meet. A few at a time, they got together in apartments when the coast was clear, or in the supermarket under the guise of grocery shopping. The one thing they could not do as planned was DNA checking, but the people with mind training grasped the truth telepathically and were willing to accept the mentors' verification.

It proved unnecessary for Ardith to speak to them all personally; the mentors and club managers recruited more believers than she did. She wondered whether it would have gone so well if Ron and Emily had not happened to be black, a fact of no consequence in their own era but significant to them from study of their ancestors. No one they told about the Elders was left in doubt about their being equals of the Earthborn. She didn't even need to mention her love for Varel.

~ 32 ~

Word about the Elders could never have spread as it did if the police had made an effort to enforce the lockdown. But they didn't. There weren't enough of them; they had always been ineffectual and had more or less given up on law enforcement when outnumbered by the street gangs; and they had no enthusiasm whatsoever for Halorun's regime. They hated him because he had given Fleet officers authority over them. As a result, they obeyed orders from above only when they couldn't get away with disobeying them, which wasn't often because there were too few Fleet officers to supervise suburban areas and most of them also despised Halorun. As long as violations weren't too blatant they ignored them.

Halorun, though charismatic enough to have once gained the acclaim of crowds, was not an especially intelligent man. Since the coup he had become a mere figurehead. The force that upheld him came from a small group of high-ranking officers within Fleet eager to seize power for themselves and ignorant of what it would take to hold onto it. Ardith soon realized that this was not the kind of dictatorship that possessed an iron hold over the populace.

To begin with, Fleet was not a military organization. It had the form of one in its chain of command, but its work was limited to the policing of space and the operation of merchant starships. It had never done any fighting because there was no one other than criminals to fight. It consisted only of officers; there were no enlisted personnel because there was no need for troops and anything else not requiring an officer's training was done by AI.

Therefore, it did not include men and women accustomed to brutality. Its officers, when ordered to intimidate innocent citizens, were not merely reluctant to do so but at a loss as to how to proceed. They were appalled by the wholesale slaughter of the gang members, which was carried out not by them but by the police under orders from higher up, and when it became evident that they might be expected to deal with rioters or even dissidents in the same way, there was talk of mutiny. Although Fleet had executed mutineers in the past, those had been isolated cases of explorer crews stealing newly-discovered resources for personal gain. It would be less easy to put down a mass uprising.

Halorun had begun to suspect this, and ignorant as he was of history, he was not so blind as to be unaware that the classic way of shoring up a failing regime is to create a scapegoat. And there was one readily at hand, since the government had always disliked the idea of psi powers and had deplored the existence of Maclairn ever since its discovery. There being ample precedent in the evil legacy of the Klan, it was not hard to get people oppressed by the regime worked up enough to call for the extermination of telepaths. All it took was to leak the news that a colony named Maclairn was a hotbed of them.

The officers ordered to attack it were not, of course, told that for more than a century Maclairn had been defended by a ship of Fleet's own. The admiral and the few others who knew that—who had not joined the coup—had already been quietly eliminated. Expecting no resistance, Halorun sent only one cruiser to demolish the colony. When to the crew's secret relief no such colony could be found, he was mystified, but sent orders that it return victorious with news of Maclairn's demise. The recorded coordinates must have been wrong, he thought, and any Maclairnans who turned up later could be dealt with.

Ardith had told Ron and Emily what really happened and all three were dismayed by the thought that other mentors might not know that Maclairn was safe. She had no way of guessing how many Jacob and Fred had told. The hardest thing she'd had to endure since arriving in Seattle was not knowing where they were and how they were doing. As for Meiko, the best she could hope for was that Liam would somehow be able to help her,

Ron and Emily had had some success in contacting the mentors in Portland, Gerard and Brielle. The telepathic link hadn't been strong, but it had been enough to assure her that they were okay and were gathering believers. The proof, apparently, had never been necessary, at least not for people with mind training. For others it would be, so little more could be done in the way of recruiting while the lockdown was in force. Relay links were slowly being set up between mentors around the world, but so far they hadn't located Jacob or Fred..

Sentiment against telepaths was running high, as Halorun had known it would, and mind-trained people were keeping a low profile, as was the now-outlawed Estelan Party. The worry was about those with no training. As in the days of the Klan, some were killed by self-appointed vigilantes and far more were in need of refuge. The mentors took in as many as they could hide, but that was a small fraction of those believed to exist. And now there was no *Estel* to take some to safety and give hope of better days to the rest.

Except that most of them thought there was. The Net posting had gone viral in its exaggerated form, and thousands of people literally believed that the Captain of *Estel* was alive and, considering his presumed age, was probably an alien. The idea had gotten into the collective unconscious.

Despite the historic connection of *Estel* with mind powers, which the postings did not specifically mention, the government censors didn't delete them. As Ardith had hoped, they were evidently assuming that putting aliens in the same class as mind powers would discredit them both. Fortunately, it seemed not to have occurred to the authorities that it might do the opposite, as in fact it did. People had little else to console them in their increasingly-chaotic world, and if the Captain of *Estel*, who was honored by those who deplored the persecution of telepaths, said aliens were something to hope for, then so they must be.

Radnor had not foreseen this. He had taken the envoys to see Terry without any idea that the visit might be the key to success in their mission. If Terry had died one day sooner it might not have happened. Which was not the only strange and significant coincidence in Terry's life, Ardith recalled. But it was in hers, and she was a little awed by it. Still, success was a long way off. While the dictatorship lasted no amount of belief in aliens would make the government invite the Elders to Earth.

She had been on Earth four months when one day Liam appeared at their door, having found her by bypassing the hack that protected her ID. Jacob and Fred were okay, he said. An exception to the rule that only people with mind training could be told about the Elders had been made in the case of Jacob's worldwide scientific contacts, who as long-term enthusiasts for contacting ETs really needed to know; and since communications were subject to surveillance he was sending them messages about his return from the expedition worded so that they could read between the lines. Derek and Galina were in Boston at Maclairn Foundation headquarters and had taken part in notifying mentors of Maclairn's safety.

The news about Meiko was not so good. "She's being held at Earthport, where Fleet has taken over a high-security prison and is using it only for political prisoners," he said.

"Have they hurt her?"

"I know you want me to be honest, Ardith. Yes, they have. Her mind training protects her and she has not suffered from pain. Nothing obscene or crippling has been done, and since she's in the hands of Fleet officers rather than terrorists it won't be. But it's not a comfortable situation to be in."

Ardith's eyes filled with tears. "But she didn't *do* anything! If only we had gotten word to her not to keep quiet—"

"She didn't, and that's the problem. She too felt that if she admitted to contact with aliens they would consider her crazy, but it backfired. They think she's pretending to be insane to cover up involvement in underground resistance."

"But surely they've checked and learned she was really on the expedition starship. How do they think she got back?"

"They laugh at the idea of aliens, so they have no choice but to believe she's an imposter. They suspect Ivanson, who verified her presence on the ship, of falsely reporting her death, thus allowing someone else to assume her identity. They have an eye on him in the belief that he's connected to some kind of plot and will lead them to the conspirators if they can't get her to name them."

"But how do they account for her ID status showing her as dead?"

"They assume it was accidentally left unchanged when the DNA profile of an imposter was put into the database, though they can't explain how that got there when the system was thought to be secure. There is something very strange about the way this is being handled—interrogators employed by a ruthless dictator would normally have killed her by now to hide their own lack of success in figuring it out."

Appalled, Ardith pleaded, "Can't you help her escape somehow?"

"We've tried, of course, but there are few options that wouldn't require killing innocent people, which rules them out. Our main tool is bribery, and so far we've had no luck. After all, it took us three years to buy Terry's freedom from the penal colony on Draconis."

Ardith bit her lip, trying to hold back tears. It should have been her! She, at least, had evidence of having actually been with an alien. . . .

Liam picked up the gist of her thought telepathically and frowned. "What evidence, Ardith?" he asked.

She told him. "I wanted to have it in case people doubted that the Elders are the equals of humans."

"Who else knows about it?"

"Only Brielle and Meiko. Brielle went with me to see the doctor."

"You shouldn't have kept it secret from the rest of us. If anything happened to all three of you it would never have been discovered."

"I didn't think about that. It was—personal, too personal to announce casually."

"May I tell the Service, and Radnor?"

"Yes, of course." Suddenly struck by a new thought, Ardith asked, "If we could show it to the interrogators would it convince them that there *are* aliens—that Meiko is telling the truth—and let her go?"

"I'm afraid not. It's possible that some already believe she is, and are afraid to tell Halorun, fearing that he'd take his fury out on them. In any case, it's too soon to use the evidence. If the government got it now, they would simply destroy it."

Liam hesitated, then went on, "All of you are in danger, you know. The authorities have your names and they know that your IDs indicate that you're dead, which marks you as associated with Meiko by more than having arrived on the same ship—in fact Ivanson probably told them you were with her in the lifeboat if they hadn't already looked it up on the Net. They also know there's some kind of organization backing you, since tracking of your IDs has been disabled. They have repeatedly entered pseudo-IDs with your names and pictures into the system, which can't be tracked either since our hack detects them, but it's only a matter of time until they locate and repair it. I think the time has come when we have to change your identity."

"That would eliminate the basis of our mission, wouldn't it?"

"The original basis, yes. But you haven't relied on your ID and DNA, have you? And now most believers are being won over by your posting about the Captain of *Estel*. Which, incidentally, was a brilliant idea, one that I'd never thought of despite having flown with him during the years he was gaining a wide following."

"It wasn't my idea, it was Meiko's! She was the one who first suggested reviving belief in him. All I did was point out that we should do it ourselves and word what we posted."

Pain distorted Liam's face. "She never told me that. We've communicated telepathically, but that never came up. I should have guessed, since her parents were Estelans." He sighed. "Somehow that makes it harder, leaving her in prison. We can't free her separately but we could bring an end to Halorun's regime if that were the best thing for Earth."

"You could?" Ardith was startled.

"Of course . . . but if we controlled the course of Earth's history it would become psychologically dependent on the Elders and in the long run its own civilization would die out. I know this, but when people are suffering it's hard to stand by and watch."

Anguish surged from his mind into Ardith's, and suddenly, with unprecedented clarity, she grasped something she had never fully understood. "*That's* what the Oath is for," she whispered. "That's why it must never be violated, even in trivial ways—why Service members must stick to it no matter how senseless it seems or what it costs them. So that when big decisions come along, you're not torn. You do what it demands without hesitating."

Liam gripped her hand. "I wish I could tell Varel

that you understand," he said softly. "But refraining from it is one more demand I have to honor."

~ *33* ~

Liam made arrangements to change the names and photos linked to the envoys' ID implants, which would keep them safe as long as they did nothing that might cause their DNA to be checked. There was no way to change the linking of their DNA profiles to their true identities.

His far larger and higher-priority task, for which he and other agents were traveling from city to city, was to warn the mentors that they must hide. A crisis had arisen because the government had just discovered that it possessed a complete list of them. When they'd arrived from Maclairn, the few officers aware of the colony had provided their IDs, and those officers had been arrested before they could destroy the record.

"Fortunately we have an agent in Halorun's office who picked it up telepathically," Liam said. "The only reason any mentors are still alive is that they're hunting them down and plan to seize them all on the same day so as not to warn anyone. Also they want to announce it to the public as a big dramatic victory over so-called occultism."

"Do they know current addresses?" Ardith asked worriedly.

"In many cases, yes. Originally they had only the Bramfield Club addresses and those are what the mentors use when signing up for online and mobile accounts, but if they own their homes, or have home utilities in their names rather than a landlord's, their IDs will reflect it. So those people will have to move in a hurry, and all mentors will need new identities."

Ron and Emily's electricity was in their own name, and that meant finding a place to move where the landlord provided all utilities in case their new IDs were ever compromised. Seattle, like all large cities, was overcrowded, and after a day spent searching it became apparent that there were no affordable vacancies even in the aging, run-down, buildings that dominated the widespread metro area. Liam had to go on to Portland to warn Gerard and Brielle, leaving Ardith to manage the move.

It was a larger and riskier task than she had been required to take on so far, and at first she wondered whether she was up to it. But gradually, as she contacted person after person seeking someone who would take them in, she became aware that she felt more capable than she had when she arrived. She was getting used to living in danger of arrest, she supposed, or maybe contact with so many who'd had mind training was having an effect on her. Or perhaps it was just because Ron and Emily trusted her and seemed to consider her in some way extraordinary. In any case, their lives were at stake and she couldn't let them down.

All contacts had to be made in person, or by the mentors themselves through telepathy, since phone calls and Net messages could be traced, and explaining the emergency proved difficult, especially since they were asking contactees to risk arrest. Harboring a known telepath had been made a crime and unlike the trainees, whose association with the Bramfield Club had been secret, the mentors were known to be its employees. Ardith did not, of course, mention aliens in these discussions, and if anyone asked whether the Captain of *Estel* was rescuing mentors, she hedged, inwardly pleased by this evidence that belief in his return was spreading.

With time running out, they finally located rooms, though not desirable ones. The only person able and willing to take refugees from the law lived in a drab complex consisting of hundreds of identical, closely-spaced duplexes in need of paint. Moving their belongings was an ordeal since it had to be done in the middle of the night, defying the curfew, and the robocab's trip record had to be hacked—a job at which their new host fortunately proved adept since Ardith would not have known how.

The hardest part was handling the bulky neurofeedback equipment, without which the mentors would be unable to continue mind training. They were forced to leave much else behind, which the officers sent to arrest them would find; but it could not lead them to the mentors. If it occurred to the police to collect DNA evidence in order to learn who their friends were, that would link her true identity to them; but it still would not reveal either their location or hers.

Between the Service's efforts and the telepathic chains that had been set up between neighboring cities, most of the mentors on Earth escaped. A few did not, and the holonews reports of their seizure and violent deaths brought horror and heartache to the rest. For Ardith it was the lowest point of the mission so far. She'd come to accept danger, but she hadn't pictured having to stand by helplessly and watch what was done to others whose fate she cared about.

She had hated Earth and wanted nothing more to do with it. Now her personal feelings didn't seem to matter. She was more concerned about the innocent people who were trapped in dreary surroundings and who were now subject to the tyranny of its new rulers. It would almost be better if she hadn't seen the Elder worlds; when she recalled them, the contrast was unbearable. But, she realized suddenly, that was probably why the Service had shown them to her. It was to make her understand that there was both need for hope and something to hope for.

Lying awake in her tiny new bedroom, she could no longer hold back her tears. Varel would be told what had happened on Earth, and he knew she would be housed with mentors. Would they be so cruel as not to tell him she was safe? Would they even tell him if she had died? *Oh, Varel,* she thought desperately, *if only telepathy could reach from star to star. . . .* And then it dawned on her that he wouldn't need to be told. Radnor would visit him, and he would sense from Radnor's emotion whether she was safe or not. It was possible to refrain from conscious telepathy, but emotion could not be turned off.

Toward morning she fell asleep, thinking of him, and dreamed again as she had on Andoval, standing once more in the light of colored suns and sensing his thought, *We will never be apart, because the worlds intersect, you see, and this place where we are now exists in all of them.* She clutched his hand and felt again the surety that even when it was dark she would be with him in sunlight. When she woke she tried desperately to hold onto that feeling, but it faded as she became aware of where she was, knowing she could never be with him again.

Days passed, and then weeks. The one good thing that had resulted from the move was that they were now in a different neighborhood where it was possible to tell more people about the Elders. Neither the mentors nor their former trainees had ventured far from home during the lockdown, fearing that it might someday be strictly enforced. Now, since Liam had said they could include people without mind training if recommended by someone who'd had it, they had many new potential contacts. Though Ardith grew weary of telling the same story over and over again rather than holding meetings as originally planned, she was thankful for the opportunity to do so.

The majority of those who heard her story didn't need much convincing. They already believed in aliens because of the Net postings about *Estel*. "Is it true?" people asked her eagerly. "Does the Captain of *Estel* really go to alien worlds, and will we someday be able to contact them?"

"Yes, most of it's true," Ardith answered. "He went to alien worlds many times, and his ship *Estel* still does. He's gone now, but when he was dying he spoke to me and my friends, saying it was up to us to bring hope for the future to Earth."

"He spoke to you personally? You saw him, as if he were an ordinary man?"

"Yes, of course. He was a very old man who was ready to die; he didn't fear it. But he wanted his message to be passed on. He wanted it known that aliens far in advance of Earth have mind powers like we're developing and that these powers are the key to our kin-ship with them. There are people on countless worlds waiting to welcome us as friends—I know this because I am one of his heirs, and I too have visited those worlds."

Some of this would find its way onto the Net, she knew—all the more now that she and the mentors were living in the home of an accomplished hacker. There was no need for her to post anything more herself. But she wondered how long the authorities would go on assuming it was nonsense.

They were blind, she felt, because they themselves thought it was nonsense. They wanted to exterminate telepaths since underneath they sensed that citizens with mind powers couldn't be controlled, but they failed to see that the mere belief in psi invalidated everything they'd been taught about the nature of the mind. The idea of telepathic aliens struck them as a useful fantasy for distracting gullible people from the oppression to which they were being subjected. It didn't occur to them that it might have enough truth in it to arouse real opposition.

In reality, the opposition was growing. Ironically, far more people believed in the Elders than would have if there had been no tyranny to cope with. Not only had she attracted a much larger audience, but those who were exposed to the idea took it more seriously than they would have while merely apathetic. In that respect, though she hated to admit it, the takeover had worked to Earth's advantage. Furthermore, she was beginning to think that belief in the Elders might not merely stir them out of apathy, but pave the way toward eliminating the oppression that had fostered it.

Had Varel guessed this? Did he have it in mind when he told her, apparently against all reason, that she and the others could save Earth? Probably not, she decided. He had spoken of dictatorship as entirely evil. On the other hand, he'd once said that as a historian he'd learned that evils such as wars sometimes lead to developments that turn out to be good, and that couldn't have been achieved any other way. That didn't make sense, but then, a lot more about the universe didn't make sense, perhaps not even to the Eldest.

If it hadn't been for Meiko's imprisonment, Ardith could almost have been happy about their progress. But she couldn't get her mind off Meiko. She was unable to make herself believe that there was nothing they could do for her.

She had just about finished contacting what people she could reach in Seattle; it was time to move on to another city and work with different mentors. Yet she had no idea where to go or how to get there despite the travel ban, and no way to contact Liam for advice. And then, without warning, the decision was taken out of her hands.

She was returning from the market with a bag of groceries when the police car drew up to the sidewalk. Two uniformed police officers got out and seized her arms before she knew what was happening. "You've got the wrong person," she declared, trying to sound angry rather than frightened. "I haven't done anything illegal. It's not curfew yet and I'm allowed to shop for food."

"You're not allowed to do anything but come with us," declared the cop. "So there's no point in pretending you're innocent."

Seeing that this was true, she got into the car without further protest. If she really were innocent she would have no reason to resist.

They took her to the police station and thrust her into a cell without bothering to book her. With sinking heart, she realized that this meant she wasn't suspected of any local crime. Had one of the people she'd told about *Estel* turned her in? No, because none of them knew she'd done anything illegal besides being a telepath like themselves, other than to help hide the mentors, and if she were accused of that she'd have been charged immediately. So how could the police have connected her with her real ID? They must have found traces of her DNA in her old apartment, but that couldn't have told them her new identity.

What it *could* tell them was that Ron and Emily were associated with her and probably lived at her current address. Desperately she reached out to them telepathically: *Ron! Emily! I've been arrested, you've got to hide again!* Over and over she called, but got no response; evidently the police station was too far from them. She could only hope that since they weren't suspected of political conspiracy the police wouldn't bother to arrest them. The government had little interest in interest in catching specific telepaths; the purge of the mentors had been all for show.

However she'd been identified, there was no denying that they knew who she was. So she was not surprised when after several hours of waiting, two Fleet officers entered the cell and put her in handcuffs.

~ 34 ~

They took her to the airport some miles from the city. Gazing out through the rain-streaked robocar window at the grey skies and occasional tall firs that punctuated the mass of flat roofs covering what once had been countryside, Ardith wondered if she would ever see even this much of a landscape again. It didn't seem likely.

She had, of course, been thoroughly and roughly searched before removal from her cell—a rather pointless procedure since she'd been arrested on an ordinary day while least expecting it and would hardly have been carrying weapons. The handcuffs were now attached to a chain around her waist, and they were heavy as well as unnecessarily restrictive. She supposed she would have to get used to that.

Only one of the officers escorted her on the flight. He was grim-faced but did not seem the sadistic sort; she could sense that he wasn't happy about this job. Turning to face him, she ventured, "Can you tell me what I'm accused of?"

"I don't know," he replied. "They just said take you to Earthport."

"What's in Earthport besides the capitol?" Ardith asked, although she knew.

"The prison Fleet took over from the old administration, the one with super-high-tech security. The criminals convicted by courts were moved elsewhere, and the powers that be have got us locking up anybody they think might cause trouble for them." He sounded bitter. *Why* am I doing this? he was thinking. *I should be flying . . . why are they wasting a jump pilot on routine police work anyway?*

Why indeed? Ardith thought. And then, her heart starting to race, she realized what she had just done. She had picked up his thought, which he had no wish to conceal and was thus angrily broadcasting. She wouldn't have guessed he was a jump pilot unless he was telepathic.

Tentatively she probed, *How long have you been stuck on Earth?*

Since we were recalled— he cut off abruptly, dismay surging into him.

He'd closed his mind to her suddenly in the middle of a thought. He couldn't have done that if he hadn't had mind training.

There was a mind training program for Fleet officers at Moonbase, an outgrowth of the original one on Titan that had trained the initial crew of *Shepard*. Like all such programs it was staffed by mentors. And mentors were extremely careful in choosing men and women to train—they refused to accept anyone who was not both psychologically fit and of unquestionable integrity. The potential of psi for misuse was too serious a danger to be taken lightly.

It was beyond all possibility that the kind of person who would support Halorun's regime would have been given mind training.

So why was this man here as a guard when he obviously didn't want to be? Just because he would be punished if he refused? Surely not; cowards did not have the psychological qualities mind training demanded. The guard must be a real member of the underground.

You don't have to hide your mind skills, she told him, *since you've already discovered that I share them.*

He stared at her. *If you were what you seem to be, you'd have the password.*

Not all people with mind training knew about Maclairn, but underground members had probably been told. *I can't say it unless I know it won't be passed on,* she hedged.

Give me a clue, then. My name is Manuel.

Did you see the pendant they took away from me? It was shaped like a flame.

Telepathy could not convey specific words as distinguished from thoughts. Barely perceptibly, he whispered, "Stewards of the Flame."

She nodded. *Are there more like you in the prison?*

Probably, but I'm newly assigned there. If you're thinking I can help you escape—

He couldn't just let her go; the plane would be met. *Could you contact other telepaths if I ask you to? Not right away, I'm not yet sure just what to tell them.*

I couldn't give you their identity.

No, of course not. I wouldn't need to know. Just pass a message on.

Okay, I could do that.

*Ardil*ready *be dead—they'd have leaked your name to fanatics instead of arresting you.*

They want information from me first.

Stunned, he looked down at the handcuffs with helpless dismay. *Their methods of getting information are harsh. I've got to think of some way—*

I have mind training, you know—I'll be okay. Just keep in touch, and do what I've asked. And if there's any way you can, get word to the two mentors I live with that I've been arrested and they're in danger. He nodded and, sensing him to be trustworthy, she gave him their names and address.

How did you come to be living with mentors? Manuel asked. *I suppose you took them in when they had to hide.*

No, it was the other way around. I came from Maclairn.

Maclairn? Oh, my God—the colony Halorun ordered destroyed, the mentors' native world? You were lucky to escape.

It hasn't been destroyed and it can't be, though Halorun doesn't know that. It has defenses he couldn't breach.

No wonder you're keeping secrets from him! Manuel exclaimed.

After a moment's thought she decided to tell him about the Elders; the underground faction within Fleet probably didn't believe the Net postings, yet it would help if they secretly encouraged them. *Manuel,* she began, *have you seen the rumors on the Net about the Captain of* Estel *and the aliens?*

I've heard of them, of course. People will believe anything when they're desperate.

Which is fortunate, because we need people to believe—you see, the part about aliens is true.

You mean there really are extraterrestrials? That's impossible; we'd have found their planets.

They have the technology to shield their planets from discovery, as they are now shielding Maclairn.

Manuel frowned. *How do you know this?*

The Elders have been visiting Maclairn for the past fifteen years. No one on Earth was told until recently; it would be a big shock, so it has to be done gradually. I am one of four people sent here to tell the people who've had mind training.

I'm finding that hard to take in, Manuel told her. *Is it what you have to keep silent about in prison?*

No. If I tell them they won't believe me—I have a friend who's been there nearly a year, telling them, and they think she's pretending to be insane to cover some sort of plot against the government. The same will be true of me. Actually there is no plot, at least not one we're aware of. We're not guilty of anything but landing illegally and using false IDs, apart from being telepaths.

So if they ever do believe, they'll let you go?

Unfortunately, no. They're aware that belief in aliens will rouse opposition to tyranny—the only reason they don't censor the postings is that they think the idea is so silly that associating it with the mind powers the Captain of Estel *talked about will discredit his legacy.*

And you think if people believed they would demand freedom?

Yes, and more—they'd demand contact with the Elders, who cannot initiate it without being invited. It's a long story, Manuel, but contact is necessary not only to end this regime, but to save Earth's civilization from future collapse. It's the only way to give people hope for the future. I have been to the Elders' worlds, and I know.

During the rest of the flight, Ardith explained it as she had done many times before to people she'd recruited. Manuel was reluctant to believe at first, but once convinced he quickly grasped the importance of getting other Fleet officers on board. *There's a lot of discontent,* he told her. *Some of us have talked about mutiny. If the Elders are waiting for Earth to invite them, that would be a focus for active resistance. But we'd need to have the support of the public.*

Yes, Ardith agreed, *that was why I started the Net rumors.*

You started them yourself? he asked in surprise.

Well, it was Meiko's idea to revive interest in him, but I wrote the first post. We met the Captain of Estel *on Maclairn when he was dying, and that inspired us.*

Manuel was obviously impressed. *You've given me a lot to think about,* he assured her. *Don't lose heart in there—I'll stay in touch with you, and I'll try to enlist more believers.*

Thank God, Ardith thought. At least there was hope that her failure wouldn't be total. Whether they locked her up forever or killed her, the recruiting effort must go on.

All too soon the plane was landing at Earthport, and then there was a long robocar trip to the prison some distance from the commercial airport; she could see shuttles landing at Fleet's spaceport as they approached. Manuel, who looked stricken, could do nothing for her as there were two armed police officers in the car.

The acres of boxlike buildings they passed through were at least relatively new, the California desert from which they had sprung having been uninhabited until the area adjacent to the port was designated the League capital. Jacob had said that the central city containing the capitol building and the university where he taught was well-planned and actually quite attractive by modern standards, treeless though it was. She wondered if he was in touch with friends here.

The prison was a huge steel-and-concrete building several stories high surrounded by tall metal fencing that left no doubt about its impenetrability. The inner gate was AI-controlled, of course; no armed guards were present because anybody trying to pass without an expected ID implant would be automatically electrocuted. She noticed that even Manuel was nervous about going through.

Once inside, Ardith was taken to a secure intake area where female guards not wearing Fleet uniforms stripped her of the clothes she'd traveled in and performed an all-too-thorough body search before thrusting her into a disinfectant shower. She wondered if she would ever see the belongings taken from her in Seattle again; they had been inventoried but it was questionable whether they had been put on the plane. She felt naked without the flame pendant.

Clad only in a tank top and panties, she was taken unceremoniously to a small cell on the third floor. It was fully enclosed, with a tiny barred window too high to see out of. There was only one bunk, built in, so she knew she would remain in solitary confinement; yet she would have no privacy since a camera eye, protected by a metal grill, was visible in the ceiling. No doubt there was a microphone as well. In fact there was what appeared to be a speaker—perhaps she would be ignored even by guards if the AI could handle routine conversation.

It was sickening to think that Meiko had been confined in a cell like this for months, perhaps without communication except for interrogation and on the rare occasions when Liam was able to contact her. That, at least, could be remedied. *Meiko!* she cried out silently. *Meiko, are you here?*

Over and over she threw her mind into the call: Meiko, it's Ardith! Are you here? Can you sense me?

Maybe she wasn't here—maybe they had killed her. Despairingly, she had almost decided to give up when the reply came. *Ardith? I was dreaming and I heard your voice.*

It's not a dream. I'm really here.

Near the prison? Is Liam with you?

No, I'm in the prison, like you. They arrested me.

Oh, my God! Have they got the others?

I don't know. I don't even know how they found me.

I do. The ceiling voice told me they'd identified you. But they hadn't caught you and I hoped they were just trying to fool me into talking.

Little by little, Meiko silently conveyed what had happened. They had indeed found traces of Ardith's DNA in her old apartment and discovered a match with the ID record of her of her arrival in Denver, for which an alert had been issued. They had then compared that ID picture with those recorded shortly before the move by all checkout machines in the apartment area. The Service hadn't used a false picture for her new identity because it wouldn't have worked where IDs were verified by facial recognition. Thus unless she never bought food or anything else, there was no way it could have been avoided short of plastic surgery to change her face. The only puzzle was why it had taken so long for them to arrest her.

It's not that I'm not sorry you couldn't get away, Meiko burst out, *and yet—oh God, Ardith, I've been so alone—*

It must have been hell, Ardith thought. How had Meiko endured it, with no way of communicating with anybody but an interrogator? *Do you know where Liam is?* she asked.

No. I hoped you did.

Even if he came there was no way he could help them. But Manuel might be able to recruit Fleet officers who could. That was their only chance of going on with their mission, and perhaps of staying alive.

Picking up the thought, Meiko asked, *Manuel? Are there guards who care what happens to us?*

Possibly, but Manuel is new. He brought me here.

It couldn't be him, then. But sometimes, when I'm feeling very low, I hear a voice—not really a voice, of course, just telepathy, so I don't know what it sounds like or whether it's a man or a woman. It . . . tells me not to worry. That I'll be okay and someday I'll be free.

It was probably the voice of Meiko's own unconscious mind, Ardith thought, an expression of her courage. But it was a good thing if she was able to take comfort from it.

~ 35 ~

Ardith had hoped she could sleep despite the hardness of the narrow bunk and the harsh light that remained unchanging. But for two nights sleep eluded her. She'd tried some of the relaxation techniques she had learned in mind training, but with small success. There was too much that she couldn't keep out of her mind.

She had asked Meiko about the questioning, aware that she must be prepared despite her reluctance to raise the subject for fear of arousing memories better left unstirred. *Meiko . . . exactly what do they do when they question you? Are the guards very—rough?*

They don't use guards. They do it with robots.

Robots? Robots talk to you?

No. Two robots come in and grab me—they're steel and have extra arms so they could subdue a strong man, but I don't fight them. And they strap me into a restraint chair, where I can't move my arms or legs or turn my head. But they don't talk, they don't even have faces. The questions come from the speaker in the ceiling.

A live voice, not a recording?

Yes, and I'm sure it's a man, not just AI. It's a strange thing, though—I can't sense any evil in him. He must be able to turn off unconscious telepathy because I can't sense his emotions at all.

What happens if you don't answer?

It makes no difference whether I do or I don't, since I don't tell him what he wants to hear. The robots—threaten me. They turn on some kind of fire lighter that comes out of one of their arms and slowly bring the flame closer and closer while the voice goes on asking questions. They aim it toward my face but they don't actually burn my face; when they finally touch me with it, it's on an arm or a leg. I think they're trying to make me believe it will be my face next time.

But they do really burn you? Ardith asked in dismay.

Oh, yes. It would take days to heal if I hadn't had the mind training that taught me how to heal myself. And it would be awfully painful if I hadn't learned how to turn off suffering. But a flame—we've touched that before, after all. It's not as scary as it would be for most people.

Most people would have cracked after the first few times, Ardith thought. What did they think of her immunity?

Meiko answered the unspoken question. *At first I didn't react because I've heard that mentally ill people are sometimes insensitive to pain and I wanted him to think I was insane. But when they kept on, I started pretending to be in agony. Now I scream when an untrained person would scream so they won't try something worse, and you'd better do that from the beginning.*

Ardith had cringed, knowing that it was a foregone conclusion that the same thing would be done to her and unsure that she would be as brave as Meiko had been. She'd lain back on her bunk, staring at the glaring white rectangle of the window near the ceiling, and wondered how long it would be before the robots came.

But by the third morning they still hadn't shown up. There was nothing she could do but sit and worry, except when she was in touch with Meiko. Did Liam know she was here? If so, did Radnor? And if Radnor found out, would Varel sense it? She hoped not. *Oh, Varel,* she thought, *if I never get out of here don't blame yourself! I had to come to Earth, we both knew that, and we both knew there was only a small chance of my accomplishing anything. This is just something that had to happen, like the love we couldn't turn away from.*

That afternoon the questioning began. It was worse than Ardith expected it to be. To begin with, the fact that the two robots were silent, totally unresponsive to any of her reactions, was surprisingly unnerving, as no doubt had been intended. More or less human-shaped but square-headed and faceless, they towered over her like the implacable machines they were—beyond influence, she thought, even by the handlers. They were AI devices, not remotely controlled but programmed to independently do what they were designed to do as efficiently as possible. They would, she assumed, respond to signals, or perhaps to just one signal: burn the victim or don't. The specific place on the body to burn, apart from sparing the face, appeared to be random.

She had not realized that the restraint chair would be so bad. She'd assumed it was just a way of holding her still while they burned her. Actually it was torture in itself to be strapped tightly around her head, shoulders, waist, wrists, and ankles, which made all motion impossible, and left there for long minutes before the questioning even started. The robots, having no consciousness, did not get tired of waiting. They stood there humming ominously until the voice from the ceiling filled the room.

"Good afternoon, Ardith," the interrogator said. "Do you have something you want to tell us?"

"I don't know what you want to hear," she replied. Her curiosity about that was genuine.

"To start with, where is Jacob Stromberg?"

"The last I heard he was in Los Angeles," she said honestly. They already knew this; it was the address on his ID.

"Don't waste our time. We need to know how to find him."

"Well, I'd like to find him, too. I'm glad to know he's not in here."

"You're taking this very casually, Ardith," the officer said. "Do you know what will happen to you if you don't cooperate?"

"No," she declared. About this she must lie, since a new prisoner wouldn't know. That she and Meiko were telepaths must at all costs be kept secret."

"Then I think we won't waste any more time before showing you," the voice stated. "After it has happened once you'll feel more like giving us some information." Oddly, as Meiko had said telepathy revealed no evil in the man who spoke. How did he manage to hide what, if not sadism, must be a chilling indifference to the feelings of others?

The robots' red activation lights came on and they turned toward her. One appendage emerged from the nearest one, at the end of which was a brilliant yellow flame fed by some internal fuel that kept it steady.

The voice continued, "It may take awhile before that flame gets close enough to burn you. If at any time you want to change your mind about talking to us, just say something useful."

The interrogator could not have known that of all threats of injury they might have used, a flame was the least frightening to her. She had passed her fingers through flame voluntarily and had not been burned. She knew with her mind that she would be burned this time; Radnor had said that it took the backing of a large group of telepaths to achieve immunity to fire. Nevertheless, remembering the candles and the torches, remembering even the pendant she might never regain, flame was to her a sacred symbol. If it must be a symbol of resistance rather than only of joy, then so be it.

And it wasn't it as if it would be painful. She focused her mind on the visual pattern Radnor had taught her and shifted easily into the state of consciousness where pain didn't hurt, and though the flame came closer and closer until she felt heat on her face before it was deflected to sear her arm, she didn't panic. She almost forgot to scream when it touched her flesh.

When she refused to say anything more the robots released her and went away. Days passed before they returned, and she realized that this was the length of time it would have taken the burn to heal naturally if she hadn't healed it herself by mind power during the first evening—she had been careful not to let her arm be exposed to the camera, as the burn's disappearance would have revealed her psi power. She guessed that the strategy was to let the victim think she was healed and then immediately burn the same area, which would be psychologically, and perhaps physically, devastating.

Despite the cruelty of the procedure, however, Ardith sensed that the main aim of using robots was to keep interrogators from having to participate at closer range than a holoscreen. Fleet officers were not sadists. They had signed up to fly starships, not extract information from helpless victims. Until the coup they had not had to do such things, and most would have been incapable of personally inflicting pain. Whoever had devised the setup had done so to stave off widespread defection.`

She knew from Manuel, who had communicated with her several times, that many in Fleet were indeed ready to defect. The majority had never supported Halorun's regime and had gone along with it only out of inertia or fear—fear for their families if not for themselves, as there had been implied threats against them. Now they were beginning to realize that conditions on Earth were only going to get worse, and not all the atrocities took place in prisons. Little by little the Fleet crews of merchant starships sent to the colonies smuggled their loved ones aboard and did not come back. Those stationed in the colonies stayed there and could not be forced because there weren't enough cruisers left to threaten them.

Meanwhile, more and more people were turning to the legend of *Estel* for comfort, and the legend was growing. Some believers were now saying that the Captain of *Estel* would return from the alien worlds bringing ETs to rescue the people of Earth from tyranny.

If only that could be true, Ardith thought. And it could be, if the Service were willing to do it. Liam had said they could overthrow the regime, but they wouldn't. Because if aliens determined the course of Earth's history its own civilization would be permanently weakened. Its people would look back and view themselves as dependent on alien benevolence. They would have no faith in their ability to influence the future.

Yet the Elders *wanted* contact with Earth. They believed the future did depend on it. Why else had the Service sent four envoys in a crazy scheme to arouse a popular demand for contact?

During the endless hours confined without distraction in her tiny bare cell, she thought about that. More and more it struck her as a paradox.

How had it been meant to work? What if there had been no coup? She and the other envoys had been instructed to tell people about the Federation, keeping it secret because the majority didn't want to think there were aliens and the government would try to suppress the knowledge. Then, if there were enough believers to influence public opinion by the time of the next election, the information would be leaked to the media. Some people would demand that the government make contact with the Elders, and if the faction willing to comply won and declared it would welcome them, Gabriel would lead a delegation to the incoming premier.

So what was different now? There were already a lot of believers—not recruited in the way originally planned, to be sure, still they were convinced that the Captain of *Estel* might bring aliens to Earth. But this idea couldn't be leaked to the media. If it were, it would be suppressed. There wasn't going to be an election and the rulers of the regime weren't so stupid as not to recognize the presence of aliens as a threat to their power. The only reason the posts about *Estel* were allowed was the censors thought they were too silly to be true.

It was a Catch-22 situation—the Elders couldn't help against the regime unless Earth's people asked them to, and the people couldn't ask them as long as the current regime was in power . . . or could they? Suddenly Ardith began to get the glimmering of an idea.

The Service had never actually said the *government* must invite them—that had merely been implied. Such decisions are normally made by governments as representatives of the people. But the current regime wasn't representing anybody but the few in power., What the Service required was an invitation reflecting the wishes of the people of Earth themselves. So if the people—a significant number of them—asked the Elders to come, they would! What the current government said would not matter.

For a few minutes Ardith was so excited by the idea that she lost sight of its unworkability. When the flaw became apparent it struck her like a blow. Of course the people of Earth couldn't invite the aliens to come. If by some miracle she and Meiko could get word out from prison and some were willing to try, they would be shut down by the government in short order, and then all Net postings about *Estel* would be erased. For it to work they would all have to ask on the same day, even at the same hour. And the Service would have to be prepared to act immediately.

To have hoped even for a moment that the Elders could help was worse than never having seen that the barrier wasn't absolute. So she wouldn't tell Meiko. Ardith decided. Meiko had suffered more than enough without being hit by disappointment.

~ *36* ~

Day followed day, week followed week. They didn't question her as much as Ardith expected, and they had stopped questioning Meiko entirely. They left them alone; it would have been far *too* alone if they hadn't been telepathic, for they saw no one.

Her food was provided from a small built-in box next to the door with a tray that slid out automatically. It stayed open just barely long enough to remove the contents. Surprisingly, it was hot food, and the beverage was steaming. After brief investigation Ardith figured out why. The box was a microwave oven with no safety latch; any hand placed in it to defeat its closing would have been cooked.

She was in telepathic contact with Manuel from time to time. He was working as a guard, and despised it; she knew that being kept from flying was almost as bad as being in prison himself. She couldn't help wondering if the underground work he was doing was worth it, but of course he could not tell her anything about that.

Finally, after about two months of imprisonment, she woke sensing a strong new telepathic presence. Liam had come at last.

I wasn't able to get here sooner, he told her. There were people in immediate danger, and you're not, until they catch Fred. They've taken Jacob, though, and he's just been brought here.

Do you know where Fred is? she asked. She was worried about Fred; if they hadn't found him after all this time and Liam didn't know where he was either, it might mean he was in worse trouble. Maybe Ivanson had murdered him, fearing that support from an astronomer would strengthen people's belief that aliens did exist.

No, I don't, Liam admitted. *But if you can fool them into thinking that you may eventually give them a clue, do so, because their hope that you might lead them to him is all that's keeping you alive. You've never wanted me to conceal hard facts, Ardith, so I've got to tell you that once they have you all, they'll probably kill you.*

Obviously he had no hope of getting them out. Why was catching them all so important to the government? she wondered. Could it be that some officials had begun to suspect they might be telling the truth? Did they realize that the regime wouldn't be safe from the proof's exposure while any of the four who'd been aboard the lifeboat still lived?

When Liam contacted her again later that evening Ardith, craving confirmation that her reasoning about how to get help had been correct though impossible to implement, told him what she had concluded. *I know you can't alter the policy,* she assured him. *But it just seems like there ought to be some way around it, when contact with Earth is what the Federation wants.*

There was no response from Liam for such a long time that she thought he might have gone away. Finally he replied, *Actually it may not be as impossible as you think, Ardith. I shouldn't be telling you this—it's a violation to give you any hint, and it may prove merely frustrating. But we've never run into a situation like this before, where a world was taken over by a tyrannical regime just at the time when contact should be made. I think bending the rules is justifiable, and I'm willing to take the consequences.*

The consequences? For him, like for Varel—for holding to the Oath best by technically violating it? She didn't want him to get into trouble, yet if it was truly justifiable to help Earth defeat the tyrants. . . .

It wouldn't be hard to get people all over the world to demand contact with aliens on the same day, he told her. *There are ample precedents, both on the Elder worlds and on Earth, not worldwide but based on the same psychology. But there are serious pitfalls. It could go very, very wrong, apart from the difficulty of instigating it from prison. You'd be taking a terrible chance.*

She waited, her heart pounding. No risk would be too great; she was likely to be killed anyway. . . .

The risk would be to the public and not just to you, and it's one we absolutely would not take if Earth were not already considered a member of the Federation. You and Meiko are not knowledgeable enough to avoid it. Jacob may be, since he's a well-educated anthropologist. But I suspect I would need to be more closely involved than the Service would wish.

If he weren't willing to be involved he wouldn't he saying any of this. *Go on*, she urged.

I think we had better get Meiko and Jacob in from the beginning, because it's complicated and will be hard to explain telepathically. She waited, trying to be patient, while he brought in first Meiko and then Jacob, who being newly imprisoned hadn't previously been in contact with her.

I didn't know it was possible to use telepathy in a group like this, conversing with several people at once, Jacob commented.

Liam replied, *Usually it's not. We can do it because Meiko and Ardith have been isolated and stressed for a long time, which increases psi power, and because I have more ability to communicate to groups than the Earthborn do.*

After explaining to the others what they were meeting for, he went on to say why getting people to demand contact with the Elders might be possible. What he told them was astonishing to Ardith though not, as he had predicted, to Jacob. Throughout history there had been many cases of large groups of people expecting some major, usually catastrophic, event to take place on a specific day in the future, or at least in a specific year. Many had thought it would be literally the end of the world. They had prepared for it, sometimes by getting rid of all their belongings because they believed they wouldn't need them. Some quit their jobs, sold their homes, and traveled to a place where they thought supernatural beings would appear out of the sky. Or they retreated to the woods with supplies and camping equipment because they thought that was the only way they could survive the coming event. When the predicted day arrived and nothing happened, many stuck to their belief; they just thought that the date had been figured wrong or that their own actions had somehow staved it off.

Most of these prophecies had been based on religion. People took portions of religious writings too literally, though different groups had different interpretations of the same texts and rejected all conflicting ones. And some were based on what were believed to be new revelations. But other predictions had been associated not with religion, but with omens like the appearance of comets or even with artificial milestones such as the year 2000.

Well, we don't want people to think there is anything religious about the Elders coming, Ardith declared.

No. You don't. But if you are not careful, some of them will. Alleged visitations of extraterrestrials have been said to involve "gods from outer space" for hundreds of years. The idea is well established in the collective unconscious. If you say aliens are coming to help Earth. that is what people will think.

Or that they're messengers appointed by God, like angels, Jacob added.

Yes. It goes without saying that such an interpretation would be disastrous, Liam agreed. *Apart from the fact that it belittles actual religious belief in help from God, it would create exactly the conception of the Elders that we need to discourage—the idea that we come as saviors instead of simply as friends.*

Yes, Ardith reflected, and it would indeed be hard to avoid. Moreover, Liam explained, there had been cults that literally believed they would be picked up by UFOs at a specific time, and some of their notions had been sick. In the most notorious cases the members had all killed themselves on the appointed day because for some reason they thought the UFOs would take only their spirits.

That's horrible! Meiko protested. *Nobody would think we're connected to anything like that.*

I'm not so sure, Jacob replied. *The people getting the message telepathically wouldn't, but the Net form of it would have to go to the general public, and a lot of people don't like the idea of meeting aliens. They might spread the wrong sort of rumors.*

How did belief in predictions spread in the past? Ardith asked. *There wasn't any Internet until near the end of the twentieth century.*

Usually there was a fanatic, charismatic leader. At first groups that specified a particular day were small. Later, or if only the year was named, it spread from writings or word of mouth. There were also cases where it happened through radio broadcasts. But once belief in a prediction had affected enough people to get into the collective unconscious, it spread even more through unconscious telepathy. And now, of course, it can reach that point much faster if a Net post goes viral.

The posts about the Captain of *Estel* were already viral, Ardith realized. And there was already a growing network of telepaths. But just spreading a message wouldn't be enough. People would have to *do* something to invite the Elders, not just wish for them to come. And if they did anything the authorities didn't like, wouldn't it lead to violence?

How could people go about demanding contact with the Elders? she asked. *They'd know better than to expect the government to listen to them.*

There would have to be mass demonstrations, Jacob replied. *People would have to gather in cities all over the world at the same time, carrying picket signs. There wouldn't be enough police, let alone Fleet officers, to deal with them.*

But there would be some. And they'd arrest people for violating the lockdown even if they didn't object to the demand.

I don't think they'd attempt mass arrests as long as the demonstrators were peaceful—there wouldn't be enough jail space. But if anyone started trouble, it might escalate.

Why would someone start trouble? Meiko asked.

Because they hate the regime and would be looking for an excuse to let off steam, Jacob declared. *That's why a lot of them would be demonstrating in the first place. It has happened over and over again in the past—any time someone organizes a demonstration for a worthy cause, troublemakers come along and turn it into a riot.*

If people who are violent get arrested it's their own fault, Ardith declared. *We don't need to protect them.*

Once they began arrests the police might grab innocents, Jacob pointed out, *and they might call for reinforcements with lethal weapons.*

The Service can put up force fields around specific areas in the major cities to prevent reinforcements from arriving, Liam informed them.

Meiko argued, *Surely there'd be armed officers on the gathering sites to begin with. The message has to be public to get people to come, so wouldn't the police be ready for them?*

The whole scheme depends on the authorities not believing there are any aliens to contact, Liam pointed out. *They still consider the idea of contacting them a useful distraction to keep people's minds off the regime—they won't dare to take action that might suggest they take it seriously.*

So would the mere gathering of crowds with signs saying they'd welcome the Elders be enough of an invitation to act? Ardith questioned.

In this case, yes, because the people have no voice in the government.

So then what will the Service do? How will it make contact that the government will try to prevent?

If the public's demand is clear, our agents can simply show up at the League capitol using personal force fields and insist on seeing the legitimate Premier.

But the agents have been modified to look Earthborn, Meiko protested. *People won't realize that they're alien, let alone learn to accept different species.*

The crew of the Service mother ship, and the agents aboard who study Earth from orbit, have not been modified, Liam explained. *We will send them, not the few who have been working undercover on the surface.*

I think the Premier may be in prison, Jacob put in.

Yes, Liam informed them. *He's in this prison, along with the rest of the elected League officials. The only action we'd take apart from holding meetings would be to get them out. And you too, of course."*

Ardith's heart lifted. Somehow she had not thought that far ahead. She had assumed that if the Service stepped in they would get her released somehow, but she hadn't pictured it being immediately as part of ousting the regime. Still, it would be a long time before such a plan could be carried out.

~ 37 ~

There was a limit to how long a group telepathic meeting could be maintained, so reluctantly they agreed to continue the discussion the next day. Ardith felt too excited to sleep, but eventually she did drop off and slept better than she had for weeks. For the first time there was hope! There was something they could actually do to affect Earth's future and make all they had gone though worthwhile—and if it worked it might mean their release.

It was still dark outside when she was awakened by an insistent telepathic call. *Ardith! Ardith, wake up!*

Liam? she responded sleepily.

But it wasn't Liam. It was Manuel. *This is important,* he told her. *Something's about to happen. You will be questioned before morning, and you must not believe what the interrogator tells you. It is all for show, and if you put on a good act you'll be okay.*

I don't understand—

I haven't time to explain, and I wouldn't even if I could. It will be frightening, and you'll react more convincingly if that's genuine. But inside, you need to know things aren't what they seem.

That was all he would tell her. *Warn your two friends,* he concluded. *I can't reach them telepathically because I've never met them, so you'll have to do it. Remember, more people than you three will be in danger if any of you reveal knowing that the interrogator won't make good on his threats.*

She had barely time to pass the message on to Meiko and Jacob before guards appeared at her door—human guards, who'd never come in the past, rather than robots. After allowing her to put on a short-sleeved jumpsuit to cover the underwear that was normally all she was given, they handcuffed her behind her back and led her through seemingly endless passageways to a small room on a lower floor.

She was left alone; the others hadn't arrived yet. It was a strange room with no outside windows but a very large one in the wall of an adjacent room that was dark. Puzzled as to its purpose, she was attempting to peer through when Meiko was thrust into the room and then Jacob. Absorbed in seeing them for the first time since their parting at the spaceport, she'd turned away from the window when suddenly a bright light came on in the room beyond. Meiko, who was facing it, gasped in shock. "Oh, my God!" she burst out.

Ardith turned, and she too gasped, for the purpose of the room was now all too clear. It was an execution chamber. She had seen similar ones in crime drama holos. It contained an empty gurney equipped with restraint straps and a wall panel behind which medical equipment was undoubtedly ready. This was where they killed prisoners by lethal injection.

The window room they were in was the witness area, where families of condemned prisoners and their victims were permitted to watch while the death sentence was carried out. "If they're going to execute us why are we here, together, and not in there, one at a time?" Meiko whispered.

Silently Ardith assured her, *They're not going to execute us. Manuel told me they would just threaten. Probably they think seeing where it would happen will scare us.*

They're right, Meiko responded.

That's good—we mustn't hide our fear. He said it's important for it to look genuine, that other people could be in danger if it were known that we were warned. But inwardly she wondered how reliable Manuel's source was. Liam had said they would be killed as soon as Fred was caught and Fred wasn't here, but he might be enroute to the prison. Or they might have given up hope of ever finding him. She trusted Manuel, but she knew that Liam had far greater resources for gathering information.

"Good morning," said a voice from the ceiling speaker. "This is the last morning you three will ever see. We are tired of waiting for you to provide us with the information we need. It's apparent that you'll never give it to us. So we are going to kill you here and now. Who wants to go first?"

During this speech Ardith had been getting more and more shaky, and now she felt her knees would collapse. It was the voice of her regular interrogator! Meiko too recognized it, and seemed on the verge of breakdown.

Something had gone wrong. Either Manuel had been given false information, or personnel assignments had been changed at the last minute. She had thought his friends might have managed to substitute a sympathetic guard for whoever was planning to threaten them, but that had evidently fallen through. And there was no chance that their regular interrogator did not intend to do what he said he would.

"No volunteers?" the voice asked. "Then since Meiko has been here the longest, she will be given the honor."

"No!" Ardith burst out. "Please, don't take Meiko—"

"Can you tell us something that might change my mind?"

The strategy was now clear. He hoped that although they wouldn't break under threat to themselves, they might be less immune to threats against friends, particularly when forced to watch those friends being killed. This was going to be a long drawn-out process. And of course none of the envoys had any knowledge of an anti-government plot. They couldn't have talked about it even if they had wanted to.

The door of the room opened to admit the robots; as always, Fleet officers would not be required to personally commit any acts of violence. The robots seized Meiko and carried her, screaming convincingly, into the execution chamber. Though it seemed apparent that Manuel's expectations wouldn't be fulfilled, they had to keep up the pretense of weakness so as not to reveal that they'd been warned. It was too bad, Ardith thought, that if they must lose their lives they could not at least keep their dignity.

Mock executions are an old ploy, Jacob declared, *though it's been done more by terrorists than in prisons. Holding a gun to someone's head and shooting blanks, that sort of thing.*

I'm not sure this isn't a real one, Ardith replied. *You're not familiar with the man's voice—*

Well, that's just it. There's a hole in his logic. He said they're tired of questioning us and are sure we won't talk, but I've been here less than two days and I haven't been questioned at all yet.

That *was* strange. Why hadn't they tried to get information from Jacob? Maybe they thought it would save time if he saw the women killed first so he'd know they weren't bluffing. It was certainly unlikely that they would kill him before making an attempt to break him.

Meiko had been strapped to the gurney and one of

the robots, revealing an arm with more dexterity than its regular ones, was inserting an IV in her arm. "Please, please don't kill me!" she begged. It was what people threatened with death usually did in holo dramas so Meiko had to, but Ardith had never seen any sense in it. No killer would pay any attention to a victim's pleas, except perhaps to take a warped satisfaction in them.

Ardith could not be sure how much of Meiko's response to her situation was acting and how much was the result of real terror, but she sensed that her terror was very intense. *Meiko, it will be okay,* she insisted. *Manuel promised me things wouldn't be what they seemed to be.*

But telepathy cannot project lies, and she was lying when she implied that she still believed Manuel.

"Last chance," the voice informed them. "What's flowing into your veins now, Meiko, is simply a harmless saline solution. Once I give the signal drugs will be added, and then it will be too late for regrets."

Ardith's knees were weak and she hoped she could remain standing until they came for her; any chairs the room normally held had been removed. Would she feel the moment of Meiko's death? she wondered. People who were close telepathically often did, she'd been told, even from miles away. And would it be painless? Radnor had said the mind training wouldn't work for a person who was semi-conscious. Oh God, she prayed, let her not feel any pain. . . .

Jacob, beside her, was keeping his thoughts to himself. His face was impassive, and she tried to keep her own equally so. She had lost sight of the need to put on an act.

The voice counted down from ten to one before the signal was given. When it reached zero Meiko's body went limp. And Ardith did feel it. She'd sensed the presence of Meiko's mind even when she wasn't intentionally communicating, and then suddenly . . . nothing. There was no sense that anyone was there.

Ardith, it could be just an anesthetic, Jacob speculated. But she was past listening. She would be taken next; even now Meiko's body was being removed. It was time, she supposed, to make her peace with the fact that her life was ending.

She had never thought much about death. She feared it because it was human to fear it. But Terry hadn't been afraid. Was that because he'd accomplished so much in his life, while she had accomplished very little even of the mission to which she'd committed herself? Or had he known something most people didn't know about what would come after? Did the Eldest know? When he blessed her, had he guessed her mission might end in death and intended her to feel that wouldn't be an irrevocable evil?

"All right, Ardith, it's your turn," said the voice. "Now that you know we'll really do it, have you anything to say?"

"Just what I've already said," she replied. "I visited alien worlds and I know that in the future Earth will be like them. There doesn't need to be a plot to overthrow Halorun—once people make friends with the aliens they'll wake up and get rid of him themselves."

"So you persist in this fantasy even in your last words. Very well, Ardith. You can't say you weren't warned."

The robots returned to the room and took her. Belatedly she remembered that she was supposed to act scared rather than defiant, just in case Manuel wasn't mistaken. But she really didn't think she looked as if she'd been told she would escape. More likely she looked exactly the way she felt—not terrified, but sad, sad for all that was left undone in her life, all that might have been, if things had been different. . . .

They dragged her to the gurney and strapped her down. As the needle went into her arm she became aware that her last thoughts would be not of the failed mission but of Varel. *Oh, God, Varel, I love you—I will love you even beyond death, if there is a beyond. But I hope you never have to know how I died. . . .*

*

When, slowly, she came back to consciousness, she wondered if this was the afterlife. If so it wasn't very promising. No tunnel, no bright light, just a dark, low enclosure and a feeling of motion punctuated by jerks. Her stomach heaved and if she hadn't known better she would have guessed that this was seasickness.

Meiko and Jacob lay close beside her. As her head cleared she became aware that they were no longer in the prison; the motion and the sounds around them made plain that this was a moving vehicle. *I think it's the medical examiner's van*, Meiko told her. *I came to in the prison garage before they put me in it, though I pretended to be still unconscious.*

Medical examiner? That's who writes death records and takes bodies to mortuaries. They're not going to cremate us or bury us alive, are they? For a moment she feared they might and was appalled by the idea of being killed twice.

I don't know who they are, but one of them is wearing a Fleet uniform, Meiko replied.

After what seemed like a long time the van stopped in a place that was silent. The rear door slid open, revealing a dimly-lit garage, and two men lifted Meiko out. Ardith heard her shriek of surprise, and then she herself was being carried and she looked up into the familiar brown face of the man who held her.

It was Fred.

Part Six: Estel

~ 38 ~

Ardith had only a few moments to be astonished at the sight of Fred before being hit by an even bigger shock. "I hope you'll forgive us for the way this had to be done," the Fleet officer told the three of them, now sitting dazedly on a bench near the vehicle in which they'd arrived. "The last part was rough, but the audio was being heard by prison authorities so I couldn't give you any hint that you weren't being executed— not even through telepathy. If they'd caught on, they'd have carried it through just to spite me."

His voice was the voice of their long-time interrogator.

"Meiko, I believed you from the beginning," he said, "but unfortunately, so did Halorun. Like many insane people he has a notion that space aliens are out to get him. When he heard that you said there really are such beings, he thought you might have telepathic contact with them and ordered us to kill you immediately. I was able to save your life by convincing him that you were involved in a human plot against him, but I knew that would work only as long as I was trying to force you to name the conspirators in a way that looked realistic."

"Andrew hated to hold you so long, but he couldn't act until we found Jacob in case he was arrested later," Fred added. "He would have been marked for execution and we won't get a second chance to rescue anyone."

"I could tell from the start that you'd had mind training and wouldn't suffer pain from what I did to you," the officer said, "and in fact I sensed telepathically that you had no fear of flame, which was why I chose it over stressors that might have been harder for you to deal with. I couldn't let my assistants question you because when you didn't crack they'd have tried something worse. By the way, the name I go by is Andrew, and under my legal name I am, or was, the prison's chief intelligence officer. I can't go back, as they may have discovered the substitution of drugs."

"I somehow knew all along that you didn't *want* to harm me," Meiko said.

"To reveal that I was faking the threats would have put us both in danger—I wasn't sure you could resist probing by other telepaths. But I tried to reassure you telepathically when I could."

She stared at him. "It was *you*! The voice that came to me sometimes—"

"I couldn't stand thinking of you locked up in there alone," he admitted. "God knows how much stress we'll all undergo while this regime lasts, but I do what I can to minimize suffering I'm forced to inflict. He turned to Ardith "I held off ordering your arrest for as long as I could, but there was a limit to the time I could get away with saying surveillance might give us leads to other conspirators."

"Is there a real underground resistance group?" Jacob asked.

"Sure there is," said Fred. "We're it. Andrew is

the leader and he brings in all the people with mind training he can find. I've been in for about a month and now you're members, too. If the government finds out about the drugs they'll hunt for you harder than ever hoping you can lead them to him, but we've got a place to hide you."

"Are you in touch with the Service?" Ardith asked.

"No," Andrew said. "Fred told us about Liam but we have no way to contact him. Until you recruited Manuel we hadn't known about the Service, or the shielding of Maclairn, or anything more about the Elders than what Meiko said. The timing of your arrest, in view of his assignment to transport you, proved very fortunate, Ardith. We needed to be aware of what was happening, and Meiko couldn't enlighten us since it would have been too risky for me to reveal myself to her."

"Liam's here now," Ardith told him. "He came yesterday, and last night the four of us had a long telepathic discussion about an idea we have for getting rid of Halorun."

Andrew stared at her in amazement. "Getting rid of Halorun? We understood from Fred that the Service can't intervene in Earth's affairs."

"It can't unless the people of Earth invite the Elders to come. It's protecting Maclairn only because the Maclairnans did invite them fifteen years ago and they've been visiting there ever since. Technically it can't tell us how to get Earth to request contact when the government won't, but I thought of a way around that and Liam is giving us more advice than he's really supposed to."

"My God, Ardith. Half of Fleet has been searching for a way to end Halorun's regime ever since the coup, and you, from prison, have figured out how to do it?"

"Well, there's no guarantee it will work, and Liam says it's risky. But we were sent here to establish contact between Earth and the Elders, and the coup spoiled the original plan. So we have to do *something*. We committed ourselves twice in formal ceremonies. We can't just give up."

Slowly, Andrew said, "I've wondered how it was possible that two young women with no apparent background in such affairs could take a prolonged ordeal as calmly as you did. I knew you weren't suffering physically and that the screaming was an act, but nevertheless you believed you were in danger of being killed—and the isolation in itself must have been agonizing, even though you're telepathic. Mind training accounts for some of your strength, but we've all had that, and I'm not sure we'd be as composed."

"We were blessed by the Eldest, the wisest and most psi-gifted telepath on the Federation worlds," said Meiko. "What he gave us can't be put into words, but it was—overwhelming. I knew while it was happening that I'd never be the same as before."

"Besides, what the Elders taught us makes a difference," Ardith said. "We've seen their worlds, seen what Earth will become if there's contact. And we've been told what will happen in the long run if there isn't."

"Then it's time for us to start thinking about your plan."

"Someone had better pick up Liam," Jacob broke in. "He'll have worried when he couldn't contact us this morning, and then if he asked around and was told we've been executed—"

"Of course. Fred, can you find him if he's near the prison?"

"Yes, we've had enough telepathic contact for that to be possible, though it would be best if Jacob came along. We'll have to get moving if we're to beat the curfew."

"Okay. Bring him to the safe house, Fred. We'll go on ahead."

They took the van, which was not a real medical examiner's vehicle but had been painted to look like one, hoping it would be less likely than a car to be challenged if they were out late. Meanwhile, Andrew took Ardith and Meiko to a safe house a short distance from the garage, and they told him what they'd discussed about getting people to gather on a given day to demand contact with the Elders.

"It might be possible to mobilize the public," Andrew agreed. "I can't judge how the Elders would respond, of course, but if Liam thinks it would work, it's worth trying—provided we can be sure that all these people aren't going to be slaughtered when Halorun gets wind of it. He's paranoid, as all self-appointed rulers are, and he'll lash out at anyone he perceives as a threat, just as he did in Meiko's case."

Ardith frowned. "It's odd that he condemned her for being a link to aliens when he allows the Net postings to stand."

"Not really. Reasoning from conventional premises tells him that aliens are mere fantasy, so he believes talking about them will distract people from the real problems his regime is creating. At the same time, his paranoia makes him think that if there are any aliens, as Meiko claimed there are, then they're coming after him and she might help them find out where he is."

Exhausted though she was from the day's stress, Ardith felt too keyed up about their plan to go to bed before discussing how to put it into effect. The relief of knowing they might fulfill their commitment after all overshadowed all other thoughts. Unconsciously she put her hand to her throat as she always did when thinking of that commitment, feeling for the flame pendant that was not there. And suddenly she was struck by the realization that it might not be lost forever after all.

"Andrew," she said, "do you have any means of getting back the things they took away from me in Seattle?"

"Possibly. They'd have been routinely stored by the police, and I have police contacts in most cities. Is there something in particular that you need?"

She explained about the pendant "We all had them, and I know Meiko has missed hers, too.. A flame symbolizes human mind potential to both the Elders and the Maclairnans; Radnor said it's a link between them."

"Radnor! Have you four seen Radnor?" Andrew asked in amazement.

'Yes, he was our mind training instructor on the Elder world Ydoril."

"He was mine too, when he was working on Earth— it's no longer enough to say 'it's a small world,' I guess! He often wore a small lapel pin in the form of a flame, but he didn't say what it meant. Now I begin to understand a little better what the goals of contact are, and why it's worth the price you and Meiko have paid, the price all of us may yet pay."

Shortly after dark Fred and Jacob arrived with Liam, who had indeed believed the three had been executed and had been about to leave the city. After introducing him to Andrew and eating a hasty meal of fast food that Fred had picked up, they settled in the living room to make plans.

"Weren't we told in the beginning to keep the

presence of aliens secret until Gabriel leaks it?" Fred objected. "Saying the Captain of *Estel* met them is one thing, but announcing a date when they'll arrive is contrary to our instructions."

"Your mission was designed before the dictatorship took over," Liam replied. "You're not obligated to follow the original plan."

"I don't see how the degree of public support for the Elders will have any effect on the views of the present government."

"It won't," Jacob agreed. "But if there's enough for the Service to step in and restore the legitimate government, it will have a big effect on its officials, who in the past were opposed to psi and presumably to contact with aliens."

"Are we sure Gabriel will go along with all we talked about?" Ardith asked Liam. "Deploy force fields, appear if the public demands contact with the Elders, and put the elected officials back in power? Maybe you should ask him before we get too far into this."

"No," replied Liam. "We can't tell him any of it. We have to force his hand. If the posting has gone viral he'll have to put up the force fields on the stated day to prevent bloodshed. And if the public does invite contact he'll have to respond because that's what the aim has been all along."

Dismayed, Ardith protested, "You're saying we'll be acting without Service authorization! You can't help us with that—they'll accuse you of breaking the Oath."

There was a long pause. Then Liam replied, "I'm already past the point of no return, Ardith. I have been, ever since I told you this might be possible."

"But you said you think it's justifiable!"

"And I do. But even if Gabriel agrees that it is, he

couldn't legally condone it, so to protect him I must keep all knowledge of it from him."

"I'm not sure what oath you're talking about," Andrew put in. "What law would you be breaking?"

"Members of the Service take a lifelong oath to put the best interests of any world they're concerned with above all other considerations," Jacob explained, "and it's assumed that intervention is never in a world's best interests unless it has been specifically authorized by the Service directorate."

"The Service can't just dismiss unauthorized action," Liam said. "If we could intervene as we choose without consequences, everyone would place their own judgment above the policies that protect the worlds we visit."

"How can policy be more important than doing what's necessary to prevent harm?" Ardith protested.

"It's not. As you yourself once acknowledged, the Oath lifts the burden of the decisions. But some-times we must carry that burden. There is a saying in the Service that the words of the Oath are anchors, not shackles. We don't give up our conscience or our free will."

"Yet they'll penalize you for exercising it, as they did Varel? Merely for helping us?"

"Do you think I'd get involved just to help you four? By advising you I'm taking on responsibility for the fate of thousands of people who are not now in immediate danger, not to mention creating a situation where a wrong move could set contact with the Elders back for many years. If I didn't feel it's this world's best hope, I'd stick to observing."

She flushed. She hadn't grasped the magnitude of the risks; she had been so thrilled by the thought of fulfilling her mission that she'd failed realize the stakes were so high. Was she crazy to think her idea could influence history—to ask Liam to incur censure by the Service to which he'd devoted his whole life?

Liam continued, "In a few rare cases of minor action that prevents serious harm, yet has no potential to cause more harm, it can be overlooked, especially if the agent is young and inexperienced. For a veteran agent who precipitates a major intervention that could easily go wrong, however, there can be no forgiveness. If that were allowed, there would be many cases, and in some of them the harm would occur, as it may in this one."

"What will happen to you when it's over, Liam?" Meiko asked.

"I will be dismissed from the Service. There is no other choice."

"Radnor said being dismissed would destroy Varel, that it would be a disgrace," Ardith said sadly.

"Varel is a young man with a long, brilliant career ahead of him and no ties to anything else. I am already retired and I spent most of my life masquerading as Earthborn, even to the extent of surgical alteration. My allegiance is to Earth and its colonies more than to Ydoril."

Tears stung her eyes. "Where will you go?"

"To Maclairn, of course. Radnor has said I'll always be welcome in his house, and I'll be happy to live out my life there, as Terry did. I can still fly *Estel;* it belonged to Terry, not the Service—when they got him released from prison they deeded it to him, and he left it to me in his will."

It took a moment before the implications struck her. Then, in awe, Ardith stated, "Liam . . . you're the Captain of *Estel!* Really. You could lead the Elders here the way people are expecting."

~ 39 ~

Ardith was feeling dizzy, partly with excitement about this new idea and partly with the aftermath of having expected to die and of recovering from drugs strong enough to have simulated death. People's voices receded into the background. Dimly she heard Andrew say, "We all need sleep before we make any decisions. We'll be safe here for a few days at least; I've got agents watching our backs."

"I suppose there'll be people trying to arrest you," Jacob said.

"Of course. But I haven't led an underground resistance group for months only to worry about having played a trick on the authorities that saved three lives. We'll be okay, or as near to okay as opponents of an oppressive regime can ever be." After a pause Andrew continued. "But I'm a little concerned about Ardith. All of a sudden she looks stricken—is it just the reaction setting in, or is she close enough to Liam to be deeply hurt by a prospect that didn't sound very terrible?"

"It's not Liam's fate that hurts her so much. It's the reminder of what happened to her lover, Varel. He broke the Oath by falling in love with her, as it doesn't allow members to make commitments to people outside the Service. The terms of his probation are that he can never again communicate with her in any way; if he violates them he will be dismissed. And as Liam said, dismissal would be worse for Varel than for him."

"That seems unjust. It sounds to me as if they punished her as much as him for something that wasn't her fault."

"Have you never caused grief to someone who didn't deserve it, Andrew?"

"You know better than to ask me that, considering what job I was assigned to."

"Then you're aware that it's not a matter of who deserves what, but of choosing the lesser of evils." Jacob went on, "Just as Meiko and Ardith didn't deserve what you put them through in prison, Ardith and Varel don't deserve the pain their separation is causing. But the Service must consider the fact that the acts of its agents affect the well-being, sometimes even the survival, of worlds. And so once an agent's self-discipline has been questioned, it must be demonstrated on an ongoing basis from that day forward."

"Ardith has come to terms with the situation," Meiko said. "She and Varel believe their love will show people who assume aliens are strange creatures that the Elders are our equals, even when there are physical differences. So she goes out of her way to tell doubters that she made love with an alien. She says she's sorry that it's genetically impossible for her to have his child."

Thoughtfully, Andrew said, "There may be some value in that. I confess to wondering, when I first heard about the Elders, whether I could view them as the equivalent of human beings. They could be good and wise and still not be suitable as sex partners. I thank you, Meiko, for setting me straight on this."

It was luxury for Ardith and Meiko to sleep in real beds again after the long weeks of hard, narrow bunks. They shared a room in the safe house and didn't wake until long after the normal breakfast hour. Fred had scrambled eggs and pancakes waiting for them, and had even been able to obtain a few bite-size pieces of synthetic ham.

They found the others in the living room, where they'd waited for everyone to be present before going on with plans. The idea of Liam flying *Estel* was exciting to all four of the envoys. "Oh, yes!" Meiko insisted. "It will attract a lot more people if we can say, honestly, that the Captain of *Estel* is coming."

"It would give exactly the impression we don't want," Liam declared. "A savior coming out of the sky? That's a classic motif of religion. It would strike many people as blasphemous."

"I don't think so," Jacob argued. "People already believe in the Captain of *Estel,* and they don't think of him in a religious sense. During all the years you traveled with him, you never encountered anyone who viewed him as a religious figure, did you?"

"No, but now that he's dead, it's different. He's at the very least a saint in some people's eyes, though he'd be horrified to think so."

"You wouldn't claim to be Terry, though," Ardith pointed out. "We'd say clearly that you are the new Captain who inherited his ship. And you wouldn't be promoting his teachings, just proving that he was a friend of the Elders. He never mentioned them on Earth or its colonies, so it's important for people who don't like the idea of aliens to know."

"That's true," Liam admitted. "But before we even talk about this I'd have to find a way to get *Estel* here, which would require me to go back for it. And that's not possible since I can't get transportation without Gabriel finding out that I'm up to something."

"Who's flying it while you're gone?"

"A Fleet officer from *Shepard* who has pledged allegiance to Maclairn. It wouldn't be safe for him to go near Earth."

"Well, now there's no reason why Maclairn shouldn't get involved," Ardith suggested. "All the reasons they didn't want to have gone away. So can't some Maclairnan bring it?"

"Maybe, but there's no way to communicate with Maclairn except through the Service ship near it,"

True, Maclairn had no ansible. "Can you communicate with that ship from here?" she asked.

"Yes, we do have the right to send private messages for transmission to family and friends on Ydoril."

"Then maybe you could send one to Varel, and he could contact Maclairn. He's allowed to do that, isn't he?"

"Od course. But Ardith, think of what you're saying! I'd be asking him to take part in a plot to deceive the Service, when he's already on probation for having violated the Oath."

Ardith gasped. How could such an idea have even occurred to her? Varel would agree to do it—she was sure of that, because it would benefit Earth—but he might well be caught. She sank back on the sofa, suddenly aware that despite the long sleep she was still depleted. Her judgment hadn't been up to par. Was anyone's? They had all been under extreme stress the past two days, even, or perhaps especially, Andrew. Andrew had seemed to think the plan was feasible, but was he now fit to evaluate it accurately?

"Don't you have other friends acquainted with people on Maclairn?" Meiko asked.

:None that I'd ask to get involved with this, even without saying why I need *Estel*. I can't be sure our messages would remain private,"

"There's another way we might get hold of it," Fred was saying. "*Promise* is still in a parking orbit with Galina registered as captain. Could she and Derek take it back to Maclairn?"

"Does anyone know what has happened to Galina and Derek?" Meiko inquired.

"The last I knew they were at Maclairn

Foundation headquarters," Liam said. "If they're still there I can get in touch with them through the mentors. They may have moved on, though, and in any case the main difficulty would be getting a shuttle up to *Promise*."

"Well, that could be arranged," Andrew said. "I have people in all branches of Fleet."

"As far as finding them goes, you could have them arrested the way you did me," Fred pointed out, "assuming Liam knows their current identities."

Liam stared at him, horrified. "I won't be a party to putting them at risk of prison," he declared. "Andrew's no longer in a position to get them out."

"I was never even in jail," Fred said. "He used Fleet resources to locate me and then assigned underground members as the arresting officers. They brought me straight to a safe house."

"Is there any doubt about these people being willing to return to Maclairn?" Andrew asked. "If not, it would be easiest to take them directly to a shuttle."

"Let's backtrack here," said Jacob. "Assuming that we might be able to bring *Estel* near Earth, what exactly do we want to do with it? Just make broadcasts? How will people know they're authentic? Anybody, in any ship, could claim to be the new Captain of *Estel*."

"Not to mention the fact that Fleet could easily capture or demolish it," Fred added. "That could be done by higher authority than Andrew's before he even knew it was happening."

Everyone froze. It was like falling from the top floor of a building without a gravity lift. "I guess it's not very practical," said Meiko in a small voice. "But it seemed so *right*, so natural a way to influence Estelans . . . ."

Ardith drew a deep breath. "And it *is*," she said.

"It doesn't matter whether it's practical. Miracles aren't brought about by being practical or logical, and let's face it, it will take a miracle to pull off a scheme like ours."

They looked at each other in silence. Then Meiko admitted, "We'd be asking Liam to risk his life."

Liam said, "Terry often told me that when it was time for him to die, he'd rather die flying *Estel* than any other way. It didn't happen like that, but I wouldn't really mind if it did for me. *Estel* is an old friend—I flew it by myself for the three years Terry was imprisoned on Draconis, you know, as well as the many years as his copilot. And if he were here for us to ask him whether this is a risk worth taking, I think he'd say it is."

"It would be a way of honoring him to use his ship and his words to free Earth from tyranny," declared Ardith.

They nodded, but then Andrew said soberly, "The goal is certainly worth considerable risk, but no risk is worth taking unless it offers a reasonable chance of accomplishing what it's meant to accomplish. Granting that Liam is willing to die for it, we still don't know if people would accept what he said from the ship as authentic. As Jacob pointed out, they'd have no way of knowing whether the voice actually came from the real *Estel* and its real captain."

Ardith's head spun. Was it just wishful thinking that made her feel so sure that they would know? It wasn't logic. Of course there could be no objective proof of who spoke from space or the true identity of the ship a voice came from; they had tampered with *Promise*'s transponder, after all. They could just as well borrow a ship through Andrew and tamper with that one.

Nevertheless, somehow people would *know*. They

would sense it. Was that the answer—psi? If psi could enable people to distinguish truth from falsehood, the world would be a different place; the answer had to be more complicated than that. Radnor would understand. . . .

"Radnor would say it has something to do with the collective unconscious," she said. "There have to be a lot of people believing the same thing for that to be significant, but when there are, other people start believing it too, especially if it's something they're emotional about."

"There are plenty of people who are still emotional about the Captain of Estel and remember how it felt to hear him speak from space," Meiko pointed out. "And a lot more who've gotten emotional about the Net postings that offer them hope in a dark time. They'll believe because they want to believe, and telepathy from us and our friends will reinforce that because we'll know it's really true."

"In other words, if I went up in a ship and said it was *Estel* and I was Captain, there'd be no grounds for believing me, but if Liam does, the fact that it's true will be drawn from the collective unconscious?" Fred asked.

"Yes! Radnor once told me that on Earth we'd be inserting ideas into the collective unconscious," Ardith recalled.

"And by now we already have," Jacob said "just by getting so many people thinking about *Estel*."

That was true, Ardith realized, and yet . . . surely they'd have to do more than that. Slowly she said, "Radnor also said we'd need mind power beyond what we consciously understand, if only to inspire others. On the boat coming back from Terry's funeral, remember? He said that was why Terry wanted us to see the Ritual."

Meiko said, "He must have meant some kind of psi. Something like the way dreams were sent to us telepathically. But only the Eldest has that power."

"We wouldn't have to send images across space," Ardith pointed out. "Just to the people in the crowd. Just what usually happens in a crowd, only focused—that's what Radnor told me ritual does. That's why we were able to touch flame." It all came together in her mind and she reached out to the minds of the others so that they too saw the connections.

After a long silence Andrew said, "I never heard the Captain of *Estel* speak and I don't know much about him, so I don't fully understand the effect meeting him has had on you. But I do know Radnor. I have more respect for him than any other man I ever met. Is he familiar with what you envoys have been aiming to do on Earth?"

"Of course," said Jacob. "He planned the mission along `with the Elders. He gave us most of our training and our final instructions."

"Then I suggest that you ask his opinion about using *Estel,* if you can get a message to him. It's not something we should decide quickly, anyway.

"We can send one aboard *Promise* if you can find Galina and Derek, Andrew," said Fred. "Then they can bring *Estel* to Earth if he thinks we should use it."

They left it at that, deciding to sleep on it before recording the message to Radnor. The rest of the day was spent drafting the Net postings they would use, deciding what cities they would target, and making lists of people they would need to contact. It could not have been done without Andrew, Ardith realized, and so Meiko's imprisonment, and hers, had been less of a setback than they had thought.

~ 40 ~

The days that followed were busy, not only with planning but with the contacting of people to whom they spoke about the Elders as originally intended. They changed safe houses several times, both for security and because it put them in range of more potential believers. The lockdown was still in effect, of course, but like the local police, they'd become accustomed to ignoring it. As long as they didn't violate the curfew they felt fairly safe.

Gabriel was told by Liam of their escape from prison, but not the details or anything about their involvement with the conspiracy led by Andrew. Ardith liked Gabriel and hated being less than honest with him, but she could see that it was necessary. She certainly didn't want him to be at risk of dismissal from the Service along with Liam.

Galina and Derek were found not at Maclairn Foundation headquarters in Boston but in Florida, where they had gone to recruit believers from among workers at Cape Canaveral's now-idle civilian spaceport. Because they had been only a few days with the envoys, months ago, and their commitment to Maclairn was recent, Andrew had insisted on interviewing them before letting them in on the secrets of the conspiracy; he was experienced in telepathically judging the sincerity of recruits. After pronouncing them reliable, he arranged shuttle transportation to *Promise* for them and saw to it that they would not be challenged by flight controllers when it broke orbit.

So the message was on its way to Radnor. It had been a major crisis for the envoys when they placed the data bracelet in Galina's hands, for they were committing themselves to a scheme that was iffy, to say the least. As Liam had warned in the beginning, there were many things that could go wrong—and they could affect the whole world. Sometimes in the night when she couldn't sleep, Ardith found herself incredulous, struck anew by awareness of what she had set in motion. Who was she to gamble with the future of Earth?

Yet Terry had predicted it. To her and Varel he had said "On you rests the future of our birthworld." She should be doing something beside just publicizing the Elders' appearance—she should be making the public *believe*. She hadn't forgotten her idea about putting images *of Estel* into the collective unconscious. Even if they didn't use the actual ship, images of it would increase awareness of new worlds. But she didn't know how to project them. At night in bed she thought of the ship, hoping to dream of it and share that dream; but she usually woke dreaming of Varel.

Liam too was concerned about what Terry would have thought. "He always was a risk-taker where it concerned what he viewed as his mission," he said. In all the years I flew with him I never knew him to back off from a chance to promote belief in future mind power, or, after I'd revealed who I am, in the importance of contact with the Elder worlds. But I can't begin to fill his shoes. When he spoke to groups it was as if he were inspired by something greater than himself, and I don't feel any such inspiration."

"He told me he didn't know what he was going to say before he said it," Ardith reflected. "So maybe the same thing will happen with you." She bowed her head, remembering. He had, in effect, passed the torch to them, and surely that included Liam, his closest friend. If Liam, who was sacrificing his career and maybe his life, didn't feel inspired, how could she?

Andrew was away much of the time dealing with

the affairs of the underground—well disguised, of course, for Halorun's backers were now hunting him and since he knew all its plans and the identities of countless members his arrest would be disastrous; his interrogators would not stop with measures against which mind training could help. Ardith and Meiko were appalled at the potential consequences of the risk he had taken to save their lives.

The conspiracy was worldwide and was taking in an ever-larger percentage of Fleet's officers. Andrew was no longer limiting recruiting to people who'd already had mind training, but was putting those who hadn't in touch with mentors who gave it to them as a condition of their acceptance. All members were told about the Elders and instructed to be ready to protect the public if any trouble occurred on the appointed day.

The day had been set during one of his return trips to the safe house. It had to be far enough in the future to allow plenty of time to recruit believers as well as to hear back from Radnor, but not so far that the people looking forward to it would lose interest. After some discussion the group chose July 20, the anniversary of Earthborn humans' very first landing on another world.

So the first of the dated postings had been put online. It had been hard to write. "It sounds like a promo for a science fiction holo," Meiko said when their first attempt was read aloud for discussion. "Save the date! Gather on July 20 to greet the Captain of *Estel*'s friends from alien worlds! They won't land unless they are sure they're welcome, so don't waste your chance to take part in the most important event of this century!'" We can't post that; it's too sensational."

Ardith thought about it, and in a few minutes

came up with something more in keeping with the earlier posts.

> There is a ship and its name is *Estel*, which means hope; and its captain visited worlds of which we know nothing. Thus he made many friends among people who are not of Earth, but are like us, whether or not their bodies look like ours. And they were called by him the Elders because their worlds are older than ours and they have knowledge we have yet to attain.
>
> It was his wish that a few of the Elders be invited to visit here and share some of that knowledge. On July 20 they will come, not to instruct us but simply as our guests. But they will not land unless we ask them to. So gather at noon Earthport time on that day, raising signs to show them that they are welcome. For the Captain of *Estel* believed that through contact with their worlds alone can we fulfill his hope of a promising future for Earth.

It had taken only two days for it to go viral. And then the problems had begun.

The first one to be dealt with was Halorun. He had been ignoring the postings so far, as he and all his advisors thought they were a good way to keep the minds of gullible people off the restrictions his regime imposed on them. But a date was another matter. Halorun began to think that something so concrete as a date just might not be total nonsense. Someone a little more astute than the usual policymakers pointed out that to ban mention of it might lend support to it by suggesting that the government saw some truth in the idea. But the conspirators knew that this respite could not last.

Andrew, who as a high-ranking officer had in the past dealt with Halorun personally, could not do so now that he was a fugitive; he was forced to delegate the job. But the strategy they came up with proved effective. As the dictator was already paranoid on the subject, it was not difficult to convince him that good aliens were coming to protect him from the bad aliens, which wasn't stretching the truth too far since if there had been any bad aliens the Service would have shielded Earth. Halorun became so eager to welcome friendly aliens that if he had had his way he would have invited contact himself, making it unnecessary to involve the public. The ruthless junta that had put him in power kept him from doing so, yet was held back from censoring the posts by his approval of them.

The next crisis came when along with online discussion in public forums among people looking forward to the Elders' arrival, there began to be some suggesting that they were coming as saviors. The envoys were disturbed by this and utterly appalled when a Net site appeared dedicated to their worship. "Look to the skies, for on the 20th of July the Great Change is coming," it proclaimed. "Be ready so that when the Holy Ones arrive you will be worthy to live in the paradise Earth will become. You who believe must gather to welcome them, and woe unto those who fail in the strength of their belief, for if they falter they will be cast out of paradise and the Captain of *Estel* will not befriend them."

"The horrible thing is that some of it's just a different way of saying what we say," Ardith lamented, "yet it puts a whole different slant on it."

"This was to be expected," Liam said. "Such ideas have been in the collective unconscious for centuries and some people are bound to attach them to the idea of gathering to await the coming of extraterrestrial beings. But it could get out of hand."

"Should we contact the administrator of the Net site, ask that it be taken down?"

"That wouldn't help—we would just be seen as the voice of evil and our own posts would be contested," Jacob said. "All we can do is emphasize in what we write that the Elders are not supernatural, but just people like ourselves."

Was this the time to go public with the statement that she had made love with an alien? Ardith wondered. No, for unions between Earthborn humans and gods were a staple of mythology and besides, some people literally believed that the human race was the result of ancient mating between primitive humans and aliens, contrary to biological fact though that was. So people who didn't know her might not assume that anyone she'd chosen as a partner must be an ordinary person like herself. She began to think that Varel's defiance of Service policy might go for nothing.

As July 20 got closer, the tension grew. They had named the cities where gatherings were to be encouraged, choosing those with well-defined public spaces around which force fields could be placed if necessary. They were still counting on there not being enough police for lockdown enforcement to be widespread and had warned the public that it was important not to show up any earlier than the appointed hour. They also warned that the Elders might not show up immediately; it would take time for them to see and respond to the welcome signs. They could not, of course, state that *Estel* would appear; that couldn't be decided until they heard from Radnor.

"What does Gabriel think about all this?" Ardith asked. "He *will* respond, won't he?"

"He's making preparations on the basis of what his agents have observed," Liam answered. "Though he's puzzled as to how the idea of aliens coming on a specific date got started when the Captain of *Estel* is viewed as history if not mere legend, he sees that they've got to show up."

"Is he angry about it?"

"No, I think he's pleased. It's what the Service aimed for, after all, though not so soon or in such a dramatic form. But he's worried lest something should go wrong."

All this time the number of people who wanted contact between Earth and the Elders had been growing, and although it was a small percentage of the population, it seemed sufficient. To be sure, there were many statements from scientists maintaining that there were no intelligent extraterrestrial beings, no doubt spread by Ivanson and others on the expedition who had given up their chance for a major discovery. But these had little impact, since the people who paid attention to them weren't the sort who read pro-alien posts in the first place. They didn't represent the reaction of the general public.

Ardith and the other envoys had almost lost sight of their original awareness that most people on Earth didn't want to meet aliens. If they thought about it at all, they felt that it no longer mattered—enough people would request contact for it to be established. So when the first active opposition appeared on the Net, they were shocked.

Previously, the opponents had simply ignored talk of alien visitors, which they considered too silly to merit notice. They hadn't gone to sites where it was discussed. Now all of a sudden it had occurred to them that maybe there really were extraterrestrials—and they didn't want Earth to have anything to do with them. "Keep aliens out of our world!" they said. "Earth is for humans. Don't let weird inhuman ETs mingle with the human race."

Racism had been extinct in human society for many generations. The current population had little idea of what the insulting word 'racist' had meant. When supporters of contact pointed out to those who denigrated advanced extraterrestrials that their comments were racist, they were outraged. They maintained that the term couldn't possibly apply to their attitude toward members of a different species, regardless of how highly evolved it was.

At first Ardith and the others were merely disgusted. After all, they hadn't expected that everyone would welcome the coming of aliens. But then there began to be calls for counterdemonstrations, and it became apparent that on July 20 the gatherings would include protests as well as welcome signs. And that was a frightening prospect. What they knew of history told them that counterdemonstrations sometimes led to violence.

"Would Ivanson go so far as to hire agitators?" Ardith asked worriedly.

"I wouldn't put it past him," said Fred. "He has a lot to lose if it's proven that the Elders exist."

The number of people who spoke out against alien contact grew, and along with diatribes against inhuman aliens, they revived the worst of the hate speech against telepaths. "We should have gotten rid of all the freaks long ago," they said. "They are the ones trying to get us to bring in beings from other worlds with unnatural mind powers."

Since telepaths were indeed behind the effort to establish contact, this claim could not be countered, and opposition to the alien landing was thus strengthened by the prejudice that had never completely died after the defeat of the Klan. "There will always be some people who are intolerant," Meiko said sadly.

"Yes," said Jacob, "but remember that for many the feeling against aliens is an unconscious mask for their fear of encountering the larger universe, and it's fear that makes it so strong."

"We can't let the percentage of opponents grow, Ardith declared. "We have to find a way to appeal to the people who are on the fence." She had to do *something*, or the crowds of supporters might not be large enough to sway the Service. The public demonstration was her idea, and it was her responsibility to make it work.

~ 41 ~

It all came down to the issue of the Elders' essential humanity, Ardith thought. Long ago Radnor had said, "We're all human in the most meaningful sense of the word." It wasn't an issue of species, innate powers, knowledge of the universe, or culture. Those things differed, but as individuals people were people, neither superhuman nor subhuman, and that was what the opponents of contact between worlds just didn't get.

And the only way to overcome their chauvinism— and their fear as well—was to make them aware that members of different 'human' species could love each other.

She had known this all along. Varel had known it when he decided that by loving her he would honor the Oath more than if he adhered strictly to its requirements. She had felt sure of it when she told

Dr. Marwen, and later some of the people to whom she spoke of the Elders, that their love had been consummated.

Some of those people, even the doctor, had been shocked at first. But they had quickly come to understand that she wouldn't have made love with someone who wasn't fully human in the ways that matter. That was the only basis on which doubters could be made to see. If despite her revelation to the few she knew, the public didn't accept the Elders as their equals, Varel would be devastated. He would believe he'd been mistaken—that his violation of the Oath that meant so much to him hadn't been justifiable. That would be far worse than what he had gone through so far. She could not let it happen.

So it didn't matter if some thought she'd mated with a "god from outer space" and others were horrified by their assumption that she'd slept with some sort of weird creature—those people weren't the ones who needed convincing. What they thought wasn't important. Their reaction would be sickening, but she would have to tell the public anyway.

When she announced her intention to the others, they were dismayed. "No, Ardith!" Meiko exclaimed. "They'll attack you, post insults in response to your message. It would be a—a desecration of your love."

"I'm afraid Meiko is right," Jacob said. "You would be letting yourself in for trouble, and it wouldn't end when contact occurs. It would follow you for the rest of your life."

"I can't help that," Ardith declared. "It would also gain us supporters, and we need them."

" Liam shook his head. "It could get worse than online attacks. You might get hate mail, even threats. In the past when racism still existed on Earth, women who had sex with members of minorities thought to be beneath them were sometimes murdered."

"Well, we're living in a safe house, aren't we?"

"We won't be, after Halorun's regime ends. I don't know where you plan to go then, but you'll be alone and very vulnerable."

Oh God. She hadn't thought that far ahead. Nervously she fingered the flame pendant, which Andrew had retrieved for her, knowing the risk made no difference—she couldn't fail to speak up for the Elders out of cowardice. Not when the consequences would be so hurtful to Varel.

It was hard to know what to say in the post. After thinking about it for some time she wrote:

> My name is Ardith and I am fortunate, for I have already met the Elders. I was a member of an expedition to investigate the mysterious interstellar message received by astronomers, and along with three others I was lost in a lifeboat. We almost died but the Elders found us, and eventually they brought us home. But first we lived with them for many weeks. On an Elder world I fell in love with an Elder, who though not of our species is no different from us in any important way. And our union was blessed by the wisest of the Elders and we were married, though because I had to return to Earth it could not be called a lifemating.
>
> So don't let anyone tell you that the Elders are not the equals of the Earthborn. Their skin color and features are different, and sometimes their size, but these are not what make people human. Humanity consists of the capacity to choose, to learn, to dream of

the future, and to love. And that, the Elders
possess in full measure. The Captain of *Estel*
knew this—and I too know, because the love
between me and the man I married is the
most important thing in our lives.

She posted copies to all the Net sites where there
was discussion of the aliens, for and against
welcoming them. Predictably, she got enthusiastic
replies from most people who favored it, though
sometimes they expressed surprise. "I didn't realize
they were enough like us to marry," one woman
wrote. "That gives me a much clearer idea of what
they are."

But there were also some who congratulated her
on having been the chosen bride of a Holy One, one of
whom had the gall to ask if she had been a virgin.
Ardith soon learned that there was no point in
arguing with these people. To them, despite
awareness that there had been interstellar travel for
centuries, the universe beyond Earth remained a
supernatural realm.

And of course, the comments from opponents of
contact were much harder to read and to deal with.

"You should be ashamed of yourself," many of
them said. "No decent woman would sleep with an
alien beast."

In vain Ardith explained that this was precisely
the point—the fact that she did make love with him
proved that he was not a beast but the equivalent of
an Earthborn human. Even her reply to the fear of
mixed-race offspring was disregarded. "You needn't
worry about that," she said. "There will never be any
mixture of species because the laws of nature do not
allow it. I'm a biologist and I know that combining
sperm and eggs with DNA that evolved on different

worlds can't result in conception, no matter how much genetic manipulation may be done in a lab." This failed to cut any ice.

Those were the mildest of the insulting comments; she did get hate mail, though only online because her physical address was not known. "Don't read it," Meiko begged when she saw her in tears. But she had to read everything, no matter how much it hurt to see Varel vilified, order to find out if her posts were making an impression.

They didn't seem to be. The people who said good things would have welcomed the Elders anyway, and the rest were not modifying their negative views. Ardith began to think that the ordeal had been all for nothing.

And then one day she got a private message to her screen name—which she hesitated to open because the private ones were almost always hateful—asking her to call. The sender was a reporter for one of the largest holo networks, he said. They were interested in interviewing her.

"Don't call," Meiko urged. "It could be a scam and even if it's not, you don't want people to see you. You would never be able to walk down the street if everybody knew who you were."

That was probably true. Moreover, Halorun thought she was dead and might want to have her killed a second time if he knew she wasn't. And she might get other threats, which would endanger her housemates as well as herself; they might have to switch safe houses again.

Yet an interview would reach far more people than the Net posts did. People didn't visit the forums unless they already had feelings one way or the other. What was needed was a way to reach those who hadn't made up their minds, or who hadn't even heard of the event predicted for July 20. A holo would sensationalize her love for Varel, might make it seem sordid, still it would attract a wide audience. Dizzily she recalled Terry's face as he declared that he was counting on them. She couldn't let him down, nor could she let Varel's sacrifice be in vain.She had come this far and now she really had no choice.

The reporter, whose name was Mike, talked to her privately in his office. He seemed interested and convinced that contact with aliens would be a good thing. At any rate, she thought bitterly, it would be a good thing for increasing his audience; it was too much to expect the media to choose stories out of concern for the public's welfare.

"But of course," he added when it was almost settled. "We would need proof. There have been many women in the past who claimed to have made love with aliens. The sensational press published their stories, but we are a respectable network and we don't present anything we haven't verified. What evidence can you provide that what you've told me is true?"

Stunned, she considered it. She could not drag the other envoys into it, and they wouldn't be believed in any case. She couldn't expose Liam or Gabriel or any other undercover Elders. She couldn't even say to contact Radnor, since Maclairn was still secret. "The people who witnessed our wedding aren't available here," she admitted.

Mike smiled contemptuously. "I thought that might be difficult for you," he said. "There's no limit to what people will say to get holo publicity. I guess I'll have to report that your story is another fabrication— we don't want the public getting excited by fake online claims."

Ardith drew breath. Angrily she retorted, "I do have proof. At least I have proof that I had sex with an Elder. You'll have to take my word for how much we love each other."

Mike looked astonished. "It's difficult to see what kind of evidence could prove that," he said.

"It's DNA evidence. I thought, at the time I asked a doctor to obtain it from me, that I might someday need to prove to the government that aliens who are similar to us exist. That hasn't been necessary, but the doctor still has a sealed record of the DNA analysis, which would be impossible to fake retroactively." She gave him Dr. Marwen's name and address. The media had a long reach, so he shouldn't find it too hard to get it from New Tahiti.

In a daze she went home and messaged Dr. Marwen with authorization to release the record to the holo network. And she wrote to Brielle in case a witness was required. Then she waited. On July 10 she heard from Mike. Her story had been checked, and the interview was on.

Waiting in the holo studio for the red light to tell her that they were live, Ardith blinked back tears. *Oh Varel, forgive me if he drags us through the mud*, she thought. *I don't think I can bear to hear our love distorted, yet you would say it's for a vital cause. . . .*

"Tonight we're talking with Ardith Moran, who has the most unique story we've ever presented on this show," announced Mike. "You may think it's a fake, but we've checked it out and I can vouch for what she's going to tell you. Ardith, is it true that you went to bed with an alien?"

"I married a man from another world," she replied, "so yes, we did what married couples usually do."

"Even though this man isn't human?"

"That depends on what you mean by human. He's not a member of the species native to planet Earth, but he's human in terms of all the other factors that define humanity."

"Does he look like us?"

"Pretty much. His face isn't shaped quite like ours and his skin color is different."

"It's not green, is it?" Mike smirked.

Ardith froze. "You must not know much about history," she said. "There was a time when a reporter could be fired for making jokes about skin color."

He reddened; evidently it hadn't occurred to him that the precedent might apply. Quickly he went on, "You don't seem like a woman who'd be looking just for a thrilling new sexual experience. If I saw you anywhere but here I'd say you were someone likely to marry an old friend from your home town. So why an alien? Is he a prince or some kind of hero?"

"Well, no. He's a history professor." She explained a little about who he was and how they'd met, no more than what she had said to people she'd told in the past about the Elders. "We tried not to fall in love," she confessed, "because we both had other responsibilities. But we just couldn't help it."

"You still love this man a lot, don't you?"

"Yes, we love each other more than anything else in the world—in any world."

"When a man and woman are that much in love, they normally want to live together and start a family. Are you going to do that?'"

"I wish we could, but I had to come back to Earth. And we couldn't have a family anyway because it's genetically impossible for species from different worlds to have offspring."

"That's right, his DNA is different, isn't it? You showed me an analysis of his DNA." Mercifully, he did not say where it had come from. "But at least you needn't be separated much longer. I understand that some aliens are going to come to Earth ten days from now. He'll be with them, won't he?"

Startled, Ardith tried to keep her face impassive. This hadn't been mentioned in what he'd discussed with her, but it was a natural assumption. "Unfortunately he won't be," she said with sadness. "He has obligations on the world where we met."

"But you've said you love each other more than anything else. If that's true, he surely would put being with you ahead of his other obligations."

"He gave his word long before he knew me, and in his culture honoring a pledge is considered more important than personal happiness." She wondered whether viewers would find this admirable or think she was merely making excuses for him.

"So when you post online asking people to gather on July 20 and raise signs welcoming the Elders, you're not doing it just for a chance to see your alien husband?"

"No, of course not," Ardith said with fervor. "I do it because contact with the Elders is important to Earth. Because people on Earth are depressed and hopeless, and only sharing ideas with older worlds can show them how much there is to look forward to in the future."

Mike's closing remarks were surprisingly positive. His skepticism seemed to have lessened somewhat, and she could only hope that the audience, too, had been swayed.

~ 42 ~

Ardith took a robocar from the studio to the safe house, fearing that on public transportation she would be recognized. Within hours the flood of messages pouring into her online account had increased to the point where it was impossible to open more than a fraction of them. Most were supportive, including many from people who had not previously heard that aliens really exist. She tried to ignore the inevitable abusive ones, reminding herself that obscenity was in the minds of the accusers and not in the loving relationship they found distasteful.

Urged by Meiko and Jacob, she decided to stay indoors until the big day, which was now very close. Fred had gone off with Andrew; she was not sure just what they were doing but it was related to preparing for the expected demonstrations. Liam was visiting as many mentors as he could, asking them to mobilize their former trainees.

They had not received a reply to the message they'd sent to Radnor. There was no knowing whether he'd chosen not to respond or whether Galina and Derek had failed to get *Promise* to Maclairn and back. And then, on the morning of July 19, all three appeared at the safe house, escorted by Andrew. The underground officers in flight control had informed him when *Estel* established orbit; he had previously ordered them to let its shuttle land without challenge.

"We've turned *Estel* over to Liam," Radnor told them, "and if this scheme works I want to be part of it." It was surprising that he had taken the time to come himself, Galina said, for Kenard was near death and Radnor had just been officially elected to assume his duties as head of Maclairn's government. Nevertheless, at the last minute he had ordered her not to depart without him.

"I see why it's necessary to deceive Gabriel," Radnor said, "but he's been my good friend for many years and I'd find it very hard to talk to him until after this is over. If it accomplishes its purpose, he'll forgive us. If not, I don't know just what will happen."

Ardith had worried about that, too. There was so much that *could* go wrong. To begin with, the government, having begun to take the Net postings seriously, was anticipating demonstrations and was determined to prevent them. Already it had Fleet officers posted in the designated gathering places with the aim of dispersing any crowds that assembled. Only the fact that most of these officers were loyal to Andrew made success in the plan even a possibility.

More and more it became apparent that it could not have been possible without Andrew's involvement. Her own ideas had been very naive, Ardith realized. Had Liam known that? Had he known that her proposal would inevitably lead to a full-scale mutiny against Halorun's regime? Because that was evidently what it was going to do. Dissident Fleet officers had been plotting mutiny for months, and this was their chance—a chance they would not have had without the assurance of Service backing. No wonder he was sure he would be dismissed from the Service. This was intervention on a major scale.

"I didn't really mean to overthrow Earth's government," she confessed to Radnor, "or to force Service people I care about to violate their ethical standards. It just—happened. And if it fails I'm responsible."

"Someone has to be responsible," Radnor replied. "That's how things do happen. Someone sees an opportunity to change the world in a particular way, hopefully a good way, and then it's like a runaway train. You can't know ahead of time where it will end up. Yet if we never took any risks the world wouldn't evolve."

"But surely it's not normal for change set in

motion by an insignificant person like me to override the policy of a huge organization like the Service that won't allow any deviation on the part of its own agents."

After a pause Radnor said, "The policies of the Service are necessary. Without them and the powerful institution that enforces them, younger races could never hold their own among the oldest. At best they and their cultures would be swallowed up; at worst there would be chaos. But at the same time, those policies are rigid, so rigid that if no one ever disregarded them no allowance for circumstances could ever be made. The Service directorate is well aware of this. They rely on there being people like you and like Liam to inject new factors into situations like this one—people willing to take personal responsibility for an outcome they can't predict and if necessary to pay the price."

"And like Varel?" Bitterly Ardith said, "Varel's paying the price without getting any credit for it,"

Again Radnor hesitated. "Don't be too sure of that," he said slowly. "Varel has more friends than you realize."

"Yet what he did may never influence anyone but me—"

"Exactly. He influenced you, and you influenced Liam, and both your actions and Liam's will influence Gabriel, who will get the credit in history books either for putting down Halorun or for committing the most disastrous breach of policy in this century. You can't escape from the net, Ardith. Nor can I, who trained you, nor the Eldest, who sent you the dreams that brought you to us. Whether it's called fate, or synchronicity, or the will of God, it's how life works."

She was silent. After a minute or two Radnor pulled a data bracelet from his pocket and handed it to her. "I've carried a message for you from Varel," he told her, smiling.

Incredulous, Ardith stared at the wide silver bracelet in her hand. "From *Varel?* But he *can't*, he wouldn't—"

"He said to make sure you got it before tomorrow. I'll leave you to listen to it in private." He crossed the room to where Meiko and Jacob were deep in conversation with Galina.

With shaking hands Ardith took out wireless earbuds and switched the bracelet on. It didn't make sense! Surely Varel wouldn't have defied the Service after all this time just to send best wishes for the success of the coming event. He could have asked Radnor to tell her that without putting it in tangible form. And why had Radnor agreed to deliver it, after telling her long ago that he would never help Varel violate the terms of his probation? Was it possible that they had released him from restrictions?

She shivered with excitement as his voice came though the earbuds.

"Dearest Ardith, this bracelet was my mother's. I would have given it to you on Maclairn, but I did not have it with me then. Let it be a symbol of our love.

"I saw a recording of the holo interview and I'm deeply impressed by your courage. Whatever good the people of Earth believe about the Elders is due to you, and this historian, at least, will make sure your role is not forgotten. I anxiously await the coming demonstrations and I only hope that they will succeed, but know that no matter what happens on that day I will be with you in spirit. I will love you always. Varel."

She clasped the bracelet to her wrist, tears filling her eyes. He hadn't said he was off probation. Was there a chance the Service wouldn't find out about the message? But he'd watched the interview, too, which must surely count as communication. And he had not sounded very confident about the success of the demonstrations—why would he be anxious? With a chill, she wondered whether he knew of some precedent that gave him cause to worry. Perhaps he had urged Radnor to come.

That night she couldn't sleep. In the morning she, Meiko, Jacob, and the two *Promise* pilots took up the picket signs Meiko had made—WELCOME ELDERS! COME VISIT EARTH, and FRIENDS OF THE CAPTAIN OF ESTEL ARE WELCOME—and shortly before noon they walked to the public plaza in front of the League capitol. This was where the Elders would land, though similar demonstrations were being held all over the world, linked by giant holoscreens Andrew had surreptitiously acquired so that people everywhere could watch.

Though both police and Fleet officers were present, only a few were making any effort to discourage people from gathering, let alone to arrest violators of the lockdown. And people did gather. More and more poured into the plaza until there was scarcely room for them to raise their signs. Their mood seemed happy, though perhaps that was just the relief of temporary freedom from being cooped up in their homes. It was impossible to tell how many had a real desire to meet aliens.

In one corner of the plaza the counterdemonstrators were assembled, with signs proclaim-ing EARTH IS FOR HUMANS, NO ALIENS WANTED and ELDERS GO HOME. There were not many of them compared to the size of the pro-Elder crowd and while they were a rough-looking bunch, they didn't appear to be contemplating violence. Several Fleet officers were keeping them separate from the rest of the demonstrators.

Andrew and Fred were not in sight. Ardith supposed they were coordinating the security arrangements. She knew Andrew was in touch with ships in orbit that he'd charged with protecting *Estel* from any attempt to stop the transmission of Liam's announcement that might be made by the government when it grasped what was happening.

Ardith, where are you? The telepathic call was strong but not wholly familiar. It took Ardith a minute to recognize Gabriel and guide him to where they stood.

He was evidently controlling his agents from here, whether telepathically or with a communicator of some sort she was not sure. "I've never seen anything quite like this," he said to her. "Even after your holo interview, I wouldn't have thought mere Net posts could lead to a spontaneous demonstration this large. Somehow you four recruited more believers than we thought you could, despite the lockdown."

"Well, it wasn't exactly spontaneous, you know," said Jacob.

"It wasn't? I know there were Net posts that went viral, but they couldn't have been intentionally scheduled or backed by coordinated real-time messages. The Estelan Party isn't capable of doing that without attracting government attention."

"We did it ourselves. The day of demonstrations was Ardith's idea, and reviving interest in the Captain of *Estel* was Meiko's. This is what you sent us here for, wasn't it? To make Earth not merely accept the Elders, but invite them?"

Astonished, Gabriel protested, "How could you know it wouldn't turn violent? And why hasn't it? When I read the Net posts I thought I'd have to provide security."

"You may yet, if Halorun's backers send in their

elites," Ardith warned. "Most of the Fleet officers here are Andrew's. They're counting on your deploying force fields around the plaza if any officers with lethal weapons approach."

"Andrew?" Gabriel looked at her as if she had lost her mind. "Who is he, and how could he possibly know we exist, let alone that we have that capability?"

"He's the head of the underground resistance to Halorun—he got us out of prison and he's been working with us. As to how we knew about the force fields and what it would take to get you to use them, we did have some advice," Ardith said. There was no need to hide it now; he was about to hear.

She didn't need to say more, for at that moment the speakers on the plaza's holoscreens came alive. "This is HS *Estel*, the Captain speaking. Stand by to record." Receivers all over the world were picking this up; Andrew had arranged for it to transmitted by the major relay satellites. "I am speaking today from *Estel* to ask you to welcome my friends the Elders as guests of Earth."

Gabriel turned white. "That's Liam's voice! He can't do that, he knows he can't intervene—"

"He knows he'll be dismissed from the Service," Ardith said. "He's going to spend the rest of his life on Maclairn the way Terry did."

Radnor, who had been avoiding Gabriel until Liam's role became apparent, emerged from the crowd. Before he could speak Jacob said quickly, "We hated not letting you in on this, Gabriel, but Liam told us we had to keep it from you to protect you from being blamed for the intervention."

The crowd hushed. Though the voice was unfamiliar to the listeners, they were too young to have heard Terry's voice and in any case he'd spoken only in the colonies, so it made no difference. The opening words *This is HS* Estel, *the Captain speaking* had been recorded in legend and for a moment many forgot the time difference, while others thought they must be hearing a ghost.

Ardith, blinking, found she'd been holding her breath; for a moment she'd lost touch with everything but *Estel's* presence. She turned to Radnor, wondering what reaction he'd sensed from Gabriel, but he seemed not to not to notice her. Oddly, he stood frozen, staring into space as if he expected the ship now in orbit to appear in the sky.

"Though this is *Estel,* I am not its original Captain," said Liam. "I am his heir, his former copilot and friend, to whom he bequeathed this ship. He was a good friend of all the Elders, of whom I am one. A few of us have been Earth's friends for a long time. Some, like me, have been made to look as if we were Earthborn, others look different. But we are all the same in our hearts.

"We all possess the things that define humanity— we make choices; we seek knowledge; we dream of a better future; and above all, we love. And because our planets are older than Earth, we have the mind powers the original Captain of *Estel* told you would someday be yours. Now that many of you have gained these powers, it is time for us to meet you as friends and bring you hope for the bright future that is your destiny. It is time for you to know that you are part of a vast Federation of countless worlds where human species have evolved.

"My hands are on the controls the original Captain used to take *Estel* to countless colony worlds and in the end, to worlds of the Elders. As his copilot I was honored to sit beside him. I am honored now to fly the ship he once flew. But there is no honor greater than to have been chosen by fate as the first to invite a ship of my own people to set down upon the world where the Captain was born. He dedicated his life to the work that has led to this day, as I have now dedicated mine to its fulfillment. I will look back on this as my happiest hour.

"So raise your welcome signs high, and soon a lander will appear in your sky, and if you desire it that lander will descend. From this day forward Earth and the Elder worlds will be united in friendship."

The crowd listened in silence, entranced. Telepathy, both conscious and unconscious, had united it, and there was no doubt in anyone's mind that this was the true *Estel*, flown by its current true Captain. Though to some *Estel* was a memory and to others a mere legend, the very name carried authority. *Estel* meant hope, and if hope lay in meeting aliens, then aliens must be welcomed. Tall white signs were thrust up like the crest of a wave, making the will of the public indisputable.

Gabriel had no choice; he sent the signal for the lander to descend. It came down, a small silver sphere sparkling against the deep blue sky of a summer day. The assembled people watched in awe as at descended, touched ground, and opened its hatch to let six Elders of different species emerge, ending centuries of secret surveillance. Official contact had been made. Earth's people were now aware that they were part of the Federation.

~ *43* ~

Ardith stood motionless, clutching her sign, still dazed with wonderment. In the instant after Liam first spoke she had *seen Estel,* seen it as clearly as if she were viewing it from space, knowing beyond doubt that it was the true *Estel* not merely because she knew the ship was in fact nearby but because she was aware that the crowd knew. And she had linked with them, pouring all the strength of her mind into desire that it would land.

This was what she'd wanted, tried night after night to insert into the collective unconscious—but surely her efforts couldn't have triggered the appearance of a visible image. Or could they? Long ago aboard *Promise* she'd been told *people have literally heard, or seen, saints and angels. In the same way people who believe in aliens have heard their voices as strongly as if the input came through their ears, and have seen beings from UFOs.* And the UFOs themselves, of course. The brain couldn't distinguish sensory input from psi.

Yet for that to happen to a lot of people at once, there had to be focus. That was what ritual provided, Radnor had said. It was what led them to draw on the collective unconscious simultaneously. Was a demonstration a ritual? He had said spectator sports could be, and she supposed anything where many people were concentrating on some immediate emotionally-important event would qualify. The sea of signs, the anticipation, the voice . . . Liam's voice had provided a focal point. But Liam had been busy flying the ship and choosing his words; he couldn't have been actively focusing the psi powers of the crowd, as Radnor said was done in Maclairn's Ritual.

Radnor. As he came toward her, his normal informality regained, she recalled where she'd seen him stand silent and detached before. On the platform by the lake at the Ritual following Terry's funeral, joined with Kenard and their lifemates to coalesce the mind power of the mourners and give them in that moment the paranormal ability to touch flame. What other ways might he influence the minds of an emotionally-engaged crowd? He was, after all, the strongest telepath on Maclairn next to Kenard, from whom he would soon take over. All at once Ardith perceived what had happened. Radnor had done the only thing that could ensure that her plan would work. That was why he had come from Maclairn himself when they asked him whether they should use *Estel*.

As she realized this he took her free hand and squeezed it. "You made it happen," he said. "They had to believe in *Estel*. All I did was make them aware that it was the real one."

For a few moments the crowd remained quiet, awe-stricken, staring at the six Elders or their images on the holoscreens. Then screams came from the edge of the plaza as people saw grim-faced officers approaching with guns drawn. The backers of Halorun, ignoring his own paranoid wish to meet the "good aliens" he believed would save him from bad ones, were attempting to regain control. Gabriel was ready for them; he had agents in place to deploy the force fields, not only here but in other cities. In astonishment the new squad found themselves thrown back from an invisible wall they could not penetrate.

Gabriel looked at Ardith. "I suppose you have an idea about what the agents who landed should do. They can't stand there indefinitely."

"They should enter the capitol and demand to see the rightful head of government. People wouldn't expect friends from the Elder worlds to talk with a despot who seized power.'

"You do know that the rightful head of government is in prison?"

"Yes, along with a lot of other political prisoners. Meiko and I have a personal interest in seeing the doors of that place opened. So does Andrew, for more reasons than you can guess."

"In other words, we are being used to put down Halorun and his backers."

"We were told long ago," Jacob said, "that dictatorship is the one thing the Federation won't tolerate and that if the people of a member world ask the Elders to come, the Service will step in."

Gabriel nodded. "That's true, though there's usually a little more formality in the decision to do it. I've wanted to get rid of that bastard since the day of the coup, and it would have been easy to manage. Yet I had to wait. Not because of policy—if it had been only that, I'd have acted as Liam has—but because of the reason the policy exists. If we'd merely appeared and saved Earth from an evil government, its people would never again have felt fully independent. They had to invite us. And you have done us and your fellow citizens a tremendous favor by setting that up."

He gave telepathic orders, and the six aliens from the lander proceeded out of the plaza, protected from the armed officers by personal force fields . After the first bullet was harmlessly repelled, those officers were too stunned to attempt further action. Although the newcomers carried no visible weapons, Halorun's supporters were not the sort of people who could conceive of there being no hidden ones. They fully expected the aliens to take over and stood frozen, waiting for it to happen. Thus the rebel officers, who outnumbered the oppressors and had long wished to be rid of them, were able to overpower them easily and put them under arrest.

"What should we do with Halorun?" Gabriel asked, turning to the envoys as if acknowledging them as representatives of the planet's population.

"I don't think you'll have to do anything," Jacob replied. "Leave it to Andrew, though he may have his hands full preventing the Fleet officers from lynching the man when they get through dealing with the junta that backed him. They've been ready to mutiny for a long time, and a lot of them were held in line by threats to their families."

The people in the crowd, not yet realizing that they were free of Halorun's regime, were slow to leave the plaza; they feared that outside the protected area they might be arrested for ignoring the lockdown. Ardith was too overwhelmed by what Radnor had done, Liam's speech, and the success of the demonstration to notice what was happening around her. In a daze she followed the others toward the capitol. When suddenly there were angry voices nearby it took her a moment to catch the words. "There she is! The woman from the holo! Don't let her get away!"

Then hands grabbed her from behind and soon she was surrounded. "Shameless slut!" the woman nearest her yelled, and spat on her. Others took up the shout. "Go back to your bestial lover, you brazen whore. You don't belong here with decent people."

Gabriel and Jacob, unaware of what was happening, had gone on ahead. Several nearby officers moved to protect Ardith, but before they could reach her the man holding her had a knife pressed against her neck. "Don't come any closer," he said coldly. "I can use this before you can touch me. And don't try your stunner either because if I see you reach for it I'll cut her throat."

Radnor, sensing that the threat was real, could do nothing beyond silently warning her not to struggle, "Take it easy," he said to the man who had seized her. "Don't make trouble for yourself. Just let her go and we'll listen to whatever you want to get from us."

"What we want is for those creatures of the devil masquerading as human to get back on their ship and never come near our world again. I'm not letting go of this bitch until I see it lift off."

Ardith's mind whirled. With half of it she prayed Gabriel would turn and see, but with the other half she hoped he wouldn't. This was the sort of situation Radnor had told her agents sometimes faced in the field—a choice between another agent's life and the best interests of the young world. The Oath would require him to let her die. But would he do that? Probably he wouldn't, not when he could send the six to the mother ship, which wasn't very far away. They could come back later. But it would lower their status in the eyes of the crowd, whose hopes had been betrayed; they might never be welcomed again. Halorun would remain in power and Andrew's people would be punished for their insubordination. Most of the good she had achieved on Earth would be undone.

She had been close to death once before and had resigned herself to it. If the respite had been only temporary, at least it had allowed her to accomplish something. Varel had been proud of her. Best to leave it at that, since they could never be together anyway. *No matter what happens I'll be with you in spirit,* he had said in the message. Had he had some sort of premonition? Was that why he'd felt anxious about the demonstrations?

The knife pressed closer to her throat; she could feel the sharpness of its edge. "I'm not going to wait all day," declared her captor, "so you'd better get those freaks onto that ship fast. When I get tired of waiting I'll kill her."

Ardith froze, wondering if she'd remain conscious long enough to feel the slash. Then, so fast that she couldn't keep her balance, she found herself freed from her assailant's grasp. Bewildered, she slid to the pavement and twisted to look back.

Another man had come from behind and grappled with the one who had held her. He was trying to pin him down, but the attacker flipped over, his right hand free, and as she watched in dismay he thrust it upward, plunging the knife into the chest of her rescuer.

Shaky with shock, Ardith stared at the man's blood-soaked shirt. She hadn't seen his face from where she lay, so she didn't grasp the full horror of it until she heard Meiko scream, "Oh, God! It's Fred!"

He had evidently been with the counter-demonstrators, placed there by Andrew to keep track of what they were doing and call for backup if action was needed to prevent trouble. He'd been ideally positioned to creep up on her captor but had waited to be sure that none of the others were watching closely enough to give warning. When his chance came he'd had to move fast. Without training or experience as a fighter, he had jumped the man by instinct, and hadn't been able to pin his arms.

The officers moved to grab the attacker as Radnor rushed forward and bent over Fred, using his mind powers to stop the bleeding. Wordless sorrow poured from his mind, engulfing all psi-sensitive onlookers, as he realized that the knife had struck too close to Fred's heart.

Ardith was in a daze, too stunned even to cry. "It should have been me," she moaned to Meiko, who helped her up and led her to a bench at the edge of the plaza. "He shouldn't have tried to save me. I was living on borrowed time after almost being executed. And I knew the holo interview would put me in danger. But Fred, he was safe, he didn't need to get involved at all—"

"Give him credit for his bravery," Jacob said to her. "He was involved in more danger than you know, doing things he couldn't reveal even to you—Andrew told me he was one of his best civilian operatives. That was his choice, just as much as your choices were yours."

Grief-stricken, she sat silently while the attacker was taken into custody to await trial for murder and Radnor arranged for the disposition of the body. Gabriel, he said, was torn by the thought that he might somehow have saved both of them if he'd been present, though he couldn't have sent the lander away because at that moment the six Elders were already inside the capitol. Ardith didn't ask what had been done with Halorun. She remained on the bench with Meiko until Jacob appeared with a car and took them back to the safe house.

As the day progressed the rightful Premier was brought from the prison and a team was sent to release government officials and other wrongfully-imprisoned people. The prison was not opened, but was used to confine Halorun and his backers. The Service played no part in that; most of its agents quietly returned to observation, no longer keeping their presence secret. The six from the lander were obliged to greet a hastily-formed committee in which the envoys would have been included, but they kept clear of the curious crowd that gathered..

Ardith was in no shape to absorb any of this. She later learned that Commander James Lexington, aka Andrew, had been promoted to Admiral and named Commandant of Fleet by the grateful reinstated Premier, thereby ensuring the loyalty of its discontented officers. Gabriel had been charged with liaison between Earth and the Elders, and an agreement had been made with the restored government for an official delegation from the Federation to visit universities on Earth in the near future. People would learn about the Elder worlds and would start exchanging ideas. They would be enlivened by challenge. The plan had been a success— all the goals had been achieved. So, she told herself, she should be joyful.

But she couldn't be. Everyone said that the overthrow of an evil regime at the cost of only one casualty was unprecedented and something to celebrate. Yet Fred had died *after* the Elders had been welcomed. His death hadn't contributed to the plan's success. Was this how life always was, hardship and sacrifice sometimes worthwhile, but other times just meaningless, leading nowhere?

"It was my fault," she said to Radnor. "If I hadn't gone on holo it wouldn't have happened. And I'm not sure my interview did any good. I'm not sure people believe aliens are like us—they might have welcomed them anyway because the Captain of *Estel* said to."

"None of us are ever sure about what causes what," Radnor said. "We make choices as best we can, and there's no knowing until later what will come of them. But sometimes unexpected good does come, even from tragedy."

Fred's funeral was a ceremonial affair, preceded by a procession of hundreds of Fleet officers—those who had been members of the underground—in their dress uniforms and the Service members in theirs, with Andrew, Radnor, Jacob, Ardith and Meiko walking behind the hearse. It was shown on the holo networks and watched by large crowds, for people had been shocked by his death and the incident that had precipitated it. Far more had been jolted into awareness of the Elders' humanity than would ever have admitted to prejudice otherwise.

~ 44 ~

Several days later Radnor, as Maclairn's new Head of Council, revealed the full truth about the colony to the public before returning in *Estel* with Liam, for whom a farewell dinner had been held. Both would be able to come back for visits, of course; from now on Maclairnans could travel openly to Earth, as the government was in no position to oppose either psi or friendship with aliens after learning the facts about its own restoration. Galina and Derek went along to become the permanent crew of *Promise*, which would resume its scheduled runs between Maclairn and Earth without the need for a stopover in New Tahiti.

"You'll be welcome on Maclairn for as long as you want to stay, and certainly to spend your last years with us," Radnor had told Liam as they finished dinner. "But I don't think you're really ready to retire. We've kept *Estel* in Maclairn's service while Terry wasn't well enough to roam from world to world, but there's a great need for it in Earth's solar system."

"Now that belief in the Captain of *Estel* has been revived, it must be kept alive," Meiko agreed. "Earth has new hope but the colonies don't, yet, and only *Estel* can give it to them."

"But I'm not qualified," Liam protested. "As I've said before, I could never fill Terry's shoes."

"Yes, you could," Ardith told hum. "I think you inherited more from Terry than his ship—you have his gift for swaying a crowd. You had to stay in the background while traveling with him as a Service agent so as not to intervene. But now you're free of that restriction."

"He would want you to carry his message on," Jacob declared. "People know that *Estel* has a new Captain, and they'll be expecting him to tell them more about the hope contact with Elders offers them."

"I guess that's true," Liam admitted. "I guess I owe it to him to try. But there will never be anyone like him."

"Even people who knew him only on the Elder worlds feel that way about him," Radnor agreed. "Yet he never pretended to be more than an ordinary starship pilot committed to spreading ideas he believed to be true."

"It's strange how one man can have such a big impact on a whole civilization, even after his death," Ardith said. "If not for him, history would be different—we couldn't have gotten people to invite the Elders and Earth might even decline into what Varel feared it might become."

"Many individuals have shaped history, as Varel could tell you," Jacob said. "But Terry's legacy is surely among the most significant, especially since it was he who made the first contact between our species and the Elders. And he inspired others to take up where he left off, which is one of the marks of true greatness."

"There should be a monument to him," Meiko said. "He was your father, Radnor. Couldn't you have one built, if not on Earth then on the planet the Maclairnans named for him? It could be made into a garden world."

"His monument is what millions of people now know, or feel, about him," Radnor said. "He wouldn't want anything more tangible, except for *Estel* itself."

After they had gone, Ardith was faced with the question of what to do with the rest of her life. There was still a lot of work ahead informing people about the Elder worlds and fighting xenophobia on the part of people unaware of the tragedy it had caused. It was her responsibility to take this on, but she would also have to earn a living. She supposed she should look for a job teaching exobiology, in which she was now the League's top expert, but she was in no hurry about it. Despite the support of a growing number of people there was still some animosity toward her, and she had yet to appear as a witness at the trial of Fred's murderer, which would bring more notoriety—especially since it was suspected that Ivanson had indeed hired agitators and would therefore be tried as an accessory.

So for the time being she and Meiko continued to live in a safe house provided by Andrew, who still used that name among friends who had first known him by it. Despite his heavy responsibilities as Commandant of Fleet he visited frequently, and it finally dawned on Ardith that he was coming to see Meiko. She had wondered why he'd taken such a terrible risk to free them from prison, becoming a fugitive and endangering more people than he saved. Now it was clear. "While she was my prisoner it would have been inappropriate for me to have any feelings toward her other than admiration of her courage," he said. "But when enough time has passed, I'd like there to be more." Meiko didn't discuss it, but she seemed happy on days when he arrived.

Now fully recovered from her ordeal, Meiko had abandoned her former career as a chemist to devote full time to the Estelan Party, which was growing rapidly. She was working in the campaign office of a candidate for the legislature and hoped to someday become a candidate herself.

Jacob had gone back to his old position as head of the Department of Anthropology at the University of Earthport, teaching considerably more about human evolution than he had known when he left. In that role he was the official host to the Federation delegation when it came, and Ardith was invited to the reception. It was good to meet Elders again, but her feelings were bittersweet. She still longed to see more of their worlds.

It had been three months since the establishment of contact with the Federation when Jacob asked her to dinner at his apartment. She debated about going, as she was weary and there would undoubtedly be other guests, but he was insistent so she agreed to come. "There's only one other guest," Jacob told her when she arrived, "and I'll leave you to talk while I fix dinner." He ushered her into the living room.

As the man awaiting her came forward, Ardith's knees weakened; she thought she might collapse from shock. "*Varel?*"

He crossed the space between them in mere instants and took her in his arms. "Ardith," he murmured. "I never thought I'd see you in this life. And then I knew life wouldn't be worth much to me unless I did see you."

"I was afraid they wouldn't forgive you for sending that message. God, Varel, you shouldn't have taken the risk just to encourage me! I would have been okay."

"But I wouldn't. I belong with you, where everyone can see that our love is genuine and not something we made up to promote contact between Earth and the Elders. Something essential to our own lives."

"Why weren't you at the reception at the University?" she asked, catching her breath after their long kiss.

"Because I'm not with the official delegation. I came on *Promise*."

"You mean they've relented and let you visit here, knowing that you'll go on seeing me?"

"No. I mean I've left the Service and will be living on Earth permanently."

Confused, Ardith protested, "I thought you weren't allowed to resign, that the Oath is binding for life."

"Oh, it is. To walk out on the Service is a very serious breach—I couldn't do that." He smiled at her. "I still have a conscience and breaking the Oath once was enough."

"But everyone said they'd dismiss you if you violated the terms of your probation."

"Exactly. I couldn't resign, but they could dismiss me. That was why I sent the message."

Abruptly, she understood, and was filled with dismay. "You shouldn't have done it, not for my sake."

"It wasn't just for your sake. Like the first time, it was partly for my myself and partly because for us to love is in the best interests of Earth. You see, I don't feel that I've broken the Oath at all. I feel that I've honored it."

"According to what Radnor once told me, you didn't really break it—its meaning takes precedence over rules. They accused you just because of politics. It seems to me the Service that's supposed to be so wise is just as blind and unprincipled as the bureaucracies on Earth."

"Oh, no, Ardith. It wasn't like that," Varel said seriously, sitting down on the sofa and drawing her close to him. "They're not stupid. They couldn't let it look as if the Eldest makes policy or has power to override Service regulations, but they saw that he was right—and they knew after my hearing that I was blameless if the love between us benefitted Earth. But they didn't say so, because it would be of benefit only if our love proved deep and lasting. If when cut off from each other we didn't turn to other partners, and we were both willing to withstand whatever disapproval it led to."

Astonished, she stared at his untroubled face. "It was all a—a test?"

"In a way. But mainly it was set up so that if the time came when aliens were welcome here I would be able leave the Service, which I couldn't do unless I was on probation. They felt that we can achieve much more as a couple than we could as onetime lovers."

So the Service's ruling hadn't been a penalty, Ardith realized. They knew that if he didn't truly love her, not communicating wouldn't be a hardship, and if he did, he'd have gained freedom to act. He must have known that in time he could come to Earth. Except . . . With shock she saw that it had been up to her. She too had been judged, and Federation citizens could not set foot on newly-admitted worlds without permission. If she had backed away from the insults, or if after the attack she'd stopped saying she loved an alien, Varel would not have been allowed to come.

"Did you know all along that they expected it to turn out this way?" she asked.

"Not officially. I had my suspicions, since no one treated me as if I were guilty. Of course I had no idea that Earth would welcome the Elders so soon—without the demonstrations it wouldn't have happened for years."

"And so you weren't really dismissed, just allowed to quit?"

"Oh, it was a real dismissal, complete with formalities. Otherwise it would have looked as if any member with a plausible excuse could break the rules and get away with it. But in private they wished me Godspeed."

Ardith frowned. "Wasn't it risky to send the message before you knew the demonstrations would succeed?" No wonder he'd been anxious about them.

Varel tightened his arm around her shoulders. "I

took a big chance by doing that," he admitted, "but Radnor was going to see you and I didn't know when there'd be another opportunity. I couldn't stand the thought of more waiting."

"You've lost your Emblem," she said sadly, seeing his neck bare of the chain. She would have a wearable flame made to replace it, she vowed—not like the Maclairnans' pins, for those had to be earned, but something comparable to her cherished pendant.

"I haven't lost what it stood for," he said.

"Radnor said dismissal would be would be a public disgrace."

"On the Elder worlds it is; in effect I've been exiled. But I don't think people on Earth will see it that way. I've been offered a professorship in Federation History at the University of Earthport and I understand that's a rather prestigious position."

"How did you manage to land a professorship on a world strange to you from so far away?"

"Well, I think Jacob had something to do with it. Now that there's contact the major universities will be seeing a demand for courses about the Federation. Oh, and as a condition of accepting the offer I insisted that they establish a new professorship in Exobiology at the same time. I wouldn't want to come to Earth and have you go off to teach on LaLande VI."

She pressed her face against his shoulder. "That's wonderful . . . but you've given up so much. Earth lacks a lot of things you've been used to since you were a child, and it's going to remain a depressing place for a long time to come. And what about the house on Everne that you were never going to part with?"

"I'll have my memories. And the price I got for it, which was paid in platinum ingots, will buy us a home of our own here if we can find one in good shape. I assume there's no doubt about your wanting to marry me."

"We're already married. Everyone who saw the holo knows that; we'll just need to deal with some red tape once you get an ID and resident status. Only there's still prejudice, Varel. Not that I'll let it affect me, but you, coming from a world where such a thing would be unthinkable— Can you endure hearing me called a shameless slut?"

"I can endure whatever I have to. It will be like going back in history, but I have the advantage of knowing that worlds do progress.'

They sank down on the sofa, still in each other's arms, and did not notice when Jacob failed to call them in to dinner.

About the Author

SYLVIA ENGDAHL is the author of eleven science fiction novels. Six of them are Young Adult books that are also enjoyed by adults, all of which were originally published by Atheneum and have been republished, in both hardcover and paperback, by different publishers in the twenty-first century. The one for which she is best known, *Enchantress from the Stars*, was a Newbery Honor book in 1971, winner of the 1990 Phoenix Award of the Children's Literature Association, and a finalist for the 2002 Book Sense Book of the Year in the Rediscovery category. Her trilogy *Children of the Star* was reissued in a single volume as adult science fiction.

Her five most recent novels, a duology and a trilogy, are not YA books and are not appropriate for middle-school readers, but will be enjoyed by the many adult fans of her work. In addition, she has issued an updated and expanded edition of her nonfiction book *The Planet-Girded Suns: The Long History of Belief in Exoplanets* (first published by Atheneum in 1974 with a different subtitle) as well as three ebooks of collected essays.

Between 1957 and 1967 Engdahl was a computer programmer and Computer Systems Specialist for the SAGE Air Defense System. Most recently she has worked as a freelance editor of nonfiction anthologies for high schools. Now retired, she lives in Eugene, Oregon, and welcomes visitors to her website www.sylviaengdahl.com, which contains many of her essays, including those dealing with her long-term advocacy of space colonization.

EARLIER BOOKS IN THIS TRILOGY

Book One: *Defender of the Flame*

Starship pilot Terry Radnor is elated to be among those chosen to defend the secret colony Maclairn against enemies who pose a threat to the spread of paranormal human mind powers. He commits himself wholly to the goal of that world, not guessing how far his effort to protect it will take him from everything else he cares about. Torn away from his family and career against his will after learning a secret too deep for its disclosure to be risked, he is forced to build a new life far from Maclairn. Yet a mysterious and extraordinary destiny has been predicted for Terry, and fate puts him in place to confront the colony's greatest peril.

Book Two: *Herald of the Flame*

As captain of his own starship *Estel*, Terry is committed to spreading acceptance of paranormal mind powers throughout the colonies of humankind. Barred from contact with his beloved planet Maclairn, he now journeys from world to world, heralding the hopeful future about which he alone knows the full truth. But the opponents of such powers are gaining strength, and on Earth the persecution of people who develop them is increasing. Soon targeted by bounty hunters, Terry risks everything that matters to him in a desperate attempt to defeat Maclairn's enemies, not guessing that if he lives long enough, he is destined for an even greater role in human history than he has played as a defender of its cause.

MORE ABOUT THE SERVICE:

The Far Side of Evil

On completion of her training as an agent of the interstellar federation's Anthropological Service, Elana is sent to the planet Toris, whose people may soon destroy their civilization. Since not enough is understood about the situation to justify any interference with their evolution, the Service has no power to act; its agents must go as helpless observers, posing as natives, in the hope of gaining knowledge that may help to save other worlds. This passive role proves intolerable to the young, inexperienced agent assigned to the same city as Elana, a city under totalitarian rule. After falling in love with a local girl who has become Elana's closest friend, he identifies too completely with the natives and unwittingly endangers the entire world by a well-meant but ill-advised attempt to intervene. Forced to assume responsibility for undoing the damage, Elana finds that only she—at great cost—can prevent an immediate war of annihilation.

Although this novel has the same heroine as the author's Newbery Honor book *Enchantress from the Stars,* it is not a sequel but a completely separate— and very different—story, which although issued as a Young Adult novel is not intended for readers below high school age and is also enjoyed by adults. The two books are in no way dependent on each other and can be read in either order.

Enchantress from the Stars

Elana, though still a first-year student at the academy of the interstellar Anthropological` Service, is elated by the chance to take part in her father's perilous mission to the medieval planet Andrecia, which is being invaded by colonists from a young starfaring Empire. How can they drive the Imperials away without revealing their own alien origin? The key to the plan is a woodcutter's son named Georyn, who believes the menace beyond the forest to be a dragon. To him, Elana is an enchantress who can give him magical powers that will enable him to defeat it. But she soon finds that this role is no mere pretense and that her feeling for Georyn is deeper than she ever expected it could become.

This Newbery Honor Book, in which the Service and its Oath were first introduced, is enjoyed by middle-school readers as well as older teens and adults. Based on both traditional fairy tales and 20th-century space opera, it offers a mythological rather than realistic view of interplanetary relations— in real life a starfaring species would not invade an inhabited world.

The Doors of the Universe

Book Three of the Children of the Star trilogy, about colonists on an unnamed planet who are not related to people from Earth. While this novel can stand alone, it should not be read before Books One and Two, in which the Service does not appear, because it contains major spoilers for them. Originally published as Young Adult, it was reissued in the omnibus edition of the trilogy as adult science fiction.